W9-BKI-486

Flash Flood

Flash Flood

Susan Slater

Poisoned Pen Press

First Edition 2003

10 9 8 7 6 5 4 3 2 1

Library of Congress Catalog Card Number: 2002114464

ISBN: 1-59058-047-8 Hardcover

Poisoned Pen Press
6962 E. First Ave. Ste 103
Scottsdale, AZ 85251
www.poisonedpenpress.com
info@poisonedpenpress.com

Printed in the United States of America

To:

All the independent mystery bookstore owners
and staff who make me feel like royalty—Special thanks to
Ed Kaufman, M is for Mystery, San Mateo, CA and
Nancy Rutland, Bookworks, Albuquerque, NM.
And to Susan Wasson who insisted
that I find a home for *Flash Flood*

Chapter One

"If that ain't a shit-eatin' grin, I never saw one. You goin' to shatter that plate glass you keep admiring yourself." The man behind the desk put his pen down and scratched under his arm while flexing his shoulder. His uniform was snug and the collar cut into the second of his chins.

"Careful, Willie. You're talking to a free man now."

"What's that supposed to mean? That makes you better all of a sudden?" A hint of querulousness, another dig at the armpit.

"Maybe. Maybe you're talking to a *rich*, free man." Eric dropped his voice and leaned over the desk before stepping back. It felt good to tease Willie a little. Tenth grade education made you eligible for shit-detail if you were born and raised this side of Lubbock, Texas. And Willie qualified. Probably hadn't strayed more than twenty miles in any direction since birth.

"You telling me somebody bought seven years of your life?"

"Maybe."

"Shit." Willie picked up the pen again. "Nobody's got that kind of money. Not for my life. Tell me, how much is seven fucking years in this place worth?"

Eric Linden just smiled. It was tempting to brag. America's newest millionaire was about to step out into the muggy closeness of a late summer afternoon. Seven years in Milford Correctional minimum security prison had earned him the right to brag. Willie was right about the years being worth something. Were the seven years a forfeit? A sacrifice? How many times had he flown cattle or semen to Central America for Billy Roland Eklund? And how many times had there been a little something hidden on the plane for the return trip? Was it just plain luck that he hadn't been caught before? Brought down at the border to have agents swarm all over, dismantle the plane before they found the cache, the discreet little bundle with a tidy street value?

"I hear all sorts of crazy things in a place like this. Time was I'd even believe some of 'em." Willie snorted his skepticism.

Now he had Willie going. But it was true. He'd been asked to take the rap, admit to helping himself, a fringe benny of flying to places like Colombia. He was offered two million by a lawyer who remained anonymous but indicated that he represented Mr. Eklund. And all Eric had to do was be the decoy. The lawyer brought the bankbook. Eric called and verified the amount. Two million had been deposited in Midland Savings and Loan, Tatum, New Mexico. The bank would act as broker, manage the portfolio, send a monthly statement *if* he pulled time. But that hadn't seemed likely.

He'd known he could get off. Talk his way out of it. He didn't have a record. He was just a pilot who couldn't resist temptation, for God's sake. He'd grown up with these people. Gone back East to get a law degree from the right school but returned to hang a shingle in Roswell, New Mexico, practice a little, do some flying, raise a family. Maybe if he hadn't handled his own defense there would have been a different outcome. But how'd he know the judge would be a Yale brother who took pleasure in cleaning up the profession?

"I suppose you goin' tell me you dumped that wife of yours to take off with the piece of ass that's waiting outside? A little quail will get you right back in here. Some men don't never learn. They just whip it out and let it lead 'em around."

The pronoun reference was clear and Willie was staring at him, mouth shut tight, accusingly sanctimonious. Andrea

Lott was twenty-three. But he wouldn't waste his breath telling Willie. And it was good to know that Andy was waiting at the curb. More than likely in that big, pink Caddy, some Mary Kay castoff of her mother's, but it'd get them back to civilization.

"Come on, Willie. You can check paperwork faster than that." He was beginning to feel antsy and tired of all the small talk.

"Hold your horses. You'd be pissed as hell if I missed something. If it's worth doing, it's worth doing right." Willie was checking dates and signatures and stamping each page. And taking his sweet, ever-loving time. Passive-aggressive came to mind, but Eric didn't push it. Wouldn't do him any good. He just needed to let old Willie play out the control thing, get his jollies by being an asshole. Besides, Eric wasn't going to let anyone ruin his day. Everything he'd ever hoped for was ten steps away.

He sat back down in a chrome and peeling padded leather chair, his back to the wire-reinforced glass partition. He didn't need to check his reflection to know that forty looked pretty good on him. And felt pretty good. Milford Correctional hadn't been so bad. There were amenities in minimum-security lockup, like the Caddy's driver, teaching assistant and highlight of the college enrichment program—and hell of a good fuck. If every Thursday at two forty-five behind the kitchen in the walkway to the freezer, fifteen minutes before the start of Culinary Arts 104 could qualify as something good. Six quickies before the course ended.

"Guess that'll do it." Willie stacked the papers in front of him, neatly aligned their edges, then slid them into a manila envelope. "They say a fool's born every day." His look said that he wouldn't mind a little debate on the topic if Eric wanted to stick around. But Eric wasn't biting. Not today.

"That ought to keep you in business." Eric grinned, picked up the envelope, stuffed it into the outside pocket of his duffle, and walked to the door. "Hey, Willie. No more advice?

Nothing about wooden nickels? Or not doing whatever the shit it is that you don't do?"

He laughed, and overcome with a delirious giddiness he pushed out of the building and stood drawing the suffocatingly hot air into his lungs. Out. He was finally out. The rebel yell caught the attention of the guard at the front gate, who watched a minute, then picked up the phone before he buzzed Eric through.

A couple pirouettes, a toss of his duffle bag in the general direction of the Caddy's back seat and he turned his attention to Andy, leaning against the hood in short shorts and halter top.

"Only one other thing might look half as good as you do right now." He lifted her and did a third pirouette as her tanned legs grasped his waist.

"There's a cooler full of Heineken on the back seat." She said, her arms around his neck, mouth close to his ear. He pulled back to kiss her, turning to make certain that Willie had a clear view.

"Woman after my own heart. But that beer's gonna have to wait." He nipped at her bottom lip, then sucked on it, then laughing, covered her mouth with his, pushing his tongue in and out and didn't come up for air until he felt her squirm.

"Oh, baby, you know how I feel right now?" He murmured into her hair. The question was rhetorical. How could anyone know unless they'd been uprooted—jerked out of society and buried for a few years?

"I could check." That breathy whisper of a voice and then Eric felt her hand drop to his crotch and knead gently. "I think you feel pretty good."

He laughed and set her down. Maybe there were limits to what Willie should see. Suddenly he just wanted to get the hell out of there.

"Want me to drive?" he asked.

If Andy was surprised at this about-face, she didn't let on.

"I'm okay." There was a hint of a pout but she slipped behind the wheel. She was West Texas pretty in a rodeo-queen sort of way. Long, straight blond hair, apple-smooth ass with cheeks that just fit the palms of his hands. Growing up he'd watch ass like that circle the show ring on the back of stud Appaloosas. He reached around and retrieved a beer, scattering ice chips across the front seat.

"That's cold." Andy jumped.

"Thought you needed to cool down." Eric leaned over and sucked up the melting specks from bare skin, letting his tongue linger on the inside of her thigh. She laughed before pushing him away and gave the gas pedal a couple thrusts. The Caddy roared into action and Andy deftly pulled a U and headed out of the parking lot.

Eric flipped open the glove box. "Got a church key around here?"

"Don't that just twist off?" Andy glanced his way.

"Yeah. Sure," Eric laughed. A church key probably dated him.

"You hungry? We could stop for something to eat?" Andy was headed southwest toward Meadow, Brownfield, Tatum, then Roswell.

"Maybe later," Eric said.

"There's that cowboy place outside Tatum. Couple hours from here."

"Sounds good."

Was he going to regret this? She'd offered the ride to Roswell but the price might include a ticket out—out of the wide spot in the road she called home. A body like hers could rot in a Tatum, New Mexico, town of five thousand, but did his plans include letting her tag along? Maybe.

He had a couple days business in Roswell; meet with Elaine's lawyer, sign the divorce papers, clean out a safe deposit box, make sure the two million plus had been transferred to the Caymans. Then he was out of there. Next stop was Miami and the best catamaran that cash could buy.

"Will you stay with your wife?"

"What?" Eric jolted back to the present.

"In Roswell. Will I be dropping you off at home?"

"No. That's married in the past tense."

"Kids?"

"One." Eric felt vaguely uncomfortable. He didn't want to dwell on what wasn't waiting for him, a son who would start college in two weeks, but hadn't spoken to him in five years.

He waited for more questions but Andy was concentrating on the highway. He let his thoughts stray to Elaine. He hadn't expected her to leave him. They had always been friends, lovers in the beginning. At forty-five she could turn every head in a room. Nineteen years was a long time.

He sighed. Andy quickly glanced his way and he smiled reassuringly, then slumped against the door intent on watching the miles roll by. Not that there was much to watch. The land was flat and scrubby—the kind that took four acres to support one cow. But this was cattle country with a few oil wells thrown in. Big ranches, big bucks. The tough plains grass had fed buffalo a hundred years ago; now prize herds of Brangus, Charolais, and Santa Gertrudis foraged among the monotonous up-and-down swing of the pumps.

Standing pools of water dotted the side of the road. This was the monsoon season. Intermittent showers would pummel the earth, and the sun would turn the moisture into steam. Looked like there was going to be more rain. To the west, virga trailed from a bank of high-flying clouds. If the temperature cooled, they could be in for a real gully washer.

The hottest damn day of the week but the first one in three that it hadn't rained half the night—only half the morning. This was not Dan Mahoney's pick of weather to tour the Double Horseshoe. He'd gone back inside the Silver Spur motel to change shirts twice. The final choice was a linen weave *guayabera*, a relic from six months in Matamoros a few years back. He wasn't wrong; the climate here in Tatum, New Mexico was about the same. This part of the country had some kind of patent on shit for weather. Hot, more hot, then when a person thought he couldn't handle it, throw in sticky-hot.

He'd gotten off the plane bitching about the heat, but if he wanted to be truthful, it wasn't just the weather. He plain didn't want to be here, a detective specializing in insurance claims out in the field tracking down some perverts who had sliced up a calf and threw her over an altar. Probably did a couple half turns to the beat of a drum in the middle of the night to boot. But he wouldn't be here if the calf hadn't been insured for two hundred and fifty thousand. So, who said it was cheap to worship the devil? Lame joke. He wasn't in the mood. It was difficult to see the humor in any of this.

What had happened to the desk job? The cushy nine to five, report every day, go home at a decent hour, have dinner with the wife and kids—only there weren't any of those. There had been a couple wives, not at the same time, but both a long time ago. Now it was just a Rottweiler who had earned the right to slobber on him now and then. And the on again, off again thing with the fifth grade teacher that was doomed, and he guessed he knew he didn't want to revive it. The sex was just so-so, but she was a Cubs fan. He'd miss the companionship.

So, what was he doing at fifty-two, somewhere out West in a one-horse town, getting ready to spend Friday and maybe a month of Fridays tramping around the Charolais cattle ranch of one Billy Roland Eklund? The money? No. Ego? Probably. "You're the best. The only one who could get to the bottom of this." His boss knew how to work him. United Life and Casualty had received three claims in three months. All for over two hundred thousand each. Any insurance company would be hysterical; his was. And there was the family thing, his boss reminded him, as if he needed reminding. He could visit his sister who lived out this way, ninety miles west to be exact, and wouldn't it be nice to combine a little vacation with business? To sister Carolyn, family vacation was an oxymoron and the only word that really fit with family was crisis. But he enjoyed Carolyn in small doses; he'd probably spend a few days in Roswell.

He looked up the street. Odd sensation to not only see the end of the main drag but the open space beyond. He'd been in a city too long. Home was Chicago; maybe he should think of relocating. But not to a Tatum, New Mexico. He liked the amenities of a city, the impersonal, get lost in a crowd whenever you want. Sometimes a person's soul needed that. Here five shops on Main Street were named after their owners: Alice's, Lil's, Jack's, Ray's, Bert & Faye's. Some sort of ego involvement to see your name in two-foot-high neon.

Halfway down the block, a pickup was backed up to a loading dock in front of the Feed and Seed Co-op. Two young men were loading what looked to be some first rate alfalfa. The insignia on the pickup's door panel read Double Horseshoe. Billy Roland's was one good-sized operation. Snatches of Spanish floated down the street as the two workers tossed the bales onto the truck bed.

He eyed the dark coolness of Jack's. A bar probably run by a second or third generation owner with the same name. Even at ten in the morning, it looked inviting. He dug the directions out of his pocket. He missed a briefcase. But somehow out here that would be laughable and brand him as a true outsider. No, boots and jeans were the uniform.

The fax paper was already breaking down; some of the lines meant to be roads had faded to an indistinct gray. Finding a ranch out here, even a fifty-thousand-hectare spread, would be difficult. He better ask for directions.

The Circle K looked promising until he read the note on the door. *Gone for aerobics—ten to eleven.* He rattled the door just to make sure, but it didn't give. He shaded his eyes and looked across the street. He'd try the Chevron station catty-corner across the way.

Ray's occupied one corner of Tatum's main street and seemed to be the only station in town. The double row of pumps wasn't quite new and the prices were forty cents higher than when he had filled up in Albuquerque. If you were stupid enough to drive this far into nothingness, served you right to pay to get out.

"Be with you in a minute." The voice came from under a Wonder Bread truck hiked up on one of two racks.

Dan found seventy-five cents in his pocket, treated himself to a root beer, and leaned against the door leading to the service bay to wait.

"Hot enough for you?" The voice belonged to someone with a massive set of arms, grease stained and hairy.

"It'll do." Dan was beginning to feel the day slip away. He was still ticked about having to wait for the fax. The home office wasn't what it used to be. Efficiency had lost its crisp edge.

"Now then. What can I do you for?" The man walking toward him was enormous; thick bull neck, jowls, and a three hundred pound plus torso. He wiped his hands on a paper towel but it was a lost cause.

"You Ray?" Dan didn't know why he asked.

"Yeah."

Brick shit house kept coming to mind but even that image didn't quite capture Ray's sheer bulk. "You want to see me about something?" The voice was losing its friendly edge.

"Just looking for Billy R. Eklund's place. Double Horseshoe."

"You got business with Billy Roland?"

Damned small towns. Everyone wants to know everything. Dan didn't let the smile slip from his face.

"Yeah. Here's my card. I'm down here to help with the investigation into the death of Grand Champion Taber's Shortcake Dream." He hoped he sounded like he'd been on a first name basis with the heifer. Chummy with its owner, too. He watched as Ray considered something, then looked up and stared him straight in the eye.

"That was some mess we found out there."

"You part of the team who found her?"

"Led the investigation. I'm Sheriff."

"Any speculation on how it might have happened?"

"Naw." A flicker of the eye said otherwise.

"This sort of thing happen before around here?"

Dan watched the man take the edge of his business card to the cuticle of his left thumb. The furious digging and scraping still left a grease-stained nail bed. Dan waited. Something told him Ray had more to say.

"One theory has it, it's aliens." His voice dropped and Dan wasn't sure he heard.

"What was that?"

"Aliens." The man didn't look up. Was this a joke?

"Are sightings common?"

"Maybe. Depends on how you think."

"Was there evidence?"

"If you knew what to look for."

"Just what exactly would that be?" Daniel could play along with the best of them. But aliens?

"Slime. No blood. All around her mouth, around the anus, was this goo. Thick stuff, clear like K-Y jelly." Probably was K-Y Jelly but Dan kept his opinion to himself. "You know they'd shoved the severed dick of a bull calf in her mouth?" Ray paused to see if Dan was with him.

Dan wasn't certain what kind of comment was expected, so he asked, "Have there been other mutilations? Ones that you've seen?"

"A couple. But it's been a few years."

"Cows carved up the same way?"

"Yeah. Exactly the same way."

Dan finished the can of pop and strolled to the trash bin. He'd seen the pictures and wasn't up to a play by play description by Sheriff Ray.

"I probably need to get going. Why don't you take a look at this map and tell me if I can find the Double Horseshoe if I follow it?"

The sheriff took the map and moved to the window.

"Shorter if you go straight here." He pointed to a section of road that intersected with County number five. Dan made a couple notes, folded the map and watched Sheriff Ray head back to the Wonder Bread truck. Dan walked out on Main Street, looked up and down the street. And then, without any real plan in mind, he walked across to the corner of Elm opposite from Ray's, and up the steps of the bank, Midland Central Savings and Loan, and pushed open the double glass doors. In a small town the bank was always a good place to start if you wanted a character reference.

Everyone, this included four people, looked up expectantly. He got that "you're a stranger" once over before a teller leaned across her wrought iron cage to inquire, "Is there something I can help you with?"

"I'd like to speak to the president."

"Do you have an appointment?" A tall man, impeccably dressed in navy suit, white shirt, and red power tie stepped around the edge of an impressive mahogany desk outside a set of carved wood, double doors leading somewhere in back. Must be a sentinel, among other duties, more than a junior clerk but not a trustee, Dan thought.

"No. I was hoping Mr. Cyrus might have a minute." Dan handed him a card. Thank God he'd glanced at the gilt-edged directory painted on the door. "I believe United Life and Casualty has dealt with Midland Savings and Loan before." A lie, but the junior clerk wouldn't necessarily know that.

"Dad, uh, Mr. Cyrus prefers a call in advance."

I just bet he does, Dan thought, this wasn't a town that would like surprises. "Why don't you check with him. My time is limited."

The clerk disappeared after a short staccato knock on the heavy doors and returned almost immediately.

"Mr. Cyrus will see you now."

Dan wondered if Junior had had to refer to his father as Mr. Cyrus since birth. Probably. Dan stepped into the room, not quite an office, but not really anything else unless there was such a thing as a one-room library. A ladder on wheels with a small railed platform on top stood just inside the door. And everywhere he looked were rows of law books.

"Awesome, ain't it?" Dan assumed the small man behind the desk was sitting until he walked toward him. A dwarf. With tailored suit, vest, pocket watch and well-trimmed graying goatee. "I should have 'Esquire' painted on the door out front. But newcomers are the only ones who don't know I'm also Judge Franklin Cyrus. Now, you here to see the bank president or the judge?"

The laugh that bounced against the bookcases was the one thing not small about Judge Cyrus. He motioned to an overstuffed chair and sat on one end of a matching loveseat, custom made with shortened legs.

"Possibly both." Did everyone in this town have two occupations? Kept things nicely accounted for if you discounted conflict of interest issues, Dan decided. "I'd like to just chat about Mr. Billy Roland Eklund. I'd appreciate it if you'd be comfortable in sharing your opinions of Mr. Eklund. Maybe, how well he's thought of around here or a little background. History of the family and ranch, that sort of thing."

"Why, I don't mind at all. Billy Roland's an open book. Won't find a nicer human being. And I emphasize 'human' when I say that, human and humane. Lots of youngsters in this town realized a college dream because of him. You know he's founder of that Bible College over yonder?"

Judge Cyrus studied him for a moment, then gestured for Dan to follow him as he walked to the only window in the room, a deep casement inset that opened out onto Main Street. "Look at this little town. We don't have poverty in Tatum. You aren't going to find drunks on the corners. Nobody is going to follow you down the street asking for a handout. This is what clean living and having a benefactor with a heart of gold looks like."

They stood silently for a moment. Dan looked for the truck loaded with alfalfa but it was gone. Ray was backing the bread truck out of the service bay and three teens leaned their bikes against the Post Office across the street before going into the building. Dull came to mind but he said, "Nice town. I don't suppose cattle money alone can do all this."

"Oh my, no. Billy R. married Texas oil money. Missy Anne was the daughter of the Governor of Texas at the time. Came from Houston, but their home was just outside Plains. There was the biggest ol' party of a wedding you'd ever hope to see." It was evident that Judge Cyrus had attended from his wistful fixed stare as he doubtlessly recounted happy days past. "She was such a pretty thing but not very well. Sickly, really. Never gave him any children. You don't go saying you heard it here, but that's the one disappointment in Billy Roland's life. Not one soul with his blood to leave everything to."

"Probably shouldn't rule out his second wife giving him some offspring."

"No can do. Tubes are tied. One of those decisions made before she even met Billy Roland."

Dan was stunned. Just more proof of the "my business is your business" mentality of a small town. But wasn't something like "tubes" private?

"Those Charolais are his babies, so to speak. Wedding gift from the Governor on Billy R.'s marriage to Missy Anne. Original herd purchased in France in 1958 for thirty-seven million. Only about fifty head all together. One happy bull and forty-nine cows."

This time he slapped his knee in mirth. "Yes, sir. That bull was happy all right. Bunch of us used to go out and watch. That bull just about went cross-eyed with happiness but he got the job done."

Dan was glad he wasn't expected to comment. The vision of a group of men hanging over a fence watching animals unite seemed a little perverted. But then he hadn't been raised on a farm, had never had a chance to get a sex education from nature. He wasn't sure but suspected it was better than the garbled street versions that he'd received.

"What do you make of the problems he's having with the cattle now?"

"Well, you're going to hear everything from aliens—" Judge Cyrus paused and looked up at him, possibly to see his reaction.

"I've already talked to Sheriff Ray, but I gather you don't necessarily share that theory?"

"Now I'm not going to rule anything out. Not yet, anyway. Only one's been mutilated so could be kid stuff, somebody from a neighboring town. Could be some sort of grudge thing, but I doubt it. Billy Roland's been pretty free with his favors. Few years back, farmer to the south of here lost some goats. He thought at the time it was some sort of satanic worship."

"Tell me about the other cows. How did they die?"

"Virus. Some virulent unknown killer picked up at a cattle show. That's how those things get started, you know, shows where there's lots of exposure to cows from all over and you can't control the new strains. Humans are beginning to have some of the same problems, wacko viruses that eat the heart muscle or into the brain. Makes you want to live in a bubble." More booming laughter. "Look, don't want to give you the bum's rush but I gotta meeting coming up. If you need any more info don't hesitate to drop by, door's always open once you get past Junior out there. Oh, in case you're wondering, his mother's regular size." This time the laughter almost rocked him off his feet but he recovered to walk Dan to the door. "It's the one question they all want to ask."

Tatum's one-mile stretch of Main Street was deserted when Andy aimed the Caddy toward the Double Diamond Bar and Grill. Friday night, and the parking lot was already crammed with mud-encrusted pickups. Garth Brooks was blasting from the jukebox but a sign announced live music at seven thirty.

She maneuvered the car to a spot six rows from the exit on the side of the weathered building garish with flashing neon tubing outlining lariats, boots, and cowboy hats. Eric noticed a group of posturing young studs leaning against their trucks, jawing and tipping back longnecks. Human nature dictated some of those conversations would turn into brawls before sundown.

They found a booth by the bar in the back of the warehouse-sized building. Nothing small about the place, Eric noted, the bar could probably seat forty with another twenty standing. Not too many were dancing; the crowd was still light. Serious partying wouldn't start before nine. It was weird to think that the place hadn't even been there seven years ago.

He'd found his appetite and put in an order for a New York steak smothered with grilled onions and home fries, green chili on the side. They might not stock Heineken but the first Coors was sliding down real nice. Eric leaned back against the cool red vinyl. He was beginning to enjoy this. He slipped an arm around Andy and pulled her close. It sure as hell beat anything he'd been doing the last seven years.

The Tercel had air-conditioning which was a plus because it took Dan an hour and a half to find the ranch. And damned if it wasn't something out of the old *Dallas* series. Big white two-story house with a wide veranda nestled in a windbreak of poplar and desert cypress. Barns better than half the houses in the United States. Pens, feeders, corrals, machinery, in freshly painted sheds. Horse flesh that represented five years' salary *if* you made a hundred thousand plus a year. Somewhere he'd read that Billy Roland kept two strings of polo ponies, thoroughbred-quarter horse crosses. Interesting how the sport was catching on out here; there was supposed to be a playing field at San Patricio a hundred and fifty miles to the west. The sport of kings—too rich for his blood.

The wood-fenced runs beside the curving drive held some real long-legged beauties. Dan slowed to watch them buck and run, slide to a stop then turn and double back, necks arched, tails floating out behind. This was the type of thing that might get him out of the city someday, horseflesh and wide open spaces.

He cursed the Tercel as he accelerated and made the wide graveled turn in front of the house. The home office had never played loose with travel expenses. Maybe, just this once, it would have been to their benefit. This was the kind of house that dictated you pull up in a Mercedes, something that cost no less than fifty thousand. And the *guayabera* had been a wrong call, too. Designer jeans, thousand-dollar boots, Ralph Lauren linen…much more correct.

He'd reviewed the players until every detail was memorized. William R. Eklund, rancher, sometime politician, founder of Wings of the Dove Bible College, top breeder/importer/judge of Charolais cattle, married to Iris Stuckey, thirty years his junior, second wife but with tied tubes; first one, sickly but filthy rich had left him fixed for life. But it didn't put ol' Billy Roland above suspicion of killing a few of his own cattle for seven hundred thou pocket change.

He walked up the front steps, oddly pristine with no paint chips, no dirt. Out here you'd have to hire someone full time to just keep the dust off. Geraniums and petunias overflowed their hanging terra cotta pots and a huge Stars and Stripes hung flaccid from a thirty-foot pole. Conservative Republican.

Possibly anal retentive, Dan noted.

There was some cutesy wreath on the door about three feet in diameter with wooden cut-outs of Charolais, those brahma-like bumps behind their heads carefully chiseled, each one nestled in corn shucks dyed a teal green to match the trim on the house.

The knocker was another Charolais, this one an anatomically correct brass bull. He let it thud against the wood.

"Yes?"

The door opened so quickly he hadn't been ready. And the person standing there wasn't a servant but had to be Ms. Iris Stuckey Eklund herself.

"I'd like to speak to Mr. Eklund."

"Not here. Maybe I can help. I'm Iris."

"Iris." He repeated her name out loud. Not because it was a pleasing sound but because it made her continue to look at him straight on, full in the face. He had her complete attention, the door between them distorting slightly what he knew was peachy skin, clear and smooth, despite the dot-matrix grayness caused by the screen.

"April, May, June, and little ol' Iris."

"Come again?"

"My sisters and then there was me and my Daddy fresh out of months. He couldn't have two Junes, now could he?"

"No, I guess not."

"So he looked around and saw a big ol' patch of purple iris in full bloom. And here I am."

Dan couldn't think of one appropriate thing to say and just stood there. Abruptly, he cleared his throat. He was there to ask questions and he better get started.

"My card." The screen door opened half an inch, and she took the card. He waited until she looked up. "I have some routine paperwork to complete. A few questions that I—"

"What sort of questions you want to ask, Dan?" She opened the door another couple inches and leaned against the jamb. He ignored the familiar use of his name. In fact, he kind of liked it when she said it.

"Routine stuff. Just need to make sure that everything's in order."

"I don't think I can help much."

"Could you have identified Grand Champion Taber's Shortcake Dream?" He knew the question was abrupt but he needed to know who would recognize a substitution—just a regular ol' cow standing in for the real thing when it came to killing.

The giggle surprised him. She leaned close to the screen, her lips brushing the harshness of the wire.

"I can't tell a heifer from a Hereford and don't plan to learn." The hint of sultriness wasn't lost on him. Little miss end-of-the-months was one hot tamale.

"Suppose the two of us might sit out here on the steps a minute or two? You could help with names and dates."

He stepped back and pulled the screen door with him. Silhouetted against the dark interior of the house, Iris seemed bigger than life. He wouldn't need to check the pubic hair to know the blond wasn't real; it was too golden and just above her ears was the shadowing of dark fuzz defying peroxide to return to nature. But the rest of the body explained why she didn't need to know the difference between anything, not even for the man who had devoted his life to raising prize-winning Charolais.

"I'm not real sure Billy Roland would want me talking to you." But she tucked the skirt of her sundress under her knees and sat on the top step.

"He's real anxious to get this claim in, isn't he? I'd think he'd welcome your involvement."

"Maybe, maybe not."

"Do you happen to know where he's off to?"

Iris shrugged; a tiny twisted wisp of a cloth strap slipped over one shoulder. The sundress covered only what absolutely had to be hidden and the lacing on the bodice had pulled apart four inches. His concentration was suffering. He'd try a different tactic.

"What, if anything, did you see on the night of July twelfth?"

The petulant look was giving way to deep thought. She raked her perfectly white teeth over her bottom lip and stared off into space. He was beginning to think she'd help when she glanced at him, and he could see that fear overshadowed all else. Billy Roland must be one mean son of a bitch. Or Miss Iris just doesn't want to fall off the chowder wagon. He was running out of ideas.

"Tell you what. If anything comes to mind, give me a call at the Silver Spur. I'll be there until tomorrow night."

He thought she nodded as she hopped up, skipping to safety behind the screen door. He felt her eyes on his backside all the way to the Tercel. She wouldn't call, wouldn't think of something. She didn't get to live in this big house by babbling what she knew, which was probably plenty.

He rolled down the windows and waited until the Tercel cooled down, considerably past the end of the half-mile driveway. But then it struck him. This ranch, this land, little Miss Jayne Mansfield look-alike, all of it was a cliché. Too rich, too macho, too Out-West big. He couldn't shake the unreality of it. Even Sheriff Ray back at the gas station was probably some kind of pawn owned by Billy Roland Eklund.

He looked past the fence posts to the right and thought he saw a rider disappear into a clump of poplar. Someone could watch the house from that distance; the grassy knoll, slightly elevated, made a good vantage point. Could it have been the master of the house? Billy Roland spying on Iris, on him, his house? Of course, he didn't know for sure, but how many times had he been wrong? Not very many.

He reached for the binoculars. Two could play this game. He realized that he didn't care if he did piss off Mr. Eklund. He hated being lied to, given some kind of cat-and-mouse run-around. He switched off the engine and, with the field glasses swinging around his neck, eased out from behind the wheel.

He marveled at the stillness. Flat land, livestock, fences. Nothing human. But he had the prickly hair on the neck feeling that he was being watched. He leaned against the top rail and took a bead on the house. Quiet. Might have been a flutter at a window on the second floor. Then again, maybe not.

Movement at the side of the house caught his attention. Coming from the back, someone was walking toward what was probably the pool. Iris. And if she wasn't naked, she had on the tiniest string bikini he'd ever seen. He knew he was meant to fog up the lens, get a hard-on just looking, take his mind off what he might have seen. But Miss Iris wasn't his type.

He turned back to the strand of poplar. Nothing. Better call it a day. Might be the kind of case that nighttime gave up more clues than daylight. He could come back this evening. Jerk. He could get shot, too. Wasn't this one of the reasons he'd opted for a desk job? Stay out of the line of fire. Coast to retirement, get out at sixty after warming a seat the last ten years, giving seminars, training some crack-ass team of agents to do field work? A smile spread across his face. He'd go back to the motel and think it over, but he was already pretty sure he'd be back out here after sundown. Habit was a powerful thing.

Three Coors later the grease had congealed along the side of the steak platter and Eric had heard twenty-two years' worth of living in Tatum, New Mexico. Yeah, he was the ticket out, all right. Only thing left around here that could make a girl some money was the Ranch, across the state line near Plains. Not an option if you had three brothers.

Andy had a friend who worked at the Ranch. And she said it reverently, not like it was a glorified whorehouse, but a privilege her friend richly deserved.

"One summer a whole bunch of Japanese businessmen took the place over. They were throwing around one thousand dollar bills until somebody from Dallas, you know, immigration or someone like that, put a stop to it, sort of suggested they move on. I've never even seen a one thousand dollar bill." She paused to sip on her Southern Comfort and Coke. "I went out there once, on kind of an interview. It's just three big double-wides behind an old farmhouse. It doesn't even look like you think it would."

"How's that?"

"Well, velvet everywhere, crystal chandeliers."

"So, what do they have?"

"A big room with cubby-holes. Floor to ceiling. Then another room with hot tubs." She turned to face him. "You know a lot of their work is therapeutic, massages, steam baths, custom-mixed lotions, stuff like that."

I'll bet, he was tempted to say, but didn't. He was saved any further discussion of the Ranch's decor by Andy saying her nose needed powdering. He stood to let her out of the booth. And then he saw him. For that split second, their eyes locked in the mirror behind the bar. Recognition? Eric couldn't be sure. There was something. The man was a gorilla, massive, thick neck; his jacket was ill-fitting but an important item if you were trying to conceal something like a gun. Eric could see the outline of it as the man bent forward to pull his drink closer. Some pretty good sized revolver? Semi-automatic?

No. This was stupid. Paranoid. Who would be after him? Andy's father? He almost laughed. Forty and he could get decked by an irate parent. He just knew for certain that it wasn't a setup by Billy Roland. He'd made a bargain with that lawyer and kept his word to the old man, covered for him.

Eric relaxed. The man at the bar seemed intent on studying the burned-in brands displayed in the wood beam above the cash register. One man carrying a gun and glancing his way didn't make an armed assassin. Not that it wasn't important to be on your toes, but it was a little too egocentric to think someone wanted you dead. He'd waited seven years for this day. He needed to start enjoying it.

The band was tuning up, and the lead singer, dripping sequins and fringe, settled herself on a stool facing the audience. Long red hair cascaded down her back and swept below her ass; her full thighs were encased in doe-soft white leather; she looked his way and waved. He nodded and held eye contact a minute. God, women could be so beautiful in these backwash places. Or was he reacting from deprivation?

Horny. That was it. That was what was wrong with him. There was nothing like getting laid to put things in perspective. Actually, no better way to start the first day of the rest of your life than with a bang. The cracked leather back seat of the Caddy was beginning to look pretty good.

Andy was motioning to him from the edge of the dance floor as the vocalist began a slow pulsating tune that had been popular a few years back. Walking toward her, he noticed how young everyone looked; mean age had to be twenty-five. Even the bartender wasn't more than thirty. It was like an entire generation of people had sprung up from nowhere. Seven years had been a long time. But then, two million was a lot of money.

Andy put both arms around his neck and folded her body into his. Holding her like this wasn't helping him put off his decision to get laid. But from the looks they were getting from some of the single women about Andy's age, Eric knew it was important for her to show him off. Even the man with the gun was dancing. Must be a local.

Andy felt good against him. Smelled good against him. If he had to take a guess, he'd say she wasn't wearing underpants.

He didn't encounter any elastic as he slipped an index finger under the cuff of her shorts. He liked that. He had found it exciting behind the kitchen; he found it exciting now. As the band struck up a lively rendition of "Cotton-eyed Joe," Eric grabbed Andy's arm, steering her toward the booth.

"Let's get out of here. I can think of a couple things I'd like to do that don't require a crowd, and music's optional."

"Am I going to like these 'things'?" A teasing smile played at the corners of her mouth. She tipped her head back and on impulse, Eric covered her mouth with his, letting his tongue barely push between her lips. It wasn't a kiss as much as an invitation. Leaving his hands clasped behind her head, he pulled back to read her expression. Just what he had hoped for. God, how he loved women to meet him head on, matching his own raw wanting. Andy grabbed her purse from the booth and hung onto his arm as they worked their way toward the door.

No motel used individual air-conditioners anymore. Their inefficiency was staggering. Dan pulled off the tight boots, stripped to his shorts, and fell back prone on the bed, letting the window unit blow full force over his body. He could have stayed in Roswell, at Carolyn's. She had offered. But knowing his sister, it was probably more gesture, the right thing to do, than anything she really expected him to take her up on.

Carolyn had married well to rancher, entrepreneur, oil-rich Phillip Ainsworth. Ski-bum handsome, Yale graduate, native of Roswell, bright enough to recognize blind ambition in a mate. Dan had wondered twenty years ago how Carolyn would ever survive in a town like Roswell. But it hadn't taken her long to groom her ticket to better things. And she'd done a good job of it. Phillip was a force in the state, charter member of a good ol' boy network.

She and Philip wouldn't be back from Santa Fe until next week and then only to kick off some fund raisers for her husband's newest project, a series of down-home Bar-B-Ques for the next Governor of New Mexico. Jason, the only nephew, was at school, so it would have been just him and Dona Mari, the Mexican housekeeper/nanny who was a self-proclaimed herbalist and whose last cleansing had left him with two days of the trots. No thanks.

Was he looking forward to seeing the future First Lady of New Mexico? Yes, out of guilt. Not really, out of truth. Dan knew she'd be totally wrapped up in this newest adventure. Carolyn was born to be First Lady of something. Dan rolled over. He had about three hours until sundown, a nap, a sandwich in the coffee shop, and then a little night work. He wadded the pillow under his head and closed his eyes.

The first rolls of thunder sounded like cannon fire. He sat straight up, dazed and apprehensive before he got his bearings. Was there anything worse than sleeping in a strange bed? A peek out the window showed patches of blue sky with some ominous gray-black clouds threatening to the west. The digital clock turned over six thirty-nine. Time to get going.

How could anyone ruin a toasted cheese with chips? The waitress was apologetic but didn't offer to make it good. Daniel left her a couple bucks anyway and walked outside. God, he was cranky. A lumpy bed, humidity you could cut with a knife—he stopped himself. Yes, those were reasons, unpleasantries, but wasn't he bugged the most by knowing he was going snooping? Taking a chance on being caught where he wasn't supposed to be?

But, damn it, they hadn't given him any alternative.

Why was it every time he was in this neck of the woods, the words to country western tunes played in his head. A little number by Johnny Paycheck was drowning out everything else right about now. He slammed the door to the Tercel harder than he meant to.

It was a great night if the rain would just hold off. No moon. Light wind. He couldn't have ordered anything better. He studied the map to the Double Horseshoe. He had an hour's drive ahead of him; he'd better get going.

The crowd spilled out of the Bar and Grill into the parking lot. A couple of discussions had turned ugly. But so had the weather. Blinding flashes of light bounced against the horizon, branching jaggedly to the sides. A series of nature's sonic booms rattled the bar's single-pane windows. The rain, heavy all around them, was just beginning here. Big splats of water hit the cement sidewalk, sending up an aroma of dust and limestone.

"We're going to have to run for it." Eric pulled Andy closer, and they darted from under the protective overhang. The air hung charged and heavy; wet slaps of raindrops stung their arms. They reached the Caddy out of breath, both scrambling to roll up the windows. Pulling Andy toward him, Eric leaned back against the leather.

"Front row seats if you like a light show."

The rain was just a loud spattering of drops, but the lightning illuminated the entire parking lot. And that's when he saw him. Again. Local or not, this guy was more than just curious. He'd started fiddling with something on the dash of his Dakota when he saw Eric look that way, but he was tailing them, pure and simple. It wasn't coincidence. Eric didn't like the feel of it. Had he been a fool to trust Billy Roland? Was this guy some hired goon?

"If you really had to run this old tank top-out, what would she do?"

"A hundred." Andy hadn't hesitated but watched him closely.

"How well do you know the back roads in this county?"

"Is that a personal question?" She pouted, then offered a small flirty smile. Andy was sitting upright facing him, her back against the dash.

"Maybe." He grinned. No use upsetting her by something that still might be just a figment of his imagination. "If we needed to ditch somebody, think you could do it?" He had her full attention now.

"It'd be easy." She started to turn her head in the direction of his gaze. Roughly grabbing her chin, he turned her back to face him.

"Can't let on we suspect anything."

"Who is it?"

"Damned if I know."

Actually, he thought he knew. How could he be so naive as to think he could do a favor, pay with seven years of his life and then be left to enjoy two million dollars? He had even entertained the idea of arranging to have a gun waiting when he got out but had thought it too risky. A gun in the possession of a felon could turn a routine traffic stop into a major event. He wasn't planning to stay in the States any longer than he had to. A gun could be purchased later.

"I think we need to change our plans. If I wanted to rent a plane, is the closest small airstrip still the one at Lovington?"

"Aerowest Charters. If they aren't open, we could try Hobbs Field."

"How long will it take to get there?"

"Maybe an hour."

Eric checked his watch. The storm might give them some time. Time to dump the Caddy and become inconspicuous. Then if they had to wait until morning to rent a plane, they'd be okay. It didn't look like the tail was too eager to move. Probably put off by Andy's being there.

"Wait at the top of the drive until I tell you to pull out on the highway."

Andy nodded, pumped the gas, and slipped the old car into gear. Slowly inching forward, they wound their way out of the lot, stopping for cars of locals turning in to park and begin the weekend. Eric had turned the rearview mirror to check the Dakota. He wasn't disappointed. It was pulling out.

"Which way is the closest turnoff to a back road?"

"To the right. About five miles down we'll intersect County Five. There's a maze of section roads that cuts through four large ranches. We'll be okay. The roads are graveled."

Eric smiled. He liked the way she had jumped right in. No questions. Just an escape plan. He was at her mercy as much as the tail.

"Let's do it." He had to yell. The rain was washing over the car in waves now. "What do you call these? Toad Stranglers?"

She didn't respond. She was intent on turning at the top of the drive. The water was already making the traction tricky for the big rear-wheel drive vehicle. The sliding didn't instill confidence, but the headlights of the pickup following them didn't either.

Damn. Dan was lost. And there wasn't a snowball's chance that he even had the slightest idea where he was. In the middle of nowhere everything looked alike in broad daylight, the dark had him totally turned around. Dan pulled over to the side of the road. He must have missed the marker. He needed to find County Road Number Five. Stay on it for thirty miles before turning to the right. He double-checked the map.

The start of the downpour caught him by surprise. He flipped on the wipers but realized they were useless. He'd have to wait it out, couldn't go anywhere in this anyway. He left on the park lights, pulled a roll of Life Savers from the glove compartment and leaned against the steering wheel. A nap? Or contemplation? He chose the nap. If he had to think too much, he might see what he was doing as idiocy.

"You okay?"

There was no going a hundred in a blinding storm, but Andy had pushed the old tank up to fifty. Her arms were rigid, hands gripping the wheel.

"I don't want to miss the turn. According to the odometer, we've gone five miles." Andy slowed, intent on the right side of the highway.

"There. Thirty feet. County marker." Eric was pounding the windshield with his index finger. Parking in high school hoping to grope and get groped hadn't made him this excited to see a county road.

"Got it."

The Caddy left the highway and slipped and swished down a short incline before leveling out onto a narrow but seemingly stable stretch of gravel. The road was slightly elevated with steep edges that allowed for good drainage. The rain seemed to be slowing. Eric rolled down the window. Squinting into the wet and wind, he watched behind for some sign of the tail. The flicker of headlights was no more than a half mile back.

"Too close." Eric eased around to face Andy. "I think we need a Plan B."

He watched as she chewed her lip. He could tell the fun was gone. She looked scared and couldn't keep the tremor out of her voice.

"Let me think. Past Elm Creek Bridge there's some silos. An access road makes a big U around the back. We could pull in and wait till he goes by. It'll work if I can see with my lights off."

Why not? They probably didn't have much of a choice. Eric was beginning to curse himself about the lack of a gun. The worst of the storm seemed to have passed. There was just enough rain to keep the wipers on.

"How far to the bridge?"

"Maybe a half mile."

The high beams were blinding and coming up fast. He was able to make out the hood ornament. The truck was practically on top of them.

"Do you think this guy's really dangerous? Maybe if we just pulled over?" Andy looked terrified.

"I think we're past having a friendly chat."

The first bullet ricocheted off the fender, making a loud ping. The second found the left rear tire. The Caddy listed but kept going on the rim.

"Floorboard her," Eric screamed. He could see the bridge.

"I'm sorry. They said they wouldn't hurt you…they just wanted to talk…." Andy sobbed and fought to control the steering wheel as the Caddy fishtailed violently.

With a jolt the front wheels connected with the bridge planking, bucking both of them into the unpadded roof overhead. The low guard rails caught the swing of the Caddy first on the left, then on the right.

Eric lunged for the wheel. Andy was no longer in control, her body slumped against the driver's side door, her head bouncing off her chest. He screamed her name, but the sound got lost in a thunderous roar as the car was thrust upward, suspended above the bridge before being plummeted downward. They were being pushed by a solid wall of water that was rolling the Caddy on the crest of a thirty-foot wave. Andy's body hit him in the side; the back of her head caught his nose. It was the last thing Eric remembered.

Chapter Two

"Assholes."

First the Caddy had gone by doing eighty with no headlights, then a Dodge pickup. It was the pickup that had forced Dan onto the soft shoulder. Thank God the Tercel's front-wheel drive kept him out of trouble. Kids. He hadn't missed anything. Only his sister thought parenting was a sacred calling. He thought it was more like an obligation you were lucky to live through. But then that was just another way he differed from Carolyn.

He cracked the window. The air smelled fresh. He breathed deeply and switched on his high beams. A ride in the country wasn't too bad after a good hard rain. He'd just passed a marker. He was on County Five.

At first the headlights looked like they were in his lane. He blinked his lights then wrenched the wheel to the right. It was the truck again, the same one that was on the heels of the Caddy. But that had been no kid driving. He could be mistaken, but it looked like Ray. Good ol' Sheriff Ray who saw an alien now and then. Sure was a shitty night for sightings, must have other reasons for burning up the back roads.

Dan goosed the Tercel up a steep incline and suddenly at the top, the headlights picked up nothing but water. "Holy shit." He slammed on the brakes and jumped out. The roar of the water was deafening. In the surreal light, the twisted steel cross bars of the bridge looked like bad Modern Art. It had been one of those Roosevelt era wooden plank one-lane jobs with concrete supports and steel reinforcements. The sign that should have said Elm Creek had disappeared. Creek? Right about now it could put the Mississippi to shame.

Dan watched full-grown trees tumble forward where the bridge had been, tossed like toothpicks up then down, singly or in criss-crossed piles of three or four. He thought he saw the four stiff legs of a cow push up through the black water to twirl in a circle before the suction of undertow pulled her down. Was he watching United Life and Casualty's millions spread across the surrounding fields? This was a killer, an expensive killer.

Then it struck him. The pink Cadillac. Had it made it across? Only Sheriff Ray had come back. Timing put it just about here when the bridge was wiped out. It'd be tough to survive all that force. If he were religious, he'd come up with something to say now, but nothing profound came to mind. He got back into the Tercel hoping that there hadn't been a loss of life. So much for a night of snooping. He'd reassess tomorrow, maybe try a new tactic: corner Billy Roland and get some answers.

"Just a minute."

The pounding had disoriented him. It wasn't light yet. What could be so important? Dan pulled on his jeans before opening the door of his motel room.

"Mr. Eklund thought you might like to ride with us this morning. Survey the flood damage. This one was a bad one. We're meeting at his place. Daybreak, 'bout an hour."

Sheriff Ray filled the door. This time there was a shiny badge on the flap of his shirt pocket right over his first name stitched in bright yellow floss. Behind him the Dakota was parked next to the Tercel. No mistake, Ray was the one who ran him off the road last night.

"Sure. Firsthand look sounds good."

"We're assuming you won't mind a little all-day horseback ride?"

"Hey, my choice of transportation."

Jesus. He'd worked summers for a dude ranch during college and the last time on a horse had cost him two broken ribs. But he'd wipe that smirk out of Sheriff Ray's voice if he died trying.

"See you there." Ray started toward the pickup. "Oh yeah, almost forgot. Bridge over Elm Creek washed out last night." Ray took his time getting the rest of the message out, waiting for Dan to react? Give himself away? "Take the highway, three turns past the Co-op, then left thirty-seven miles. Can't miss it."

Dan kept his face impassive. God, he hated this "he knows that I know" game. He saw me out there last night. But the question is why was he chasing the Cadillac? Speeding teenagers? An old pink Caddy surely couldn't be confused for a spaceship. He watched Ray leave the motel parking lot. He'd skip breakfast and get going. Could be Miss Iris would be serving up something hot off the griddle. He caught himself humming in the shower.

If he were the type to reflect on nature's injustices, the havoc of a flood had to be second or third on the list behind, maybe, a tornado or hurricane. The early morning sun revealed acres of gray-brown silt. Silt was clinging to everything. Milo lay flat in a field with a gray-brown mud wash plastering it to the earth. He'd spotted two dead calves, bloated, tongues swollen, eyes covered with flies, their coats scruffy and mud-stiff.

The county road was surprisingly well-drained, a puddle or two in low spots, but overall, safe going. It'd be awhile before anyone could get equipment into the fields though. He didn't try to hurry; he figured the inspection team would wait. He had a sneaking feeling that this ride was organized for his benefit, anyway. A chance to meet Mr. Billy R. Eklund in action, a lord of the manor scenario—let me show you how much of mother earth I own. See the good old boy in the midst of devastation and then out of conscience pay off those claims and go home. He'd see.

Dan counted about twenty cars, mostly pickups, lining the drive in front of the house. One was a vet truck; the enclosed back made it a clinic on wheels. Lot of the large animal docs were going to that—a portable phone and an outfitted truck. Progress. Always something new.

He hadn't reached the top step before the front door was thrown open.

"Mr. Mahoney. I understand we've been missing each other. Billy Roland here."

Like it had to be announced. The beefy hand he held out sported a two-carat diamond pinky ring.

"Glad we're finally touching base."

"You just let me know how I can help. You need any information, I want you to know that you can come to the source. That's important. No need asking questions of others, just come right on out here and chat with ol' Billy. Now, come along. There's a buffet in here that'll knock your socks off."

Well, it hadn't taken Judge Cyrus long to share their little conversation. Dan followed Billy Roland into the house. A gaggle of male voices—excited laughter, a couple bass guffaws, the back-slapping kind, probably the judge—boomed out from a room off the end of a long hall. Was this some sort of Old West thing? Eat hearty, then ride out to survey the damage? Count the dead livestock? His own appetite waned thinking about what was ahead.

He followed Billy Roland past the polished oak bannister at the foot of the stairs that curved upward out of the parquet oak floor. The chandelier threw rainbow chips of light across the Persian entry rug. No adjectives came to mind that quite captured the opulence. This sure wasn't his apartment in Chicago.

"Everyone? Listen up. This here's Mr. Mahoney. I 'spect you all to show him some kindness." Billy R. had pushed open the two paneled doors and entered a massive study, a man's room all hunter green and brass, dark stone fireplace, marble bar, walnut desk to match the walls.

Dan acknowledged the hellos and shook hands with half a dozen friendly types who pushed toward him. Judge Cyrus led the pack. There was a stale smell of tobacco and bourbon. Even Billy Roland was nursing a tumbler of pale golden liquid over ice. Dan checked his watch. It was seven nineteen. He didn't need to bolster the old testosterone this early. In fact, he'd have a hard time putting away the heaping plate of scrambled eggs and biscuits someone had handed him.

"If you don't mind, I'll just trade this in for a cup of coffee, black." The uniformed servant didn't bat an eye; the plate disappeared and Dan had his mug of steaming coffee before he could be urged to take seconds on the eggs.

He watched Billy Roland work the room. A slap on the back here, a whispered word and an explosion of laughter there. One of the servants interrupted and indicated the phone. Billy Roland took the call at the bar. Must be difficult to get away from business. There was no sign of Iris. Probably wouldn't be at these all-male gatherings, sort of a cross between a roundup and a foxhunt.

"Let's you and me push back from that buffet table and think about getting this show on the road." Billy Roland had returned to stand by him. Dan was wondering how the man could look just like he thought he would. A combination of a past President, someone who could get into swinging a beagle by the ears, and his grandfather who looked over his glasses, fixed him with a stare like he was taking a sighting off the end of his nose, a bulbous large-pored thing that dominated his face.

But that's where the comparison to his grandfather stopped. Billy Roland was something else. His posture screamed intimacy. An arm thrown around Dan's shoulders, leaning just close enough to rub that belly-muscle slack paunch against him, voice conspiratorially low when he wanted his attention. Dan fought back an urge to make sure he still had a billfold.

"I'm going to take Dan here on down to the barns. You all join us real soon now, you hear?" With that pronouncement Billy Roland steered Dan through the kitchen, a high-ceilinged monstrous room with assorted clerestories, ignored the genuflecting servants whose jabber in Spanish had abruptly ceased, pushed through the back door, crossed the porch, a screened affair filled with expensive outdoor furniture, and covered the distance from the house to the closest barn in a dozen strides.

"Hank. Thought you'd be saddled up by now."

Hank must be the vet, Dan thought, unless all the ranch hands wore a lab coat over chaps, but Billy Roland was more intent on walking down the long row of stalls than introducing him.

"Here we go. Baby Belle. Hell of a smooth ride, just like her long-backed mama. She'll do you just fine."

Dan thought that Hank blanched and started to say something. But knowing which side the bread was buttered on probably buttoned his lip. Baby Belle in the meantime had reared and struck the front of the stall a couple times and Dan hadn't seen her ears stand up once.

"Ray was saying you know your horseflesh." He was handing him a halter and lead. "Saddles over there, tack room on the left."

One time forty years ago when his parents moved to the suburbs and he had had to change schools he felt this same way going out at recess. The wall of sixth grade boys had bloodied his nose, kicked him in the shins, bruised a kneecap but accepted him because he didn't yell "uncle." Was it too late to yell now? He slid the stall door open wide enough to step inside and eased the lead rope over Belle's neck. The horse eyed him, sized him up, let him buckle the halter in place before lashing out with a sidewinder-fast front hoof, catching him a glancing blow below the knee.

Without dwelling on what he had to do, Dan stepped her out into the walkway, grabbed her head, a hand on each side of the halter, and muscled her backward, pushing hard, not letting her get her bearings.

"Coming through. Little attitude adjustment."

He backed the mare through the crowd entering the barn, wheeled her around and headed her backward to where they started. Then he released her, leaned close and whispered, "One more kick and you're Alpo, sweetheart," in his best Bogart imitation.

But the mare had broken a sweat on her neck and had both ears forward. Leery respect, Dan decided. He'd won one and might not be tested again. He tied her to the stall door and went to get tack. Was it his imagination or was Billy Roland struck dumb? That's a man doesn't like his fun ruined.

The riders waited in twos and threes before falling in behind Billy Roland. Sheriff Ray was conspicuously missing but, as if on cue, a rider appeared to the right beyond the strand of poplar and cantered toward them.

"Most damage seems to be in the back forty. Lots of fences down, twelve calves dead or dying." Ray's horse breathed heavily. Ray must have been in a hurry to report in. It seemed strange that the county sheriff would ride fences and not a foreman.

"I'll pick up some extra syringes. Y'all go on. I'll catch up." The vet turned back toward the barn.

The first couple miles were uneventful. The damage was extensive to crops, but they had only seen one dead calf, the distraught mother standing guard, bawling her anxiety. Telephone poles were down or leaning precariously. The creek water had receded but wasn't contained. The sun was now almost overhead, and the swollen earth steamed. And so did Dan. He had taken off his jacket, next the vest and rolled his shirt sleeves above his elbows.

At the first sign of black gnats, he'd rolled them back down. The gnats were merciless. They hung in the air in undulating swarms sometimes drifting over the horse's ears, sometimes humming above his head. He moved Belle out away from the others and sought relief from the insects by steering her to higher ground.

The ridge seemed to please Belle, who stretched her neck forward to catch a nibble or two of grass and gave Dan a vantage point from which to survey Elm Creek and its path of destruction.

At first he missed the pink Caddy mired in the mud listing badly to the right, water running freely through its windows. Only the hood, the roof, and the left rear fender were above water. With a coating of silt, it blended with other debris choking the edges of the field.

"Over here." Dan yelled and pointed, then goosed Belle down the slope, keeping her at a trot until they were a few feet from the car.

"Oh Lord." Billy Roland sloshed around the perimeter of the Cadillac. "This here's the Lott girl's car, isn't it? You don't think she could be in there, do you?"

Sheriff Ray seemed reluctant to act or offer an opinion.

"I think it'd be a good idea for you to check, Sheriff."

Dan watched as the sheriff eyed the water and muck then handed his reins to the man closest to him and dismounted with a splash. This called for a new pair of Justins; as Dan watched, the water rose over the tops of Ray's boots.

"Need help?" Two others were wading toward Ray. Then the three of them circled the car in the now waist-high water, one man taking a gulp of air and ducking under the surface to check the car's interior.

A hand broke the surface of the water. You didn't need to be a coroner to know it belonged to someone dead, Dan thought, a dead woman not very old. It took the three men another five minutes to bring the body to the shallows and then pull it out of the water. The vet did a cursory once over and offered an opinion that her neck had been broken. Probably one of those point of impact things, instantaneous, no suffering.

"Should we check for anyone else?" Dan thought Sheriff Ray gave him a long look. Probably with good reason. Dan could have sworn that there had been someone on the passenger side last night. He urged Belle closer to the wrecked car. She shied at the upended tree that held the Caddy anchored, and it was then that he saw the manila envelope stuck in its branches. The envelope had had time to dry but the contents were stuck together. Dan pulled a couple pages apart, ordinary prison release papers, and then he saw the bank book.

Seven years ago someone had deposited two million dollars into an account at Midland Savings and Loan in Tatum, New Mexico, Judge Franklin Cyrus's bank. Some sixth sense nudged Dan to commit the account's seven-digit number to memory. Could be worth looking into, but he didn't quite know why.

"Looks like we might find an Eric Linden, if we look a little longer."

Dan watched Billy Roland move his horse toward him. He had tucked the flap of the envelope inside to suggest he hadn't opened it. Something told him that was safer. Just read the name off the front. Billy Roland's expression wasn't pleasant, and he knew without being told that Billy Roland was familiar with this Eric Linden. Knew him and didn't think much of him. Odd. According to the papers, Mr. Linden had been locked up for seven years.

"Oh Jesus, that's just like Andrea. Give a lift to any poor soul needing it."

Billy Roland reached for the envelope, opened it, quickly checked the contents, then stuffed it into his saddlebags. Someone had ridden back to the Double Horseshoe for a winch and tractor. Dan and the others waited on dry ground. There was a sack of sandwiches and a cooler of iced beer, but

Dan couldn't have found an appetite with both hands. There, that sounded Texan. He was getting better at this.

Someone must have called the dead girl's father because he arrived with the tractor. A short swarthy man who had to be restrained. He seemed more angry than grief-stricken. But who could say how anyone should act at a moment like this. The Creek reluctantly gave up the Caddy. After four or five false starts the car pulled free and slid to shallow water.

It was empty. Probably a miracle that the girl's body stayed put even with seat belts. There wasn't one square inch of glass left in the car and the passenger side door was doubled back against the front fender. Dan tied Belle to a tree branch and walked over for a closer look.

There had been a time when he'd pulled this kind of detail every day. Rookie claim adjuster, appraise the damage, assess a dollar value....Something was bugging him about the Caddy. Left rear wheel was gone. Not just the tire, the whole damned rim. Where the water had washed it clean of mud, there was bright metal, like someone had lifted the wheel off. Other than the front right tire being flat, the other tires were still on the rims.

Dan bent down to take a closer look and his hand bumped across a groove in the car's fender. He straightened to look.

Fresh crease in the paint. He'd bet just about everything he owned that Andrea and her passenger had been a shooter's target. Might explain the left rear wheel being gone. If so, someone had come out here pretty early and rearranged the evidence.

"Got something there?" Billy Roland leaned over the saddle horn.

"No. Just reflecting on how severe nature can be." Dan heard the creak of leather as Billy Roland shifted his weight in the saddle.

"Just plain awesome."

"Any idea who this Eric guy was?"

He thought Billy Roland started to say something, then changed his mind.

"Just somebody who wanted a ride into town, I'd say. Ray says he saw 'em at the Double Diamond around seven. As to why they were out here, well, son, I hope I don't need to spark your imagination." Billy Roland turned his horse toward the road, then suddenly wheeled the big gelding back around. "I can't believe my lack of hospitality. I meant to say something this morning. I want you to pack up and get out of that motel. Spend your time out here at the Double Horseshoe. I know there's some paperwork needs going over."

Conflict of interest came to mind, but Dan also saw the benefit of snooping in the open. "I'll take you up on it."

At the moment he couldn't get this Linden guy out of his mind. Spend seven years locked up with two million waiting and then get gypped out of spending it by some freak act of nature...or a bullet. Dan would probably never know which.

Billy Roland's house exuded grandeur. Dan sat on the veranda in the coolness of early morning and enjoyed its Victorian charm; the high-ceilinged porch offered the perfect view of green fields and crisply white barns. He'd slept in a hundred-year-old canopy bed with crocheted edgings on the sheets and goose down in the pillows. It was the best rest that he'd had so far.

His adjoining bathroom had a claw-and-ball porcelain tub, probably another original, and matching pedestal sink. The bordello red of the flowered wallpaper was muted by real walnut wainscoting and varnished wood floors. If you had to live out in nowhere, this was the way to do it.

The breakfast table had been set up on the east side of the house to catch the morning sun. Silver and china rested on real linen. Everything had a turn-of-the-century look to it. Not newly purchased antiques, but rather, a grow old with the house feel like the wicker chair he was sitting on. This must have been Billy Roland's family home.

"Billy Roland's awful sorry. He should be back tomorrow night."

He started. Dan had almost forgotten about the woman who sat across from him. He could be wrong but the hair seemed freshly done. Iris sounded apologetic, so why wasn't he convinced about Billy Roland feeling remorseful about stranding him?

Dan reached for the orange marmalade. "I'd like to spend some time today with the vet. Hank, isn't it?"

Iris nodded and poured the two of them more coffee. Amazing, but the servants seemed to be gone, too. Their intimate breakfast on the veranda hadn't been interrupted once.

"I'd like to show you around, first."

"As long as it doesn't include any saddle time. I've 'bout had my quota for the next five years."

Iris pursed her lips and leaned forward. "You know Billy Roland thought you might need a rub down."

He couldn't argue with that, but he hoped it wasn't in Iris' repertoire.

"I was supposed to call over to the Ranch. I got a friend who does that Japanese stuff—Shih Tzu, I think."

"Shiatsu."

"Whatever. Does that sound good?"

"Why not?"

He watched Iris walk into the house to set up the appointment. The view to his right took in the swimming pool and a half dozen cabanas with thatched roofs. To his left must be five acres of pasture; huge irrigation wands swept back and forth in lazy one-hundred-and-eighty-degree arcs.

"Ten o'clock, okay?" Iris had opened a window in the study.

"Sure."

Time for a swim, loosen up the old muscles then let an expert untie any knots that were left. He could get used to living like this.

"You know Billy Roland thought we might like to go over to the fair this afternoon."

"Fair?"

"County Fair at Harper. Just the other side of the state line. The Charolais are going to be judged. Some important guy is here from back East supposed to really know his stuff."

He didn't know if he liked someone planning—no, wasn't a better word *controlling*—his day? But, actually, why not? The show might help him get a feel for the Eklund investment.

He helped the massage therapist set up her table in a sitting room on the second floor. The orange tube top and crinkled gauze skirt gave her a hippy look. Not that that was a word in vogue today, but she reminded him of times when girls looked like that. Soft long brown hair fell over her shoulders. She seemed shy, reticent to start a conversation.

He stepped into a guest bath off the hall and returned draped with an oversized towel. She was waving lighted incense in a circle from the center of the room.

"For purifying." She smiled through lowered lashes.

He wondered if one tiny stick would be enough for the Eklund residence.

"Let's start with you face down," she said.

Her strokes were firm and even and lulled him into losing track of time.

"Finished. Unless there's someplace I missed?"

Was this some kind of code he was supposed to respond to?

"I'm fine. You're great."

She leaned over him, her hair tickling his chest. It was obvious he'd missed his cue. "I've been paid to stay longer." Her mouth was about three inches from his. She waited for him to say something, put an invitation into words, he guessed. "I mean, if you'd like a nooner?"

He sat up slowly pushing her back to stand in front of him and knew he looked stupid trying to keep the towel from slipping. She'd just offered to jump him, and he was being Mr. Modest.

"I don't think so."

"The money puts you off, doesn't it? I mean it's being paid for already." She continued to stare at him, then with a laugh added, "I'm probably the same age as your daughter and I can tell you're the type that that would bother."

He almost groaned out loud. What type was that? Too old for anything under thirty-five?

"Course, there's always Miss Iris." For being tight-lipped a couple hours ago, she was positively loquacious now. "But I never said that," she added, then winked.

He slipped off the table and went to retrieve his clothes. By the time he got back, the massage therapist was gone. He hadn't even tipped her. That was probably taken care of, too. He found himself getting angry. Just that slow burn that comes with being used. Wasn't this some not so subtle way to get a person in the right camp? Provide a little nooky in exchange for looking the other way during the investigation? Well, Billy Roland had miscalculated. He wasn't about to throw away a career for loose change and free ass.

Harper was the Roby County seat. The two-and-a-half-hour drive from the Double Horseshoe was taken up mostly by listening to the vast collection of Country Western CDs that Iris just happened to have on hand. He got the distinct feeling that she'd been coached to keep a tight lip. Which was all right with him. After the morning, he welcomed the silence.

The town was bigger than Tatum, more prosperous looking with a town square. The courthouse in the middle of a half acre bordered by red-orange zinnias appeared to have had a European influence with its cut stone walls topped by turrets and rounded parapets.

"We can grab a bite in town or go on out to the fairgrounds."

"I can wait." Dan checked his watch. Two twenty.

At first glance there didn't seem to be a parking space left in the lot to the side of the entrance. But a gate attendant recognized Iris and waved her through then pointed to a VIP spot behind the dairy barns.

The fairgrounds must cover four or five acres. Dan admitted his surprise to Iris.

"This land is part of a co-op. 'Bout five ranchers went together. They have some real big shows like calf roping and bull riding in addition to livestock judging—all national level."

Lunch sounded good even if it meant standing in line to get a mug of root beer and what the sign said was the best bratwurst and kraut on a bun to be had, anywhere. They ate at a picnic table, one of ten set up as an outdoor dining area. It seemed to take Iris forever to finish. She was preoccupied with wetting a finger and snagging every stray strand of cabbage that had escaped to the paper covering the bun.

"You think I'm wasting my life stuck out there on the Double Horseshoe?"

He hadn't been prepared and wasn't sure he'd have the right answer even if he'd thought about it, but he did take a couple seconds to get organized.

"What else would you like to do?"

"Oh, I don't know. Travel, I guess."

"People who travel always come home to somewhere. Seems like you could travel and still live at the Double Horseshoe."

The answer hadn't been the one she wanted to hear, Dan thought, judging from how quickly she stood up, wadded up the lunch papers, and dropped them in a trash barrel.

"C'mon. The judging's about to start."

Dan followed Iris single-file through rows of booths, all selling chances on something. Calliope music blared from a midway of rides to the right. The cow barns were ahead and Iris walked directly to the covered arena in the center and climbed six rows up in the bleachers behind the judging stand.

"I just love the smell in here." She kicked off her sandals and wiggled tanned toes sporting bright red polish before propping her feet on the seat in front.

Dan tried hard to see what could be so appealing. Cow patties and sawdust left a little to be desired. The arena had been divided into three rings and a group of judges were making their final selections. Dairy cows, probably yearlings.

"You want a program?"

"That would be helpful."

Iris skipped barefoot down the bleachers and disappeared through a side door. It was thirty minutes before she returned.

"Hank says we're on in fifteen minutes."

"How's Hank?" It wasn't that Dan cared, but he thought they ought to talk about something. It was apparent Iris didn't want to watch the judging.

"Okay. Could you stand another root beer? Coke, maybe?"

Iris was absolutely wired. On something? It was hard to tell. But her energy level had certainly jumped.

"I promised Hank I'd bring him something back."

"Nothing for me."

He'd had to shout because she was already at the bottom of the bleachers. Maybe she was just excited. But she hadn't shown that much interest in cattle. The whole thing was getting a little crazy.

The Charolais judging started at exactly three thirty. It didn't take a program to see that the bulls were first. Iris was nowhere to be seen, so Dan matched the numbers on the entries to those listed in the program. Immaculately dressed young Hispanic men in white shirts and pressed jeans led Billy Roland's entries around the ring, posed them, backed them, and stepped to one side so that the judges could move in closer. Each used a slim silver baton to urge the bull to place a hoof just right or retreat a certain number of paces and turn a certain way, and each handler stayed on his toes, always aware of just how the bull looked from every angle and how to bring the animal's best profile forward at the twitch of a tail.

This was a cadre of trained experts. Teams of young men and animals who practiced long hours together. Fifteen entries came from eight different ranches; two ranches outside Dalhart and Dumas rivaled the Double Horseshoe for total number of blue ribbons when the first round of judging was completed.

As they left the ring, Dan spotted Hank leading a particularly fine animal through the double doors to line up waiting his turn to be judged. Must be something special to be shown by the resident vet himself. But Dan could see that special something from where he was sitting. The bull's coat was gleaming silver with a darker gray mottling on his legs. Hooves were a distinct black and shone like patent leather. The bull had been polled but a lack of horns didn't take away from the sheer size, the frightening largeness of the animal that made a statement of raw power.

But he seemed as tame as a kitten. Dan vaguely wondered if they were allowed to use drugs. Could training keep this animal docile and compliant? Over the loudspeaker, an announcer was summoning all Charolais bulls two years and over. Dan glanced at the program. Hank moved into the ring with Mountain Run's Cisco Kid.

Directly across from him about twenty businessmen in suits, boots and western hats lounged in an air-conditioned glassed-in viewing box. Two of the men looked to be Japanese. Interesting. Dan was suddenly caught by the enormity of the cattle industry, its internationalism for lack of a better word. He knew that Billy Roland was a renowned judge and worked competitions from Columbia to Japan, but seeing the mix of interested bystanders brought the point home. Considering that the judging had started at seven a.m., there had been one hell of a lot of beef traipse past the stands in eight hours.

Hank was now moving his young bull to the center, backing and turning it with the finesse of someone who seemed to be an extension of the animal itself. A young man followed at the heels of the bull urging it onward working in unison with Hank. Hank's muscled forearms pushed at the four-snap cuffs of his western shirt. His lanky frame was supple and handsome in western slacks and ostrich boots. Couldn't be too many years out of school, Dan surmised, a young man somewhere in his early thirties, already set for life working for Billy Roland. There wasn't even a sweat stain on his hat band.

Dan watched the judge start his rounds, checking his clipboard as he eyed each entry. Hank and the bull were posed perfectly. There couldn't have been a hair out of place. Then with his mouth wide, the bull gagged, shook his head, gagged again. The third gag reflex pushed the bull's tongue out of his mouth, strangling a tortured bellow as his legs folded beneath him.

It took a second to realize what had happened. Hank was all action. Someone ran to him with a plastic case of medicines and syringes and he plunged a long needle into the bull's neck, then another under the right leg. The bull didn't even twitch. Dan didn't need to check any papers to know that the animal was insured. Something in six figures, high six figures. He'd bet on that. What galled him was the audacity of it all. Billy Roland planned for him to see it. Treat the insurance dick to a little unexplained death. Dare him to figure out how he did it.

A machine that looked like a forklift hoisted the limp bull onto a flatbed hospital cart pulled by a tractor. Dan took the bleachers in twos. He wasn't going to let the bull out of his sight. But the first thing would be to get another vet involved. That all-important second opinion.

"I want a complete workup. Blood, tissue...you guys know your business." Dan directed the team of lab assistants and conferred with the show vet, leaving Hank stewing on the sidelines.

"You can't keep me away from my own animal. At least let me do an examination." Hank's cheeks were flushed and he'd grabbed Dan by the arm as he walked by.

"If you so much as touch this bull, the insurance policy is null and void." Dan should probably watch his anger but at the moment he had no reason not to suspect Hank.

Two hours later, fifteen vials and an assortment of plastic containers packed in dry ice were handed over to FedEx for overnight delivery to Chicago and an identical set to Texas A&M. The judging had been canceled and the arena posted No Entry. Dan sat in the bleachers and watched a team of specialists collect samples of sawdust, tap water, and flecks of paint from the gates and from any surface or foodstuff that might have been consumed or even licked. He'd placed a call to Chicago to verify the bull's insured sum; he had been right, six hundred thousand.

After the team left, he continued to sit staring at the empty arena now bathed in shadows. Iris and Hank were long gone; back to the Double Horseshoe, to confer with Billy Roland? Congratulate each other on a job well done? Dan had a sinking feeling that he might not ever figure out how they did it.

The clang of metal echoed around him. Someone had opened a side door in the corrugated steel building.

"No one's allowed in the arena. Judging will resume in the morning," Dan called out then waited.

No answer. The door clanged shut. The silence was comforting. He could hear the muffled screams of kids on the midway. Rides. As a teen he'd dump more than a week's allowance on that thing where you stood at the edge and thanks to centrifugal force were sucked flat to the sides as it whirled vertically—then tossed your cookies after it stopped.

"Don't turn around."

The voice was male, low pitched and not familiar, coming from someone underneath him in the darkness. Dan realized the hair on his arms was standing up.

"Do I know you?"

"You will. I'm going to put a piece of paper on the seat behind you. Don't pick it up until you hear me leave."

"What's this about?"

"I think you know."

Dan listened to the sound of someone reaching up and placing something on the bleacher behind him. There wasn't any easy way to get to the man. He'd be out of there before Dan could squeeze through the plank seating and drop to the floor. Besides, curiosity had replaced fear. There was something about the man. Maybe he had the answers.

"Is there more?"

"Could be."

"How can I get in touch?"

"Leave a map on the dash of the Tercel. Circle where you'll be."

Dan waited a full minute after he heard the door shut before turning around. Who was this man? How did he know what he was driving? Could be a hired hand at the Double Horseshoe. Some disgruntled cowpoke looking for revenge. What did he care as long as the information helped nail Billy Roland?

He leaned back and picked up the folded piece of paper. A company's insert—the kind of detailed disclaimer that came with a boxed drug. He smoothed the creases and could just make out *sucostrin succinvicholine.* A muscle relaxant. Then penciled in the margin were two words: "tail vein." Virtually undetectable. Dan knew that was what had happened to Mountain Run's Cisco Kid. Could he prove it? No. But he knew and the knowing might be power enough.

He'd had the drive back to formulate a plan but the driver of the cattle truck had been talkative, filling him in, almost reverently, on how Billy Roland's neighbors revered him.

There were tales of scholarships, new church pews, operations for the indigent...he could do no wrong. It was just an echo of what the judge had said. Oh well, the bigger they are, the harder they bounce.

The Double Horseshoe was ablaze with light. Dan had barely stepped inside before Iris caught his arm.

"He's in the study."

Dan thought Iris looked tired. For the first time, he noticed little lines etched around her mouth and a gray puffiness below her eyes. Being Billy Roland's wife could be a tough job.

"Looks as though you been rode hard and put away wet." Billy Roland's attempt at humor fell flat. Dan wasn't in the mood.

"I don't think we need to talk about this for very long. We'll meet in the morning. I'll need full financial disclosures. Everything. You can bring a lawyer in. I'll take your statement under oath."

He left the room before Billy Roland could react. Upstairs, he packed everything he'd brought and carried it out to the Tercel before going back down the hall to the study.

"I want you to be thinking about something. Sucostrin succinvicholine. Sleep tight." Dan closed the door behind him.

Billy Roland made no move to detain him.

He got his old room back at the Silver Spur. Before going to bed, he unfolded a map of New Mexico and circled Roswell in red. He paperclipped a business card with the local office phone number on the back to the upper right hand corner and left it on the dash. The map was gone in the morning.

"I'm not asking you to understand, son, I'm asking you to believe me. I don't have any problem with your muscle-relaxant theory. It's as good as any. But what son-of-a-bitch would do such a thing?" Billy Roland was on his second Glenlivet over.

"I need to tape this session." Dan placed a recorder on the edge of the desk.

"All right by me. You got any problems with that, J.J.?"

The lawyer looked up from an accordion file on the coffee table, nodded his assent, and went back to pulling out papers. Dan had instantly disliked the man. Italian shoes and a silk shirt which was open just one button too far to show a quarter-inch-thick gold chain. His dark hair, all the same length to below the ear, was combed straight back and plastered into place. His round tortoise shell glasses looked more for show than a prescription for myopic sight. J.J. stood for Juan Jose but that's as much as he knew; he guessed home was Mexico.

"Start by stating your full name, today's date, and where this deposition is being taken."

While Billy Roland was doing that, Dan opened the file that J.J. had just handed him on Mountain Run's Cisco Kid. It wasn't like no one was cooperating; he was bowled over by the eagerness of both Billy R. and his lawyer. Made Dan think there might be some honest to God remorse at work here—at least in regard to the Cisco Kid.

Dan pulled an advertisement and attached bill of sale from the folder.

"Let's start with where and when you bought the Cisco Kid."

"September 23, 1998, from Cecil Tucker Farms, Green Valley, Arizona."

"Asking price and price paid?"

"I, uh, Hank, you want to intercede here, explain to Dan what the circumstances were at that time?" Hank started to step forward.

J.J. pushed the file folder aside. "I didn't hear any questions from Mr. Mahoney." He scrutinized Dan. "Are there any?"

"I suppose there should be. Asking price for a six-month-old bull calf, seventy-five hundred dollars and price paid, fifty-five hundred—amount insured, two hundred thousand at eighteen months and six hundred thousand at age four.

My question for the record is, what takes the worth of a bull calf from fifty-five hundred to six hundred thousand in under four years?"

"Because there were some medical issues at the time of purchase that impacted price. Hank, scoot a chair on up here and talk into this thing." Billy Roland pushed his own chair out of the way.

Hank, looking like he'd just buried his best friend—which might be the truth, Dan thought—pulled his chair closer to the desk. Without his customary hat, his curly dark blond hair made him look young, vulnerable even.

"When I first examined Mountain Run's Cisco Kid at approximately six months of age, he appeared to be Cryptorchid."

"Cryptorchid or Monorchid, because it says here—"

"Let me finish. Originally, Cryptorchid. There were no testicles in the scrotal sac. But it was observed that under stimulation, one testicle would descend. It was also determined at that time that Cisco Kid had viable sperm being produced in both testicles."

"But this would still be considered a serious fault? Something highly suspect as a genetic factor, and definitely something you wouldn't want in your herd?" Dan asked.

"True. But Mr. Eklund and I were convinced that an illness suffered soon after weaning might have caused the condition. In short, the only thing that we've done wrong—against show rules, that is—is operate and surgically tighten the ring that keeps those testicles outside the body cavity."

"That's illegal?" Dan said.

"Against show rules. But who's going to find a half-inch suture scar on that part of a bull's anatomy. Who's going to even look for one?"

"So, in yesterday's show, the judge could have dismissed the bull if such a scar had been found?"

"Yeah."

"Has Cisco Kid's ability to sire been tested?"

"He has five on the ground from last spring and we're expecting ten come April next. Quality of offspring helped get us insured by United Life and Casualty. He was outstanding, prepotent—he could have rivaled the best."

"So his condition once corrected didn't cause any problems?"

"We discovered that his sperm count was somewhat lower than what one would hope for in a normal bull of the same age, but this poses no problem with live-cover."

"Are you saying he would not have been a good candidate for A.I.?" Dan followed up for the recorder, "A.I. stands for artificial insemination or the transport of semen to the cow to be bred without the bull being present."

"Might have had some problems," Hank said.

"Now, I'd like you to relate what happened yesterday when you were away from the bull, and who if anyone was left in charge, plus your actions when it was determined that the bull was critically ill or injured. List all medications used, their purpose, generic name, and the lab that produces them."

Dan dropped in a new tape and Hank started to recount the day.

"Dan, could you an' me step out of the room for just a minute. Something I want to show you." Billy Roland picked up an envelope from the table and motioned toward the hallway.

"I want you to look at this."

Dan opened the envelope and saw a transfer of title and a bill of sale for Cisco Kid dated one month ago. The sale price was one million U.S. dollars and the new owner was an Enrico Salazar Garcia, address Venezuela.

"I hope you can see how some son-of-a-bitch cost me four hundred grand."

"Why was the bull even in the show if he was sold?"

"New owner wanted the stamp of approval, a critique, if you will, by the judge yesterday. It was the only time we've shown Cisco Kid. If he got high marks, he would have been air-shipped tomorrow."

"Should we be talking about enemies? Who might want to do this to you?"

"Any man who's got more than his neighbors sparks some jealousy."

Dan thought Billy Roland seemed old there in the half-light of the hallway. Worn out. And it was easy to believe him. Believe that he wouldn't throw four hundred thousand away just to get six and make a point. No, Billy Roland didn't get where he was on bad business deals.

"I'll get back to you with the results of the tests on Cisco Kid. I'm going to be in Roswell for a couple days setting up shop. I'll keep in touch." Dan went back in the study leaving Billy Roland leaning against the wall.

Chapter Three

We are gathered here this morning...

Elaine slipped a stockinged foot out of a black high-heel and absently pressed it into the thick dewy grass. The coolness felt good on her arch. The bright New Mexico sunlight washed the surrounding marble markers a startling white. She adjusted her sunglasses and stole a glance at the crowd. She was surprised at the number of people who had shown up. The curious, mostly.

...to pay our final tribute to this man, your servant, who...

Had she been wrong to choose a religious ceremony? It was bad enough she was burying an empty box, missing the sense of closure that comes from viewing a body. Should she have made it secular, too? What was the worst that could happen? Eric would come back to haunt her?

...strayed from your flock...

Understatement. Fucking understatement. Oops. She was trying not to even think in curse words anymore. It was tough.

Was her shrink right? That she still had to work on forgiving him—even after he was dead? Forgive him for throwing away his family? Maybe she was just upset that she needed a shrink. If this had happened a thousand years ago, she'd pay someone to toss a couple doves in the air and read their flight pattern. Easier, much easier. Just more proof that she was an anachronism.

...but deserves our compassion and understanding...

From the grave? Wasn't she ready to just walk away? Start over? Send Matthew off to college, take that sabbatical. Finish the anthology of poetry she'd worked on for five years.

...as we overlook his trespasses...

She wanted to scream. Even in death he was forcing her to play a part. But to be fair, he hadn't twisted her arm, made her buy the black cap of a hat with a chin length veil and three-digit price tag, the perfect accessory to the black linen suit and tailored pumps. Grieving widow might be her best wifely role. The Emmy for best widow, singly or in a series. God, not a series; once was enough.

High fluffy, gray-white clouds floated over the sun, blocking its glare. She kicked off the other shoe and tried to concentrate on the minister, who droned on extolling the virtues of the air-space contained in the box in front of him, pausing for effect to touch the coffin every fifth sentence. My God, she was so cynical and maybe even on the verge of hysterics. She just wanted this over. A burial of Eric, however symbolic, so that she could get on with life.

But would she have gone through with the divorce had he lived? Or would he have talked her out of it? More promises of repentance, how he needed her.

The first glittering slice of rainbow appeared just above the minister's head, a second to the left and a third just peeked through the clouds between them. Solar halos. It was a sign. It had to be. Her life couldn't be such shit without promised help. Maybe it just attested to her state of mind, but the parhelia were as good a sign as any. Sundogs wouldn't lie.

"No."

"Dan, please."

"God damn it, Carolyn—"

"I hate that language."

"I'm trying to stop."

"Well, it doesn't sound like it."

"Truce?"

"Okay. But I don't know why you won't do this one thing for me. For yourself."

"Have I been wandering around here bemoaning the lack of a love life?"

"You're her dinner partner, for God's sake, you're not taking her to bed."

"That's it, Carolyn, I'm going to get a bar of soap. I will not tolerate that language." The last was said in a pretty good imitation of his sister's voice. And it got the result he wanted. Carolyn burst out laughing.

"Now tell me why this is so important."

"She's my friend. Her son is the same age as Jason. She's a widow."

"I think I hear violins."

"Dan be serious. She's perfect for you."

"Remember the last time you played matchmaker?"

"That was in high school."

"Disasters are long remembered."

"I know you're not gay."

"Thanks. Is that Philip's opinion, too?"

"Don't be snotty. I wish you two would get along."

"We do. Sort of." Carolyn's husband was a little too officious for him, but there wasn't any out-and-out animosity.

"So, we can count on you? You'll sit across from her at dinner and make some kind of small talk, then walk her to her car."

"Hey, who said anything about walking anyone to a car?"

"Okay." Carolyn threw up her hands. "Just the small talk. You don't have to see her again."

And probably won't, Dan concluded to himself.

Dan had been in Roswell two days and he was already restless. His sister had set him up as "dinner companion" to some friend of hers, probably a hopelessly small-town socialite with small-town interests. Bet she'd never heard of the Cubs.

He'd hoped to hear from the informant but there had been nothing. The results were in on the Cisco Kid. Again nothing, not one thing showed up in any test that smelled of foul play. Death was attributed to a bronchial virus. Simple act of nature. He'd drive out tomorrow and tell Billy Roland.

He'd called Midland Savings and Loan. Another dead end. There was no account for an Eric Linden, never had been. Or it had been closed out. He had talked with Junior. Made it seem pertinent to his investigation because he had witnessed the drowning—or almost. But unless he was being lied to, though that didn't make sense, the two million didn't exist, which made him suspect that the two million had not been gathering interest for seven years, had never been deposited. Might be just as well the poor bloke never found out. Talk about being ticked.

So Roswell, instead of soothing his soul or whatever with its high dry sparkling sunshine, was making him feel caged. Antsy to do something and he wasn't even sure what that was supposed to be. He was anxious to get the investigation over with. He still needed to meet with Hank, tour the barns, start the inventory. Carolyn was probably right. Maybe, he did need a diversion.

He pulled a loose-fitting sweater over his head. A splash of Polo and he'd be ready to meet the guests—correction, guest. The fifth grade teacher had called last night. She missed him. He probably should have told that massage therapist that his current love interest was thirty-two. And that he was old enough to be her father. Actually, who cared?

He didn't think he had too many hang-ups with age. He'd read that graying around the temples instilled confidence. But somehow now the temple grayness met behind his head. Could be time for that Grecian stuff. But then again, maybe not. A head of thick gray hair was better than a shiny scalp.

There was a hint of thickening around the waist. Now that was something he did need to work on. The NordicTrack was probably still folded up under his bed. He tugged the Levis in place, still a thirty-two, snug or not. Carolyn had assured him that the dinner wasn't a dress affair. He'd take her at her word. He reached down to tie his Nikes.

Carolyn had gone to pick up Phillip. Something about his car stalling. But Dan smelled a rat. More like let's let Dan meet date by himself. Give them some time alone. Get the amenities over, start to feel comfortable, establish a rapport—

The doorbell interrupted. He better get going. Dona Mari was on one of her yearly pilgrimages, wouldn't be back for awhile, so door-answering duties were all his. He decided against the splash of Polo and reached for the Lime, then let the doorbell ring a second time before walking to the front of the house.

Later he would ask himself why he couldn't stop staring, but maybe he knew the minute he opened the door. Opened the door, held out his hand, and made contact. Real skin to skin and for a split second, he didn't want to let go, drop her hand, break that buzz of feeling.

Dan led the way to the kitchen. He'd been asked to open the wine, let it breathe before dinner. And she followed him, then perched on a stool at the breakfast bar and kept him company. As easily as if she had been doing it all of her life. At one point he wanted to ask if she felt the same uncanny comfort in being with him. But that would come later. And there would be a later; he was sure of that.

"Your work sounds dangerous, exciting even."

From anyone else Dan would have dismissed the comment as patronizing. But it only made him open up more. He was halfway through the 1987 case of a jewel theft on Long Island when Carolyn and Phillip walked in.

Even the watchful eye of his sister didn't slow him down. He was witty, dug back into the recesses of some forgotten poetry class to comment accurately on iambic pentameter, then segued that neatly into why Faulkner and the Southern angst was a milestone in American lit. He caught a "What the hell?" glance between Phillip and Carolyn, but he didn't miss a beat. And what was even more remarkable, neither did Dr. Elaine Linden.

Everyone else might as well have been invisible. The eggplant hors d'oeuvres disappeared and the beef Wellington, but somewhere between the Guatemalan coffee and bananas Foster Dan was admitting to himself, he was smitten. Rocked right back on his heels by this vivacious, long-legged woman whose dark hair escaped a side part and curled toward her face and whose throaty laugh made him think of reaching for a cigarette after sex.

They talked. Phillip and Carolyn finally excused themselves and went to bed and Dan and Elaine moved out to the patio by the pool. The conversation was children and jobs and city versus country living. She pulled her hair back with some kind of gold sliver of a barrette and let the slit in the front of her long skirt divide to cool her legs. He loved her mind, but he stared at those legs.

It was two a.m. before she "really" had to go. He walked her back through the house wondering whether a kiss would be too much, too soon. Wondering how he would stop with something chaste. Decided against it, too risky, but continued out the door to her car, reiterated the time and place where he was picking her up on Wednesday evening, opened the car door, leaned in the window to say how much he'd enjoyed the evening, then watched her pull out of the driveway and turn left at the first corner. Suddenly, New Mexico was looking pretty good.

"There are a dozen roses on your desk."

The line was delivered in about the same tone that could have announced: "a tarantula has been found squashed underneath your blotter." So, who was this work-study to pass judgment? To say she couldn't get flowers, roses, two weeks after her former—for God's sake she had served him with papers—husband had been buried?

Elaine just smiled in wide-eyed sweetness and said, "Oh?" Why even give a hint that it might not be an everyday thing. Hundreds of suitors lined up on her lawn tossing long-stemmed beauties at the balcony outside her bedroom. She felt giddy. Silly, if she was into admitting things. And, yes, the roses were perfect. Not red, but a glowing golden peach. And the card read simply, "Looking forward to Wednesday."

She pushed a few papers around on her desk. She wasn't in the mood to stay cooped up all day in her airless, sometimes cool, sometimes not, office. She'd gotten the final okay for the sabbatical. September 1 and she was free. Exactly fourteen more days. Until then, a little paperwork, some editing on the anthology and…a cruise? A carefree tramp across Europe? A mystical "Stonehenge to the Nile" month-long tour by a psychic? She had seen that tour advertised in the *Albuquerque Journal.*

Or, would her love life take off and…and what? Somewhere along the line reality had to set in. Just because she was drawn to some man she'd just met…but there were the roses. And he didn't seem to be the type to send roses to just everyone.… And she knew his sister. Had counted her a good friend at one time.

This was making her crazy. If she closed her eyes, she saw a tall man with a head full of graying brown hair, handsome in a casual khaki sweater and jeans, with eyes that creased almost shut when he smiled and, yes, twinkled. There Jude Deveraux, his eyes twinkled. God, she was being stupid. Maybe, if she dwelt on his ears being a little too large, the faint smattering of pock marks on one cheek, some badge earned in puberty, or the cologne that made her sneeze and think of margaritas.…

She gathered the roses, placed them back in their box and locked the door behind her. She needed to wire Matthew some money before three, do laundry, pick up some wine, return a shirt...and keep her mind off of what might not be.

He'd traded in the rental Tercel for a red Jeep Cherokee and instantly felt better. He simply noted "need all-terrain vehicle" on his expense report. He doubted that it would be questioned. His boss thought he was at the end of the earth anyway.

When he'd called Billy Roland that morning, he'd gotten an invite to a polo game in San Patricio. One-thirty, picnic lunch provided. He needed to hand over the report on Cisco Kid anyway, might as well enjoy the afternoon to boot.

The drive took a little over an hour. It was some of his favorite New Mexico scenery, rolling hills, old farm houses, stone fences, apple orchards so ancient that the exact names of their fruit were lost—Smokehouse reds, Rallin's greens. He used to like to visit Carolyn in the fall and take a box or two of those oldtimers back to Chicago.

The village of San Patricio was timeless, beyond old with its hand-plastered gray-white adobe walls, and well-swept dirt courtyards, set below the highway, its tin roofs clustered together. He angled the Jeep down the steep incline and drove between the Catholic mission church and school then followed a winding dirt road back toward the Rio Hondo. The river was more like a stream this time of year, but he knew the water was cold and clear.

The polo field was in front of the Hurd Gallery. Pricey oils and water colors by Peter and William hung side by side with those of Henrietta Wyeth. Oils a little pricey for him but he did have a nice collection of prints, many signed. The two-story adobe building backed up against a wooded area separated by a garden of perennials, mostly roses, some free standing, some espaliered against the gallery, others tumbling over each other along the fences. But all in brilliant bloom in shades of pink.

Horse trailers were parked near the road and the cars of spectators—an ample sprinkling of Jaguars, Mercedes, and Lincolns—lined the single lane that led to the announcer's stand and covered viewing area. He parked the Cherokee and walked toward the pavilion, a blue and white striped canvas-topped tent open on three sides. Picnic wasn't exactly the word he'd use to describe it, but he did see a number of rattan baskets sitting on a back table.

The game, it appeared, hadn't begun. Two groups of mounted players, sticks in hand, huddled at opposite ends of the field. Strategy time, Dan guessed. The wraps on the legs of the horses matched the color of their rider's uniform. This wasn't just a bunch of guys who got together once in awhile on weekends, this had the look of professionals.

"You're my date for lunch." He hadn't seen Iris slip into a folding chair beside him, but there was no mistaking that breathy little-girl voice.

"Lucky me." He tried to sound convincing.

"Luckier than you know." With lips parted she leaned close, the wide brim of her straw hat keeping her a discreet two feet away. Hat matched dress, and shoes matched hat, everything black and white in combinations of dots and stripes. The same outfit would look just fine at the Kentucky Derby, Dan thought. Out here it just seemed overkill. But he noticed as he looked around, the other women were wearing Derby finery, too.

"Wine cooler?" She handed him a glass that contained something pink with a sprig of mint. He'd thought he would chase down a beer, but took the glass anyway.

"Do you like polo?" He was stretched for conversation topics with Iris and never felt exactly comfortable with her.

"No. But Billy Roland does." She pulled her full skirt up above her knees and stretched tanned legs out in front of her.

No nylons, Dan noticed, but then who was looking. Those legs couldn't hold a candle to Elaine's. He was seeing Elaine tonight and couldn't fight down a little surge of excitement. Movie, dinner, good conversation, and if he was lucky....

"Must be a leg-man."

"What?" Dan was startled out of his reverie.

"These things." She pulled the skirt even higher. "How's this? Better look?" God, he must have been staring.

"Do they have restrooms around here? Or do I need to go back to the gallery?" He stood quickly, broke the spell or whatever it was that Iris was trying to set up, and looked around, spotting an elaborate bank of Port-o-Potties beyond the pavilion. "Hold my chair."

There was a line and he chose to wait over by a group of tables, baked goods offered by the local Presbyterians, ceramics by the Methodists, some sort of knit things, could be animals from the V.F.W. wives, horse jewelry in silver and gold, an elaborate rack of dried flowers, garlic wreaths and herbs directly in front of him, all set up in the shade under a group of old cottonwoods.

"Dona Mari."

He hadn't meant to half yell out her name, but he was surprised. He hadn't expected to see the old crone. He thought Carolyn had said she'd gone home to Chihuahua. But there she was sitting in front of the dried-flower display behind a card table draped with white cloth; a basin of water in the center held a white chrysanthemum that floated lazily around a thick lighted candle. The scent of orange blossoms filled his nostrils. Small leather pouches tied with long strings, amulets holding God knew what potions, surrounded the center piece. It must be good luck charms today and it appeared that business had been brisk.

"Your sister said you was back." She looked old; even her gypsy finery and jangling bracelets couldn't hide puckered skin, sunken eyes and the fact that the hair pulled back from her face had turned white. She still pronounced sister with an elongated double "e."

"Someszing for the love life?" The old eyes still sparkled and the laugh still sounded like the wadding of dry paper. She held up a lavender leather bag with feathers sewn to the sides.

"Don't think it's a match with what I'm wearing." Dan held it against his shirt before handing the pouch back.

"Always ze joker. Someday you find out how smart you aren't."

Dan hated her predictions; sometimes, like now, he felt they had already come true. She'd been with Carolyn since he could remember. Visits over the years included finding the withered feet of various animals and small birds on his pillow or feathers and rocks in his shoes. His sister swore by her. Dona Mari could do no wrong. He wished he felt comfortable around her.

"Here, you keep anyway." She thrust the pouch at him. "You need bad." He had no idea why his love life should be her concern. And he didn't like the laugh that followed, but what the hell? He reached for his wallet.

"No. Is gift. You no bad man, maybe head is hiding from the light too much. That is all."

Could be. More than once someone had suggested he had his head up a part of his anatomy. He thanked her and turned back toward the field; there was still a formidable line in front of the rest rooms. Billy Roland was talking with Iris and someone else was riding his horse. It looked like Hank. He headed over that way.

"Don't tell me you didn't bring an appetite. Look at this here spread." Dan nodded appreciatively and agreed with Billy Roland that everything looked great. Which it did. He'd bet Iris hadn't gone near the kitchen to prepare it either. They had moved to a table covered with a checkered cloth. The heaping platter of fried chicken was crowded by the bowls of potato salad and baked beans.

"Don't be bashful, now. Just dig right in. Iris, honey, you fix him up a plate."

Dan sat next to Billy Roland and watched the game. Hank was good, an expert horseman. From the cheering and foot stomping, his benefactor agreed. It was probably a young man's game or an idiot's. Dan flinched when one of the players was decked by a mallet.

"I'd like to come out in the morning and tour the barns. Would that be a problem?" Dan had handed Billy Roland the test results on the Cisco Kid and watched as he scanned the papers before quickly putting them in his pocket. His expression registered raw pain. Was this some ace acting? Or was the loss of the young bull that traumatic?

"I'll tell Hank."

Dan thanked Billy Roland, said good-bye to Iris, and walked toward the Cherokee; he didn't see Dona Mari. She must have folded her tent and left.

Elaine pushed the door open and pointed to the portable phone at her ear.

"Shouldn't take too long," she whispered, then waved him to follow her and they walked back into her study. "Go back a page. What was the last thing…Um hmmm…I don't think it belongs there. Henry, I have a guest…okay, one more page…." Dan felt her tug on his sleeve, and he turned back from the floor to ceiling bookcase, Sheridan to modern day in a thousand, give or take, volumes.

"My boss," she mouthed then shrugged and covered the mouthpiece. "Can you do me a really big favor?"

"Sure."

"Take Buddy for a walk." She handed him a leash.

Obviously, Buddy was a dog. Where was he? Elaine was pointing behind a leather couch. Dan leaned over the back.

The black Lab looked a hundred and ten in dog to human years but shuffled upright and waddled out of his hiding place.

"You're grayer than I am."

He thought Buddy gave him an approving once over. This wasn't how he had imagined the evening starting. He'd have been content to sit back and watch Elaine in action, maybe casually stare at her long legs, tanned, encased in nylons, three-fourths of them showing from where the mini-skirt ended. Instead, he slipped a choke-chain over Buddy's head and snapped the leash in place.

He found a park about a block from the house and followed Buddy as he sniffed and watered a dozen obviously crucial spots before wanting to head home. Buddy had a wheezing spell on the front steps, his lungs filling and collapsing, forcing air out the sides of his mouth in bubbly puffs that brought Elaine outside in a rush.

"Asthmatic. Has been since a puppy but it still scares me."

Buddy seemed to recover under slow rhythmic strokes to his head and chest and now just leaned against Dan in a sort of "I like you" form of doggy acceptance, breathing easier, a trail of saliva dripping to Dan's slacks.

"He likes you." She seemed impressed.

"Probably smells Simon. The Rottweiler that owns me."

Dan followed Elaine back in the house. He was faintly sorry she had traded in the mini for a pair of form-fitting Levis, but only faintly.

"Give me five more minutes."

He would have given her however long she wanted. Strangely, time was no big thing. Not as long as she was sharing it with him. They were going to a standard dinner and movie. Nothing out of the ordinary, nothing with subtitles—including the dinner. He didn't want her to order for him in French or Italian or whatever it was she spoke fluently. He didn't want to worry about being monolingual, not tonight. He was thinking along the lines of Bar-B-Que and a Bruce Willis, but even that could be modified to a steakhouse and something with Anthony Hopkins.

But the theater was an artsy-fartsy one that brought back oldies but goodies. And played to an elite crowd of university types. *Farewell My Concubine* caught him off guard. He hadn't seen it whenever it first came out—just not his type of movie. But he liked it; the subtitles didn't make him lose track of the action, possibly because three English words seemed to equal a prolonged minute of Chinese.

And dinner? Not steak but whatever that stuff was with artichoke hearts and capers, he'd do again. They shared a white chocolate cream something or other and two cups of cappuccino and talked until the restaurant closed.

He didn't know he could remember as many fascinating cases as he'd related in four hours. And she seemed to enjoy the stories. Not just pretend-enjoy like the fifth grade teacher, but really get into, ask the right questions, the kind of enjoy that went right to his ego. Something to be said for someone a little older.

It wouldn't have taken the offer of another cup of coffee to get him back to her house. They both knew it would end up that way. Kid gone, two consenting adults, house to themselves. They stood on the porch as she fumbled for the key, than stepped inside. He put his hand over hers, stopped her from turning on any lights. He hadn't driven the last two miles with a hard-on to have to spend time with more small-talk. He was taking a chance that she felt the same.

"Matthew left some condoms…" Neat relationship for a kid to be that open, that adult; but he had already thought of safety, and tried not to hear the voice of Pam, the fifth grade teacher, admonishing him to not take chances. New ball game. New ball park. He pulled her to him and kissed her.

They were somewhere in the hall between a bathroom and a bedroom. He was surprised and aroused by her eagerness. Not a lot of fancy teasing moves but just plain old "I want you inside me" which was what she whispered before sinking to the floor after slipping out of jeans and blouse. He found this openness blindly stimulating even on the floor in the hallway. Screw his knees which had gone out the second year of college varsity. He swallowed the pain, kicked free from the last of his underwear, made the Guinness Book of World Records for getting the condom on, and rocked forward as she guided him in.

It had been a long time since he'd seen rockets, maybe even heard them—and this over the pain in his knees. It didn't last long enough. But the feeling of softness, the scent of floral, the muskiness of bodies slick with sweat lingered. He was too old to ask if it had been good. He already knew the answer to that. He rolled to one side, propped on an elbow, then said, "Is that offer still good for coffee?" They convulsed laughing. And then she seemed embarrassed. Too aware that she'd tripped him to the floor in the hall. Had let her guard down, had let him see her wanting…her eagerness.

They were both quiet as they gathered up clothes. She pointed out the bathroom and disappeared into one of the bedrooms at the end of the hall. He reached the kitchen first, found the canister marked decaf, and started the coffee maker. He got milk out of the fridge, two mugs from the glassed-in cupboard above the sink, and sat at the kitchen table to wait. He'd just carried his cup of coffee into the study when she appeared.

"Hi." She looked sheepish but freshly scrubbed beautiful with her hair wildly loose around her face.

"Coffee's ready."

When she came back he held a framed picture of Elaine, what was probably her son at about age ten, and a strikingly handsome man. The three were posed in front of some cathedral that looked familiar. The vacationing American family in Europe.

"Handsome family."

"Thanks." She reached out to take the picture and he watched as she put it face down on the mantle. "Someday, I've got to put these little reminders away."

"How long ago did your husband die?" He had asked it idly, not wanting to pry but assuming the years must have taken the edge off of her grief.

"Three weeks."

Dan hoped he hadn't overreacted. But he was sitting up straighter and had kept the coffee from sloshing onto his crotch. "I didn't realize it had been so recent."

"We'd been separated for seven years. I had filed for divorce. The death thing was a little anti-climactic. Our life together had been dead for some time."

She pulled a package of cigarettes out of the desk drawer, tapped one out and lighted it.

"I only do this when I'm nervous."

Dan waved aside the invitation to join her; this was his ninth year without smoking and it had almost stopped bothering him. Almost.

"How did he die?" It wasn't that he wanted to prolong a discussion that was painful for her, but curiosity had kicked in.

"You won't believe this. A flash flood. The car Eric was riding in was washed away when a bridge collapsed somewhere to the north of Tatum."

Dan didn't hear the last part. *Eric Linden.* He had just boffed the wife of the man whose body he'd helped hunt for, the man who had some pretty lousy friends. Ones who would shoot at him and help themselves to his money. Or the two million might have found its way into the accounts of the beautiful wife....Dan was pretty certain that someone had wanted Mr. Linden dead.

"Is there something wrong?" She sat beside him on the sofa. "I guess I thought that Carolyn would have told you. It was pretty scandalous when Eric first got caught." She stubbed the cigarette out and pulling a leg under her, turned to face him.

"What did he do?"

Why was he asking? What kind of bizarre coincidence was this? If he had any smarts, he'd just get up, walk to the door, smile some thank-you, and get the hell out. Not run any risk of a complication. Life—it never failed to surprise him by dealing unfair twists.

"This bothers you, doesn't it?" She was staring at him now, then broke eye contact and got up and reached for another cigarette, not waiting for him to answer. "Eric was greedy. I should have seen the depth of it, that anything to keep up with his friends attitude, the world owed him...." She stopped with her back to him fumbling with the pack of cigarettes and didn't continue.

"I have no right to pry." He got to his feet and checked his watch, made a big deal out of being surprised. "Whoa. I can't believe the time. Tomorrow's a full day at the office, get things set up, then back out to the Double Horseshoe."

He moved toward the door but she didn't turn around. It wasn't the best exit, made it seem like he was running away—well, wasn't he? "I can find the door." Not that she offered to show him; she just lit a cigarette and walked around the back of the desk to put the pack away. She didn't even look up.

He walked down the drive past her Benz. New, a 300E but still expensive enough to set someone back forty-odd thousand, and the two-hundred-thousand-dollar home and the clothes. And where had Carolyn said the son was going to school? Boston College? That was another twenty plus grand a year. Even with a full professorship, fifty or sixty thousand a year could get stretched pretty thin. Or not make ends meet at all.

He sat behind the wheel of the rental and realized how angry he was. Pissed that something with the potential of being so good could have turned to shit. Jesus. What stupid luck. He thought of the feel of her body under him, of her passion, and realized how much he had wanted this to work...turn into....He reached in his pocket for his keys and pulled out the small lavender leather pouch and cursed Dona Mari, then started the car and drove back to Carolyn's.

He slept in fits and starts, jolting awake, his mind busy with a thousand details, questions...pain. Elaine, the wife of a felon, living beyond her means—most people's means. Someone killing prize cattle costing the company he worked for hundreds of thousands...Billy Roland? Hard to believe he could do it. Kill what he'd worked to perfect all these years. So, who? Could the informant tell him? He hadn't heard from him in five days. Had something happened to make him change his mind about talking?

The sunlight surprised him and he awoke with that shock of disorientation that comes with lack of sleep and checked the clock on the bed stand. Six-thirty. Shower, shave, cup of coffee, and he'd be at the ranch by eight.

Hank met him in the corrugated steel building that had a regulation-sized show ring in the middle.

"Looks like a lot of expense to go to, but buyers like to see their purchases paraded around, compared to others. Helps some make up their minds."

Dan nodded and looked at poster-sized pictures, advertisements, of various breeding bulls hanging on the wall behind him.

"Impressive."

"Some of the best."

Dan listened as Hank extolled the virtues of the bulls, giving a brief history and an update as to their whereabouts. Billy Roland's stock was everywhere. All over the world. More than one top-grade herd got its start right here at the Double Horseshoe.

"Let's go on back to the breeding barns."

He let Hank lead the way through insulated steel buildings with stalls opening onto paddocks, pens filled with scrubbed-shiny calves, young bulls kept separate, some with individual handlers who worked with them daily and slept in a bunk room not far away. There was a lab, full veterinarian hospital with racks and lifts and tie-downs, and two other vets on call who had access to the operating equipment.

"Used to feed milk." Hank was pointing to a walk-in cooler room. "Sort of a veal approach for the general herd, but now feeds are more scientifically balanced. You can get that off-the-mark growth spurt with combinations of grain, pellets, and grass. But we used to keep about thirty Guernseys, still have the milking equipment." Dan looked through a glass window into a room with pipe stalls, rubber mats for traction and drains down the center aisle, and a jumble of hoses and stainless steel vats.

"Now here's the nursery."

Dan was not one to think of cattle as cute but the five little guys in the center of the room could pass for adorable without even trying.

"They're up here for their weekly physical, weight, temperature, shot of BST—"

"BST?"

"Recombinant bovine somatotropin, the genetic copy of the hormone that occurs naturally in cattle but when increased through injection, gives the little guys a real kick in the rear. Growth rate is substantially higher."

"This stuff legal?"

"You mean has the FDA approved it?" Dan nodded. "Last fall. Then slapped a moratorium on its use, then lifted that last month." Hank paused and leaned against a freshly painted railing. "This is a crazy way to make a living. If you're not regulated to death, you lose stock by natural disaster, or unnatural...."

This seemed as good an opening as any, Dan took it. "Any ideas who might want to hurt Billy Roland?"

Hank shook his head. "Whoever it was had some inside information."

"Such as?"

"Oh, the worth of the stock, not just in money but in breeding potential. He hasn't lost an animal whose death won't be felt. Shortcake Dream, the Cisco Kid—the end result of years of work to introduce the right combinations. Can't be duplicated."

"And you don't have any idea who it could be?"

"I've gathered the employment records, they're in my office. Thought they might help. But, honestly? I can't think of anyone who would want to do this."

"What about competitors?"

"Makes sense. I've thought of that. But where do you look? A lot of the market is overseas. Japan, France, not to mention South America."

"So you're saying that the mysterious virus that killed the first two heifers could have been intentional?"

Hank just nodded. "How'd you pick up on sucostrin succinvicholine?"

Dan swallowed. "One of those theories that came out of an investigation back East." He hoped he sounded convincing.

"I was impressed. You know your stuff."

Dan didn't quite know how to react. He hadn't been trying to fool anyone; his knowledge was limited. It was the informant who knew his stuff.

"Do you feel you have enough protection for the barns?" Change the subject, get Hank talking about the ranch.

"We should. Mr. Eklund hired on ten new hands last week."

"Am I going to find working papers for the guys I've seen so far?" Dan said it with a half-smile; it wasn't meant to be threatening.

Hank looked sheepish. "Papers are in progress. But it takes awhile."

"Are you comfortable with Mexican nationals working with the herd?"

"Some have experience. All are good with animals. It's always worked out before. Some of the regular hands have been here for years, twenty or more."

"You know, I need to inventory this entire operation."

"No problem. It's going to take awhile."

"Can we set a date? Start first of next week?"

Dan waited while Hank seemed to consider something and watched as the vet scooped a pinch of tobacco out of a pouch in his breast pocket. "I'll need to have some men on standby. We're talking about rounding up a lot of stock." Hank pushed the wad between his cheek and gums.

"I'll go over those records on past workers first, do what I can around here, get the office stuff out of the way. I could put off the bulk of the herd for a month probably, if that would help."

"Yeah. I'll be in Caracas next week."

"Cattle delivery?"

"Mr. Eklund sweet-talked Señor Garcia into taking two cows in calf by the Cisco Kid. A four for the price of one package."

"Who's your pilot?"

"Yours truly. Safer to have a vet on board during transport. Works to Mr. Eklund's advantage if they're one and the same."

"I'd also like a list of all vets who might have had access to the stock, here at the ranch or at shows over the past year. Maybe a list of competitors, too. Anyone who might possibly stand to gain." Not to mention Billy Roland himself, who was pocketing the insurance money, but Dan wasn't convinced that the money was the cause of it all. He was looking at a multi-million dollar spread. How could a few hundred thousand be that important?

Dan spent that evening finding an apartment in Roswell. His contract allowed that on extended road trips. And it got him out of Carolyn's hair. She'd balked, insisted, at first, that he stay there at the house; then, thinking he was seeing Elaine and needed privacy, drove him nuts trying to pry out the details.

The apartment was furnished. That was being kind; it had furniture was more like it. But it would do. Side entrance off a fire escape served as a back door. He was one story up and to the back with a panoramic view of the stables and training barns belonging to New Mexico Military Institute. All this from the fifties-vintage bay window.

He'd probably stay at the motel in Tatum most of the time during the inventory. Driving a hundred and fifty plus miles every day round trip wasn't his idea of working expediently. He'd had a phone put in at the apartment. So he could call Elaine? He hadn't made up his mind. But it surprised him that he couldn't keep from thinking about her. So, her husband had been a felon, did it really make that much difference? Wasn't he being a little tight-assed about the whole thing?

He got up a half hour earlier the next morning and walked to work. Now that was something he couldn't do in Chicago. He liked towns with turn-of-the-century buildings. Old red brick two-story structures that oozed history and displayed their conception in a chiseled stone corner block.

Roswell's courthouse had a weathered green metal dome that could be seen for miles perched on top of a three-story stone, wide, rectangular-shaped collection of offices placed well back from the main street and surrounded by hundred-year-old elms. Across the street and down two blocks, the local office for United Life and Casualty occupied the second floor of a refurbished Victorian, resplendent with wine and green trim, shutters to match, the brick recently sandblasted to capture the patina of soft rose. The cornerstone read 1889. Upstairs the offices were high-ceilinged, all with fans and the original embossed tin tiles, their floors gleaming a varnished oak.

"Visitors. I put them in the conference room."

Dan smiled his thanks and followed the receptionist's pointing finger and continued toward the back of the suite.

The conference room contained a mahogany table so long that it was rumored it had been built right there in the room, a ship in a bottle. Dan was never sure the story was true but it could have been. The two men sitting at the table looked like Mormons, a little old maybe, but still with that crew-cut, clean-shaven good looks. But he knew he'd be wasting his time looking for bicycles. It was funny how agents and missionaries could look alike.

"Mr. Mahoney? Roger Jenkins, FBI. We'd like a little of your time."

So what was he going to do? Refuse? Dan closed the door behind him and held out his hand.

"Tom Atborrough." The second man rose, leaned across the table and shook hands. Dan pulled out a chair and sat opposite two open briefcases.

"I'll get right to the point," Roger said. Must be the dominant one, Dan thought, as he watched Tom lean back in his chair. "We've heard the tape, Mr. Eklund and the vet explaining their investment in the bull that died last week. Frankly, we have no reason to suspect that it isn't on the up and up. The insurance part of this is of no interest to us." Roger paused, then pushed back from the table and stood, towering over him before he continued. Setting up a psychological advantage, Dan noted; these guys couldn't put much over on him.

"We have reason to believe that Mr. Eklund is using the cattle business for a cover-up. Seven years ago we were pretty certain that it was drugs, deals with Colombian drug lords. But then they pulled that little sacrifice, gave us their pilot on a platter and backed off." Roger paused to pick a folder out of his briefcase. "We have a copy of the report you sent to your home office in Chicago. Apparently, you witnessed the possible drowning of that pilot, Eric Linden? Saw the car he was in being chased by the county sheriff? And later inspected the car and ascertained that the car had, in all probability, been a shooter's taget?"

Dan nodded.

"One of our snitches at Milford Correctional said a bank statement was delivered every month and two million dollars was collecting interest in Midland Savings and Loan in Tatum, New Mexico. The bank was to have been in charge of managing Mr. Linden's investments. I don't need to tell you that the money has disappeared or didn't exist in the first place."

Dan didn't need to ask how they knew that he knew; Junior probably shared their little conversation. Or maybe Judge Cyrus.

The community was more than a little inbred.

"We do know that the Lott girl was hired to set Linden up. The plan, obviously, went wrong."

"Who hired her?" Dan was curious.

"The sheriff."

"We're betting with Mr. Eklund's money and endorsement," Tom chimed in.

"Are you sure?"

"Prisons are funny places. People hear things all the time. Sometimes the information's worthwhile," Roger said.

"Seems like Miss Lott was sent to provide a little entertainment for Mr. Linden while certain people looked the other way," Tom offered.

"I'm not sure I understand."

"Miss Lott was encouraged to engage Mr. Linden in sexual acts."

"While in prison?" Dan felt a twinge of sympathy for Elaine. The husband was a real winner.

"Yes. A guard was bribed to make such encounters easy. They all took place in the two months before he was released."

"All to set up Mr. Linden once he got out? Set him up to be killed?"

"It would appear so."

"Do you know whether he was killed because of the two million not being where it was supposed to be, or because of what he knew in general?"

"Both, maybe. We'd been keeping an eye on our friend Mr. Linden, given him ample chances to share what he knew. When we found the two million missing, we thought we'd have some leverage, but someone beat us to it."

"What makes you think this Eric Linden knew something?"

"He used to do some part-time work for Mr. Eklund. Maybe once, twice a year fly livestock to South America, sometimes Canada. If not the whole bull, then semen from some prizewinner. We don't think it was an accident that Eric pulled time in a posh white-collar crime prison just two hours from Mr. Eklund's ranch. Somebody needed to keep an eye on him."

Dan was thinking fast. Billy Roland had pretended not to know Eric Linden. When Dan had found the manila envelope beside the Caddy after the flood, Billy Roland had insinuated that he was just some drifter Andrea had given a ride. Why the lie?

"What's the FBI's interest now?" Dan knew they'd get around to it, but all this talk about Eric Linden and the two million was giving him a headache. It made Billy Roland out a liar, and it didn't make Elaine look like an innocent bystander, either. But, somewhere inside, even though he knew the consequences, he couldn't help wanting to protect her.

"Three months ago, there was a drug bust in Dallas, a big one, seemed like a new pipeline had opened up, a connection to South America that was capable of flooding the streets of major cities across several states. A flight plan was found that indicated the private air strip on Mr. Eklund's land had been used for refueling."

"Have you questioned Mr. Eklund?"

"Doesn't deny the refueling. Says his people told him it was a handful of good ol' boys who strayed off course flying to a turkey shoot, said they stayed around long enough to toss back a few cool ones, then took off."

"For a minute you sounded just like him," Dan offered, but neither agent cracked a smile. "I guess I still don't see what this has to do with me."

Roger swung a leg over a high-backed oak chair, straddling it and looking Dan in the eye.

"Frankly, we like the position you're in. You've got access to the Double Horseshoe and the books. As a matter of routine, you'll be running an inventory of stock. You'll be privy to what goes on out there."

Tom leaned forward. "And, there's that little matter of Eric Linden's wife. We like your position there, too."

Dan bit his tongue. God damned spies. Agency, my ass, they're just glorified spies. He didn't say anything. Let them make the next move.

"The proposition is this...." Roger had pulled papers from his briefcase.

Dan tuned out. He knew what was coming and knew that he wouldn't have the opportunity, the luxury, of turning them down.

He'd be working for the federal government and United L & C. But he knew right now which one took precedence.

"So, wine and dine Ms. Linden, you'll be on an expense account, wear a wire whenever possible, and check in at least once a week. We have a suggested itinerary." Roger passed Dan a manila envelope. "Look this over, then destroy."

No one wasted time with handshakes. The deal stunk. Dan was caught and they knew it.

Another morning and he hadn't called. Elaine had stopped crying just as the sun broke through the tangle of russian olive branches outside her bedroom window. Stopped crying and resolved to get tough. How could she have let someone get so close so quickly? Could she be that desperate? She splashed her face with water and walked out into the patio. The peach blush of dawn spread across the horizon. It was calming.

She fixed bagels and cream cheese, a pot of coffee, and sat at the patio table and contemplated the sabbatical. She needed to make a decision, but her thoughts kept straying to the evening with Dan. Maybe, he'd call. No, she'd seen the look on his face. He wasn't going to be eager to get involved with some ex-con's wife...almost former wife. Damn Eric. Would she ever get away from him?

What if she called Dan? Carolyn had said he'd gotten an apartment, sort of hinted that it was for privacy reasons. But what would she say? What was there to say? The roll in the hay was dynamite, sorry my old man was a felon?

This was the first time in forever that she'd been alone. Matthew was in Boston; she might not see him until Christmas. She had a year ahead of her all to herself. Could it get any better than this? But she knew the answer. Two weeks ago she would have said an unequivocal no, but now....

The flowers arrived about noon, at the house, an eye-boggling arrangement of orchids all in white. Sprays of Phalenopsis, Cattleyas, Dendrobiums, truly a conscience-provoked peace offering. The note read simply, "I'll call tonight." Six more hours but Elaine couldn't stop smiling.

Chapter Four

At eight o'clock on Friday morning, a grease-stained sack of Spud-nuts sat in the middle of the front seat of Roger Jenkins' plain vanilla, not to be conspicuous, car that blended with the eight to ten other cars parked in front of the Circle K convenience store. Great place to people-watch, if Roger just wanted to kill some time. Which wasn't a bad idea.

He needed a little time to collect his thoughts, run some ideas past his partner. He watched as two cops pulled beside him and gave him the once over. Small potatoes, graduates of some po-dunk academy out here in nowhere. He'd even match 'em firepower, what he had in the trunk versus what they had. The cop who got out of the passenger side paused, rolled his toothpick to the other side of his mouth, then walked on in the store.

Just a kid. Graffiti detail was probably the toughest duty he'd pulled. Roger watched a woman stop next to the gas pumps directly in back of him. She was having trouble getting her gas cap off. Roger was just about to offer his services when the two cops came out carrying cups of coffee. The young one seemed to know the woman and went to her rescue. In small towns these one-on-every-corner stores were magnets for human interaction.

Roger absently glanced at his watch. What could be taking Tom so long? He was going to take a dump, get two cups of coffee and a newspaper. Maybe the johns were busy. Being on the road was the pits. His own constitution was never the same. You didn't eat right, sleep right, it was irritating but maybe it'd be over soon. Either that Mahoney guy would come up with something quick or they'd pull out, chalk the Linden death up to tough luck and try another avenue. Still, the evidence implicated Billy Roland, the use of the air strip and all.

He'd worn a short-sleeved shirt, sans tie, and had parked his jacket in the back seat. Sweat still covered his face and neck with a fine, itchy mist. He envied indoor, air-conditioned work. And he envied the guys who drew the big jobs, a shakedown in L.A., or Seattle. Now there was one neat city. Water, cool weather, mountains close by. He wasn't going to waste time trying to think what amenities Roswell, New Mexico had. He didn't want to strain his brain.

Roger played with the folders in front of him balanced against the steering wheel and compulsively lined them up then fanned them out before he pulled them together to begin again. They were disappointingly thin.

"So, what do you think?" Tom Atborrough opened the car door and slipped into the front seat. He carried a large plastic covered cup with the Circle K insignia on the side and started to hand Roger an identical cup. Roger waved him away.

"You solved the world's problems yet?" Tom was busy emptying sugar and two creamers into his coffee.

Roger hated Tom's attempts at humor but aside from that he wasn't bad to travel with. "Any minute now."

"Are we lucky to have this Dan Mahoney on the inside or is he just one more idiot to watch?" Tom had stopped fiddling with his coffee.

"Nice guy. Probably won't know what hit him if this thing breaks the way I think it will."

"So he is a plant?"

"Yeah, you could say that. But I'm not sure why. His boss says Billy R. asked for him. Made it real plain that he was the man, no substitutes allowed. Asked him not to mention it."

"You sure the old man isn't just concerned about his cows?"

"How long you been in this business? That's chicken feed. A few hundred thou doesn't measure up to the millions to be had on the street."

"Okay, okay. Think Dan's going to be a team player?"

"Yeah, until all this hits too close to home. But he's the best we got." Roger squirmed away from under the wheel and propped a knee on the seat. "I just hope he's not in it in some way with the Linden woman."

"So we watch him. We're doing that already."

"I think the question is what are we looking for?" Roger reconsidered the coffee and leaned over to pick the cup up off the glove compartment tray.

"With Linden out of the picture, we don't have anyone to squeeze."

"What about his wife?"

"I still don't know that she knows anything. We got a tap on her phone and bugs in the house. So far, she's clean. Two more weeks and we pull out."

"Hey, the sex was just getting good."

Roger chose to ignore the invasion of privacy part of his work and let Tom's remark slide. "With her husband out of the picture…still, seven years ago I thought she knew more than she was saying, had some ideas about who suckered her husband into the drug deal."

Roger shifted back to rest his forearms on the steering wheel. "Jeez, I gain weight just looking at these things." He opened the car door and tossed the bag of doughnuts into a trash bin in front of the car.

"Wasn't there a chocolate one left?"

"Be my guest." Roger watched Tom fish the sack out of the garbage and shake a few coffee grounds off the sides.

Dan had picked up groceries, lunch meat, cheese, quart of milk, and run home for lunch. The light on his answering machine was blinking. He halfheartedly hoped it was Elaine. Calling to say thank you for the flowers. Would he have gotten in touch if it wasn't part of the assignment? He didn't know. But he thought he might have. He pressed the play button. He was just putting the grocery sack on the counter when the message stopped him.

"Hear you sold out to the big boys. Dangerous game. I didn't find any firearms in your apartment; maybe you better get weapon. Wouldn't want you to try to save my life with nothing to back it up." Maniacal laughter then, the click of the receiver. That was it. He played it again. The informant. He was vaguely ticked that the man had the audacity to let himself in and poke around the apartment.

But the advice was probably sound. Dan needed a gun. It wasn't standard issue for work in insurance fraud, but his new business arrangement put a different spin on things. He wondered if the expense account would cover it. He popped out the tape and slipped it in a drawer. At least the informant seemed to be a secret from the FBI. Wonder how they'd missed that one? Unless it was someone from the Bureau, protected by them, set up to use him because Dan had access.... He sighed. Just one more reason that retirement looked good.

The bulk of the gun felt odd. A bulge at the waist that he didn't need. But he had put a hundred rounds through it at the range that afternoon and the .38 was beginning to feel "like an extension of his arm" if he could quote the instructor, some yesterday Marine who probably led NRA sit-ins at the Capitol. Then there were the two new jackets, cut fuller to conceal the weapon, and some shirts, which led to matching socks and a tie. God, buying a gun could change your life. Not to mention...but he wasn't going to think about Elaine. It was business now. Cut and dried. But he was finding he had to keep reminding himself of that.

Carolyn called. Her choice of topic for the day, after she caught him up to date on Jason the wonder child, was the ominous decision of a nursing home future for their mother.

"I was out there last week. She simply can't live alone much longer."

Dan chose not to answer. He'd visited Mom at Easter and had felt he'd interrupted her bridge routine. Five afternoons and two evenings of assorted foursomes crowding the living room and he'd stopped worrying. She was a little fanatical, not crazy or infirm. Her apartment in Scottsdale was in a seniors-only section; her life was good.

"I don't think a nursing home would let her keep that hair color." The bottle of dye he'd found in the bathroom cabinet had read "Flame."

"You belittle everything. What happens to my mother isn't funny."

Dan almost smiled. Now that their mother had become the sole property of Carolyn, she'd drop the subject for awhile.

Actually, Carolyn was being civil, invited him to dinner on Saturday. Would he like to bring Elaine? He'd think about it. Then she said that Dona Mari was back. Said she'd seen him at the polo match. An inquiry about the investigation, and she hung up, friendly, a little sisterly curiosity.

Time to call Elaine. He couldn't kid himself; he was looking forward to seeing her again, excited about seeing her, even. He'd thought drinks might be okay, go easy, no sex, just get to know one another. Keep it simple and away from the home fronts, no temptations. A hotel lobby, maybe. He'd decide later whether or not to wear the wire.

She'd answered on the second ring, excited, breathless, obviously glad he called. He had a couple fleeting mental images of her legs, then stopped himself and concentrated on the conversation. They'd meet at the Radisson at eight. He'd just have time to shower.

At first, it was simple chitchat, tentative, self-conscious small talk aimed at masking the awkwardness. The orchids were wonderful; she had never seen flowers so beautiful; he had made a perfect choice; she'd never forget them. Then, back to safer ground, was the work going okay? Would he be staying at the Double Horseshoe? Would the investigation take a long time?

He had been enjoying how the silk skirt of her shirtwaist rode above her knees, billowed actually, as the deep cushioned lounge chair enveloped her in teal leather. Then he just said it, said what he was thinking, what he needed to know. What had been bugging him since the feds had told him about Eric and the sex in prison.

"Tell me about your relationship with Eric."

She paused as he watched her; then, she met his gaze and held it. Deciding, maybe, to duck the request unless she saw some sincerity or could measure how much of the truth he really wanted to know? He couldn't be sure, but she must have seen some validation because she smiled one of those tentative half smiles and took a deep breath. "Any particular starting point?"

"Your choice."

It took her a moment to begin. He almost said forget it when he saw the pain. But he didn't; he waited.

"We both lost our parents when we were young. It was a link, gave us something basic in common. He was raised by an aunt. I lived with my grandmother." She paused to shake her hair away from her face. "We met in college. I was, uh, am—I can't seem to get the tense right now that he's dead." A nervous laugh. "I'm five years older than Eric. Not a lot of difference but I've let it bother me."

The way she said it made Dan think of other women, younger ones she assumed were competition, ones like the Lott girl, Andrea. He must have made younger women a hobby in prison and out.

"I got pregnant right away. I was twenty-eight. It seemed okay. I was very much in love."

"Eric wasn't?" He wanted to grab the words back. She looked thoughtful and didn't react like the question was out of place. She just took a little more time before she answered.

"I wanted to think so."

Dan listened as she talked about Eric at Yale. A friend of his aunt pulled some strings to get him in, but he just squeaked by. A lawyer was something he wanted to be, not necessarily work hard at. And yet people liked him, were always willing to bail him out, forgive him. Was she talking about herself? Dan didn't know.

After she took a sip of her drink, she continued. Flying was his passion. There had been a succession of small planes and money lost. The aunt bankrolled some of his ventures. She had been permissive, always hoping something would take. He'd find his calling, so to speak. But nothing did really. There was a long string of "sort of" successes, but more failures.

"Was he close to Matthew?"

"When Matthew was young, but he missed out on seven formative years."

This might be as good an opening as he would get. Dan leaned back. "Did you have any warning that Eric was into something that was illegal?"

"I should have. I still can't believe that I just tuned out. Didn't see...." She stirred her drink.

"Didn't see?" Was he pressing too hard? Was that a flicker of suspicion when she glanced up?

"His recklessness, his desperation." Dan waited while she took a sip of her margarita. "Actually, I've always thought his friends knew more than they said." She absently studied something on the edge of the table. "I never thought he did it on his own, worked alone. I said that he did, I corroborated his story for the investigation, but I never believed it. Eric was a follower. He wouldn't have initiated such a thing."

"Some kind of friends."

She just nodded and finished her drink. "I suppose it's all right talking about all this now that he's dead. Actually, it feels good." Her smile was radiant. Dan wanted to stop right there but felt he had to ask the obvious.

"Tell me more about his friends."

Her look was disconcerting. Suddenly, after the self-purported cleansing, she was clamming up, looked uneasy.

"I wasn't thinking when I said that about friends. I don't want you to think I'm implying...."

"I'm lost." And he truly was. She obviously thought he knew what she was getting at.

"Well, Phillip, Billy Roland...."

"Stop a minute. Phillip?"

"Carolyn's husband. Didn't you know he and Eric were inseparable? One of those male pal things. Because our children were the same age, it became a family thing."

Had he succeeded in keeping the shock out of his face?

Was he glad he wasn't wearing a wire? Phillip. God damn it. She had just implicated his brother-in-law.

"I've said something wrong, haven't I?"

"No, I'm just surprised."

"I guess what I should have said was that I always thought Phillip must have known, and should have tried to talk him out of it. I know Eric would have confided in him."

"Did you ever confront Phillip?"

Elaine was staring into her drink, absently poking a bar straw through the holes in the ice cubes. He waited.

"Not really, I guess. We talked. Things were pretty strained for awhile. With Eric in prison, I didn't see much of them. Jason and Matthew were still pals and I saw Carolyn fairly frequently, but it wasn't the same, if you know what I mean."

Dan thought he knew exactly what she was trying to say. He knew Carolyn and the importance of maintaining that squeaky clean image—too much at stake, the state's first ladyship.

"Eric always tried to keep up with Phillip. Have the same plane, take the same vacations, but there was no way he could match Phillip's money."

"No. There probably wasn't." Dan was quiet a moment thinking about his sister's husband and thought even he was naive when it came to putting a dollar amount to what Phillip was worth. Two million? Five? Ten? A lot, he knew that.

"What about Billy Roland?"

"Billy Roland?"

"You mentioned him a minute ago. Do you think he was involved?"

"He was Eric's employer, sort of on again, off again. But, more than that, he was a longtime friend of the family. I find it hard to believe that he would be involved in drugs. Yet, the plane was his, the assignment. I've always had that nagging suspicion that Eric, at least, thought he was taking a fall for the old man."

"Would he do that?"

"That's another side of Eric, give you the shirt off his back."

"Or seven years of his life."

She smiled but didn't offer to continue.

"I'm sorry. I didn't mean this to turn into a grilling."

"No problem. I'm just glad we can talk about it. That's important to me. It's going to be important to any new relationship I have. I don't like secrets."

He reached out and took her hand, and got that same zing of pleasure he'd remembered. "I'm glad you agreed to see me again. I apologize for bolting the other night."

"Understandable." She shifted in the chair but didn't remove her hand. "You look tired," she said finally.

"Too much work."

As good an excuse as any to bail out for tonight. Dan needed to stop touching her before he went back on the promise to keep this drinks only and heard himself suggesting something else.

"How about dinner on Sunday?"

"I'd love to."

She reached for her purse before she stood, slipping her hand out of his. But then she paused and said almost shyly, "Thanks for the drink. I enjoyed it. This was a perfect evening."

He thought what she left unsaid was thanks for not pushing me, not making me do something I want to do making me risk getting hurt. But then wasn't that what he was thinking? And being tired wasn't a lie. He followed her past the front desk and then around the side to the parking lot. The powder blue Benz didn't have a speck of dust on it.

"Nice car."

"One of those nice things that Eric made possible."

Dan felt himself going on the alert.

"How's that?"

"His aunt left her estate to me. Wrote Eric out of her will. It was sort of a last straw when he went to prison. She actually put in her will that I was to buy a new house and car. I think she took responsibility for how Eric turned out, thought the money would make up for hard times." She smiled before slipping behind the wheel. "See you Sunday."

Dan watched as Elaine pulled out into traffic. For the first time that evening, he felt relieved. Maybe she didn't need the two million.

The phone was ringing when Dan walked in the door of his apartment.

"It's probably time we had our little chat. But I'm not sure your phone's clear. Give it about five minutes, then walk across to the gas station. Pay phone's in front."

The informant again. Dan suddenly wasn't tired anymore. He needed the information that this guy could give him. He slipped into jeans and a t-shirt, locked his front door, and walked across the street.The station was deserted. A guy in a pickup putting air in his tires but otherwise all the islands were empty. Dan didn't have to wait long before the phone rang.

"Do you have a name?"

"Not important. I have information, the kind of stuff you're looking for."

"On the scam to defraud United L & C with the death of a few select Charolais?"

"I don't give a flying fuck about a handful of cows. You and I both know the feds aren't talking beefsteak. But, yes, that among other things."

"So, why don't you tell me what they are interested in." Dan hated the guy's attitude but informants were rarely the cream of humanity.

"Drugs. Money. Anything illegal."

"How do I figure in?"

"You're going to get the proof."

"And if I say no?"

"You won't."

"How do you know?"

"Trust me. You're already in up to your dick."

Dan thought of Billy Roland, then Phillip and the feds. Maybe he already had a vested interest. The asshole was probably right.

"What happens next?"

"I get back in touch. When do you go back to the ranch?"

"Monday."

"You'll hear from me."

Then the phone went dead. He walked back across the street and unlocked the door to another ringing phone. Wasn't his night to get any rest, it seemed. He could barely recognize Elaine's voice through the sobs, something about Buddy being dead and someone breaking into her house. He said he'd be there in ten minutes, told her to call the cops and stay put.

The first thing he saw when he pulled in her drive was the car door open on the Benz and a purse lying on the ground about two feet away, open, with its contents spilled across the driveway. He hit the back door, burst into the kitchen and heard the sound of crying coming from the study. Elaine was sitting cross-legged cradling the body of Buddy in the middle of the floor, surrounded by an unbelievable mess of papers and books and overturned furniture. Her head was buried in the fur of his neck and her shoulders shook convulsively. The dog's eyes stared unseeing at the ceiling and his legs were beginning to stiffen.

He called her name. She looked up startled, then wiped at her eyes.

"Are you hurt?" Dan dropped to his knees. She shook her head. "Have you called the police?"

"Nothing's missing."

"Are you sure?"

"TV's here, CD player, computer...."

"Jewelry?"

"Nothing's gone. They said to fill out a report at the station."

"And Buddy? I think we ought to have a vet check him. Find out cause of death." When she agreed, he called a twenty-four-hour emergency animal clinic and said they'd be there in twenty minutes. He was glad he'd rented a Jeep; Buddy was a good seventy-five pounds or more and even wrapped in a blanket, difficult to maneuver into the vehicle.

While they waited for the results of the examination, Elaine told him how she'd come home to find the back door open and heard Buddy howl, just one long painful cry. Like he'd been waiting on her. He'd died in her arms. There were fresh tears, but she was regaining composure. The vet assured them that he'd died of overexertion. Something excited him, frightened him, but he'd probably not been touched. Just one of those old age and shock things.

Elaine spent a few minutes saying her good-byes and then chose to let the vet cremate him. Dan heard himself offer to dig a grave in the yard; he knew it was past midnight, but

Elaine just thanked him and said that this was all right. They drove home in silence.

He helped her put the house back in order. Book cases were replaced, repaired in one instance, and papers sorted. Elaine was right. Nothing had been taken but the next question was—what was someone looking for?

"I don't know what I could have and not even know it."

"Something of Eric's?" There it was again. His name. The ghost between them. He couldn't forget he was here partly because the feds wanted him to be. Wanted him to look for anything that would give them Billy Roland.

"Were there any papers, I don't know, something Eric had kept here at the house?"

"No. I bought this house after he was gone. He never lived here. Never saw the place. I stored his personal things. I wanted this place to be mine, no memories."

"Were there any personal effects? Something they would have sent you from Texas?"

She was shaking her head, then looked up, "The bank called last week and said I should come get the contents of a safe deposit box, one I didn't even know he had. It was in his name only. I had to provide a death certificate to take the stuff with me."

"What was in it?"

"Nothing unusual. A passport. A picture of his parents. A ring of keys."

"Keys?"

"I recognized the ignition key to his Jaguar. A car he sold twelve years ago. Kept it for sentimental reasons, I guess."

"Did you recognize any others?"

"No. I thought one was to the back door of our old house."

"Where are the keys now?"

"I tossed them in a drawer at the office."

"In the morning you're going to the office, get the keys, and put them in your safe deposit box. Okay?"

She nodded. "Do you think they're important?"

"Who knows?" He didn't have to say with Eric's background, anything might be important. They finished cleaning up. He insisted on staying the night. She didn't protest. There wasn't even a question of sleeping in the same bed. The sadness over losing Buddy put a real damper on the evening. He gathered up a comforter and sheets and slept on the daybed in the spare bedroom. It was three before he turned out the lights.

Elaine was up before he was. He found her in the kitchen, perched on a stool by a breakfast bar that separated kitchen from dining room. She didn't look like she'd slept very well.

"Promise me those keys go into a safe deposit box first thing this morning?"

"I promise." She tried to smile but wasn't exactly successful. The temptation was there to kiss her. But this kind of hurt was beyond kissing and making it well.

"I have to run by the office. I promised Carolyn I'd have dinner with them tonight. But, I'll call later."

He couldn't say she'd been invited too, but that he wanted to question Phillip about Eric and it wouldn't exactly do to have her there. Then before he got to the door, he turned back and made an offer he'd been thinking about. One that would make him feel a whole lot better if she'd take him up on it.

"Want to do something for me?" He waited till she nodded. "I'm going to be out here a month. Would you mind doing a little dog-sitting?"

"Maybe I'm not ready for another dog yet."

"I'd feel a lot better if I knew you had some protection. Whoever did this to the house last night might come back." Dirty tactics to play on her fear, but he could see it had worked.

"I suppose you're right."

"I'll get back later."

◇◇◇

Dan stopped at the office and called good old Roger and gave him a piece of his mind about scaring everyone half to death, about the dog, about the house being in a mess. Yes, the dog was old but that was no excuse for leaving him dying. Roger had Tom get on the other line. Both vehemently denied breaking and entering. But had Dan expected them to stand up and come forward? No. Not the feds. Not when they were desperate for evidence, grasping at straws.

These were just a couple guys probably getting pushed by their superiors. But that was no excuse. He finally slammed down the phone. But he knew they couldn't be threatened. They hadn't found whatever it was they were looking for, which was probably anything that would implicate Elaine. or friends. And they just might be back. That's why Simon was important.

His next call was to Jonita, the long suffering, longtime employee who kept his socks in order and everything dusted and even looked after Simon during his short trips. Yes, she'd get him out of the kennel and have him shipped out. She'd leave a message as to when to meet the plane if she missed him later. She'd try to have him on his way tomorrow morning. He thanked her and told her to put it on the household plastic and was glad he'd left a card with her for emergencies.

He felt good about bringing Simon out. Being away a month or two was hard on him. Both of them. The kennel, a real doggy Club Med on Chicago's north side, encouraged leaving a video of you and your dog especially if separation was over two weeks. There was even a resident viewing room. He'd never left Simon with home movies, and he'd seemed to do okay. But then, maybe, he just took the teasing from the other dogs, took the ribbing from the snooty Afghans he'd seen there once or twice before. Whatever, it would be good to have him close by.

He called Elaine, but she was out. He hoped putting the stuff of Eric's into a safe deposit box. He left a message inviting her to go into Albuquerque tomorrow to pick up Simon; he planned to leave late morning. Then he confirmed with Carolyn that dinner was at seven.

Dan struggled with the wire. The tape irritated his skin and kept popping off. He told himself that he was only testing it tonight, it was unlikely that Phillip would say anything that would interest anybody. Or was he hoping that Phillip wouldn't?

He was ambivalent about his brother-in-law. They didn't have a lot in common. Mostly, he had just ignored Phillip over the years. They had spent the usual stilted holiday dinners together. Everyone being courteous to one another. Carolyn and Phillip were both nice to each of his two wives; they always exchanged inane gifts that usually had to be taken back, but that was Carolyn's doing. Her taste and his never had been the same.

But, their lives were so different. Phillip started his own electronics firm, manufactured some gizmo that made him rich. Filthy rich probably captured it. Then he'd inherited the family ranch. Put it all together, and you came up with a net worth of a few million. But the money wasn't a problem, not between them anyway, even though Dan had chosen a four-year degree in criminal law from a local college, and Sis was Smith all the way.

No, when Dan got right down to it, it was Phillip's back-slapping—"never met a man I didn't like"—that forever campaigning stance that drove him nuts. He always thought it covered up a slightly superior attitude. Out West breeding but Back East education.

The fakey, but expensive, English Tudor commanded a full unfenced acre of the Country Club Estates, Roswell's grouping of upper-class homes around a golf course. Carolyn met him at the door and gave him a sisterly peck on the cheek. Their mother must be doing fine this week. Dan followed her into the living room. The house's forty-five hundred square feet held priceless art work, some Hurd oils he wished he had. The rugs, bright colored kilims, were perfectly placed, blending with the richly polished wood floors.

"It's nice enough tonight to eat out back. Mosquitoes aren't too bad."

They were passing through the kitchen and Carolyn had handed him a covered casserole and gestured toward the French doors leading to the patio. "Phillip's grilling his fabulous salmon. You've had it before."

"Don't think so."

But, then, would he have remembered? Dan stepped out and placed the dish on the table and almost bumped into Dona Mari, who gave him a sour look.

"Hey, old man, can I fix you up with one of these?"

Phillip was waving a bottle of Samuel Adams but it was the fake British thing. That was also on the list of Dan's dislikes, part of that hale and hearty glad-handing approach.

"Sure." Dan stretched out on a lounger and tipped up the ice cold beer. "Good." He nodded Phillip's way but the man had already turned back to the grill. He studied his brother-in-law and marveled at how little he'd changed over the years. Maybe the teeniest hint of a beer gut belied youth, but it was the same tapered western shirts, calf-roping buckle from a junior rodeo in '59, five-hundred-dollar Tony Lamas fresh out of the box, and styled hair. Maybe that was it, styled hair and manicured fingernails.

This was a man who prided himself on being an operator. A sweet-talker who got his way. Always. Dan watched as Phillip did a fancy two-step and hummed some country-western tune all the while brushing the salmon with a brown liquid. Carolyn had said that they had been promised the party's top position on the ticket in two years. Dan wondered how much of the campaign would be funded by Phillip, a sort of under the table, not-to-be-reported million or so.

Dona Mari was setting the table, large gold hoops weighing down her earlobes, a tiered multi-colored skirt making swishing sounds when she passed him. She acknowledged him but seemed grumpy and withdrawn.

The salmon actually was fabulous, but so was the saffron rice and green salad with cilantro dressing. Cooking was obviously an interest that Carolyn shared with Phillip. Funny. He'd never thought about what they did together before, besides promote one another. In that, they were perfect. But what hobbies did they share? He realized he didn't have a clue. He remembered Carolyn's fear of small aircraft. That must have caused a problem over the years given Phillip's preoccupation with flying. He could never imagine them in bed.

Dessert was a crème de-something-or-other. Totally satiated, they sat by the pool and enjoyed the sounds of a desert night. Dona Mari hovered about clearing the table, folded the table cloth, then went back to the kitchen.

Phillip was just offering him a cigar when Dan said, "Tell me about Eric Linden." There it was. Straightforward. The same request had worked before. Only this time it backfired.

"I would think Elaine would tell you anything she wanted you to know." This from sister dear. Letting hubby off the hook or just naively stepping in?

"I'd rather get Phillip's impression."

"Why?"

Even in the half-light Phillip seemed nervous, or was he imagining things? The tip of the cigar glowed bright red.

"I suppose because I wouldn't be certain she was telling the truth."

"You really like her, don't you?" Dear Carolyn, always the romantic but maybe it wasn't such a bad cover to let them think he was just trying to be careful about his love life.

"I'm reluctant to get involved if there are any skeletons in the closet."

"Nothing that would involve Elaine." Finally, something from Philip.

"How well did you know Eric?"

Phillip pulled on the cigar and exhaled slowly before he answered. "He was a childhood friend, and business acquaintance. Later on, he did some legal work for the company. We flew together, founded a club for single-engine enthusiasts, that sort of thing. Our sons were the same age." His cigar smoke drifted over Dan.

Dan could see Phillip enjoying the company of another man. Someone with the same hobby. Maybe that was it. He could see Phillip as the consummate good old boy. A cigar, good Scotch, a few loops over the barn in a Piper Cub. It was a lot clearer picture than Phillip the father, the family man, the husband in bed.

"Was he in love with his wife?" God, where had that come from? That wasn't exactly what he had planned on asking, but Dan found himself very interested in the answer.

"He was a womanizer. Screwed everything in skirts. Took advantage of women. Played on their defenselessness." This from his usually prissy-mouthed sister. "It was terrible for Elaine."

"Why'd she stick around?" Now, he was honestly curious.

"Elaine is one of those women who sign up for the duration. Until death do us part. Seriously, she's a great one for honor and commitment. Thought divorce was admitting defeat, wouldn't be good for Matthew. Can you imagine?"

Dona Mari had brought coffee and a tray of liqueurs. He chose a crème de cacao cut with half and half, a maraschino cherry floating on the bottom.

"*Beso de Angeles.* You weesh." Dona Mari muttered then passed him the drink and laughed that low cackle.

"Elaine deserves the best. She's been through so much," Carolyn said.

It crossed his mind to ask if he qualified, but he didn't; maybe he was afraid of the answer. He just asked the question that he'd come to ask: "So, was Eric framed? Doing a little work for his employer that he didn't know about? Or, were the drugs his? Just a way to line his pockets without anyone knowing?"

"His." Phillip didn't waste time in answering.

"How do you know?"

"I don't really. He didn't confide in me, if that's what you're thinking. I just know how much he wanted money. Not needed, really. Elaine had a good salary. His aunt took care of him through the trust set up by his parents. No, I believed him at the trial. Temptation became too much, he helped himself. And, if you had known Eric, that fuck-the-world attitude—he never thought he'd get caught, let alone do time."

"Seven years seems pretty stiff for a first timer."

"You don't know Charley Aspen. Judge Aspen. Wouldn't have been so bad if Eric hadn't been a lawyer. Aspen's a stickler for cleaning up the profession. Tell a lawyer joke within fifty feet of him and you're dead."

"You seem to know him pretty well."

"Old deer hunting buddy. Known him for years."

"Didn't you try to talk to Charley, on Eric's behalf?" Carolyn asked.

"Nothing illegal. I just thought the sentencing was a little severe."

"What would Eric have done once he got out?" Dan saw Phillip hesitate like he started to say one thing, then reconsidered.

"Elaine had finally served him with papers, so I don't think he would have come back here," Carolyn said.

"What do you think, Phillip?"

"He had something set aside from when his aunt died a few years ago. Should have been enough to start over somewhere."

What had Dan expected? Some admission about the two million? Wouldn't Eric have confided that? He got the feeling that Phillip knew more than he was saying.

Dona Mari stepped onto the patio carrying a bucket of ice, then stopped, gasped, dropped the bucket and began to shriek in garbled Spanish. She was pointing toward the edge of the lawn where the desert reclaimed its territory and sand met lushness in stark contrast. And there was the figure of a man, some seventy feet away, only partly concealed by a piñon as he gazed toward the house.

Suddenly Dona Mari was running, around the pool, past the changing area, moving unbelievably quickly for someone her age burdened by a long skirt. Dan took the other route behind the diving board to try and head the intruder off; Phillip stayed with Carolyn.

And then when he was still twenty feet away, Dan heard the pop of a gun, something small, like the derringer in Dona Mari's hand. Jesus. She could get them killed. And the man hadn't moved, simply stepped back into the shadows of the tree and then out again, letting Dona Mari see him before he turned and ran over the lip of the arroyo into the darkness of the eighteenth green, keeping his back to Dan.

The derringer's second shot was squeezed off as Dona Mari fell to the ground. Swoon came to mind but Dona Mari seemed to be in shock, both eyes were wide open but unseeing, a trace of spittle rolling out of her gaping mouth.

Phillip and Carolyn were beside her now. Carolyn on her knees cradling Dona Mari's head, whispering encouragement.

"Did you call the police?" Dan asked.

Phillip shook his head. "I'm reluctant in my, uh, present position to get the law enforcement involved."

Of course, might not look good to have the housekeeper of the future governor emptying guns into would-be intruders.

"You don't think she hit the guy, do you?" Phillip was truly upset.

"Doubt it. Lucky for him a derringer's not too accurate."

"I never knew she carried a gun. I'm truly shocked." Dan believed Phillip.

Dan knew he wouldn't have used it, but so much for leaving his gun in the glove compartment while out with family. It took Carolyn to help get Dona Mari to her feet and the three of them to half carry her toward the house. Dan and Phillip waited downstairs while Carolyn fussed with ice packs and smelling salts and then, exhausted, came back to the living room and fixed a double bourbon over ice and ran back upstairs.

When she came back, it was to fix a drink for herself and sink down on one of the couches.

"She's quiet now. Refuses to go to a hospital." Carolyn sipped quietly on her drink. "You know, she's a healer in her own right, actually distrusts Western medicine."

"She may not be so strange after all."

"Don't joke, Dan. I'm so upset." Carolyn's chin quivered and tears rolled down her cheeks. "You know how much she means to me."

"You know Carolyn credits her with saving her life," Phillip said.

Dan had heard the story a hundred times. Dona Mari had delivered Jason when they couldn't get to the hospital in time and devoted day and night to the new baby and mother.

"It's just the hocus-pocus baloney."

"Everyone is skeptical of what they don't understand," Carolyn said.

Defensive. He knew he'd lose this one if he didn't stop but then just like when they were kids, he continued, couldn't resist.

"And you do understand?" There, throw down the gauntlet, amazing how he still got pleasure out of baiting his sister.

"Yes. I do." At least the sniffles were gone. Dan noted the chin that now stuck out defiantly.

"So explain."

"She's a Santera. It's a religious system that honors ancestors and recognizes a direct contact between man and nature."

"Do they have a church or temple or whatever they would call it?"

"The rituals, magic, really, are practiced in a forest, sometimes sacrifice—"

"Sacrifices?" She now had his attention. Grand Champion Taber's Shortcake Dream had been found on an altar in the woods.

"Oh, it's not what you think. A sacrifice can be symbolic, fruit, flowers, candles, that sort of thing. If it is animal, it means that there's great danger about, great forces are involved, and there is some sort of major undertaking about to happen. She's had these spells before. She's delicate, fragile, even. She just can't overdo."

Now that he'd had a few minutes to recount what had happened, that wasn't exactly the way Dan had seen it. It wasn't some kind of spell. For all the world it had looked like Dona Mari recognized the intruder. Recognized him and, if the derringer had been accurate at twenty-five feet, would have shot him point blank. He clearly recalled how the man had stepped into plain sight, confronted Dona Mari. Dan's running up must have interrupted. But even he couldn't help but think the man's profile had been vaguely familiar.

"I better be going." Dan rose. Carolyn didn't get up; Phillip offered to see him out. Looking down at his sister with her shiny chestnut hair and glowing pink cheeks, he thought of the dark, mysterious woman upstairs and couldn't repress a shiver.

The first thing Dan did Sunday morning was call Elaine. Simon would land in Albuquerque at three fifteen. He'd pick her up at noon for the trip. Good old Roger had called. Suggested breakfast. Meet him at the Village Inn at ten. He checked his watch. He'd have time to run by Carolyn's. He thought it might be good brotherly policy to see how Dona Mari was doing, maybe question her about animal sacrifice if she was up to it.

The house looked deserted from the front when he pulled up. The drive curved around to the side and ended in front of three closed garage doors. Dan picked the far one to block and pulled the Jeep snug with the building. Flagstone steps continued around the side to the pool area and hearing voices, Dan started in that direction toward a wrought iron gate.

At first he was startled by the blood. A dead chicken was lying on the flagstone step with strange black charcoal markings in a circle around its body. Dona Mari. Keeping God knew what evil spirits from the house. But this was promising; she must be better. He opened the gate.

He'd just stepped through when he was tackled from the side by a three-hundred-pound thug who pinned him to the ground and took his gun.

"Armed, Mr. Ainsworth. I think we got him."

"Oh, for Christ's sake, that's my brother." For someone who didn't like foul language, Carolyn was doing pretty good, Dan admitted as he rolled to a sitting position. Carolyn looked agitated and stood in front of him arms folded.

"I'll take that." He struggled to his feet and reached for his gun.

"No hard feelings?"

At least the thug held out his hand, but Dan ignored it. Carolyn immediately began brushing his jacket but he waved her aside and simply slipped it off and shook it a couple times.

"Is this necessary?" Dan waved toward the thug, who now stood a discreet distance away.

"I think we need protection." Phillip moved to stand beside Carolyn and placed a protective arm around her shoulders. "You know last night might not have been a fluke. In my position, with the upcoming elections, a bodyguard is a hell of a good idea."

"I totally agree," Carolyn added, but she didn't sound convinced.

"All this because some guy took a peek at your backyard?" Dan said.

Phillip turned away and Carolyn corrected him, "Threatened Dona Mari, you mean."

Dan let it drop. It was amazing how four people saw the same thing and could have such different interpretations. But it was interesting how fast Phillip could come up with a bodyguard on a Sunday in a town like Roswell.

He didn't see Dona Mari and decided not to ask to see her. He inquired after her health and then left, stepping over the chicken on his way to the Jeep.

Roger let him get halfway through the plate of eggs overeasy and corned beef hash, homemade, not out of a can, before getting down to business.

"I hope you believe me when I say we know nothing about any break-in at this Eric Linden's house."

"It's his wife's house. He never lived there. That's why you couldn't find anything of his." Dan buttered a second piece of toast.

"Look, have it your way, but that's not how the Bureau works."

"Okay." Damned if it wasn't, Dan thought. But he had to admit, they didn't usually leave a mess.

"How long will you be in Tatum?"

"However long it takes. I've got to inventory every individually insured piece of livestock on the Double Horseshoe and check those others covered under a blanket policy."

"So what's that mean? Pictures? Vet consultations? Go over breeding records? Match ear tags? Computer chips?"

"All of the above."

"A month? Maybe two?"

"If the weather cooperates." Dan signaled for the waitress to bring more coffee and to take his plate. He was feeling human and a little sanctimonious that he'd left food on the plate, hadn't felt he should wipe it clean. Wasn't that the first step to losing a little weight?

"How's wearing a wire going?" Roger had just changed the subject, he better pay attention.

"Haven't had any real need to test it. Haven't done anything that would be of interest to you guys." Dan knew what Roger would say, and wasn't disappointed.

"Leave that to us. We're not asking you to be discriminatory. We get paid to make those decisions."

Dan waited while Roger added a second packet of sugar to his coffee, ceremoniously tapping the side of the tiny white sack to get the last granules. Must be something big coming. He's taking too long to get to the point.

"When you go over the books, we want to know about any bills of sale to anyone south of the border, or any imports from those countries. Get us dates of delivery, size of shipment, actual copies of transport papers, vet's health certificates, names of exporters or importers...and inspect the plane. We'll accept a deposition, but pictures of the plane would be better."

"Don't want much, do you?"

The sarcasm was lost like he expected it to be. He hadn't even seen an airstrip. But he knew they were on to something.

The Cisco Kid. He would have been on his way to Venezuela if he hadn't died. Maybe Billy Roland was telling the truth, he didn't know who killed the bull, but Dan was certain for the first time that United L & C's claim was chicken feed when compared to the kind of money that could be made.

"Get back to us when you have something. If that's the first day you're there or the last. We expect to hear from you."

No good luck. No pep talks. Just get this done, buster. The "or else" was always implied, a between the lines reading that was vague but none the less threatening. And Dan never knew exactly what it might be. He always supposed someone could fix it so that he was audited on his income tax—every year for the rest of his life. That was incentive to do what they wanted.

The plane was late and Simon had clearly had it with travel for that day by the time he was checked in. He whined and pawed at the door of his crate until Dan let him out. Then in some predestined moment in time, he romped past Dan and skidded to a stop in front of Elaine, who had dropped to her knees and was hugging his basketball-sized head and allowing more slobbers than even Dan could have put up with.

"He's a puppy."

"Eighteen months, but he doesn't chew. Got an A at obedience school." He didn't think she was listening to him, but what was amazing was how Simon obeyed Elaine's every command. He'd never seen the dog heel, sit, stay, whatever, better. The trip back to Roswell went by quickly. Simon rode in the back but would lean over the seat in half hour intervals to snuff the back of Elaine's head. Reassured, he'd settle back and put his wet nose on the window glass.

They talked, relaxed and at ease with one another, and stopped for dinner at a drive-up in Socorro, laughing as Simon inhaled three double burgers and begged for more. It was dark by the time they got to Elaine's house, but she insisted on taking Simon to Petsmart to make sure she got the right size bed and see what toys he might like.

He had the house to himself. And the only thing he could think of was making love, not that primeval scream of body contact they did in the hall a couple weeks ago, but a slow prelude to a relationship Dan wanted to have. Screw the feds, he didn't care if this woman had a past. He just wanted to be involved in her future. He was finished rearranging the room by the time they got back.

"What's this?" Elaine laughed but was clearly puzzled. She stood in the doorway to the study taking in the room's new carpeting—sofa pillows, bed pillows, throw pillows—every cushion in the house now covered the floor. Votive candles flickered from saucers on the window sill, and shelves and tops of the bookcases—probably meant for next year's luminarias but he didn't think she'd mind his borrowing them.

"Just protecting my knees in case you're a floor-only type."

She laughed, "Let me check on Simon. Don't go away."

When she came back, she had also managed to shed her clothing. And she let him look, walked toward him slowly before dropping to her knees, then sat there taking in every naked inch of his body with her eyes. Coolly she reached out and touched him, ran a hand over the stiffness before she straddled him and lowered herself slowly, ever so slowly, all the time eyes locked with his.

And that's when the calculated moves ended. He pulled her down hard; one mouth bruising the other, tongues searching, her hips rhythmically pushing against him. Muffled sound, little groans of pleasure. Her? Him? He didn't know and didn't care. Everything was motion. He rolled her over pushing deep inside pinning her hips in the softness of a pillow. She clung to him pulling free to whisper, "yes, yes…" before meeting his thrusts in that perfect timing that usually doesn't happen without lots of practice.

There was no slowing things down, holding back, going for some greater high. There was no controlling the wave of feeling that seemed to start at his toes and roll upward across his body exploding in his groin but spreading a tingling warmth through his chest and down his arms. He'd always thought the "mutual climax" an overrated myth but knew by the way she'd arched against him emitting a scream that brought Simon snuffing and growling to the door that some kind of magic "oneness" had occurred.

He felt she was reluctant to let him go, separate, pull out of that mind-altering state and rejoin reality, so he nuzzled her face, neck, ran his tongue around a nipple, tasting the saltiness of their perspiration. She was still but moved her hands down his back and lightly pressed his buttocks, brought him closer to her, then snuggled against him and held him there.

It was a long time before they moved, broke the spell, and then it was without words, just a shifting, a pulling apart but bodies still touching. He dozed, then slept. When he awoke, the candles were sputtering, some with wicks already drowned in liquid paraffin. He looked at Elaine, and beatific came to mind. Not a word usually in his vocabulary, but it seemed to fit. He found the bathroom in the hall without turning on lights and managed to step over a snoring Simon without mishap. The shower felt good, stinging pings of hot water from a hundred tiny jets. He hadn't felt this good in so long he couldn't remember an exact date. The gray of dawn was just pushing the night aside when he walked back to see if Elaine wanted coffee.

She roused, opened her eyes and slowly smiled. "Do you suppose I could have seconds?" She pulled him down and pushed him gently onto his back, knelt between his legs and took him into her mouth.

This time when he awoke, the sun streamed in catching the swing of the Austrian crystal hanging in the window and making rainbow patches of light dance across his chest. Elaine absently traced one with her finger, then said reverently, "I think I've found the pot of gold."

"Is that some veiled comment about my anatomy?"

Laughter. They tumbled together, too relaxed, too sated to want more, finally getting up to stumble over Simon on their way to the kitchen. It was eleven o'clock before they had coffee on the patio. A perfect night, a lazy day—it all made Tatum seem like a thousand miles away.

By the time he headed for Tatum, it was early afternoon. He'd called ahead, rented the same motel room. He'd check in about six, they'd leave the room unlocked, key under the mat. No need to bother them at the office.

He didn't know if he'd be invited to move out to the Double Horseshoe again. It would make things easier if he were. He left a message for Billy Roland, said he'd be out Tuesday morning. But for now he just wanted to think about Elaine: last night, this morning and all the other mornings he hoped would come.

The seventy-five mile drive from Roswell to Tatum was one of those mindless stretches of highway. He hadn't seen it patrolled and the average vehicle did eighty. Usually, but not today. He fell in behind traffic trusting the truckers with fuzz-busters. Scenery consisted of oil wells, and the smell of burning natural gas. Flaming torches dotted the horizon in four directions.

There were few houses to be seen. Oversized decorative metal entries, cutouts depicting cattle or horses and spelling out the ranch's brand and the owner's name, arched over gates across roadways to mega-acre ranches. And to the naked eye, the roads looked for all the world like they led off into nothingness.

For a late Monday afternoon, it was business as usual in Tatum. Main Street had half a dozen cars parked in front of Lil's Mercantile and another half dozen at the grocery mart. The Silver Spur had one new car parked in front of number eleven. Dan pulled the Jeep into the parking slot in front of room twenty-two. He found the key, then shouldered his bags and pushed the door open.

"Welcome back. Come in and shut the door."

The man sat on the opposite side of the room in almost total darkness. Blinds pulled and lights off. Only Dan's opening the door had cast a long streak of late afternoon sunlight into the room illuminating the man's legs. The informant. He would finally be able to put a face to a voice. Dan wished he'd have been a little more open about meeting him. He was having to take a couple deep breaths just to calm himself. He let the bags slip to the floor.

"Sit on the bed. Don't turn on the light."

Dan followed instructions, fluffing the bed pillows before he stacked them against the headboard and leaned back. God, he was tired. And he wasn't in the mood for this. He hoped the meeting wasn't going to take too long.

"Before we get started, I have a request."

Dan didn't like the hardness of his voice.

"Okay. What's that?"

"Quit fucking my wife."

The man flipped on the table lamp beside him and Dan looked into the face that he'd seen in the picture at Elaine's, seen at the edge of the pool at Carolyn's. And he couldn't seem to stop the feeling of something crushing his chest and realized that the strange noises were his own short gasps for breath. Eric Linden.

In the flesh, his handsomeness barely altered by a fresh scar half hidden in his hairline, the nose curving slightly from a recent break, the corner of his mouth drawn down in some kind of permanent smirk.

"If this is going to work, pal, you'll do as I say. I'll give you everything the feds want and maybe some things you haven't bargained on. But I call the shots. Is that understood?"

Dan nodded numbly.

Chapter Five

Eric lit a cigarette and offered one to Dan. If ever there was a time...but he refused. He couldn't stop himself from thinking of the consequences with Elaine, stop the inward cursing at his bad luck. Bad luck? Wasn't this more like disaster? He tried to stem the increasing feeling of bone-weary numbness that was spreading, paralyzing him, making him sick to his stomach with a cold dread that Elaine was lost to him.

"Are we clear about Elaine?"

"How does she figure in all this?" Dan avoided the obvious, simple answers, like yes or no, he needed to make Eric spell out Elaine's involvement.

"You'd really like to know wouldn't you?"

"She thinks you're dead."

"And now I'm not."

"But you'll tell her?"

"Eventually. When I need to."

Dan studied the man. It was more than curiosity about Eric's part in all this; he wanted to know how dangerous he was. Could he kill someone? Put Elaine in danger? It didn't help that his Robert Redford handsomeness made him look fifteen years younger than Dan, an easy fifteen, maybe more. This was a man women wouldn't be able to resist.

"You could turn state's evidence," Dan finally said.

"And not live to tell about it, or look over my shoulder the rest of my life while I enjoyed some penny-ante job provided by the government."

"What are you going to do?"

"Maybe it's more like what you're going to do." That smirk again. Dan watched as Eric leaned back and brought his hands together to steeple his fingers, smug, cocky, in control. "I figure my information is worth two million. And you're going to make sure I get it, this time. You'll provide me with the bargaining chip."

Eric's game plan was simple. Fuck the bastards who had fucked him, shot at him, tried to keep him from getting the two million. He thought there was lots to be had on Billy Roland and friends, but most of it seemed to be conjecture, hearsay. Nailing Billy Roland or anyone else would involve Dan's getting the evidence by following Eric's directions. Eric was going to stay dead. Work from undercover. Play both ends against the middle. Blackmail Billy Roland to reclaim the promised two million plus interest.

"You know there probably wasn't any two million deposited in the first place to gather interest." Silence. Dan could feel Eric studying him.

"How do you know?" Steely calm, the voice of someone who knew it was the truth but didn't want to believe.

"I found your bank book after the flood. I did a little checking."

"There were statements every month. Descriptions of stocks in the portfolio."

"Easy to duplicate would be my guess."

"And the whole thing was a sham."

That was all he said, and it wasn't a question. Dan watched as Eric leaned back in the chair and contemplated something on the aging acoustical tile above his head.

Dan broke the silence. "What's in it for me? If I'm supposed to gather this evidence."

"Stupid question. I think you've been 'in it' just fine."

"Is that supposed to be some reference to Elaine?"

"You might say that."

"Leave her out of it." Dan half rose off the bed.

"My, my aren't we the chivalrous one. She's not a bad piece, wouldn't you agree?"

Dan fought the temptation to deck him, probably because he knew he wouldn't reach him before Eric would have picked up the semi-automatic on the table beside him.

"Don't push me on the Elaine thing. The feds expect me to continue to see her, expense account and all that. I'm not going to disappoint them."

"They don't expect you to get in the sack."

"I don't like being told what to do."

"It'd be easy to kill you. Now, not mess around. They'd play hell proving who did it." Laughter, then Eric pushed the gun away. "Listen, maybe we can't be good buds but nothing says we can't work together and both get what we want. Truce?" Eric's smile was genuine. "C'mon. So I was a little shocked to see my old lady in bed. That pillow thing with all the candles? Class act. Maybe I'll use it sometime." That smirking smile, then, "'sides your dog loves me. Let me make myself at home looking in the window."

"Actually, you need me." Dan wanted to keep him talking about business. He was sick and tired of wondering who was peeking in the windows at all the wrong times. "If this little plan is going to work, I'm your insurance person, no pun intended."

"You're right. After I get my two million, I don't care who you tell what to."

"Did you see who killed the Cisco Kid?" Now was as good a time as any to test his information.

"I was there."

"Meaning what?"

"I killed him. They're still trying to figure that one out."

"Why'd you do it?" Dan felt shock and anger. He couldn't understand people who could harm animals. It had even kept him a vegetarian until a few years ago.

"Could call it revenge. Cost the old bastard a few hundred thousand. Have him see what it feels like to lose something he cares about for a change."

Dan hated the bitterness, didn't trust the man who felt he had been double-crossed. But there was one last thing that he needed to know, had to know.

"How do Carolyn and Phillip fit into all this?"

"You don't really know anything, do you?"

"I suppose I don't. You going to enlighten me?"

"Sometime. Soon, maybe. But not tonight. Forget about Sis for now. Let's say it's more of a private matter."

"When do we meet again?"

"Tomorrow, maybe. Here or I'll leave a message. Now, I need to get going. Work to do." Eric paused at the door. "Think about what I've said. You've got a lot to lose if this gets fucked up. Elaine, your sister.... Play it cool and it's just another job. You can live happily ever after." More laughter as Eric closed the door.

Dan didn't even get up to lock it but just sat staring into space, trying to formulate a plan of his own. The odds weren't real good that he could come up with one. He was a plant by the feds and coerced by a dead man, not to mention being responsible to United L & C who paid his salary. His sister and brother-in-law seemed to be involved, and worse—Dan was in love with the dead man's wife.

He fought the urge to drive back to Roswell, confront Elaine, tell her that her husband was still alive. But then what? Could he trust Eric not to harm her? No. Of that much he was sure. The man he was working with was bitter, enraged, and wouldn't necessarily stop at anything to get what he wanted—his way.

◇◇◇

He hadn't needed to set the alarm. He was up by five thirty Tuesday morning. And he couldn't shut out the night before. He felt an urgency to do something and knew there wasn't anything he could do. Wait to see what Eric's next move was, not call Elaine—that was the worst, trying to keep her safe by staying away.

When he pulled into the long drive that led to Billy Roland's house, no one had to tell him something was up. A group of eight men on horseback was gathered around the front steps. Dan had met them all before, only this time they were packin'—every rider had a pistol on his belt and a rifle tucked into a case on his saddle. Billy Roland came out of the house with Sheriff Ray close behind.

"Got a little problem just south of here. I'd welcome your input. Wouldn't take a minute to get ol' Belle ready to go. What do you say? You with us?" Billy Roland leaned in the passenger side window and the scent of bourbon and after-shave drifted over Dan.

Dan nodded, cursed a body already reeling from a lack of sleep, and pulled the Jeep around to the back to park next to the barn. Belle nickered when she saw him. That was positive. She even seemed eager to go for a ride. He saddled up but left his gun concealed. The snub-nose Ruger wasn't in the same league as the firepower out front. As he trotted Belle around the house, Billy Roland gave the signal and the group moved out cantering past the irrigated fields then turned south at a large windmill.

Air rushed past as Belle settled into the ground-covering gait. They seemed to be heading west but angling to the south.

Then Dan saw the airstrip. Not elaborate, just one enormous hangar, quonset-hut style, a couple windsocks and a strip of asphalt that stretched farther than he could see. There was room to land something of pretty good size. There were no planes to be seen. But he was struck by how well kept it was, and well lighted. This was a strip that was used—and not just once in a while, and not just in the daylight.

They had gone over some kind of rolling stretch of low hills so he couldn't see the house from where they were, but he estimated they were no more than a mile, maybe a mile and a half, from where they started. Billy Roland waved for everyone to follow him across the strip and Belle only shied once about putting her feet down on something black with strange white stripes before dutifully trotting across with the others.

They seemed to be headed toward a thicket. If that's what you would call a strip of wooded land that followed a stream bed, dry now with only a trickle, a foot-wide ribbon of water that snaked through the center of its sandy bottom. By the looks of the twigs and debris, some caught six feet up in the trees lining the banks, this artery had raged out of control during the flood.

Billy Roland was slowing now. The mad dash from the house was either some kind of male posturing or a way to settle the horses, wear them down a little. Belle had broken a lather on her chest and seemed to welcome the opportunity to walk in the coolness of the trees.

No one spoke. Whatever it was they were going to see, he was probably the only one not in on it. The horses were walking single file now, Sheriff Ray in the lead, and the thicket had turned into woods with a dense brush floor. They had turned away from the stream and the scrub oak and cottonwoods had closed ranks to make progress difficult. There were no animal sounds, no birds singing, just this oppressive silence broken by the horses stepping on twigs and rotting vegetation.

The clearing couldn't be seen from a distance; it simply popped up suddenly, a circle some twenty-five feet in diameter with a pile of stones, altar, Dan supposed, in the center. The trees at the edge leaned over the area, branches almost touching overhead, a natural canopy of green. But no one was enjoying the beauty of a hidden woodland retreat. All eyes were on the altar.

◇◇◇

"Shit." Sheriff Ray leaned over his saddle horn for a better look.

"Hank. Get over there and give us the particulars." Billy Roland then turned his horse and moved closer to Dan. The humidity and lack of a breeze made the fetid odor hang over them. Hank dismounted and walked around the altar.

"Dead maybe two days. Female caucasian, probably Hispanic. Somewhere between fifteen and twenty. Predators, coyotes and the like, have done a pretty good job of helping themselves. Cause of death…" He leaned closer and pulled a piece of filmy white material away from the face. "I'd swear the neck's been slashed. And…." Hank paused to remove more of the drape. "Follows the same pattern, certain organs have definitely been removed."

"Same pattern as…?" Dan asked.

"This isn't the first time. This here's a ritualistic slaying. They come along every once in awhile, a little human sacrifice important to some wannabe Aztec war God or whoever else wanders up from across the border bringing their heathen ways with them." Billy Roland shook his head. "Usually, these fanatics work farther south. Remember Matamoros a few years back? Got that college kid on spring break?" Dan nodded. "We're going to have to be extra careful. Maybe I should assign some patrol duty. Jorge?" Billy Roland looked around then gestured to someone behind them.

Dan watched a young Hispanic man back his horse away from a knot of riders and move alongside.

"Dan, this here's Jorge. Helps Hank with the stock. Comes as close to a ranch foreman as I got. He's the one who found this mess. Chasing down a calf and stumbling onto this. How's that for shit detail?"

"Me gusto mucho, Señor." Dan shook his extended hand.

"You get some of the boys and check these woods a couple times a night. And keep an extra close look-see on the barns."

Billy Roland dismissed his foreman with a wave of his hand. "Good man. No bullshit. Speaks English, by the way, just lets on he can't till he gets to know you. He'll be helping you with the inventory."

"So, what happens now?"

"You mean with the corpse?" Billy Roland acted vaguely surprised that he would even inquire. "Handled by the book. The sheriff makes his report. The newspaper will get ahold of it, send a couple reporters out. It'll be headlines for a few days. The body will be sent on to Roswell for a once-over by the coroner. Won't nothing be found. Fingerprints won't be in the books. Some effort will be made to send a description to authorities in Mexico, but it won't come to anything. Body will be held a decent length of time, then an unmarked grave. Guess some family will always wonder what happened to their daughter. Sad, when you think about it." Billy Roland abruptly spurred his horse and trotted toward the edge of the clearing, giving orders before starting back to the house.

Dan joined the group of men as they trooped across the front porch of the Double Horseshoe after turning their horses over to ranch hands to be cooled after the ride back. He accepted the tumbler of scotch and walked out on the porch to sit in the swing. He still couldn't quite accept what he had seen.

"I heard about what they found in the woods."

Iris had opened the study window from the inside and pushing the curtains back, swung a leg over the sill and sat there beside him, straddling the casement. She was barefoot, in scanty shorts and top. He turned back to look out across the fields.

"You know why they kill someone? Someone young like that?"

"No, why?" He didn't want to admit it, but his curiosity was piqued.

"They needed someone innocent to go to the other world and keep the spirit of a dead man from coming back."

"I'm not sure I understand."

"If someone sees a ghost, and if this ghost could cause some harm, a go-between is used to beg the spirit to go away, continue his travel to the other world and leave the living alone. If the ghost is a man, they use a pretty young girl."

"Who told you this?"

"Maria, in the kitchen. Most of the people believe in the Santeria."

Dan sat bolt upright. What had Carolyn said? Dona Mari was a Santera. Dona Mari had seen Eric. Did she think she was seeing the dead? Was she behind the killing of this girl? A sacrifice to keep a very much alive 'ghost' from coming back? To keep Eric from hurting Carolyn or Phillip? She was that devoted. He thought of the dead chicken. She was already using magic to keep evil from the house. Her involvement in all this wasn't as far-fetched as it seemed.

"I'm supposed to tell you to move on out here soon as you can."

Dan was jolted back to the present. Here was the invitation he'd been waiting for. Nothing against the Silver Spur but the drive was time consuming, not to mention the motel's faulty air-conditioning and easy access for unexpected visitors. He wasn't looking forward to seeing Eric again soon.

"Thanks. I'd like that."

"Billy Roland thinks it'd be easier for you to do the inventory. Work out here. Not have to drive back and forth. Get three squares, and not in some coffee shop."

Iris could sound seductive without trying, he decided. She just oozed come-on and probably didn't know it. He turned to look at her full pouty lips, trying not to stare at the two perfectly rounded breasts that pushed up over the halter top. The barest sprinkling of freckles over each.

"Thank him for me. But I don't want to put anyone out."

"You won't be." Iris was running her tongue over her upper lip, mouth open forming a rosy "O." Maybe the seduction was calculated after all. He turned away. He couldn't shake the feeling that somehow Dona Mari had had something to do with what he'd seen earlier. Did Carolyn or Phillip know the extent of her involvement?

"So, we're all set then?" He hadn't heard Iris step over the casement to stand behind him.

"Yeah." He stood quickly. Better to have her in view than not. "I'll go into town this afternoon and check out."

It hadn't taken him long to pack, a couple suitcases, a box of work-related folders, computer print-outs, notes on the case, his laptop. He'd left a twenty-dollar bill for the maid and returned the key before he put into words what was bothering him. He wanted to talk with someone about what he'd seen that morning. And who better than Judge Franklin Cyrus? Someone, besides Billy Roland, who had lived in Tatum all his life.

The judge was busy, but Dan didn't mind waiting. He took the old leather overstuffed chair offered by Junior, who had slid it closer to the window.

"Thought you might like some light."

Dan wasn't sure for what, but the view wasn't unpleasant. The space between the bank and Lil's Mercantile on the north had been blocked off to form a garden hidden from view to those on the sidewalk in front. Dan could see white benches next to a sundial and to the right of a birdbath. A tangle of elms with old climbing roses winding up their trunks caught his eye, splashes of red against the brown. It looked like a memorial garden. Dan vaguely wondered to whom.

"Pretty, isn't it?"

"Very. Who's the gardener?" As long as Junior wanted to be chatty, he'd go along.

"Dad. And, sometimes I plant a few things. It's supposed to be a copy of an English garden."

"I'd say you were successful."

"We need more rain. Everything does so much better with rain water."

Dan thought they had just about reached the limit of his green thumb knowledge or interest; anyway, he had a couple questions he'd like to ask.

"Did Eric Linden keep an account at Midland Central?"

Junior pushed his glasses up on his nose. "I don't know whether I'm supposed to let out that kind of information."

"Let out what kind of information?" Judge Cyrus boomed from the doorway to his office. Fantastic hearing, Dan thought.

"He was just asking—"

"Just curiosity." Dan smiled at Junior, who seemed to pale and back toward his desk.

"Well, I bet I know what you're curious about. Good idea to talk with an expert. C'mon in." The judge was waving him toward his office. "Who told you I was up on my witchcraft?"

"Overheard someone mention your name this morning," Dan lied, but was beginning to feel his luck had changed.

"Nasty business out there. I heard about it. Couldn't get away to have a look myself. Course, wasn't the first time. This sort of thing happens. Goes with the territory if you live this close to the border."

Dan wasn't sure how to start, but was saved any uncertainty by the judge's eagerness to discuss it. So he just sat back across the wide desk and let the judge continue.

"I suppose we've been plagued with this sort of thing about thirty odd years now. Doesn't seem possible it could be that long ago, but it must be." The judge paused, picked a cigar out of the ashtray and thoughtfully sucked on a well-worked end before lighting it. "Had ourselves a real Voodoo priest in our midst back then. Started out harmless enough. The Methodists sponsored a family from Haiti. Brought 'em here to start over after one coup or another. That country has more crazy trouble. Everyone in Tatum was behind it. Billy Roland offered the man work along with his wife over at the Double Horseshoe."

"Did they have children?"

"Two girls. Want a little something to wet your whistle?"

Dan shook his head but watched Judge Cyrus go to a liquor cabinet built into the bookcases. He brought a cut-glass decanter of whiskey back to the desk.

"Well, the first thing to happen was the wife died. I'm not sure I even remember what from. Something she came over here with, jungle fever. But the husband blamed us, the hospital and doctors here. Next thing we started hearing about were strange rituals out at the McCandless place."

"McCandless place?"

"Herb McCandless, deacon in the Methodist church. He and his wife, Jane, gave the poor unfortunates a home. Shack, really, but with running water, out behind their house 'bout five miles out of town."

"What kind of rituals?"

"Coming to that, hold yer horses." The judge poured a generous two fingers of whiskey into a glass.

"All of a sudden-like, Herb and Jane quit coming to church or even into town more than once a month. Might not seem strange to you but, let me tell you, that had some tongues wagging. So, I get talked into taking a group and riding out to their farm to have a look around."

"I'll never forget it. You've lived long enough to see some bizarre stuff in your life, I'll bet—" the judge didn't wait for Dan to comment before going on— "but this will beat anything. Anything."

"When we rode up, first thing we saw was ol' Herb McCandless standing inside a circle drawn on the ground with flour out under a tree in his front yard, barefoot, in his boxer shorts and undershirt. Just standing there under an old elm with this Voodoo priest dancing around, covered with feathers and beads and body paint, sweating up a storm and chanting some convoluted scripture in a mixture of Creole and Latin." The judge paused to pull on his cigar.

"I don't need to tell you we all just about dropped our teeth."

"Where was the wife?"

"It gets even stranger. Jane wasn't in the house and from the mess things was in didn't look like she'd been paying much attention to it for some time. So, a couple of us started scouting around. And we found her, all right, cowering behind the outhouse, stark naked 'cept for a loin cloth out of some sort of goat's skin. And she was got up bad as the priest, feathers, paint, and totally wacked out. God knows on what. But it took weeks to get her straight again."

"What did you do?"

"It was touchy. We slapped the priest in jail. Probably a mistake. He drove everybody nuts, yelling curses, exorcising the deputies. Another family took in the two young girls. But we couldn't really hold him. Without the McCandlesses bringing charges, we didn't have a thing. And Herb and Jane refused. They never were the same. In the middle of the night about six months later, they just up and pulled out. Had a cousin take over the farm."

"What did you do with the priest?"

"Turned out to be a halfway decent guy. Stayed on at the farm, worked the fields. Finally went down to Chihuahua and brought back another wife, older Mexican woman probably in her forties at the time. His girls got raised and moved away. A bunch of us always thought he just needed to understand that the United States was different. We didn't practice a religion like his over here. Anyway, we never did have any more trouble."

"What happened to him?"

"Died, finally. Maybe twenty years ago, now. Old age. Hard to know how old those guys are. They don't look their age. You ever take a close look at a National Geographic? Can't tell the young bucks from the old."

Dan decided the question was rhetorical, and asked what had been bothering him. "And the girls?"

"Never did see them again. Never came to visit that I remember. The second wife's still around, though. That Dona Mari who works for your sister. She must be seventy-five by now, if she's a day."

"Dona Mari?" He was glad he was sitting down. He wondered if Carolyn knew the story about Dona Mari's husband. "Did she ever practice Voodoo that you know of?"

The judge's laugh boomed out, "Some say she does, even today. Some won't invest a penny without consulting her, getting some kind of good luck charm. She's harmless, if that's what you're thinking."

"But, in the woods this morning—"

"Don't think there's a connection. No, your Dona Mari is more of a fortune teller. Folks swear by her as an herbalist, too."

Dan wasn't so sure. But then he was the only one who knew the connection with Eric. Dan thanked the judge for his time and headed back to the Double Horseshoe.

"Should we start with the paperwork first?" Wednesday morning and Dan was finally getting started on the inventory.

He was moved in, back in the room upstairs at the Double Horseshoe, and had slept like the dead, only that wasn't a good comparison anymore. Not after yesterday morning and the girl in the woods.

He hadn't called Elaine, had fought with just showing up on her doorstep and saying…but that's as far as he got. He hadn't heard from Eric; it obviously made meeting more difficult with him being at the Double Horseshoe. But he felt better being out here. The less he saw Eric, the less risk of inadvertently putting Elaine's life in danger. Good common sense told him he should just step out of the picture altogether and let husband and wife figure things out.

"I thought you might like to take a look at Taber's Shortcake Dream." Hank seemed to be the designated guide.

"I've seen the pictures."

"I mean the carcass. We froze it. Thought we should save it until United L & C sent someone down. The UFO museum in Roswell has asked for it. Guess that's where it'll end up...depending on you guys, of course."

"UFO museum?"

"Corner of Third and Main. Opened up about a year and a half ago. Good place to have one if you remember the incident in 1947."

Dan was going to assume that Hank didn't think he was old enough to remember '47 clearly, which was the truth. But he had read about the sighting of a spaceship and the possibility of a government cover-up of an alien survivor.

"Suppose you're right. What will they do with it?"

"Put it on display. They've got a replica of an alien, you know, one of those little guys, comes up to about here," Hank paused to point to belt-buckle level, "with those big slant eyes, almost no nose or mouth. It's one of the most popular things they got. People all the time are getting their pictures taken standing beside it. An honest to God mutilated cow might be even better. Bigger draw."

Seemed he'd hooked up with an expert, but what the hell, a good investigator never ruled anything out. "Do a lot of people around here believe in the sightings?"

"Not just around here. Thousands have visited the museum since it opened."

"Have there been a lot of mutilations in this area?" He needed to keep Hank on track. He could always visit the museum himself.

"Haven't been any for years. Then starting last spring we had two and the Johnson spread had one."

"I show no record of any loss at that time due to mutilation."

"Naw, I know. If the cow's not worth over a couple thousand, it's not reported. Ranchers get tired of the skeptics. It was a fluke that Shortcake Dream was out that night."

"How so?"

"Her handler had to go home to Chihuahua and a new kid was with her. Somehow, and I'm not saying the heifer didn't do it herself, the paddock was left open, and she just skittered on out and wandered off."

"Where was she found?"

"In the woods."

"Where the girl was found?"

"Yeah. That's what makes it look like the work of Masons or one of those groups from across the border. Aliens usually just leave the bodies out in the open."

There was no doubt that Hank was a believer. But Masons?

"What do you mean by Masons?"

"Masonic Temple in town. Ol' Judge Cyrus heads it up, wife's in Eastern Star. I know he's a friend of Mr. Eklund, but I've never trusted a...."

Dan thought he was reluctant to say dwarf but made a note to check his story. Wouldn't that be something. Local banker, judge, and civic leader slices up a cow now and then in the woods.

He certainly hadn't said anything about that yesterday. But wasn't it more plausible that satanic worshipers, someone from across the border, was responsible? They were close to Mexico. Maybe less than two hours' drive. That would rule out Dona Mari, too. At least, he hoped it would.

"Is witchcraft practiced openly around here?"

"Depends on what you mean by witchcraft. You comfortable with the supernatural?" Hank stopped just outside the clinic area to let two young men pass leading a yearling bull between them before he pushed open the door that exposed an absolutely spotless hospital operating room.

"I'd like to think I have an open mind," Dan said but some might not agree to that; he thought fleetingly of Dona Mari as he followed Hank through the door.

"I've grown up with it. Once when I was seven, I came down with a high fever. My mother called in a *bruja* who was also a nurse. She put a raw egg in a glass of water and put the glass under the cot I was lying on then said some words. Before morning the egg was cooked solid and my fever was gone."

Hank seemed to be waiting for him to say something. Difficult to discount firsthand information. "Sounds like she saved your life. Is that the calf?" Dan didn't wait for Hank to add anything more to his story but walked toward the bloated carcass of an eight- or nine-hundred-pound heifer in the middle of a heavy, green canvas tarp on the floor near a drain.

"Yeah. I had the boys bring her in earlier. They can help move her if you need a better angle."

Dan thought the angle was probably just fine. It was the smell that needed some work. Rotting flesh and antiseptic. Shortcake Dream hadn't been frozen fresh, that he knew, and having her out here in the barely air-conditioned clinic wasn't doing her any favors.

There was something wrong with the head, but it wasn't until he moved around to the front of the calf that he saw what was puzzling him. All the skin had been removed from the jaw, pulled right down over the nose with a precision cut appearing surgically perfect and starting just below her eye. One ear was missing. Completely gone. A perfectly round incision with neat, smooth edges and a circle the size of a fifty cent piece was all that was left.

"It's like laser surgery," Hank said.

"What?"

"Cuts like this one." Hank knelt by the cow's head and pointed to the missing ear. "And this eye socket, this eye was removed with instruments, sophisticated ones. Trust me. It took medical training to do this."

"The tongue's missing." It wasn't so much a question as a comment.

"Weird, huh? The DNA and chromosomes of cattle, though, are close to human. So, some like to think that all this is done in the name of alien science. But, what do you think they'd do with an entire eye, or ear, or tongue?"

Dan didn't answer, and had an idea that Hank would tell him if he kept quiet.

"It's almost like they're collecting replacement parts for some of their clones," Hank said.

"Clones?"

"Theory is that those big-eyed small guys are just clones. The real 'people' stay back on the ship. They say that's why that one they found alive in '47 wasn't saved. There wasn't anything to save."

Dan studied the carcass. There hadn't been much, if any, blood. It could have been suctioned off or it had retreated to the major organs. Then there were the sex organs, or rather lack of them. They were gone. Another surgically perfect hole in her udder, teats missing, rectum intact but anus cut away. And there was a penis, the tip of a penis from what was probably a very young bull calf, tucked in her throat.

"Anyone ever find the bull calf?"

"The one who gave up a part of his anatomy? No. We looked, too. Didn't seem to come from our herd or anyone else's nearby."

"Was there anything else you noticed about the body when you first saw it?" Dan remembered the goo described by Sheriff Ray.

"As usual, the mouth and rear had this clear jelly around it."

Dan let the 'as usual' go by. It was obvious that this wasn't Hank's first brush with a so-called alien killing.

He hadn't called. Elaine had checked the answering machine a dozen times. It was working. She'd left a message at the Silver Spur, and it wasn't returned. Daniel Mahoney was not going to get back in touch, at least not for awhile.

And she was absolutely baffled. How could she be so far off? Wrong in her assessment of character, in her assessment of how much this budding relationship meant to him. She had relived that night a thousand times. The chemistry was explosive. She could not have improved upon the love-making. It was the same for him. She knew it.

Could he be one of those types who got immersed in his work? Forgot about all else? Well, she wasn't one to sit around. Serve him right if she wasn't there when he decided to call. And she knew he would. Someday. When chasing down clues about dead cattle got old.

Simon nudged her arm for another bite of French toast.

"If and when your father comes back, you better remember what you learned in school and don't tell him about begging at the table."

It was like she had been abandoned with a child. At least she knew he'd come back for his dog. Comical. It smacked of junior high. Will he call? Should I call? Guess things were a little more straightforward today. She remembered the calls that Matthew got, girls on the regular line, girls on call waiting. She'd given him his own phone two years ago.

Still she wasn't exactly knowledgeable about the rules. She'd been married for almost twenty years. Maybe she had misread the situation with Dan. One thing was for certain, she needed to get on with her life. Make decisions about the sabbatical, get away for a few days. No more waiting around looking eager.

"Simon, how 'bout a trip?" At the sound of his name, Simon pushed to a sitting position and watched her intently.

"Why don't we go to the woods? I bet a certain city dog hasn't chased a squirrel outside a city park."

The chairman of her department had a cabin in the Jemez Mountains northwest of Albuquerque, an easy half day's drive from Roswell. He was offering it all the time. Well, she'd take him up on it. Just three or four days. Solitude, long walks, maybe some fishing. Simon would love it. She would love it. No phones, so she couldn't be caught sitting around waiting for one to ring.

It was set. The cabin was vacant. She loaded camping equipment into Matthew's pickup, thank God she'd talked him out of taking it with him; food for one human and one dog, fishing poles, tackle, a cooler of ice and soft drinks and was on the road by two. She'd left a note on the back door and a message on Dan's answering machine at his apartment. Didn't want to get caught dog-napping.

Simon was thrilled. He sat beside her on the front seat for the first one hundred miles then leaned against her and sort of slid down to sleep with his head pushed into her side. He felt good; she missed Buddy. This was just the sort of trip Buddy had lived for. She wasn't certain that Simon had too many car-trips under his belt, but he was a trooper. With frequent stops and a couple snacks, the four and a half hours whizzed by.

They reached the cabin just as the sun was setting. Elaine emptied the car then returned to the cabin's roughed-out front porch to watch the rose and cream of the sky spread above the mammoth evergreens. Everything smelled fresh with a lingering scent of pine. Simon couldn't seem to stop running, investigating one tree, marking it before bounding further into the woods and then racing back to make sure she was still there.

Elaine poured herself a Diet Coke, grabbed a sweater, and returned to the porch. Solitude. Somehow she was feeling better already. Simon finally tired and lay beside her sprawled on his side, feet twitching with some happy puppy dream of game that got away.

It was cold before she went inside and lit the oil lamp so that she could see to build a fire. Rustic was perhaps an understatement. The cabin's log frame needed repair. There were chinks between the beams that framed the two windows. A good reason it was best to visit in the summer. The first week in September was pushing it. The one room was spacious—for two people or one and a dog. There was running water and a tiny bathroom to one side of the kitchen. Sparse, but perfect. Exactly what she needed.

Simon watched her as she spread the foam cushion in front of the fire, unrolled the sleeping bag on top of it, and stretched out. Simon flopped down at the foot of her floor-bed and was instantly asleep.

Watching fires had always been soothing. She roused once to throw on another log and let Simon out. While she waited for him to return, she slipped into a long flannel night shirt. Simon came snuffling back to the door and was asleep before she had gotten back into the sleeping bag. She was beat but relaxed and felt better than she had in days.

She hadn't brought a clock but her watch said eight when she awoke to the sun pushing its way across the floor. She hadn't meant to sleep away the day. Simon wolfed a bowl of dry dog food and begged to go out. She fixed coffee and sat on the porch listening to the birds. It was so unbelievably tranquil in the woods. She always wondered why she didn't get away more often. She'd make sure the sabbatical included lots of getaways.

The fishing poles were a little worse for wear. She couldn't remember when they had last been used. It had been years. She and Matthew had wet a few lines together. She could remember him so well at ten or twelve. How did he get to be eighteen?

The Jemez river was no more than thirty feet from the back of the cabin. She almost tripped over Simon as she half climbed, half slid down the steep bank. Once at the bottom she followed the narrow river to a bend that formed a deep pool around a cluster of rocks. Perfect for trout.

The day was warming rapidly so she stripped to a cotton short-sleeved shirt and shorts, discarding sweater and jeans on the bank. This was more like it. In fact, wading seemed more inviting than fishing. At least Simon thought so. With all his splashing, the fish were probably in the next county by now.

Slipping off her hiking boots, Elaine stood at the edge of the river where the bottom was covered with small smooth gravel. The water was like ice, joltingly fresh.

She walked upriver collecting rocks, ones with sparkling mica caught in layers or their surfaces tumbled shiny by the river; she lost track of time but knew that she was at peace, that she didn't want this feeling to end. She whistled for Simon. He'd disappeared into the woods on the opposite bank and had been gone too long. She whistled again. No dog.

Then she saw Simon in the distance walking beside a man still half hidden by the trees. Dan. Yes. Didn't she have a feeling that he'd find them? She'd left a map with her note. But as she watched, she knew it wasn't Dan. But how could this person be so familiar? When she first heard the screams, she had no idea they were hers, no idea that she was stumbling backward cutting her feet on sharp rocks, scrambling up the bank to safety. Safety? How could you be safe from a dead man?

And then she stopped. Stopped the running, the screaming and sank to her knees in the tall grass and stared. She practiced taking long deep breaths until, when he was splashing across the water to join her, she could say, "I should never have buried an empty box."

His laugh hadn't changed. He stood there looking down at her, amused, more handsome than she remembered with a body chiseled from years in the prison gym. Self-contained, self-centered or both. The smirky smile, the lock of hair that fell forward, a world of memories blocked her from thinking clearly.

"So, what's new, kiddo?"

She laughed, leaned back, a hand shielding her eyes. Here was Eric, alive, standing in front of her like nothing had happened. Like he hadn't been gone for seven years; like he hadn't died. Laughter bubbled up from some recess, not a reaction to humor but that first step after screaming when the conscious mind doesn't want to believe. And she could feel herself slip closer to the edge of some cliff, some abyss, a black hole she'd never get out of. She mentally kept this vision from fully forming, struggled to push it far back where it couldn't come forward to envelop her and simply said,

"Something tells me your life's been more interesting."

He held out his hand to help her up and she hesitated, maybe only a nanosecond, but she felt reluctant to touch him. It was sort of like someone had held out a bowl of peeled grapes at Halloween and told you after you'd felt them that they were dead men's eyeballs. But his hand was warm and very much alive. Yet in a rush she realized what was trying to sift to the surface of her thinking—she was feeling disappointment. Bitter disappointment. She had wanted this man dead, out of her life. She was rocked by the enormity of it. Could she really be thinking that? What kind of person rejoiced in another's misfortune? Or was it like her shrink had said, it was easier to accept death as an ending than continue to work through her feelings and reach conclusions, however painful?

"Should we go back to the cabin?" Eric said.

She nodded, then pulled her hand away. "I need to find my shoes."

Eric talked on the way back of the flood, how lucky he'd been to be washed free of the car, how he'd been living on a little money he'd put away but was stealing what he could, food, clothing, gun, the motorcycle he'd ridden up here. There was a lot of bravado, but then hadn't there always been?

Eric dragged another chair onto the porch. They sat in silence both watching Simon patrol the edge of the woods. Elaine found herself curious about what Eric wanted to do now. There was still the question of why he had waited this long to step forward. Why had he wanted to stay dead? Still wanted to, it seemed. Elaine broke the silence first.

"What advantage is there to hiding?"

She thought he looked like he might not answer. The muscle in his jaw in front of his ear twitched, then stopped. But she knew she would demand an answer. She wasn't going to play games, ones that could ruin her reputation, cost her her job. Maybe she had made some decisions without knowing it. But she had to be on guard, keep herself from relaxing, slipping back into the old familiar, not questioning, just "going with the flow" behavior of so many years.

Eric finally began to talk, not looking at her, staring straight ahead at the trees, Simon's antics, the cloudless sky. He insisted that he'd been set up seven years ago, but couldn't prove it. No doubt there had been many flights when he had unknowingly acted as messenger, delivery boy. The offer of two million had seemed the least Billy Roland could do. The fact that the two million never existed or was withdrawn kept him in hiding. He would get it back with threats of exposure.

"Do you have evidence of Billy Roland's involvement?"

"I'm working on getting it."

"Then what?"

"Confront him. Demand what I'm owed."

"Isn't there a better way?"

"Damn it, Elaine, I was shot at. For all I know Andy would be alive today if someone hadn't shot out the tires on the car." She watched him as he paused, realizing he'd mentioned the girl. Let him feel awkward. She was past caring one way or the other. It wasn't the first female; it wouldn't be the last. Finally, she said, "I'm not comfortable with all this secrecy."

"You're not comfortable? What the bloody hell do you think this is?"

He'd leaned over and grabbed her arm, jerking her to face him, his fingers digging into her biceps. "This is my life. How can I make it any plainer? Someone wants me dead." He released her arm but continued to look at her. Defiant, belligerent, angry, an anger that was slowly slipping over the boundaries of right or wrong almost as Elaine watched.

"So, what happens next?" She moved to the porch railing and sat facing him.

"I need the keys and passport from the safe deposit box."

"That's what you were looking for when you broke into the house? The night Buddy died."

"Sorry about ol' Bud. He got pretty excited at seeing me. I was afraid he'd have a stroke."

"But didn't wait around to help."

"I don't play by your rules, anymore. I have two goals, stay alive and get what that bastard owes me."

"Did you ever play by any rules?" She said it quietly, maybe more of a question to herself but searched his face, watched the eyes for an answer.

"I'm not going to say the marriage was perfect."

"A lack of perfection made you throw everything away for two million dollars?" Sarcasm. It felt good. Then she leaned back, rested against a support post and said, "You know, the only one that ever got to me was Carolyn. All the waitresses and secretaries, the girls you smuggled across the border…you never brought them home, never flaunted them, but my so-called best friend? The wife of your best friend?"

"That was eight years ago. It's forgotten."

"Time doesn't erase everything. Maybe takes the edge off…."

"Had I been in my grave, I wouldn't have been cold before you started fucking around."

The calculating iciness of his voice surprised her. How did he know about Dan?

"I think I'm entitled to a life."

"You're so stupid, Elaine. For all the degrees, all the surface smarts, you're fucking naive."

"Should I ask you what you mean or could anything stop you from telling me?" A wash of anger left her skin tingling.

"You're being used. Your insurance dick works for the feds. You're a part of the payroll, get close to the poor wife who just might know more about all this than she's saying. Wear a wire, wine, dine and fuck the poor thing. Just a mercy hump for the needy, but then maybe she'll tell you what she knows."

"You're lying."

"You know I'm not. The asshole hasn't even gotten back in touch, has he? Fills a room with pillows, spends the night screwing the grieving widow, then disappears, leaves poor little Elaine sitting by the phone. Frankly, it was a good idea to come up here, saved you from looking too pathetic."

She ignored his meanness, the biting crudeness designed to hurt, and simply said, "Dan wouldn't use me."

"Then explain this."

He pulled a folded paper from his wallet and handed it to her. It was a copy of an expense report. A Federal Bureau of Investigation, government form and two items had been circled in red. One, an electronic device, a wire; and two, a seventy-eight dollar bouquet of orchids, white, miscellaneous types, sent to her address. The signature at the bottom was Dan's.

She couldn't say anything…couldn't stop the tears that came from nowhere and burst through tightly closed eyes to run down her cheeks. She wadded the paper and rocked back and forth trying to keep the sobs from pushing up her throat and making any sound. Then abruptly, she said, "You know I'm the one who told Phillip." She said it softly, swallowing hard. He had to lean forward to hear. She blew her nose on a Kleenex she found in the pocket of her shorts.

"Told Phillip?"

"About the affair with Carolyn. I made copies of all the letters I found, yours, hers, and went to see Phillip." She had his attention but couldn't read his expression. "So, maybe, turnabout is fair play."

He continued to stare. Disbelief? Disappointment that she'd been able to take the edge off of his little surprise about Dan.

"Phillip never said anything."

"But things seemed to cool down pretty quickly."

"Carolyn ended it. But it was over by then anyway. It didn't mean anything. It wasn't a threat to you or to Phillip. Carolyn was bored. Needed some excitement in her life."

She couldn't keep the sarcastic laugh back. "And you? Were you bored?"

"I didn't say that. I always thought we were good in bed."

"Maybe in the beginning."

She was tired of all this. She needed time to lick her wounds in private. Think about Dan without getting angry about being used. And think about Eric.... "What do we do about the divorce?"

"Depends on whether I stay dead, doesn't it?"

"How soon will that decision be made?"

"I don't know. Depends on how quick our old friend Dan can come up with the evidence."

"Dan?"

"Yeah. You might say he's an employee of mine. He needs information for the feds. I need information to get on with my life."

"You know, you haven't asked once about Matthew."

"I try not to dwell on what I've lost."

She let it pass. It was still too painful to confront him about dropping out of his son's life. And she felt exhausted. She'd go back to Roswell, get the keys and passport, call a travel agency and get on with the sabbatical.

Chapter Six

Dan rode to Roswell with Hank to deliver the remains of Shortcake Dream to the UFO museum. He had all the pictures, measurements, and samples he needed. It was becoming important to get her embalmed as soon as possible; the museum would take care of that. They planned to use a new freeze-dry chemical that would preserve her indefinitely. When he'd called, they promised to set aside some videos on mutilation for him. All in the name of research. Well, curiosity, too.

He'd gotten the message from Elaine saying she would be in the mountains for a few days. At least, he didn't have to worry about her. Simon was having more fun than he was. The sheer volume of records, some on disk, most hard copy, at the Double Horseshoe would keep him out of trouble for some time.

Hank filled up at the Texaco station just inside Roswell city limits before delivering his cargo. The town was bustling. They turned north onto Main, then took a left on Third. They could see the fork lift in the alley waiting on them.

"Can we assume that you're a supporter, too, Mr. Mahoney?"

Dan looked down at the tiny lady with blue hair and three strands of pearls draped over the bodice of her black dress. She had opened the alley entrance to the back of the museum and directed the unloading of Shortcake Dream, informing them that she was a volunteer every Thursday. Last year she had been a docent at the zoo, but she'd moved on to aliens the end of January.

"I keep an open mind."

"My, I'd think you would have to in your work. I just bet you have hundreds of fascinating stories."

Did she bat her eyelashes? Dan was beginning to think his tour guide was some seventy-five-year-old coquette. But the eyelashes weren't seventy-five. The outside corner had come loose above the right eye and poked stiffly straight across, looking more like a tiny misplaced moustache. But he decided against telling her.

"We just don't know how to thank you for the calf. It's the biggest thing we've ever had here."

Dan didn't think she was talking about size but he wasn't sure how they were going to display the animal.

"I think we'll put her in with Freddie."

"Freddie?"

"The replica of the clone." She smiled and motioned for him to follow and took off in that clipped gait of older people, posture erect and stiff, the result of wearing orthopedically correct oxfords for half a century.

Freddie wasn't exactly what he expected. Maybe it was the shade of blue, bright and luminous that made him look… he was thinking unreal but how could a four-foot-high egg-headed being look real?

"You know they aren't real." What was this, mind reading? True confession? He watched as she absently patted Freddie's head. "These little guys are just messengers, scouts, they don't have any insides so to speak. It's just empty." She tapped on the side of her head. "They communicate with the mother ship telepathically and all look alike. Real aliens look just like we do. You can't tell the difference."

"I see." He didn't see. He just didn't want to argue. But he wished that for the sake of effect, he could sprout an antenna above each eye, that would give his guide a thrill, or a heart attack.

"We're thinking of putting the glass front freezer case there. Perfect, isn't it?" She was pointing to the opposite wall.

Dan nodded his agreement, then followed her to the viewing room. He was ready to kick back and view some blood and gore, only those were the two things that were never found. They had the Linda Moulton Howe tape, one of the most definitive on the subject. So he watched forty minutes of actual footage on mutilations and interviews, every example looking exactly like Shortcake Dream. But if he could check out the tape, so could anyone else—an aspiring alien, someone wanting to throw an investigator off track.

He'd have to come up with something more concrete for United Life and Casualty. Alien mutilation wouldn't get past the first level of underwriters. Maybe it would be better to check on the Masons.

"You need to do anything else in town or can we head back?" Hank stood in the doorway.

Dan thought of leaving a message for Elaine, but pictured Eric's anger and decided against it. He'd check in with Roger instead.

"Just let me make a phone call."

He used the phone in one of the offices out front. He guessed the number was for a motel somewhere in Roswell and wasn't disappointed. Tom answered but went to get Roger, who asked where he was calling from before talking. Was there just the slightest hesitation when he said the museum? Some urge to ask what the hell he was doing there? Must have mastered his curiosity because he launched right into what Dan still needed to do after a brief acknowledgment of what he'd sent so far to the P.O. box in Roswell.

"Got the copy of the schedule. Two of the five trips down south last year coincide with big dumps on the street. Could be coincidence, could be something we can use. You need to go over that plane. Pictures, fabric swatches from the seats, random samples of engine fluids, air from the tires, you know the routine. Use a vacuum whenever you can, then put everything in envelopes or lab containers. I've sent a package of materials out to the Double Horseshoe, including a camera. Let's say you get that stuff to me day after tomorrow. We'll meet at three, courthouse lawn."

"Okay by me." It wasn't, but it was easier to reassure than argue.

"One more thing. That Enrico Garcia? It's just like you suspected, big connections with Columbian drug lords. Stay on it. You could be close."

Roger wasn't going to waste time on small talk. He hung up after reconfirming the time they'd meet. It was just as well, he could see Hank leaning against the pickup by the curb.

Dan had promised he would have everything. That could be a lie unless he went out to the hangar tonight. He sat a moment and tried to decide what was bothering him. He felt pressured, that was one thing; then, there was this looking the gift horse in the mouth, staying at the ranch, sucking up Billy Roland's hospitality while he was waiting to nail him. But wasn't he trying to nail him on the cattle thing? Somehow, that was different, in the open, straightforward. Billy Roland was helping him find the answers, just like an innocent man or someone incredibly cocky.

For some reason, Hank was talkative on the ride back and Dan decided to take advantage of his mood. He'd picked up a six pack, offering a beer to Dan as he threaded his way through the late afternoon traffic on Highway Three Eighty, pushing the pickup over seventy when he could.

"Did you know Eric Linden, the pilot who worked for Billy Roland about eight years ago?"

"Before my time, but I heard of him. Combined a little business with personal interests. Smuggling, wasn't it?"

"Yeah. You fly to Central America. How easy would it be to bring something back?"

"Probably easy if you had connections."

"Have you ever been stopped at the border, the plane searched?"

"Twice. A few years back and just a couple months ago. Nuisance. Clean as a whistle both times."

Dan popped open a beer and contemplated his next question. Hank's input could be helpful, unless he was in on it, too. But he hadn't seen anything that indicated Hank was not what he said he was, a hard-working vet who was also a pilot.

"Do you think Billy Roland could be behind smuggling drugs?"

"No way. He's a straight shooter. Hates that sort of thing."

Hank hadn't hesitated. And his answer hadn't seemed rehearsed. But maybe false insurance claims fall into another category, Dan mused.

"This Garcia guy in Venezuela. Was he happy with the cows that you delivered last week?"

"It wasn't exactly the Cisco Kid, but I think so."

"Do you stay with the plane while you're there?"

"It's guarded. I stay up at the villa, private room, a little live entertainment if you know what I mean."

"Not sure I do."

"Women," Hank grinned sheepishly. "All shapes and sizes, I have my pick."

The beers had loosened Hank up, but Dan could only think of Eric enjoying the same live entertainment years ago.

"Has Mr. Garcia purchased other stock from the Double Horseshoe?"

"For many years."

"Before you came?"

"Years before. His herd rivals Billy Roland's."

"This the same Enrico Garcia who's rumored to be tight with the drug lords down that way?" Dan was fishing but it didn't hurt to check. Maybe Hank had noticed something before or after the live entertainment.

"Can't say. All those guys have skeletons in their closets. But the money spends the same."

"Got another trip planned soon?"

"You thinking of coming along?"

"Might. I've always wanted to go to South America. See the last of the rain forests."

"You'll probably have time to finish your investigation at the ranch first, nothing's on the calendar until late September."

The six pack was history. Hank had downed four to his two by the time they pulled up in front of the barns.

"See you at supper." Hank's apartment was behind the first set of barns. A fairly small four rooms with private patio that put him just fifty feet from the clinic. That was taking your work home with you.

Dan walked back to the house. Supper was a family thing, Iris, Hank, sometimes Jorge, sometimes someone from town. Billy Roland really got off on having a group around him at meal time. Making up for not having a family, Dan thought. But, whatever, the meals were sumptuous. Not that Dan needed mashed potatoes, gravy, and meat every night.

He was crossing the veranda when he saw Billy Roland reclining on a chaise lounge in the shadows next to the house. The ice sounded like tiny bells as he swirled his drink and rubbed the cool glass across his forehead. "Can I fix you up with something?" His voice sounded tired, spent, in pain, even.

"Sure, why not." Dan walked toward the stocked sideboard and poured himself a scotch. Billy Roland hadn't moved.

"Drag up a chair. We're overdue for a little chat, wouldn't you say?"

"Could be." Dan chose to sit on the steps.

"You ever have migraines, son?"

"No. A couple nasty hangovers in my youth probably don't qualify from what I've heard."

"Well, if you do, this here stuff's the only way to go." He handed Dan a vial that read Banamine.

"A painkiller for cattle?" It was then that Dan saw the syringe and a disposable needle on a tray table next to the chaise.

"Yeah. Dosage is a little tricky. Hank helps me. If I get a jump start on these things, I can lick 'em before I'm flattened. Now, why don't you humor an old man and tell him how you're doing. Just let me lie back here with my eyes closed."

Dan wasn't sure where to start. He was thinking about how he could check what was in the syringe. Wouldn't that be a kicker if the lord of the manor was a user?

"I've looked into the alien thing. Just got back from delivering Shortcake Dream to Roswell."

"Tell me the truth, son, you believe little blue people cut up my heifer?"

"I have a couple other leads."

"I bet you do. You struck me as one who'd think that spaceship stuff was malarkey. But you live out here long enough and it happens more than once, it's hard to ignore. I never sighted anything twirling around in the sky, but some of my friends have. Good upstanding citizens, hard to discount their stories."

Was he telling Dan how to report the death, or just making small talk?

"I thought I'd check out the Masons."

"Judge Cyrus would love to help you there."

Was that a chuckle? For someone with a migraine, old Billy Roland seemed to be enjoying this.

"I'll keep you posted." Dan stood. He needed a shower before supper.

"No, no, sit a while. Supper's going to be late cuz of my noggin, anyway." Billy Roland sipped his drink. "You're the best. I know you'll get to the bottom of all this. I wouldn't have asked for you, if I didn't think you could do it. I did my research, and I haven't changed my mind."

"You asked for me?" Dan sat back down. He hadn't been told. This was the first he'd heard that he was handpicked.

So, why would the person being investigated want the best? Yes, a little bit of ego to let him consider himself the best.

"You have any idea how small and how intimate the cattle community really is? The big ranches, other Charolais breeders, the circle of judges? Well, let me tell you. You have gas on Monday, they know it by Tuesday. A few big claims and I might as well have farted in their faces, they know it that quick. And then there's the speculation. Old Billy Roland's in need of money. Who's got it in for him now? They're sharks, son, circling for the kill. I already feel like there's a chunk of me in the water. Innocent or guilty, the reputation suffers."

Dan waited while he took a long sip of his drink.

"Fix me another one of these, son, if you would, please. Lots of ice."

"Could someone from that community be doing this?"

"I can't imagine anyone from the circuit killing the Cisco Kid. We didn't show him. He was one of those best kept secrets, you know, every breeder's dream, a little something in the backyard that'd wipe ass from here to Sunday. Next to Shortcake Dream, his death hit me hardest. You got any leads?"

Dan hadn't been prepared and almost let the bottle of scotch slip from his hands. He didn't just have a lead; he damned well knew the killer but couldn't say. He'd tried to forget Eric's place in all this. He still hadn't made up his mind how he'd report it.

"Looks like that bronchial virus thing the labs came up with. I don't have anything better."

"You know there are times when all this gets to be too much. Losing what you've worked for, thinking your friends might be to blame. Doesn't help the headaches."

He said it softly, rubbing the glass back and forth again across his forehead. Dan didn't say anything. He could understand how a man like Billy Roland could get depressed.

And he felt sorry for him. That surprised him. He really didn't want this man to suffer more. So, was he on the verge of letting feelings get in the way of good investigating? He couldn't be sure.

"What can you tell me about Eric Linden?" Dan asked.

Billy Roland put his glass down and seemed to be thinking about something. Dan waited. He wasn't in any rush.

"You mean the man who was killed in the flood?"

"Hank said he used to work here, was flying for you when he got caught." Again, Billy Roland stared off into space, seemed to be choosing his words. At least, Dan knew he couldn't pretend he didn't know him. Not anymore. Dan knew their connection.

"You believe some people are just born no good? No Puritan work ethic, no morals, no consideration of other people's property?"

Dan nodded. So far he hadn't said anything about Eric that he couldn't agree with.

"Well, that doesn't even come close to sizin' up your Mr. Linden. And I'm a Christian man. Like to see the good in a fella whenever I can. Look for it, even. Give someone a second chance."

"I take it that was hard to do with Mr. Linden?"

"Nigh onto impossible. I watched Eric grow up. Knew his aunt, great lady, she stepped in when his parents were killed in that car accident. I even helped 'em out a little when he was having trouble at Yale. Made a few calls, that sort of thing, nothin' much but it seemed to help."

"You knew him all his life?"

"Gave the bride away at his wedding. I sure thought that would settle him down. You ever meet his wife?"

This was out of the blue. Dan stammered, "Yes, nice woman, smart."

"Bet your sweet bippy. Elaine's nice as they come. And pretty, don't you think?" Billy Roland had turned to look at him.

"Classic beauty." That wasn't a lie. He thought that.

"It's the legs. Never seen a heifer with a better pair."

"But I take it that didn't keep Eric around the house?"

"Maybe at first."

"But later?"

"Everything just kept turning brown, if you know what I mean. He was an ambulance chaser. His practice never did take off. Oh, he did some work for your brother-in-law, nothing challenging, glorified bookkeeping. But he'd rather play. He burned through his inheritance on one plane or another. He was a good pilot. A lot of us tried to keep him busy, crop dusting, delivering cattle, odds and ends like that."

"Guess it wasn't enough."

"Nothing would ever be enough for Eric."

Dan thought of letting things drop, not question him about Eric anymore, then he decided against it. Why not go for it? What did he have to lose?

"Did you have any idea he was smuggling drugs?" He was curious as to how Billy Roland would answer. If he had offered the two million and then took it away....

"I still get hot under the collar. He threw everything in my face—all the help, all the years of knowing his family. Used my plane, even. He deserved to get caught. God knows how many trips there'd been where he'd sneaked through. And you know what's funny? I never suspected. I just didn't think he'd do anything like that. Goes to show you, you can be dead wrong about some people."

You can say that again, Dan thought. He scanned Billy Roland's face in the half light of early evening. The pain was etched deeply around his eyes but he couldn't see the guilt, couldn't hear it in what Billy Roland was saying. How could this man pretend innocence? It was his connection with Enrico Garcia. Eric was just his pilot.

"How'd the family take it?"

"'Bout killed his aunt."

"And Elaine?"

"Devastated."

"But she didn't divorce him."

"They don't make 'em like that anymore. She'd stood by him through affairs—"

"She knew about his philanderings?"

"Looked the other way. Every once in a while, Eric would slip across the border with some little thing. Underfed, underage, wanting a chance at a good life. I'd find something for her to do here. But he never fooled me. I always knew he was getting a little special thank you, if you read me." Billy Roland paused to look up at him. "There just wasn't ever any keeping it in his pants. Hornier than a three-peckered billy goat."

"Do you think he was working on his own?" Dan was finding himself vaguely uneasy with all these references to Eric's sex life. And the old man seemed vehement about not being involved, not even knowing about the drug smuggling.

"Don't know. He said he was. But who could believe him?"

"What do you think?"

"Part of me wants to believe he was set up. That he wouldn't get involved in drugs on his own. It's hard to say. Roswell has a few secrets, but its leading citizens don't push drugs, that I know."

"Was it unusual that he pulled time so close to home?"

"Now that took some doing. Judge Cyrus, his brother-in-law, a little help from yours truly—took a lot of clout to pull that one off. Thought it'd be better for Elaine and Matthew."

"Was it?"

"Maybe at first. But, you know, she and the boy never visited him after the first year. Just stayed away, went about their business, but never went back to Milford Correctional."

"Wonder why?"

"Guess I always thought she finally gave up. 'Bout the time he was supposed to get out, she served him with divorce papers. Probably couldn't see the rest of her life with a felon. With Matthew off to college, guess she thought she'd start over."

"Probably a good idea."

"You know she deserves a good man, a good life."

Dan was glad he didn't have to answer. He wanted to be that man, and now things were out of his control. And he didn't see any way of changing them. Would Eric talk to Elaine? Would she still leave him?

"You all going to sit out here till morning?" Iris stepped out onto the porch. "Supper's getting cold."

"Iris, honey, I didn't know you were back from town. What you got on that table in there?"

"Couple of your favorites, yams with apricots and a pork roast. Some of that crusty old French bread you asked me to get."

"Now, that does sound worth moving for. Dan give me a hand here."

Supper was quiet. Billy Roland picked at his food but blamed his loss of appetite on the headache he'd recently circumvented, said that's what happened, he'd get rid of the headache but be a zombie the rest of the evening. He excused himself before dessert and went upstairs to bed.

Hank had lost the loquaciousness he had shown driving back from town but offered to stick around to play cards even though he couldn't stop yawning. Jorge declined and left without dessert. Iris said she wanted to go to bed early, and Dan said he needed to do some reading. The peach cobbler was eaten in silence, and everyone left the dining room without coffee.

He had the study to himself. Dan picked a leather recliner and pulled down two books on Charolais cattle, then another on Coronado and his trek through this part of the country in 1541. That ought to put him to sleep. Actually, he needed to plan his evening. He found the box of supplies Roger had said he'd mailed on the hall table. He'd go through it when he was certain everyone was asleep. Tonight might be the best time to look at the plane.

He waited until midnight then started out on foot. It had crossed his mind to saddle Belle, but he might have made too much noise in the barn. He didn't want to explain why he felt the urge to go for a night ride all of a sudden, burdened with an assortment of plastic containers with labels, a camera, and a mini-vac. It'd be better if no one saw him, coming or going.

He wore a denim, long-sleeved shirt and jean vest, its pockets crammed with supplies. The flashlight and gun were in separate hip pockets, each reassuring in its own way. He estimated the walk to the hangar would take forty-five minutes. The night was perfect, clouds obscuring the moon, no wind.

At first he kept to the row of poplar and hedge along the fence leading away from the house to the south. Billy Roland had ordered a mounted patrol of the property after the incident in the woods. The rider seldom came close to the house and made one wide circle of the property once a night.

He stood for a few minutes behind the trees watching until he was satisfied that no one had seen him leave. The house remained dark. From a distance its silhouette loomed on the horizon, secure, inviting, nestled into an extended windbreak of trees, the only inhabited shelter for miles. There was no sign of the patrol. Still a little early.

He jogged part way until his knees let him know enough was enough. He decided to approach the hangar from the west, follow the edge of the woods until he could cut across the runway to the back of the building. He wasn't sure how he'd explain this snooping; he just hoped he wouldn't have to.

The moon popped out for a few minutes and he hung back shielded by the thick underbrush and waited for clouds to float over it again, then dashed forward to the corner of the building before pausing. Again, he listened for noises by sucking in his breath and letting it escape through his mouth, all the time straining to catch some unfamiliar sound, some indication that he might not be alone.

Something that could have been a coyote sang in the distance. An answer came from over his shoulder to the east.

But there was nothing else. He flattened his body against the cold of the corrugated steel and inched forward; his rubber soled shoes crunched on the gravel path along the side of the building.

The door at the back of the hangar was locked. He'd expected that and reached into his tool kit for a screwdriver. This lock wouldn't even be a challenge. It was not a talent he was proud of, but one that came in handy. It took less than ten seconds to open the door.

Dan quickly stepped inside and closed the door behind him. The echo of steel on steel sounded like an avalanche as it rolled through the building, gradually faded, then stopped. He continued to wait by the door before moving on, letting every sound register and implant on his brain. The creaks and groans of the large wood truss and steel sheet building gave it a language all its own—and it talked to itself. Unnerving if you were by yourself and weren't supposed to be there, Dan thought.

The building covered five thousand square feet at least, a warehouse, hangar combination. Something rustled overhead. Pigeons, probably. Maybe a bat. His flashlight illuminated a collection of droppings on the concrete floor under one beam. Boxes stacked at the back had the logo of farm equipment, could be replacement parts. He'd check later.

But first the plane. Only in this case, planes. The cargo plane was easy to pick out with its pregnant-looking undercarriage and ramp doorway underneath in the back. The second was a surprise. A Lear jet. It seemed to be in mothballs. Its engine was dismantled and in a few thousand well-ordered pieces, some in trough-like trays with numbers and notes tacked to the sides, some, bigger, unwieldy, on the cement floor, and still others in crates. But it hadn't flown in awhile, that was for sure. It looked like it hadn't been worked on in awhile, either. Dan wondered who the mechanic was, a hobbyist, maybe?

The cargo plane showed signs of use but was well-maintained.

Dan walked underneath it, then around to the front. It could hold two to four passengers and probably another two or three four-legged creatures. The outside walls were obviously reinforced. The plane was heavy. From its shape, it looked like it shouldn't be able to fly, sort of a bumblebee that would heave itself into the sky and stay airborne against all odds.

The ramp doorway was locked from the inside but the cockpit was open. Someone had left a ladder in place and Dan hurried on board, shutting the door securely behind him. He'd need to muffle the sound of the battery-run vacuum however possible. He was fifteen feet above the hangar floor. He squatted down beside the pilot's seat and waited for any unfamiliar sound before switching on the flashlight.

The plane wasn't new, just well cared for. The buttery soft leather upholstery and wood instrument panel belied the plane's age. They just didn't make them like they used to. Dan dropped to hands and knees to inspect the flooring, a long strip of rubber mat glued in place at the edges and immaculate. A person could eat off the floor.

But in keeping with why he was there, Dan revved up the miniature vacuum and ran it under the seats and along the sides of the walkway leading to the cockpit. He emptied a minute amount of particles—three grains of sand, the stem of a crushed leaf, a knotted piece of string—into a plastic container and labeled it appropriately, then moved on to repeat his gathering in front of the pilot's seat and beneath the instrument panel.

It was slow going. He glanced at his watch, one twenty. He worked his way backward to the cargo hold, lowering himself into the padded stalls. These would be time consuming. Here, he scraped paint and metal from the tie-downs to collect dried saliva as a precautionary measure. Probably would tell the lab what they used to sedate the animals, and who knew whether or not that would be important. Next, he pulled threads from the canvas-covered padding that lined the walls, using a hollow needle to go between the seams to sample the stuffing.

The cleanliness astounded him. Here was a good example of safeguarding the animals…or destroying evidence. The plane was beyond clean. Dan supposed it helped to have a plentiful supply of cheap labor.

"Fancy meeting you here."

There had been times in life, like now, that Dan was pleased that he had strong sphincters. In spite of his heart pounding crazily, he quelled the fight-or-flight reaction and turned slowly to look at Eric leaning over the top of the opposite stall.

"I could say the same."

"Just lending a hand."

"Things not moving fast enough for you?" Dan squatted down to poke the suction tube between the circles of rubber making up the two-inch-thick mat that each animal stood on. Heavy cushioning for heavy cargo. Eric didn't seem exactly chatty. Dan ignored him as he continued to work.

He was just finishing up the first stall when he saw the crystals swirl up through the mat, enter the tube and clink into the clear container attached to the back of the vac. He knew it wasn't beach sand. Three more holes, three more tiny caches of an illegal substance. They seemed out of place in these immaculate surroundings. Then it hit him. He knew why Eric was here.

"Busy evening."

"What do you mean by that?"

"I think you know. I just collected a substance that probably wasn't here an hour ago." Dan tried not to sound accusatory, just keep his voice even, statement of fact, what he thought, and nothing more.

"Sorry, can't pin that one on me."

"Can you tell me what you are doing here if it isn't to plant a little something where I'd find it?"

"How 'bout I just thought you needed help. Thought I'd go over the plane myself. I'm not exactly impressed with a few schedules, copies of bank statements, and a list of South American contacts from eight years ago. You got to do better than that."

"Give me time."

"I don't have time."

"I'm not reporting this."

"The hell you're not. This will keep your friends happy and you in expense account money for awhile. Oh, speaking of expense money, I showed Elaine a copy of the report that included a billing for the orchids. Believe me, you're not going to be getting any for awhile. She's feeling just a little taken about now. Probably why she's decided to spend some time with me. Maybe nothing permanent, but then again, you never know."

Laughter, then silence. Dan willed his arms to remain at his sides and let the anger wash over him. He didn't have anything to say, nothing that would take away the sick feeling in the pit of his stomach. He could only imagine how seeing that report had made Elaine feel. Would he get the chance to explain?

He dismantled the vac and loaded the camera. He'd finish quickly and get back to the house. He took a number of close-ups where he'd found the crystals. Crack? It had to be crack cocaine. But he knew he should let a lab decide.

Eric disappeared. He'd done what he came to do, made sure Dan found the evidence. Dan had ignored him, not trusting himself to confront him. He heard him open the cockpit door and climb to the hangar floor. Dan's mind was racing. How could he explain to Elaine why he sent flowers on the taxpayers' money? Without admiting he'd been paid to court her? Jesus. She must have been shattered. So, would she go running back to Eric? Better the devil she knew?

He snapped two rolls of twenty-four exposures. Nook and cranny shots, changing lens for the in-tight, up close, small stuff. Roger would be pleased. Roger would be more pleased with the plastic canister of crystals. He wished he didn't feel so strongly that Eric had planted them.

He backed down the ladder and saw Eric in the shadows by the Lear. Dan had hoped he was gone.

"Beautiful, isn't she?"

Dan supposed he meant the plane. Eric ran the beam of his flashlight along the silver fuselage.

"Not my thing."

"You know, this one's mine."

"How's that?"

"Flew Billy Roland to an auction. Some Texas biggie went under and the Lear was practically given away. I talked him into getting it restored. Had it hauled here and I had just gotten started reworking it. Sent the engine off for an overhaul."

Eric's expression looked wistful in the surreal light of the flashlight as it played across his face. "Those were happy times."

"And you believe a man who would buy a plane for you to tinker with would set you up?"

"People do a lot of crazy things if they're cornered."

Dan hoped he wasn't talking about himself, because that's exactly what Eric was, cornered. Dan adjusted the vest full of containers and left by the back door.

As he neared the house, he saw the light on in the study. Three-thirty. Must be Billy Roland. Hopefully, he'd be back in bed by the time Dan had stashed everything in the Cherokee. But, he wasn't. Billy Roland was standing on the veranda waiting for him.

"Nice night for a walk." Dan spoke first.

"Son, you don't have to lie to me. I took a peek at that box that came for you yesterday. United Life and Casualty wouldn't have kept you on all these years if you weren't thorough."

"Probably true. And I admit to liking to work at night. By myself."

"There's a lot of loner in you. Ever marry?" Billy Roland motioned for him to pull up a chair as he sank heavily onto the porch swing.

"Couple times. Didn't take."

A chuckle, then, "I'd imagine it wouldn't. I can't see you taking up with any ordinary filly."

They sat quietly. Billy Roland didn't suspect him of doing anything not required by the insurance company. Good. He wasn't quite ready to explain old Roger and Tom. Not yet. Billy Roland probably didn't know he had gone over the plane. Should he tell him? No, he had another topic of conversation he wanted to bring up with his host, a little question that was long overdue.

"Earlier this evening when we talked about Eric Linden, there was something I wanted to ask you."

"Shoot."

"When we found the Caddy after the bridge washed out, there was a manila envelope stuck in the brush. Did you ever take a look at the contents?"

"Yep, and saw the same bank book that you did."

"But no two million ever existed."

"And someone was about to be caught in a lie. If Eric had lived." Billy Roland had stopped the swing and crossed his feet at the ankles; the heels of the cloth bedroom slippers flapped against the painted boards of the porch flooring. "You think that someone was me?" There was no anger in his voice, just a matter of fact what-do-you-know tone.

"Could be, if you had something you needed covered up. Something big enough to bargain with a man for seven years of his life."

"I can see how I'd be high on your list. My plane. My contacts. But it just didn't happen that way. I answered enough questions after Eric's arrest to last a lifetime seven years ago."

"Were you straight with me earlier when you said you doubted any locals put him up to it?"

"I've come to believe Eric initiated it, set up the deal with outsiders."

"And the two million?"

"To keep his mouth shut, maybe. The two million didn't come out in the trial."

"I wouldn't expect it to."

"Son, I want you to level with me. You think I could be behind ruining a man's life? Then have him killed on top of it?"

"I don't want to think that." And that was the truth. Dan liked this man, found it difficult to believe he'd jeopardize his position. Throw his life away when there was every indication that he didn't need the money.

"I thank you for that. You want to look at that bank book?" Dan followed Billy Roland into his study and waited while he fiddled with a small wall safe behind his desk.

"Here it is. Other than supposedly being issued by Midland Savings and Loan, there's no evidence of who made the deposit."

Dan switched on a floor lamp and held the book under the light as he turned the pages. He didn't know but guessed that the notations had been made by Eric based on the statement delivered to the prison each month. In one instance, a loss on utilities was noted, in another, a gain in pharmaceuticals. The math was straightforward. Two million invested, interest and dividends reinvested with a nice tidy sum at the end of seven years totaling almost another million dollars on top of the original two.

"Do you trust Judge Cyrus?"

"With my life. Known him forever."

"So you don't think he knew anything about this?"

"I asked him. Took that little black book over to him and demanded an explanation. He was as shocked as I was. Course, a book like that would be easy enough to come by."

Dan would have liked to have said that Eric verified the deposit before going to prison. Talked with someone at Midland Savings and Loan, then heard once a month for seven years from someone representing the bank. Or supposedly representing the bank. Maybe Dan should ask Eric a few questions. He handed the book back.

"You find everything you need out there tonight?" Billy Roland closed the safe and twirled the dial.

"And something I didn't need."

"How's that?"

Dan knew he was taking a chance, tipping his hand if the crystals were part of a stash; but if they had been planted….

"You tell me."

He'd kept the vial of crystals, didn't leave them in the Jeep, wanted them with him until he decided what to do. This wasn't what he'd planned, but it might prove interesting. He tossed the small container to Billy Roland and pulled a chair up opposite the desk. Billy Roland was silent. Not "What's this?" "Where'd you find it?" Nothing. He just sank into the high-back, ergonomically correct swivel desk chair and stared at the contents. Then picked the vial up and shook it watching the nuggets clump back together at the bottom. Dan waited. It was Billy Roland's turn to say something. And the longer he didn't, the more guilty he looked. Finally, he sighed and looked Dan in the eye.

"Guess I might have some explaining to do."

Dan nodded.

"I'm guessing you found this in the clinic out back. Good eye. My surprise is that it's probably crack, not cocaine already refined."

"You suspected that I might have found cocaine?"

"Hoping you would. More than one reason I asked for you—told your boss it was you or no one."

"I'm not following."

"Guess I better start at the beginning. You want anything? Drink? Cup of coffee?"

"I'm fine." He watched as Billy Roland got up to pour himself another scotch. The cocoa-tan striped silk robe with corded maroon trim looked rich but did nothing to hide the slack skin of a hairless, pasty white chest. This was a man old for his sixty-odd years. Old and spent.

"I'm gonna tell you a little story, then let you decide how to use it. I'm relying on your integrity. I know I'm not wrong, son, you're a fair man."

Dan didn't say anything. Obviously, he was about to hear a confession. He hadn't planned on this.

"My suspicions are that this belongs to my wife."

Dan must have looked startled and about to say something, because Billy Roland waved him silent and went on.

"My Miss Iris is the most beautiful creature on the face of this earth. But beauty has its price." Billy Roland paused and looked at him, but Dan was too stunned to open his mouth and just nodded for him to continue.

"You ever know any beauties who just couldn't handle it? Hollywood's full of them. Too beautiful and too weak of character to take care of themselves. The Marilyn Monroe syndrome. Women like that need help. Need someone strong to help 'em get along in life, resist the temptations and ne'er-do-wells who just wait to prey on their weaknesses."

Billy Roland stopped to take a drink then swirl the ice in his glass before continuing.

"Five years ago I founded The Wings of the Dove. Bible College outside Carrizozo. Bought a small ranch with a grouping of old buildings nestled in the hills, then brought in a crew of caretakers, cooks, groundskeepers, and the like—even found me a Bible thumper whose wife doubled as dorm mother and a couple teachers. Nothing radical. Just straightforward fundamentalist teaching. There's a need for that in this world, good straight talk from the Bible." He paused and sucked down half the scotch before continuing.

"Well, before I know it, the place becomes a retreat. Falwell rented the whole thing one summer. So, in addition to bringing lost souls along in the teachings of the scriptures, the place sort of gets a name for itself, among the in-crowd, TV evangelists. And that's when Miss Iris shows up. She'd been saved by one of the biggies—Robertson, if I remember correctly—and then just became a religious groupie, glorified word for a hanger-on with no real purpose in life, and showed up here."

Billy Roland rummaged in the top drawer of the desk and pulled out an eight-year-old *Playboy*.

"Lookee here." The centerfold had obviously been admired before and fell open with little help. And there was Miss Iris.

Longer hair, a little darker blond. A trifle thinner in the face. But then who looked at the face? The full breasts, implant-perfect, the freckles covered by makeup, was the first thing a casual viewer would notice. She was reclining in a bed of Japanese iris; the stark purple blue of the flowers with their yellow-gold stamens hugged the curve of a naked hip and bunched between her legs leaving something, at least, to the imagination.

The face looked young, even for twenty. And guileless. Dan was struck by the freshness that emanated from the page. Untainted, unspoiled, a girl next door with a perfect body. He scanned the bio. The usual. Her hobbies included eating pizza, watching movies, and bowling. No surprises there.

"I married her six months after she showed up on my doorstep. I had to, had to own that perfect animal no matter the internal flaws. I breed all the time for the perfect specimen—that one beauty that no other can have. Something I can flaunt at the shows. And then all of a sudden, I had perfection in my own house. Next to me every night. Son, I don't have to tell you, I was in heaven."

Dan let the past tense slip by. He already knew that paradise wasn't what it once was. The gilt was off the Iris, so to speak.

"Then what happened?"

"About two months after the honeymoon, I discovered she was addicted. Cocaine. Been using since she was fifteen. Left Wisconsin and landed in Hollywood in a world too fast for a youngster. Got the rush from a few shady producers—B movie stuff, glorified porn in one case."

Billy Roland took one last look at Iris among the iris and put the magazine back in the drawer. It was obviously a prized possession.

"We checked out all the sanatariums. Found one in Mexico, near Guanajuato, that fit the bill. She was gone six months. Course, I visited. And she recovered. It was tough. I never want to see someone go through that again. She almost died and I couldn't help her. Well, when she came back she stayed clean. Worked at the college. Helped with booking travel arrangements for some big names who came this way to relax, take a few weeks to drop out of their world.

"I should have known the temptation would still be there. I guess I made it easy for her. Last year I suspected she was hooked again but didn't say anything. Just cut back a little on her allowance. Then the cattle started dying—"

"I don't see the connection."

"Yes, you do. Think about it. You know the first three heifers to die were listed in her name. My little present, trying to get her interested in the Double Horseshoe, give us something together despite the age difference. Shortcake Dream was the best I'd ever produced. Thought my present of the best would show her how I loved her."

Dan was kicking himself. No, he hadn't known whose name the cows were in. He would have found out eventually. But he had assumed. And had missed a clue, a giant clue. Was he losing his touch?

"I've suspected she's planning to leave me. Just under a million and she'd have a nest egg. She couldn't ask me for it. Knew I'd know what she was up to. She knows I'd fight her on divorce. Besides, she signed a prenuptial that lets her out with the clothes on her back, and not a hell of a lot more. I thought at the time I needed to protect my first wife's money. So, that's where you come in. An outsider, ace detective, I knew you'd find out. I wouldn't have to point a finger at my own wife. But I had to stop her and you'd do it for me."

Dan was amazed. All this time, he had been part of a plan to trap the errant wife.

"You believe she killed those cows for the money? But how? She had to have help."

"Now, that's for you to figure out, isn't it, son?"

"But you must suspect someone?"

Billy Roland just shrugged and downed the last of the scotch in his glass. The silence was oppressive. A grandfather clock in the hall boomed out five strokes. The servants would be coming up to the house soon. What could he say? Billy Roland spoke first.

"Forgive me. I'm weak. Just don't have the stomach for a fight anymore. But I don't want to lose her." His voice was barely above a whisper, choked with emotion. "Can you understand that?"

Dan nodded. He did understand. He remembered Iris's behavior at the stock show. Her mood suddenly up shortly after they got there, after she'd queried him on whether he thought she was wasting her time out in the sticks. No, he had no reason not to believe Billy Roland. He knew his story was true. But, now what? He had the motive, the name of the person who stood to gain; what he didn't have was the evidence to nail her.

"What do you want me to do?" He looked across the desk at Billy Roland who sat with his head in his hands.

"What you have to, son, no more, no less."

Dan stood, started to say something comforting but didn't find any ready words that would make a difference, so he leaned over the desk and picked up the vial of crystals. Then put it back down.

"Why don't you put this in the safe. I need some time to think." Then he left the room.

Chapter Seven

Dan tagged every sample, neatly arranging them in a box along with the two rolls of film. He thought he'd be early but could see Roger waiting by the WWII Mauser, a memorial that took up the northeast corner of Roswell's courthouse lawn. It was a quarter to three.

"Bingo, baby. This is going to keep yours truly in the land of mesquite and sand, but so what? I can stand a little more deprivation for a bust."

"What are you talking about?" Dan had felt Roger's excitement when he walked up.

"Hey, don't be so modest. Good idea to drop the stuff off ahead of time. Gave us time to give it the once over. And you're right. Crack cocaine. How much did you find?"

Dan stared at him. God damn Eric. Eric must have suspected he wouldn't turn the crystals over to the feds. And he was right; he wouldn't, not under the circumstances. So Eric took it upon himself to give the feds something to whet their appetite, something to stick around for. Giving leverage for Eric to pressure Billy Roland into coughing up the two million plus. Only it was looking more and more like Billy Roland had nothing to do with Eric's drug bust or the two million. So, the only thing his overzealous behavior did was hang Dan out to dry. "How 'bout we go over to the bank parking lot across the street. Don't want to attract too much attention here."

A reprieve. Think. He needed to put them off. He saw Tom waiting in the car. Riding around Roswell in the back seat of a car with two federal agents wasn't his idea of a fun afternoon. "Hi. You did good." Tom was leaning back to open the door behind the driver's seat. Dan got in. What else could he do?

"How's a Dairy Queen sound?" This from Tom who turned right at the corner not waiting for an answer. It was all small talk while they waited in the drive-up line. Two car loads of people in front of them ordered fries and hamburgers and colas.

"You know this is a nice little town. Great place to raise kids." Roger seemed in good spirits, ebullient even. Dan thought he knew why. He was about to get a promotion, probably based on his timely wrap-up of fingering a major supplier. Only Billy Roland wasn't a supplier, major or not. He had no idea what was going on. He was just one sick old man with a cocaine-using wife who killed cattle to keep her habit going and maybe stockpile enough money to leave him. And until Dan uncovered evidence to the contrary, it was none of the feds' business.

The icy treats were sweet and cool. Not like real ice cream, a passion of Dan's, the cones lacked the richness and flavor he would have preferred. But they were free. Roger, the last of the great spenders, forked over the three seventy-five. But wasn't it Dan's money anyway as a taxpayer?

"What say we take a little cruise up Highway Seventy?"

Dan didn't care. Tom could motor them wherever he wanted. It wasn't going to get any easier.

"So the lab said it was crack?" It would be best to stay in control. Ask the questions; direct the conversation.

"Top grade."

"Any idea what country produced it?"

"Probably Colombia. Matches some stuff that showed up in the East last month."

"How much more is there?" This from Tom.

"None that I know of."

Dan said it calmly, offhandedly, like the crack was just something he'd stumbled across, which was exactly what he was going to make them believe. He caught Tom's expression in the rearview mirror. If they hadn't been on the highway, Tom would have parked the car in about one second and turned on the passenger in the back seat. His eyes registered surprise then turned hard.

"Tom, why don't you take that road up there to the right. We need to find a quiet place to talk." Roger took the news better. Mr. Calmness pointed to a dirt road leading off in the distance. It didn't look used. His voice was even, a practiced modulation meant to mask emotion, Dan thought, taught and practiced during training, no doubt. When they were out of view of the highway, Tom pulled over and stopped, started to speak but must have gotten a signal from Roger because he abruptly opened the car door and got out. Dan waited.

The tiny tape recorder made little clicking noises as Roger fiddled with the buttons and finally pressed play. No "would you mind?" or "hope this doesn't bother you"; they were beyond that. He was now facing two men who probably felt they were getting jerked around. And their fuse wouldn't be very long. He fought a crazy urge to cross his fingers, doubles, using both hands.

"Suppose you start by giving any background pertinent to finding the sample of crack cocaine that you delivered to our motel room on the night of September 27. Begin by stating your full name, occupation, and time of this conversation."

Dan complied, then said what he had planned to say, and prayed it would be convincing.

"The sample in question was found in its entirety and in its present container in the glove compartment of a truck, part of a fleet of six, belonging to the Double Horseshoe ranch owned by Billy Roland Eklund and located—"

"We've got that, go on." More fumbling with the recorder, then Roger said, "Who, for the record, would have had access to this vehicle?"

"Quite a few including the ranch foreman, resident veterinarian, owner, his wife, and various ranch hands numbering over twenty-five." A barely audible "shit" came from outside the car where Tom leaned against the hood.

"What do you plan as follow-up to this discovery?"

Dan droned on about one-on-one surveillance, a stake-out of areas frequented by the ranch hands, interviews. He referenced the packet of materials he had turned over an hour ago, glorified bullshit that he hoped would get him by and promised more. Finally, Roger seemed convinced that the sample was indeed random, but it, at least, placed illegal substances on the Double Horseshoe. They had more than they had had last week.

The ride back to town was quiet. Before they dropped him at his car, they set up a time for another chat. "Chat" was Roger's word; Dan would have chosen "grilling." It wouldn't be so easy next time. He only hoped Eric wasn't planning the delivery of another surprise package. If possible, Dan needed to make certain that he wasn't.

By the outskirts of Tatum, Dan knew one other thing he was going to do that afternoon—drop in unexpectedly on Judge Cyrus and discuss the two million. And include a little unplanned, catch him off guard, if possible, discussion of what was going on in his county among its upstanding citizens.

Dan pulled in next to a sixtyish Lincoln, something old enough to have fins, and marveled at its mint condition. A glance at the steering setup said it was designed for someone not of normal stature—not a bad euphemism for "short." No doubt the judge was in.

Junior apparently was the designated welcoming committee but this time he ushered Dan to the back without checking with his father first.

"Saw you pull up. Just finishing up here. Be with you in a sec." Judge Cyrus continued to sign papers then handed the stack to Junior and waited until he had left the room before speaking.

"Been a little disappointed that you haven't dropped by. No more questions on Voodoo?" The hearty laugh boomed out. "How's that inventory going? Billy Roland keeping you busy enough?"

All just meaningless small talk. An answer didn't seem necessary. The judge was pulling a cigar from a humidor on the edge of his desk and seemed engrossed in rolling it between his fingers, sampling its aroma with his eyes closed, then snapping back to the present before cutting the end.

"Join me?"

"No thanks." Dan knew that lighting the end of anything and putting the other in his mouth would mean buying a pack of cigarettes when he left and another in the morning.

"I get the feeling this isn't exactly a social visit, am I right?"

"I'd like your help. That's probably more in the business category."

"Give it a run. I don't have any secrets."

That's the first lie, Dan thought, but as long as he was here, "I need to know that there aren't any surprises for United Life and Casualty when it comes to Billy Roland's former pilot, a Mr. Eric Linden—no reason that Billy Roland was trying to amass a little extra cash this past year."

"Go on."

"When was the first you heard about the two million plus that Midland Central was supposedly handling for Eric Linden?"

"When the request came in, a coded wire-transfer order, the morning he was released."

"Who placed the transaction?"

"Well, it had obviously been sanctioned by Eric. It was all on the up and up. Only there was no money, of course. Request came from a bank in the Caymans."

"What happened next?"

"Called an emergency meeting of Midland's board of directors. President of our affiliate bank in Roswell. An owner/broker of an investment firm over in Hobbs. Billy Roland. Your brother-in-law, Phillip. A lawyer representative from the Petroleum Trust. A group in Portales. That was it. Two parties were absent."

"I imagine everyone was surprised."

"Let's call it shock. I don't think we really believed it, thought there was some error until Billy Roland found that bank book after the flood."

"Was there any attempt to contact Mr. Linden the day of the transfer?"

"Too late. He was unreachable, already being processed out. So, it seemed reasonable at the time to assume we would just meet with him when he showed up on the doorstep. And that, we all felt certain, he would do."

"Was there any speculation about the money? Where it could have come from? Why it was supposedly invested the day he went to prison?"

"We're not a bunch of dunces. Had to have something to do with his serving time." A gray cloud of smoke circled overhead, the layer dividing the room into two five-foot segments, an upper and a lower. "We all guessed he was in with some mafia-type group that could afford to buy him off, pay him for doing time and keeping his mouth shut."

"How had the account been opened in the Caymans?"

"Interesting you should ask. I checked on that a few years back. Eric's aunt left him fifty thousand when she died. The money was first deposited here. Eric had left an account open, but within a month transferred the fifty to this here bank in the Caymans."

"Did that seem strange?"

"Naw. Can't stop a man from putting his money where he wants to. Guess I figured he was planning on starting over down there someplace. Time was a pilot could make a good living in the islands."

"And the fifty now?"

"That's where things get interesting. I checked. Thought I'd get Elaine everything that was coming to her."

Or there might be other reasons, Dan surmised. He didn't rule out the involvement of this man in some overall scheme.

"It's gone. Supposedly, a Mr. Linden withdrew principal and interest two days after we know he died. Just about started an international incident when I suggested that might be real hard for a dead man to do and that I'd be happy to supply the death certificate to prove it."

"Did you ask for copies of the transaction?"

"Yep. I gotta show you this."

Dan waited while Judge Cyrus unlocked a long, narrow black metal box.

"Look here. This is Eric's signature just as sure as this one is, and that one is. The first was signed in this office in front of me." He pointed to identical loops and tails of letters below the line. "Wouldn't you say these signatures are the same?"

Dan held the papers to the light. They were exact. No hint of forgery at least to the layman's eye.

"Making allowances for maybe here he was having a bad day—these are exactly the same."

"This here document was recorded when the Cayman account was opened four years ago, this one is a little over two months old."

"I can't tell the difference."

"These were done by the same man. No doubt about it. Now, how you figure they did that?"

Dan didn't comment. This wasn't the time to hint that the man in question might be alive. Instead, he asked, "How was the fifty thousand collected?"

"Wire-transferred to a bank in El Paso. Picked up by someone no one remembers clearly. Other than his hand was taped, some sort of injury. And wouldn't you know it?

Surveillance cameras were out that day. Now this signature is almost unreadable."

He pushed a copy of a receipt across the desk. The squiggles were there but bunched together. The first name was just an initial, not spelled out. The E and the L at the beginning of Linden were intertwined. It didn't look much like the others, but hadn't the judge said the man's hand was bandaged? If you had just survived a flash flood, you wouldn't be in real good shape. Dan moved a lamp on the desk so that he could illuminate the signature from underneath.

"What do you think? Done by the same person?" The judge bent over the lamp with him and peered closely at the signature.

"Could be. Then again, might not be. What are you going to do?"

"Already acted. Did what I thought was best. I contacted Elaine. After all, it was her money. And, you know, she thanked me for thinking of her best interests, for being concerned but then said to drop it. Just like that. Drop it and stop dredging up the past. Oh, she said it in a nice way, but you could see the hurt, the pain right near the surface. Said she thought anyone who impersonated the dead would get their reward, that she wouldn't have to do anything."

"Probably right." Dan thought of Eric. Convenient for him that Elaine would go along with his duplicity. Was he seeing a side of her that he hadn't known was there? Or was she being threatened?

"Nothing more I can do about it. But it sure galls to think someone's enjoying fifty grand just because he read the obits and took some action. Could have been someone in the slammer with Eric, knew a little something about his money, had a copy of his signature. Could have been in for forgery." The judge's laugh sounded lame, lacked his usual wall-bashing gusto. "Guess we'll never know."

"Maybe not."

Dan rose to go. Today didn't seem like the right time to ask about the Masons. He'd come back. He still had to prove how Iris killed the cattle—if, in fact, she did.

"Am I gonna see you at the Bar-B-Que tonight?"

Bar-B-Que. It was ringing a bell. Damn. Tonight at Carolyn and Phillip's. The big campaign kick-off. Carolyn had sent an invitation. Was he going? Judge Cyrus was looking at him expectantly.

"I'll be there." Then just before he reached the door, he turned back. "You think Phillip has a chance to be governor of New Mexico?"

"A chance? You sure don't know the politics in these parts. I'd just about bet the bank that your brother-in-law will be a shoo-in. Between lobbying for the Bureau of Land Management grazing rights, and his ties with the labs, both Sandia and Los Alamos, there isn't an interest group in this state that doesn't want him elected."

Dan hadn't thought about Elaine's being at the party until he found himself looking for her car and realized he was relieved when he didn't find it. What would he have said? What hurt was how much he wanted to see her. But not here, in a crowd. He wanted to talk her into getting away from the craziness and go off somewhere, the two of them. Then, as always, he thought of Eric.

There were no dead chickens in front of the door; that was promising. Someday it might be interesting to talk to Dona Mari about her Voodoo priest husband. She was standing just inside the front door as he walked up. She was taking coats and depositing them in the study before ushering people out to the pool area. He followed a group of well-wishers looking for Phillip and saw the guest of honor standing over an open pit supervising the unearthing of a singularly aromatic roasted pig. There was loud clapping and cheers as it was lifted above ground.

Dan looked at the crowd. Billy Roland hadn't arrived yet, but Judge Cyrus was deep in conversation with two men by the pool house. The half-acre backyard had been groomed to perfection. Paper lanterns swung from draped electrical wiring ending at the edge of the pool, a half-dozen insect torches burned along the edge of the patio. A decorated platform took up space beyond the pool; must plan on speeches later judging by the sound system with speakers poised on poles around the yard. Cardboard cutouts of elephants ringed the podium. Party affiliation was plainly displayed, as if it took any guessing, Dan thought.

Chairs had been strategically placed in intimate groupings of three or four around small tables with red, white and blue checked cloths—convenient for the constituents to have that friendly chat, or just get to know one another while fawning over the candidate. Nothing had been left to chance.

"I invited Elaine."

Carolyn was at his elbow, smiling out at her guests but obviously not finished with what she had to say to him.

"I'll never understand you. This is another example of running away from a situation that could be perfect for you. You're afraid of love, of giving anything remotely smacking of emotional support to someone else."

Dan didn't interrupt. It wouldn't do any good. She was on a roll.

"You're a cripple. Mother agrees. Those bimbo wives when you were younger. We both thought you were mature enough for a relationship now." She paused long enough to kiss a woman on the cheek who was gushing on about how perfect Carolyn would be as the state's First Lady. Dan watched his sister graciously accept then turn back to him as the woman moved on.

"I feel invested in this. I'm the one, for God's sake, who encouraged poor Elaine to go out with you. If I had known you would use her, get her hopes up, then be unavailable—isn't that what you've been? Or do you have a better word for it? Maybe that all-important work seventy-five miles away just keeps you overwhelmed."

She stopped and looked up at him sweetly. "Aren't you just a few miles from the Ranch? Maybe it's just easier to buy it. That's certainly a non-investment of emotion."

This last surprised him. He almost laughed. Was that a taunt of some sort? The idea that he needed to pay for a little sexual pleasure made Carolyn seem out of touch. Archaic, even. Certainly out of touch with what he was about. But was this Carolyn's interpretation or Elaine's? They were friends. Maybe, they talked. He missed his chance to question Carolyn as Phillip walked up to claim his wife to help him serve.

Dan followed and put off questioning Carolyn until later. He joined the line and piled a plate with roast pork, baked beans, and potato salad, grabbed a beer from a tub of ice and accepted the judge's invitation to join two other men in one of the groupings of four chairs and table by the pool.

"Don't know who you know, and who you don't. This here's J.J. Rodriguez, attorney, and Bob Tyler, president of the Stockmens Association."

Dan acknowledged seeing J.J. again, and shook hands with the six-foot-tall burly man beside him in an ill-fitting western shirt that strained across a beer gut.

"I hear some of our good citizens are talking you into believing the stories about aliens." Bob chewed with his mouth open. Not a pretty sight. Dan tried not to notice.

"Don't want to overlook any leads."

"Well, don't let 'em pull your leg. Any good vet could have done what was done to old Shortcake Dream. You get my drift?"

Was Mr. Tyler implicating Hank? Or another vet at the Double Horseshoe? Not that that hadn't crossed Dan's mind.

"You ask old J.J. here what he thinks and he'll tell you the *bruja* did it. Cast some spell to ward off evil. That was one hell of an expensive spell, wouldn't you say, J.J.?"

Dan noticed that J.J. looked uncomfortable; he was bent over his plate and appeared preoccupied. Mr. Tyler seemed to think he had just said something immensely funny and bits of pork sprayed from his mouth as he laughed. J.J. chose not to comment. Dan wondered about Bob's using *bruja*, the feminine for witch. Was he referring to Dona Mari? Did she have a following? Or was there another local into witchcraft?

"Bob, let Dan get away from his work for awhile. This here's a celebration. His brother-in-law's going to be number one someday."

Funny. Being related to Phillip gave him some kind of stature. Hadn't the judge just given Bob a veiled warning, sort of a verbal kick under the table? A reminder of whom he was talking to? Small town dignitaries, all of them. Power politics in the burbs. He couldn't believe it.

Dan finished his plate and rose to get another beer. He had just knelt down to fish a Budweiser from the bottom of the tub when he saw her, alone, in the doorway. The sleeveless high-necked dress was classy, casual with sandals, adorned by one long rope of gold beads. Her hair was drawn back, away from her face, and tied with a silk scarf.

And so much for being an emotional cripple. He should call his mother; she'd be happy to know that his heart was racing and he wasn't sure he could trust his legs to stand. He wanted this woman. But it wasn't just lust. And he would get her, but not if it put her in danger. He had to be careful. But he had to know if she felt the same way, could overlook the orchids on the expense report and realize that he was telling the truth when he said he was in love with her. That what had been business was now personal.

He stood, and the motion caught Elaine's attention. She stared at him, started to take a step forward, then abruptly turned back into the house just as he pushed, not too gently, through a throng of people directly in front of him and half ran across the lawn to the back door. She was leaving.

Dona Mari glanced up as he ran through the kitchen and dining room then continued down the hall, across the foyer to the study. From the doorway, he saw Elaine reach for her jacket on the couch. He stepped inside, closed and locked the door, and leaned against it.

She didn't turn around. Just held her jacket close to her body and waited.

"We have to talk." It wasn't the romantic thing he'd hoped to say, but it was the truth.

"I don't think we have anything to say." Her voice was low, flat without feeling.

"Elaine." He was by her side, turning her to face him, brushing her neck with his lips, finding her mouth, kissing, crushing her to him, fleetingly wondering how long it would be before someone would need a coat, try to open the door.... She turned her head away and said, "No." He was surprised by her strength. Both forearms were against his chest pushing him away.

"Why?" He'd never thought that he suffered from a lack of eloquence, but he seemed to have a problem now.

"I shouldn't have to explain."

"Eric...?" Another monosyllabic reply. But wasn't that it? More than the orchids and the expense report? She took a step toward the door; he caught her arm.

"Don't leave." His voice sounded choked, barely audible. "Don't throw away what we had. Trust what we felt together. It was real. It's our lives that are unreal." Good. She was looking at him. Did she agree?

"I don't know whether I can trust you. I don't think I know you anymore. You were using me to get information."

"I don't deny it. But I didn't expect us...to be so good together." What had he wanted to say? I hadn't expected us to fall in love? That was the truth. But this wasn't the time. He prayed there would be a time...later, when the craziness was past. "I came out here to look into possible insurance fraud. I didn't anticipate the rest. I didn't want to get mixed up with Eric."

Elaine put a finger to her lips. "I don't want to talk here. I need time. I'll get back. No promises, though, things may not work out."

And then she stepped close, took his head in her hands, and pressed her mouth to his, hard, tongue searching, pulled back an inch and whispered, "I promised Simon I'd give you a couple wet puppy kisses if I saw you. He misses you."

She wasn't talking about Simon. They both knew that. And the puppy kisses were probably the best he'd ever had and she pulled away just as another part of his anatomy woke up to say hello. She smiled, a little sadly. That she couldn't stay? Couldn't pile on top of a hundred coats and jackets and screw his brains out? He wanted to think that.

"Elaine…." He took her arm again, but she gently pulled away and unlocked the door.

"I don't know when I'll see you again. I need to help Eric." She had lowered her voice which accentuated its throatiness.

"*Need* to help him?"

"It's hard to understand. Maybe I don't understand it myself. Duty?" She shrugged. "Some father-of-my-child link to the past? I don't know. But he stands in the way. Our way. I don't want anyone hurt."

She opened the door just as a guest knocked inquiring about her coat, and was gone before Dan could follow. But didn't he have to let her go? Too many unanswered questions. And didn't he have to find some of the answers, make some of the decisions? And what did she mean by not wanting anyone hurt? Was she protecting Eric?

Dan walked back out to the party and ignored Carolyn's inquisitive looks. He found a beer and wandered toward the miniature grandstand, might as well listen to the speeches. In fact he found himself a little curious about the kinds of promises that politicians in New Mexico might make to their followers. And, it would keep him from thinking, from dwelling on what he had to do.

The party broke up about one. Carolyn seemed to have forgotten to interrogate him about Elaine in her attention to visiting dignitaries. The honored guests included a senator and congressman from that district. He watched Carolyn, transformed into the perfect hostess, flit from table to table. This was her element.

A select group stayed past one. Some pre-campaign caucus that included the judge and Billy Roland and a handful of others. Dan left as Phillip moved the group into the study and opened his liquor cabinet. Must be getting ready to talk money. Dan left after thanking Carolyn. He'd stay in town tonight at the apartment he seldom used and catch up on sleep and laundry. Not too exciting. Had he hoped when he saw Elaine that the evening might have turned out differently?

As usual, there hadn't been any warning that he had a visitor, but Dan wasn't surprised to see Eric sitting at the kitchen table in the dark. In fact, he was hoping he'd show up pretty soon.

"I was just guessing you'd spend the night here. Glad I was right. But I didn't think you'd stay for the whole frigging thing."

Eric had helped himself to the last beer in the fridge.

"Don't turn on the lights," he said as he pushed a chair out from the table. "I prefer to talk in the dark."

"I'm taking for granted you haven't dumped any more surprises on the feds." Dan was still angry about the crystals showing up on Roger and Tom's doorstep.

"Not this week. But you have to admit it was a hell of a good idea since you're fucking off."

Dan didn't answer. He'd promise himself he wouldn't rise to the bait.

"I got something better for you this time," Eric said.

Dan waited while he finished the beer.

"You know that lawyer I met with? The one who set everything up seven years ago, more or less said he represented Billy Roland?"

"I remember."

"Well, he was there tonight."

"He was where?"

"At the party, Carolyn and Phillip's."

Dan tried to untangle his thinking—was Eric there with Elaine, lurking around outside, while…? He made himself concentrate on what Eric was saying.

"What's his name?"

"I may not know his real name but he used Jon, without the 'h'."

"And that's all you have? Just a first name?"

"Jonathan James Reynolds. Law firm out of Dallas. Byers, Northmore and Reynolds."

Something was nudging his memory. J.J.R. Initials awfully close to Juan Jose Rodriguez.

"Describe him."

"Dark hair, combed straight back. He sat next to you. Across from Bob Tyler. Course when I knew him the hair was curly, fell forward over his eye, and it was blond."

"Juan Jose Rodriguez. Are you sure that's the man? It's been seven years. You could be mistaken."

"I wouldn't forget."

"You're right about one thing, he is Billy Roland's lawyer."

Eric had gotten up to lean against the sink.

"The fact that he's using a different name should tell you something."

"I only have your word for it." That seemed to slow him down, Dan thought, then added, "That's probably our biggest problem in all this, your insisting on staying undercover."

"Got to. I have more leverage this way."

"I'm not so sure anymore."

"I wouldn't last one day without protection. You forget I was shot at? That someone wants me very dead. I'd need round the clock protection. And nobody's going to give me that until I have the evidence and it would have to be big time. And if I have the evidence, I'll be able to put a little pressure on Billy Roland myself, get my money and be out of here and won't need anyone's goddamned protection." He kicked back against the sink with the heel of his boot.

Utter frustration, not that Dan could blame him; didn't he feel the same way? He waited a moment and then asked for what he should have demanded their first meeting: a play by play account of what happened seven years ago.

"I know you've heard this before, but don't leave anything out. I'll be the judge of whether it's useful information." Then Dan lowered his voice. "And don't fucking lie to me." He knew there wasn't any hope of using a tape recorder, so he got a couple legal pads out of a drawer, put the date and Eric's initials in the top right hand corner, and sat back down at the table.

"Ready?"

Eric hadn't moved, just stayed standing by the sink. He nodded in the light from a streetlamp that came through the open miniblinds above the sink.

"Give me the circumstances around the bust. What you were doing, and for whom."

"I was returning from Venezuela. I had flown three yearling heifers to Senor Enrico Garcia, stayed two nights on his *finca* outside Caracas, and returned with an empty plane on a Friday afternoon."

"Did you ever check the plane before takeoff?"

"I kept an eye on mechanical things, personally checked gauges, that sort of thing. I handled the refueling."

"Did you file a flight plan?"

"Not always."

"I mean that trip."

"No."

"I take it Mr. Garcia had an airstrip."

Dan looked up as Eric nodded, then continued, "Was there anything that made that trip different?"

"Nothing. I've thought about it a lot. It was routine. I'd probably flown down there a dozen times over a four-year period. Nothing. Absolutely like any other trip."

"Was there live entertainment provided the last night you were there?" Dan thought Eric hesitated before he answered.

"The usual. Girls, a few drinks, just the fringe bennies of working that kind of job."

Dan bit back a comment about the wife and eleven-year-old waiting for him at home.

"So, you didn't bring anyone back with you that trip?"

"No stowaways, if that's what you mean."

Dan let the term go. If that's what Eric called his occasional imports, that was his business. "Would it be safe to say you were a little hungover on the flight back?"

"Maybe. What are you getting at?"

"That anyone could have had access to the plane before you took off. You wouldn't have necessarily noticed anything."

"I wouldn't have been looking for anything."

"That's true, too. But it would have been easy to put something on board. How was the stuff packaged?"

"The usual. Clear plastic inside paper bags wedged into the panels separating the stalls, buried in the padding."

"So you were brought down at El Paso, at the border?" Eric nodded. "Then what happened?"

"Didn't take them long to find what they were looking for. I always thought the border guards had been tipped."

"And they took you into custody there? In El Paso?"

"Yeah. But this Jonathan guy was there. Met with me the first night. Said he was my lawyer, needed to talk with me and would see about bail in the morning."

"Didn't you think it was odd that he was almost waiting on you to be busted?"

"Not at first. Lots of those guys just work the borders. Always around waiting for a quick buck."

"So when did he say he represented your employer?"

"The next morning. And, funny, that's exactly what he said—he represented my employer. Even told me my employer would remain unnamed. He never mentioned Billy Roland."

"Let's go back to your first conversation. What was said?"

"That my employer felt badly about what had happened and wanted to make a deal with me. You know the rest."

"Tell me again." Only this time, I'm taking notes, Dan thought.

"He, this Jonathan representing my employer, offered two million deposited in the bank at Tatum if I would say that I had initiated the whole thing. My greed, my need for big time money."

"And you said yes, just like that?"

"I didn't think I'd get any time. Clean record. Impress the judge with my background. That's when Billy Roland stepped forward. Said he'd pull every string to get me into Milford if it should come to that. Told me he would pray for me and that he'd forgiven me. Said he understood the seven deadly sins." Eric laughed. "I bet he did. But all this was done in front of an audience. Made him look good."

"And you got seven years?"

"Reduced from twelve."

"And you checked with the bank before the trial?"

"Bet your life. Talked with some twit who gave me the account number and verified the amount."

"Did the twit have a name?"

"Ed."

"Just Ed?"

Eric nodded.

"Did you sign any papers? Anything at all to verify what you had agreed to?"

"Sure. The wording sounded a little like a confession. I agreed to accept sole responsibility for my actions, which included piloting a plane found loaded with cocaine, and the amount of two million would be deposited in Midland Savings and Loan to gather interest while I was in prison. The reason I knew it was Billy Roland, besides the fact that he would be one of the few people around here with that kind of cash, there was a stipulation that the money would be left to Elaine in case of my death. She was always a favorite of his."

"I don't suppose you have a copy of the papers?"

"My copy was on file at the bank. But, I have this."

Eric unfolded a much worn yellow sheet of lined paper torn from a legal pad. Dan could see nothing in the near darkness of the kitchen. Then Eric struck a match and he saw black pencil tracings that outlined the signature of what looked to be a Jonathan James Reynolds beside a date in April seven years ago.

"How…?"

The match went out. Eric sat opposite him at the table.

"Funny to think that proof of any of this comes down to a copy of a signature that I'm lucky to have. Lucky because some asshole who wasn't who he said he was pressed hard enough with a ballpoint to leave a replica on the pad underneath. And I was smart enough to save it."

"I need a copy."

"Already thought of that. Look at these."

Again, match light flickered over a much more distinct black on white copy of the signature. No mistaking the Jonathan James Reynolds now.

"What are you going to do?" Eric asked and watched him as the match burned down to his fingers, and he blew it out.

"Don't know yet. But, one more thing. The monthly updates. Who brought them? You got one a month?"

"That was slick. I got to give that to them. That took some planning. Every month I'd receive copies, pages cut out of investing magazines, or stock updates, supposedly, the ones in my portfolio. Then, like clockwork, Mr. Reynolds would call with that month's figures. I had received a bank book and I recorded the figures, sometimes a gain, sometimes a loss."

"So, your only point of contact was this Jonathan?"

"Yeah."

"These calls. Would they be recorded somewhere in prison records? Like who called and when?"

"White-collar time is a little more lax. You forget I was low risk. Don't think anyone cared who called or who didn't."

"Do you have these pages on stocks? What did you call them?"

"Pages torn out of *Value Line* or *Standard and Poor's*. Any schmuck could have gotten them at a library. No, I tossed them."

"Were they mailed?"

"All postmarked Tatum, envelopes part of bank stationery."

"And you're telling me this Jonathan Reynolds, maybe a.k.a. J.J. Rodriguez, called every month for seven years?"

"Kept me quiet, didn't it?"

Dan didn't answer. All he had was a copy of a signature but it might be fun to run it by old J.J. just to see the reaction. Or better yet, compare it with a recent signature, and he thought he had one of those on the deposition he took over the Cisco Kid.

"How would you describe your working relationship with Billy Roland Eklund?"

"Good. Really good. He was like a father. Had helped me out a couple times."

"No apparent reason he'd want to screw you out of a promised two million?"

"I always considered him a square shooter. I always knew he spent money like water but I never thought drugs was behind it. That really shocked me. Guess when he asked me to take the fall, I thought I owed him one. And he's apparently stayed clean the last few years."

Clean or never dirty, Dan thought. It was also hard for him to imagine the old man into anything illegal.

"You ever meet Iris, the second wife?"

"After my time. I didn't even know the first wife very well."

"Anyone else who would have liked to see you behind bars? Out of commission for a while?" Dan didn't know what he was fishing for; it just seemed like a logical question to ask.

"Can't think of anyone."

"Maybe a client who thought you screwed him?"

Eric slowly shook his head. "I wasn't the best lawyer, but most of my work was done for corporations, not private parties."

"Think about it. Maybe you'll come up with something."

Dan stopped by the Roswell office in the morning to check his mail. Nothing urgent. Then he dialed information for Dallas. Byers, Northmore and Reynolds had a number. Was he surprised? He was more surprised when he found himself holding the line for a Jonathan James Reynolds. What was he going to say?

"Jon Reynolds, how can I help you?"

"Dan Mahoney here, investigator for United Life and Casualty out of Chicago. I'm trying to locate a Jonathan James Reynolds who represented an Eric Linden arrested on smuggling charges a few years back in El Paso, Texas."

"Eric Linden? Name doesn't ring a bell. Don't think I'm your man though, I specialize in divorce. Should I have my secretary check our records?"

"Yes, if you don't mind. And one other thing that would help clear this up, would it be possible to get a copy of your signature?"

There was a pause. Uncertainty? Reluctance?

"I suppose so. I'm not sure I understand."

"We have documents signed by a Mr. Reynolds supposedly from your firm, but have reason to believe the signature is forged. I would appreciate it if you could send that copy to my office in Roswell along with a sample of your letterhead."

The man finally agreed. Dan had only to wait. This certainly made things interesting. Billy Roland's lawyer impersonating a lawyer from Dallas. He left instructions for the secretary at United L & C to call him the minute the letter came in. Then he called the office in Chicago and asked that secretary to fax a copy of the deposition that had the signature of J.J. Rodriguez. When he had them together, he'd check with a crime lab expert. It could prove interesting. In the meantime it was back to the ranch and time to start that inventory.

The Double Horseshoe was quiet. Billy Roland was off to Chicago accompanied by Hank for an international symposium on worldwide cattle markets. Dan left a message at the barns that he would be ready to begin the inventory in the morning; Jorge just needed to give him a time. He wasn't looking forward to the days in the saddle, but it would be good to get away.

He asked a visiting farrier to check out Baby Belle. He'd be putting her under a lot of stress for a few days, subjecting her to mixed terrain, some rocky. He didn't need to be out in nowhere with a lame horse.

Hank had shown him where the overnight equipment was kept, sleeping bags, utensils squeezed into canvas carrying cases, plastic slickers, pup tents that folded to no bigger than a Sunday newspaper made of a material to withstand hurricane-force wind and rain. He was in charge of packing his own gear. And as he collected the items and signed them out, he felt the beginnings of something like excitement. More than a look forward to something new, this was adventure. For a few days he would be matching ear-tags to computer lists and enjoying the countryside, not worrying about crooked lawyers, or drug busts gone awry and errant husbands showing up unannounced.

He would be roughing it, sleeping in the open, eating in the open. A chow wagon would meet them at designated dinner spots. Breakfast and lunch, something in packages, would be handed out for the next day at each stop. Billy Roland left a flask of scotch on the dining room table with a note that it might be appreciated. Dan slipped it into his pocket.

They were taking two pack animals but carrying space was limited. The laptop computer would stay with him, the extra batteries could be transported separately. Modern technology meets the Old West. Or something like that.

Jorge came up for dinner that night. Iris decided to cook steaks on a grill outside, sort of a prelude to their trip. It wasn't like she prepared anything. Thawed steaks and left them on the counter in the kitchen and warmed a pot of beans. The potato salad was in the fridge, fixed before the kitchen help took off for the evening.

Dinner was quiet. Dan wasn't sure he felt at ease with Jorge but chalked up any reservations that he had to the man's quiet manner. But in some ways that was a relief, nothing worse than getting caught with a non-stop talker when you're trying to concentrate on business and happen to be a captive audience.

There would be five ranch hands riding along. They would act as scouts, spot the cows, then the five of them would round them up, drive them to holding pens if there were any close enough and help with checking the ear tags. One of the men was a vet.

Dan expected to check over a thousand head in the next few days. Many would be mixed-breeds, Brangus, Braford; only a few Charolais and polled Hereford mixed in the herd that scrounged for food and congregated at one of a hundred stock tanks. These were range-fed beef cattle being prepared for a market later in the fall.

Jorge said he should be ready to ride at six and Dan turned in about nine after a shower, something he might not have for a while. The bed felt good. He had left a window open and a breeze played with the corner of the sheets. The moon was a perfect crescent, and he watched as its light cast dappled shadows across the quilt. And that's all he remembered before slipping into the sleep of the weary.

He dreamed of Elaine. The two of them together, running across a field, then tumbling down a hill to wrestle body against naked body in tall fragrant grass. Her hair was swept back from her face and she was teasing him, reaching between his legs, grabbing then releasing him to run a hand across his abdomen. He reached out and drew her to him murmuring her name as he pressed his head between her breasts.

"Shit."

He sat up. He was awake and focused and pissed all at the same time. "Get out of this bed. Now." He wasn't even worried about keeping his voice down.

"You weren't so all-fired anxious to get rid of me a minute ago." Iris could pout like no one he'd ever seen before, full bottom lip slightly curving downward, eyes watery, imploring—no, begging—blond hair tousled spilling over her shoulders, down her back giving her a wayward urchin look. But then there were the breasts, nipples erect, thrust forward by the curve of her spine as she sat back on her knees at the foot of the bed but aware, very aware, of exactly how she looked, how provocative the pose.

Dan swung his legs over the side of the bed and stood with his back to her and wished he believed in pajamas or, at least, slept in shorts. He pulled on the pair of Levis thrown over the chair next to the window, then not knowing what else to do, sat down.

"What are you doing here?"

"Funny, you have to ask." She swung a leg around to settle cross-legged, facing him.

"Damn it, Iris, get out."

"No one's here to see us."

"That's not the point. I'm not interested."

"That's just real hard to believe." She put extra emphasis on hard.

"I'm not into playing games." She didn't seem to be in any hurry to move. Would he have to carry her to the door?

"Who's Elaine?"

It caught him off guard. This reference to someone he wished was sitting in the exact same place as Iris and in the exact same attire—nothing.

"Friend."

"Sure. Close friend, maybe?" Giggles.

"Why do you want to go to bed with me?" Maybe, the direct approach.

She stared at him a moment, then, "Are you going to investigate me?"

"What do you mean?"

"As the owner of those cows that died."

"Should I?"

"I don't know anything."

"Then I'll find that out, won't I?"

"Will I get the money?" Now, the real reason for being here was coming out, Dan thought.

"If I don't find reason to suspect foul play."

"When?"

"When what?"

"When will I get the money?"

"One month. Maybe two. As soon as I wrap up the investigation."

She sighed. "I need the money now." And then he did something he'd been wanting to do, been curious about ever since the talk with Billy Roland; he took a step toward the bed and grabbed her by the arms. Pulled her arms out toward him and even in the pale light could see the infinitesimal dots in the creases of both forearms.

"I bet you do."

She pulled away and flounced off the bed and left the room slamming the door behind her. Dan didn't lock it. He knew she wouldn't be back. But it was another hour before he got back to sleep.

It must have rained before dawn. Lawn and flowers glistened with a heavier than dew coating of moisture. And the smell of freshness enveloped him as he headed toward the barn. Great day for a roundup. When he thought of last night, he almost laughed. Shouldn't there be a medal for passing up sex with perfect bodies? But the sadness of it stopped him. A young life in trouble without a promising future.

"You be ready in five minutes?"

It was a question, not a command. Jorge stood in the breezeway of the barn talking to five men whose horses were already saddled. Must be the hands going with them. Dan nodded when he saw that someone had saddled Belle and brought her up front.

The pack horses were tied outside. One of the men handed around a thermos of coffee and sweet rolls, then Jorge swung lightly onto his horse, started down the drive, and waved them to follow. Belle sensed Dan's excitement and sidestepped the first fifty feet before he goosed her into going forward. The time together would be good for both of them.

The first half day netted a hundred and fifty steers found clustered around a stock tank about two miles from the house. All had ear tags and all were numbers in the computer. By late afternoon they had checked an additional hundred and seven. The chow wagon was already parked and waiting for them at the designated spot by the time they finished.

"The bulk of the herd is probably on the *Llano Estacado*." Jorge trotted his horse alongside Belle. "This area is called the stockaded plains. If you look carefully, you can see the fortress-like appearance of escarpments, there..." Jorge pointed in a circular motion to the west, "and there." He pointed back to the east. "We'll get over closer to those ridges tomorrow. Then the real work begins."

There was a beauty in the sparseness of the land. The natural boundaries contained the herd in a basin stretching miles in every direction. A wooded area in the distance marked a stream, an oasis-green dot starkly outlined against the dusty sage of the prairie grass. One, maybe, two hundred years ago, buffalo roamed this same area in herds big enough to cover several acres.

They had passed a line of migrant worker shacks. All vacant, looking like they hadn't been inhabited for awhile. Dan thought they might stop there for the night but Jorge pushed on saying they were later than expected. At the next rise Dan saw the paneled truck waiting on them in the distance.

Dinner was already being served when Dan dismounted. He rubbed down Belle, gave her water and feed before he went to get a plate for himself. There was an iced keg of beer, fried chicken, more beans, and more potato salad. But everything tasted great, something about being outdoors. There was a hint of chill in the September night air. After the dinner wagon left, in this case a panel-backed Land Rover, someone built a fire.

Jorge sat with the men who worked the cattle, but Dan didn't feel left out. Jorge just seemed more comfortable speaking Spanish. Not that his English wasn't perfect, it was. Probably educated in the States, Dan surmised. The right qualifications for being a ranch foreman this close to the border.

Everyone turned in early. But Dan didn't know when that was; he had left his watch in one of his saddlebags. Time was the last thing that mattered out here. He unrolled his gear next to a clump of prairie grass—a sleeping bag on top of a two-inch-thick foam pad laid out on sun-hardened caleche clay and sand—and he'd never sleep better.

The second day was a repeat of the first. Only this time they found larger pockets of cattle milling around remote water tanks each marked by a windmill and easily seen from miles away.

As they approached a herd, Jorge would ride forward, push through them looking them over, sizing them up? Dan didn't know. But he could be looking for any that might be diseased or lame. The man was thorough.

It was late in the afternoon when they rode over the crest of a low rolling hill and spotted about fifty head moving single file toward a water tank in the distance. Their leader was a particularly large black steer. But he wasn't the one that caught Dan's attention. At the rear and about fifty feet back from the rest was a youngish looking heifer. A straggler not accepted by the others.

As Dan watched, she stopped and looked his way, more interested in the riders than following the group. Dan dismounted, pulled out the computer and walked toward her.

"Nice Brangus heifer," Jorge offered. "Need some help with her?"

"I might be able to do this one all by myself." The heifer still hadn't moved by the time Dan stood in front of her, even though Jorge hovered behind him on horseback as a precaution.

"I'll be over here if you need help." Jorge seemed reluctant to leave.

"No problem. I'm okay." Dan put the computer down and reached out to pet her. She was in poor condition, slack skin, her coat which should have been a shiny black was dull with loose hair and flakes of dander; there were signs she was suffering from diarrhea. Only her eyes were clear and warm. She even made a grunting noise as he patted her back and moved to check the ear tag.

Dan didn't know cattle but this one seemed different. Even in her condition, better than the rest. A certain look. He pulled an ear toward him; the tag had been mangled. It was barely readable. Whatever this heifer had been doing out here, she'd had a rough time of it. He punched in the number 5141 from the tag and saw that the Brangus-Charolais cross heifer was one of Billy Roland's, raised on the Double Horseshoe, and was three years old.

Absently, he scratched behind her ear just in front of the hump characteristic of Brahma and Black Angus mix cattle. The hump was less pronounced than in Charolais but still very much present. Only Charolais were completely silver or mottled white in color, like the hairs around this heifer's eyes. Maybe that's what caught his attention, the owl-like appearance of her eyes that leapt out at him against the jet black of her coat.

He patted her on the right shoulder and she moved sideways. Not to get away from him but to square up, better place her feet. Suddenly, Dan's mind was racing. He picked up a stick and tapped her flank just like he'd seen Hank do in the show ring. The heifer, keeping an eye on him, collected her mass and moved her left hind leg back to line up with her right hind leg, then pulled herself up and out over her front legs, showing chest and neck to the best advantage.

Dan stood back, praised the heifer, and took in the perfection of this badly treated animal whose good breeding came through in spite of condition and a lousy dye job. Then he followed a hunch—more than a hunch. He pressed in the number 5747. If someone had filed off the points on the sevens, the number would look like 5141. But he didn't need to wait for the records to come up on the screen. He knew without looking that standing in front of him was Grand Champion Taber's Shortcake Dream.

Chapter Eight

The men in the Land Rover had dropped off dinner and raced back to the house for the hospital truck, a well padded stock trailer with wide, woven canvas bands of support that criss-crossed beneath the animal, gently keeping it on its feet, aiding it in standing during the ride back over rough terrain.

Meanwhile, the vet who rode with them went over her. Of course, she'd been exposed to who knew what on the range, but he thought she'd be fine with good food and care. Lucky to have found her when they did because he didn't think she would have lasted much longer. Shortcake Dream needed little encouragement to hop into the trailer. It was almost like she knew she was going home, Dan thought.

They were met at the barns by Hank, who instantly took over backing the heifer gently out of the trailer and quickly moving her to the clinic. There were two other vets helping him as he began collecting blood samples and preparing injections of antibiotics. Another ranch hand tempted her with some kind of mash in a stainless steel bucket while he rubbed her nose and whispered encouragement. Dan thought Shortcake Dream looked content. Happy to have all the fussing. Life was back to normal for her.

But if Shortcake Dream looked happy, Billy Roland was ecstatic. Tears had rolled down his cheeks when he watched her being unloaded. He did a cursory check of the heifer himself, exclaiming over her condition, and then Hank ordered him back while his team took over.

"How can I thank you?" Dan and Billy Roland had walked back to the house.

"Just a little matter of everyone being in the right place at the right time."

"More than luck, son. You recognized good breeding and thought to question a situation that didn't look right to you. I'll forever be in your debt."

Billy Roland said it reverently but the excitement seemed to have left him spent. He slumped into a deep leather chair in the study and leaned against the high back.

"Suppose you could find a little something to put in a glass over there? I'd be much obliged." He waved toward the bar but Dan was already moving in that direction. He figured they both had earned a scotch over.

"Spell it out for me, son."

"What?"

"What you're thinking. About who's behind this. Who's trying to put one over on the insurance company."

Dan didn't answer immediately. In all the excitement he hadn't necessarily tried real hard to decide who he thought was behind the switch, number 5141 for 5747. A little switch that would have grossed about three hundred and fifty thousand for Miss Iris. But who masterminded it? And what would have happened to Shortcake Dream? He found it difficult to believe that she would have been left to die on the plains. Not after someone had gone to all the trouble to disguise her.

"I could ask you the same question, couldn't I?" Dan handed Billy Roland the glass of scotch.

"Assuming you think I'm innocent."

"Are you?" Dan hoped his directness wouldn't be misunderstood.

"In some ways I am, in some ways I'm not."

"Care to explain that?"

The sigh was deep. Dan was almost afraid that Billy Roland wasn't going to continue when he pushed himself out of the chair, crossed to the bar and brought the bottle of scotch back and placed it between them.

"Might need a little refresher later on," he said and sank back down and picked up his glass.

"When those first two heifers died unexpectedly, I had my suspicions. Like I explained, the money would come in handy for Miss Iris. But I didn't say anything. I just wanted to bury my head in the sand, not believe what was right in front of my nose." Billy Roland took a long drink of scotch. "When Shortcake Dream was found mutilated, I'd liked to have died. My whole life was in that heifer. I'd never signed over my best if I hadn't thought the gesture was worth even more. Like some old fool, I thought I could buy a love that never would be there for me." He paused to down three swallows of scotch.

"But I couldn't believe that Iris could have had that heifer killed. Couldn't let myself believe it. It would have meant that Iris never did love me or she couldn't have hurt me that way. Killed a beautiful living being. You don't know how hard I was hoping that alien theory would pay off." A wan smile and another swallow of scotch.

"So now what am I left with? I got Shortcake Dream back, but now I know that Miss Iris was behind it. Miss Iris and some stud who also sucks up my hospitality and draws a paycheck, probably. But luckily someone who just didn't have the heart to kill a fine animal."

The first crash of breaking glass startled both of them. Dan reached the door of the study first and headed toward the kitchen. Iris didn't see him standing in the doorway but heaved another piece of dinnerware in the direction of the man standing in front of the butcher block island in the center of the room. She was out of control. Her face was red and splotchy and distorted by screaming.

"You can't do anything right. Can't even kill a god-damned cow." Another plate shattered into a hundred pieces after sailing over the head of the man and banging against the wall. Then a cup and saucer followed. Iris was hysterical and from the center of the room, Jorge's eyes never left her.

"I needed that money. You told me everything was taken care of. You and your god-damned promises. You didn't tell me you decided to spare that stupid piece of shit. What's a cow? I'm dying out here. I'm dying." Iris sank to the floor sobbing uncontrollably, her head on her knees.

"I'll be out of here in the morning." Jorge said it matter of factly to Billy Roland, who stood in the doorway behind Dan. "There's been no damage. Shortcake Dream will be fine. Glad you finally got around to doing the inventory. She wouldn't have lasted much longer." This he addressed to Dan. Then he turned to go. "Oh yeah, Hank will back me up on this. The first two heifers really did die of virus. That's when Miss Greedy decided to go for a lump sum and then split. Take little old Shortcake Dream out and disappear."

He left by the back door. Dan made a move to follow, but Billy Roland stopped him.

"Let him be." He stood looking at Iris. "I want you out of here, too, come morning. You'll get what's yours from the first two heifers. Put it to good use. There won't be asking me for any more."

Dan watched the old man go down the hall to his study, but he didn't follow. If he had to guess, he'd say that Billy Roland would probably kill the bottle of scotch and wouldn't want any company when he did it. Dan crossed to the back door. He'd go down to the barns to check on Shortcake Dream. He stepped over a subdued Miss Iris on the way. Tangled lives. Wouldn't be the first time an insurance investigation had turned into soap opera.

The kitchen table was covered with travel brochures but she wasn't kidding herself. She wasn't going anywhere. Not immediately, anyway. She switched off the overhead lamp and pushed bare toes into Simon's soft fur. Close to midnight according to the clock above the stove. This wasn't how she thought the sabbatical would be. Christ, this wasn't how she thought her life would be. In limbo. Decisions that had to be made were sliding away, just outside her reach.

She was feeling a need to get on with things. To take control. Stop waiting for Eric to dictate the next step. Was she even sympathetic anymore? Did she care that he felt he'd been cheated out of two million dollars? Couldn't she just go to someone, authorities maybe and tell them about Eric and then walk away?

But what if he was killed? Because of her, what if he really died? Or what if he turned on her? Threatened her life for double-crossing him? That was another possibility. Or maybe he would harm Dan. She didn't put that past him.

"Got any coffee?" She hadn't heard Eric get up. He slept most of the day on a bed in the spare room and would get up after dark to do whatever it was that he did; she didn't ask.

"I'll start some."

"Maybe you should take that trip or whatever it is you have planned." Eric sat at the table leafing through a booklet on Ireland.

"I'm not sure this is a good time."

"Might not be a better one."

"Eric." She paused. "What are your plans? When will you be out of here?" She could feel him staring at her in the darkness illuminated only by the yard light next to the garage. "I'm tired of this. I want out."

"No can do. You know that."

"We're adults. You can't hold me against my will."

"Is it against your will? Just because you don't want your house to burn down or your boyfriend to end up missing...."

Elaine willed herself not to say anything. Idle threats. She had to believe that they were meaningless. So, why didn't she take action? She filled the coffee maker with water and turned back to face the figure in the shadows.

"Do you mind telling me what you plan to do next?" Besides eat, sleep, and drink a six-pack a day around here, she added to herself.

"I'm sure as fuck not getting any help from your friend."

The allusion was to Dan. He was always referred to as her friend. She knew Eric met with him occasionally. Funny, it was her only contact with Dan.

"Let me help." Elaine paused. Did she mean it? She had been thinking of a plan, part of a plan, that might help.

"How?"

"Let me talk to Billy Roland. If you're not willing to confront him, I will. In a nice way, just to see what he knows."

"I'll think about it."

"I want an answer now."

"Pushy, aren't we? What would you say to the old man?"

"That you told me about the money while in prison. I can say I've decided to look into finding out what happened to the two million that should have been mine."

She could tell the idea appealed to him. He wasn't getting anywhere this way. She poured two cups of coffee and sat at the table.

"Okay, but I'm going with you. I'll be outside."

Was this because of Dan? Probably. But she didn't care. She was taking action.

"Tom, come here." Roger Jenkins was leaning over the tape equipment that recorded every phone call made by Dr. Elaine Linden and could barely contain his excitement. So far, the tape had proved worthless. Two phone calls from students concerning incomplete grades, one call to the hairdresser, several to a travel agent in Albuquerque, other miscellaneous small town business calls, and that was it. The sum total for all of last week. Nothing of any importance to the investigation of Billy Roland Eklund.

"This is it." Roger pointed to the tape, rewound it and played it for Tom. The call was short. The formalities, then an invitation to supper that evening. Roger played it again for Tom.

"Sounds like she hasn't talked to him in a while."

"Or making it sound good in case someone's listening."

"I don't know. The wife seems to be exactly what she is, a college prof who just buried her shit of a husband."

"Maybe. But one thing's for certain, we'll be there. This just might be what we've been waiting for."

Roger could tell Tom didn't share his enthusiasm. The assignment was going stale for Tom. Sometimes he didn't think Tom had what it took to advance, that sort of bulldog tenacity and an uncanny sixth sense. No, Tom was wrong on this one. He could feel it. He didn't know when it would be but they were getting close to cracking this nut wide open. And, tonight could just very well be their lucky night.

She had called the Double Horseshoe in the morning. Billy Roland seemed happy to hear from her. She had to come to supper. He wouldn't take no for an answer. It had been far too long since he'd seen her. They'd make an evening of it. He had someone he wanted her to meet.

It wouldn't take three guesses to figure out who. She hung up looking forward to it. She wasn't exactly certain what she'd say, but felt confident that she'd think of something. And she'd see Dan. Spend time being in the same room with him. Decide without hormones getting in the way whether he was telling the truth about not using her, about wanting her.

She left Roswell about five and arrived at the ranch at seven. She hadn't pushed the Benz but took the time to formulate a plan. Eric slept most of the way, or at least kept quiet. He was in the back seat, covered with a blanket, and only roused when they turned into the curving drive leading to the house.

Eric told her to park on the south side of the house. Try to get everyone into the study after dinner. She'd see. She locked the car and walked across the porch to the front door. It had been years since she had visited. Five to be exact. She'd driven out with Eric's aunt the year before she died, but nothing had changed, not one petunia in one hanging pot.

"Elaine." The door flew open before she reached it and Billy Roland wrapped her in a bear hug that almost took her breath away. The same enthusiasm that she remembered, but he looked so old. He felt thin through the western-cut jacket.

"It's been too long," she said.

"Took the words right out of my mouth. And if it's possible, you're prettier than ever. How'd you get the old hands on the clock to move backward?" He held her at arm's length to admire her, then turned abruptly to the man standing in the shadow of the doorway. "Dan, you're the resident expert on heifers with good breeding. Wouldn't you say this one is pure blue ribbon all the way?"

Elaine smiled and held out her hand as Dan stepped forward. Thank God, it was dark enough to hide her blushing.

"Elaine." It was all he said but his eyes filled in the blanks. And the touch of his skin. She withdrew her hand. Had Billy Roland noticed anything? Leaving her hand a moment longer than necessary in Dan's? She felt Billy Roland's arm go around her.

"Let's not dawdle out here over long. I can see you two would be seeing more of each other if I didn't keep Dan locked away. But, then, who am I to play Cupid, got a piss poor track record myself."

Elaine didn't understand the reference but knew he hadn't missed her attraction to Dan. Billy Roland insisted on a mini-tour of the barns before eating. He did nothing to hide his admiration of Dan and his thrill at having Shortcake Dream back. He told and retold how Dan had been smart enough to recognize good breeding and had saved the heifer's life.

Billy Roland walked with his arm around her pointing out animals or new additions to his barns. He seemed truly pleased that she was there. She tried to catch Dan's eye. She'd like to tell him that Eric was in the car. Maybe it wouldn't make any difference. But she would be more comfortable if Dan knew why she was there.

They looked at the horses first. Elaine was treated to the stories about Baby Belle and how she was now a one-man filly, thanks to Dan. There seemed to be some barely concealed innuendo linking Elaine with Dan, comparing her to the filly, hinting that Dan might be able to work that same kind of magic on her, too. Billy Roland's attempt at humor was a little embarrassing under the circumstances, but she laughed when she saw Dan roll his eyes skyward and shake his head.

Elaine enjoyed the tour. Somewhere between admiring the clinic and stepping into the stall to pet Shortcake Dream, she realized how happy she was. Dan put his arm around her waist and they watched as Billy Roland checked the heifer and coaxed her into eating a little mash. Dan thought she already looked better and said so. Billy Roland agreed but thought there was a long road ahead of them before she could be bred, let alone shown.

Dan whispered that he'd missed her. She whispered back that Eric was in the car and felt his arm slip from her waist and his body pull away. The gesture almost made her cry out. It was wrenching how much she wanted this man and how screwed up everything was. Billy Roland finally tired of coddling Shortcake Dream and the three of them walked back to the house. She thought Dan had to be at least ten feet from her. But maybe that was wise. She knew Eric was watching.

Supper was private. Just the three of them sharing a good Bordeaux with the steaks. Conversation bounced from Matthew to Elaine's sabbatical and back to the Double Horseshoe. Dan was quiet. With his back to the window, he never took his eyes off of her. She liked that. She was comfortable and was almost lulled into forgetting why she was there and who was standing outside. Almost, but not quite. Eric was taking all this in; she could feel it.

And, she came so close to just saying, I have to go now, no dessert, coffee, after dinner drink; but she didn't. She heard herself agreeing to coffee in the study. Sweaty palms and all, she pushed back from the table and followed the two men down the hall.

"Would you feel comfortable talking about Eric?" She waited until each of them had a drink and Billy Roland had settled on a striped settee to her right.

"Of course, darlin', is something troubling you?" Billy Roland looked up expectantly.

She ignored Dan, who sat across the room facing the windows, but hoped that he was aware of what she was doing. Not that he could help, he couldn't without giving Eric away unless he was willing to talk about seeing the sheriff the night of the flood. Maybe, there'd be an opening....

"I've had seven years to think about this and now that I'm here, my nerve isn't." She smiled nervously in Billy Roland's direction and didn't look at Dan. She took a deep breath. "You know, he always thought he was going to prison for you. Felt that he owed you one. Since he got caught with your cocaine, he would help you out, take the rap for you."

"That's hogwash. What on God's green earth gave him an idea like that?" Billy Roland sloshed half his drink onto a Navajo Yei rug as he pushed himself upright.

"Maybe because the lawyer who met with him said he represented you."

"I didn't send a lawyer. I offered, but Eric wanted to represent himself."

"This wasn't someone to represent him. This was someone who had papers that assured Eric of two million invested for a plea of guilty."

"Do you have a copy of these so-called papers?"

"No. Like the two million, they don't seem to exist."

Billy Roland had gotten up to fix another drink. Elaine waited. He was angry; she could tell that by his posture. Had this been such a good idea? Dan had walked along the row of windows opening onto the veranda and pulled the blinds—shut one of the windows and made certain that no one could see in. Eric would be beside himself, but she had to smile.

"Let me just make sure I understand you. Eric told you that a lawyer saying that I'd sent him, offered him two million to plead guilty, sort of indicated that the cocaine was mine?"

Elaine nodded.

"I may have the name of that lawyer, Jonathan James Reynolds," Dan said.

"Never heard of him."

"But you do keep a Juan Jose Rodriguez on retainer."

"You saying J.J. used an alias?"

"Not exactly. I think J.J. impersonated Mr. Reynolds."

"Do you have proof?"

"I may have by the end of the week."

"How long has J.J. worked for you?" Elaine asked.

"'Bout seven or eight years now. Would have started work for me just about the time that Eric got sent up to Milford."

"Did someone recommend him?" Dan asked.

"Two folks had been using him, Judge Cyrus, and your brother-in-law, Phillip Ainsworth. Fact is, J.J. is a nephew or some relative to that housekeeper of your sister's, Dona Mari. But then, so is my ranch foreman, Jorge. Former foreman, right, Dan?"

Dan nodded but looked pensive. Elaine watched as he seemed to be contemplating something. Was there something about linking this Jorge and J.J. with Dona Mari? What did that mean? All had access to the major players, all were in interesting positions to—

"What kind of evidence you planning to come up with?" Billy Roland asked.

"I may have a copy of the signature that was on papers left with Eric seven years ago. It may not prove anything, just places J.J. at the scene, and leads to more questions."

"I suppose the sixty-four-thousand-dollar one is why. Why would anyone bribe Eric to take a fall…I suppose you both have considered the possibility that Eric is guilty? The cocaine really was his…." Billy Roland looked thoughtful.

"But then there's the bank book," Dan said.

"I tend to believe Eric. I mean, I believed him when he told me all this seven years ago," Elaine said.

The muffled thud, like a sack of feed being thrown on the porch, startled the three of them into silence. They listened, but there was nothing else, no scuffling, crashing into anything, just the one sound of mass connecting with the porch. Elaine pulled back the heavy drapes and looked through the blinds. It was too dark to see much of anything. But the porch swing was moving sideways like someone had bumped it in his haste to get off the veranda.

"Anything?" Dan was beside her.

"Nothing."

"Could be Hank's black Lab. That hound's always thumping around up here on the porch at all hours," Billy Roland said.

"I'm going to look around." Dan started toward the door.

"Me, too." What was she thinking? If Eric was tempted to do something threatening, she'd be there to stop him? Something like that.

"Hell's bells. You can't go off and leave your host." Billy Roland grabbed his drink and followed. When the three of them reached the porch, Elaine was struck by the serenity of the evening. All seemed perfectly calm, a night bird's call, clouds that draped the almost full moon in a feathery haze, a calf that bawled in the distance. Silence. Then a few answering woofs from what was probably the Lab down at the barns. Idyllic. As they watched, the moon slipped out of the clouds to illuminate the porch, the drive, and surrounding fields.

"I'm going to take a look around." Dan walked down the steps.

Elaine and Billy Roland followed the curve of the veranda to the area outside the study. The swing was now still. There was no hint that anything had been disturbed. Elaine stooped to look under the windows. If someone had been standing there not long ago, it was impossible to tell now. No dust to give up footprints. There was no evidence of a struggle.

She thought of checking the car but didn't know how she'd explain what she was looking for. So, she waited with Billy Roland, sat in the swing and let her feet skim along the floor as she pushed, then released and enjoyed the stirring of the still air.

"False alarm. Can't find anything out of place." Dan joined them, then caught her eye and shrugged his shoulders before turning to sit beside Billy Roland on the veranda steps. A message that she interpreted to mean he hadn't found Eric. Odd. She wondered if he had looked under the porch. Could Eric have tripped and fallen against the house? Then quietly crawled underneath? No, the noise they heard was more like someone being knocked to the ground.

They sat enjoying the night. No one seemed interested in pursuing the subject of Eric again. Elaine didn't say anything. Curiosity as to where he was vaguely bothered her. If he wasn't in the car when she left, what then? Billy Roland stood and stretched and allowed as how an old man still needed beauty rest.

Elaine hugged him. She was sincere when she said it had been a great evening. She walked with him back into the house, got her purse and jacket and returned to the porch.

"I'll walk you to your car." Dan waited in the shadows. "I'd like to make sure Eric is all right," he said as he took her arm.

"You think he's in the car?"

"Only place I didn't check."

The Benz was unlocked, with the blanket draped over the front seat. But the car was empty.

"Now what do I do?" Elaine couldn't keep the frustration out of her voice. "You don't think he'll try to approach Billy Roland on his own?"

"Unlikely. But maybe I'd better get back. Are you going to be all right?"

She nodded and slipped behind the wheel.

"Call me when you get home. I'll wait up."

"Thanks."

"Elaine. I want all this to be over. I…."

She put a finger to her lips then mouthed "Me, too" before turning the key in the ignition.

"You know who this is?" Roger hissed the question between huffing under the dead weight of the man they were carrying between them and trying to keep from stumbling as he pushed the pace. They needed to reach the protective cover of the poplar before anyone in the house came looking. He hadn't anticipated the man they found looking in the window to go down so hard. Roger hadn't even planned on hitting him until he saw the gun tucked in the back of his belt. Training had taught him to ask questions later. But when he had shone the flashlight in the face of the man on the porch, he knew. He knew and could hardly keep his excitement under control. What did this mean? He couldn't even speculate, but it was big. He knew that. He wanted to say I told you so to Tom, but he'd just gestured for him to take one side of the fallen man and help Roger drag him to cover.

After sprinting down the drive, they paused in the poplar to watch and catch their breaths. Only Dan left the porch to circle the house. They hadn't left a trail, not in the gravel of the drive. Roger had risked the sound of crunching rock in order to cover their immediate tracks. They waited, staying hidden in the windbreak about seventy-five feet from the house.

"Damn it. Go back inside." Roger watched the group settle on the porch. He was plainly stressed and anxious to get his prize back to the van parked about a half mile down the road and didn't want Elaine and party to wait around too long. He didn't want to have to hit the guy slumped between them again.

"Looks like they're there for the night."

"No, wait. Billy Roland's getting up. Okay, party's over. That's right." Roger's whispered encouragement seemed to work. As they watched, Elaine and Dan walked out to the car. Then as Elaine nosed the Benz down the drive, Dan went back to the house.

"So far, so good. But we still need to be quiet." Roger was breathing easier. He motioned for Tom to help him hoist the man into a sitting position before pulling him up between them. He couldn't wait to question this man.

"So, who is this?"

"C'mon. You don't know? This, Tom, is a dead man come back to give us some answers."

"No shit? Eric Linden?"

"None other, alive and well."

It was difficult to hide his smugness, so Roger didn't try. He'd felt this case was his. His to solve. He was banging on the door to that promotion, just lacked the exposure that would get the attention of his superiors. But this, this could do it. Hadn't they wanted to question Linden about the two million? Squeeze a little and see where it got them? Everybody would be wetting themselves; and he'd take the credit.

Roger sent Tom into the office at the Silver Spur to rent a room for the night. The no vacancy sign flashed on as Tom came back out.

"That was lucky. Got some convoy of truckers going through. Number Twelve's the last one." Tom climbed back into the cab of the van then squeezed between the seats and squatted by Eric's body. "Think we're going to attract attention trying to get him out?"

"Not if we're drunk."

"Good idea."

They didn't try to be quiet. A trucker parked along the perimeter of the motel swung down from his cab just as they pulled Eric upright but turned back to check his tires and didn't watch as they walked Eric between them to the door.

They dumped Eric on the bed and Tom went out for soft drinks and to scout the surroundings. Roger remembered that there was a vending machine next to an ice maker at the end of the first row of rooms. Eric was going to need an ice pack and quick to stop the swelling knot on the back of his head. But to anyone watching they looked liked three guys who pulled off the road to continue a little partying.

The ice pack seemed to have revived Eric by the time Tom had set up the recording equipment from the van. Eric was functioning, if only painfully so, but could handle a few questions, Roger decided.

"Thought you dicks had given up and gone home."

Roger smiled. "I'm glad we didn't."

"Am I right in thinking I'm going to be detained against my will?" Eric held up manacled hands.

"Is that lawyerese for under arrest?"

"On what fucking charge? Surviving an attempted murder didn't used to be a crime."

"Oh, let's say violation of parole. Carrying a concealed weapon—which just happens to be stolen, I'll bet." Roger was aware that Eric knew that gave him every right and then some to lock up his ass, take him back to Milford or some federal penitentiary. Roger hadn't exactly decided what he'd do. Probably depended on Eric's cooperation. He needed him safe and out of commission. "But I think you might have some interesting things to tell us. What happens to you might be negotiable. Let's say I could have found this piece along side the road."

"If you get what you want?"

"Something like that."

Roger looked over at Tom, who popped a small cassette into the machine. The push of a couple levers and he was ready.

"Who set you up on the cocaine deal seven years ago?"

"Billy Roland Eklund."

"Proof? Besides this lawyer who guaranteed the two million for taking a fall?"

"Crack cocaine found in the mats on the plane."

"When?"

"Two weeks ago."

"Damned Mahoney. Did he know about this?"

"Yeah. But he's in pretty tight with ol' Billy Roland. And he's the type who wants the show to himself. Resents you guys nosing around."

"I could have told you," Tom interceded. "Insurance dicks are all the same."

"Let's hear more about the crack."

"Ran across it myself when I was going over the plane. Found out quick that our friend, Dan, wasn't going to be of much help. That's why I got it to you guys soon as I could. Anyway, rumor has it the second wife's a user. But I think the original hauls were to pay off debt. A few million lost in bad investments, stock market in '87, a few dry wells. I used to do a little tax work for Billy Roland. That spread is a multi-million dollar operation. It takes some big bucks to keep it going."

Roger nodded. An idiot could see that, the reason for Billy Roland needing money. And from what he'd seen of Miss Iris, keeping her in drugs might be the only way of keeping her at all.

It made sense. He knew that it would. He just needed a break to prove it. And the break turned out to be an eye witness. No wonder Billy Roland wanted this man killed, sent the sheriff to do the job. This was dynamite.

"What will you do?"

"Search warrant. Subpoena the books."

"What's in it for me?"

"Besides staying out of the slammer?"

"Something like that."

"Well, it's not going to be money. You can kiss that two mil goodbye forever. Let's say your reward this time around is for being Joe Citizen, just an honest stiff doing his civic duty."

"Fuck you."

"Thought that might be your reaction."

"I want my identity protected."

"As if you have any bargaining chips, my friend."

"I've been shot at."

"We know. That's why until this is over, protective custody is probably our best bet."

"I'd be more useful out there undercover."

Hadn't he lived long enough to recognize a loose cannon when he saw one? No, Roger thought to himself, you'll stay hidden for now. The man couldn't keep the bitterness from his face. This was one pissed-off joker. And that kind of anger could make a man do something stupid.

"I can better protect you if I know where you are."

"Fuck you."

"You said that before. Not very original. Tom, give a call to Milford. I think we need to park our baggage for a few days. But make sure he'll be accessible, phone in his cell, that sort of thing. Ask for the honeymoon suite." Roger laughed. "You know, I've never been happier to see someone alive. You've been a great help." There, an attempt at sincerity which from the look on Eric's face fell flat, Roger thought. But who cared? The man was an ex-con, took a dive to protect someone else probably, but he was slime. You just had to look at him to know what kind of values he had.

Dan had checked the house after Elaine left then took another turn around the grounds. He had distinctly heard the sound of a body hitting the deck when they had been in the study. It was muffled by closed windows and drapes, but still not a sound that could be easily confused. He hadn't wanted to alarm anyone. He couldn't very well say he knew that Eric had been snooping at the window.

But there was nothing—no footprints—the ground was hard and unyielding from a lack of rain. He checked the barns and accidentally awakened Hank, who had just gone to bed. He'd been working in the clinic and hadn't heard anything suspect. Dan felt uneasy. Some feeling of dread that he couldn't shake. Elaine called around midnight. There hadn't been any hitchhikers on the way back and no phone messages. She shared his uneasiness.

He went to bed but couldn't sleep. He got up, dressed and grabbed a flashlight. This time he made a larger circle of the property: house, barns, the corrals immediately to the south, then the county road that flanked the property starting at the end of the circle drive. At the point where the county road angled closest to the house just behind a stand of poplar, he thought there were tire tracks. Longer axle width than a car, bigger tires. A truck or van, probably.

But it might not mean anything. Whoever it was had backed into an entrance to the field in knee deep weeds that covered any footprints. Could have been a farm truck. He had seen some hands working over this way earlier in the day on a faulty irrigation pipe. They would have used this entrance to the field, too. At best a few tire tracks were inconclusive. Eric had simply vanished—with or without help.

It was the why that Dan didn't want to dwell on. At least knowing his whereabouts had given Dan a sense of security. Eric believed that he could better handle the investigation alone, on his own, that Dan knew. And didn't Dan feel his vindictiveness had already gotten in the way? Whose idea had it been for Elaine to show up to play twenty questions?

Actually, he couldn't blame her. She was trapped by this man and probably just wanted to help. And wasn't he also interested in the answers? Only, he'd just about decided that Billy Roland couldn't have had anything to do with the cocaine on Eric's plane. But how could he get Eric to listen? Maybe this J.J., Jorge and Dona Mari link would prove helpful. He could hope anyway. Dan walked back to the house.

It wasn't until three twenty the next afternoon that Dan knew exactly what had happened to Eric. He knew the minute the federal marshals pulled up, fanned out, guns in hand, waiting for Roger to give orders to search and confiscate. Roger and Tom seemed to have gained new importance poised against a backdrop of heavies. Dan noted more than a little swagger as Roger approached the front door.

Dan walked down the hall to the study and told Billy Roland that the feds were on the front lawn with a fistful of search warrants. Dan didn't try to explain, tell Billy Roland what he thought had happened. How could he? Eric Linden was supposed to be dead. He just followed the old man back down the hall.

"Mr. Eklund, I've got a feeling that this doesn't surprise you. Must have been expecting our visit." Roger stood at the foot of the front steps, smug, crew cut standing perfectly straight, the sun reflecting off the distortion-free, optical-quality gray lenses that masked his eyes.

Billy Roland looked shell shocked, Dan thought, and suffering from a migraine. He was in a bathrobe and slippers. He shuffled forward stopping at the top step, shaded his eyes and surveyed the army of uniformed men in the drive.

"What's this here all about?"

"Let's just say we have reason to believe that crack cocaine has been discovered on your property and there's a strong indication that we'll find more."

Billy Roland swung around to Dan. "You promised, son. You said you wouldn't use it. It was just our little secret about Miss Iris." His voice mixed disbelief with hurt and Dan felt like he had been stabbed. He opened his mouth to say something, then shut it. Maybe the less said right now. Billy Roland's words hadn't been lost on Roger, either, who bounded up the steps, shoved the papers into Billy Roland's hands and proceeded into the house after one smirk at Dan.

And that's when the screaming started. Later it would seem funny but at the moment, uniformed men pushing into the house struck terror in the hearts of a dozen Mexican workers—probably all without papers—who ran yelling *"Policia Militar,"* scattering in a dozen directions, the troopers on their heels. Out the front door, around the sides of the house; it was like turning over a beehive.

Roger tried to get his men organized, but no one could hear above the bedlam. Roger collided with the cook in the hallway, who clung to his leg begging him to spare her children. It took Tom to peel the woman away only to have her grab him around the waist and continue to shriek hysterically while immobilizing Roger's right hand man.

The marshals didn't know whether to chase down the Mexican nationals or begin the search of the house. Most stood outside the barns uncertain without orders what they were supposed to be doing.

"Tom, damn it, where are you?"

Roger pushed past Dan to look in the study. Dan could see Tom pleading with the cook to release him, the two of them entangled just inside the kitchen door. By now they had run out of what few words of English they had in common.

"Get over here." Roger stuck his head out the door of the study and had caught sight of Tom. "Now. What the fuck's wrong with you?"

Roger ducked back into the room, obviously relishing the fact that he had the prime location all to himself, Dan thought. Dan couldn't see where Billy Roland had gone, but he decided to go down to the barns, get out of the house.

"Sorry, pal, nothing I can do." He pushed past Tom and the cook.

He had just reached the back steps when he heard the explosion and within seconds saw the flames. The office or the clinic. He couldn't tell which. Maybe both were on fire. The first barn of horses was bedlam. He paused to slip a halter on Baby Belle, then grabbed the lead ropes of two other horses tied in the breezeway and ran with the three outside. Others were pounding against their stalls and whinnying in that shrill high-pitched call of alarm.

A nearby corral was open, and he unsnapped the leads before he turned them loose and ran back to the barn. A number of stable hands, Dan thought he counted five, were working as a team and emptying the barns of livestock. Dan helped with two geldings, and was almost trampled by their eagerness to escape the tendrils of smoke that seeped through an air duct and hung in the still air above the stalls.

The corrals closest to the barns were filling up. In the distance Dan could see calves and adult cattle being herded into the surrounding fields. As he headed toward the clinic, he fleetingly thought of Shortcake Dream and hoped someone would be with her. But, for now, he had to help with the fire. Hoses attached to mini compressors were already pumping water in a steady stream both on the inside and the outside of the building, directly onto the clinic.

Dan stood back as Hank ordered a group of men to take axes to the outside door and then cut holes in the roof. Aluminum ladders had been dragged from somewhere and now each leaned against the building. The smoke continued to billow outward and upward, but there were no flames.

"What happened?" Dan asked Hank, who stood next to him, his eyebrows singed off and streaks of soot in his hair.

"Iris used to do a little free-basing. I was going to destroy the evidence, tipped over a bunsen burner. I had some chemicals on the counter. The place just went up."

"Jesus." Dan didn't say more. This was just fodder for Roger. He'd jump all over a suspect fire in a clinic and if he found any traces of drugs....

"Look, I'd do anything to protect that old man. He means everything to me. He gave me a chance, a lot of responsibility right out of school."

"I know. I feel the same way."

Dan and Hank moved back to make room for two men pulling a hose to be handed up to those on the roof. He knew they wouldn't have long to wait before Roger was on the scene. Dan watched as Roger gave orders to a man standing outside the kitchen then trotted toward them. Showing academy form, Dan noticed, elbows tucked, landing on the balls of his feet.

"What's going on?" Roger was out of breath.

"Everything's under control," Hank said.

"That isn't what I asked." Roger swung to face Hank. "What the fuck was on fire?"

"The clinic."

"You in charge?"

"Yeah."

"What started it?"

"Carelessness. Moving some volatile chemicals from a cupboard to the counter."

"You responsible?"

Hank nodded.

"You know what kind of trouble you'll be in if we so much as find a whiff of drugs in that mess?" Roger gestured toward the blackened interior of the clinic, smoke still rolling out through the battered door. "Ever hear of tampering with evidence?"

Hank just stood there. Roger, infuriated, pushed Hank against a support post.

"Don't jerk me around."

Hank's face was completely impassive, Dan thought. Then Hank broke Roger's grasp. Not roughly, but with authority.

"If you have something to discuss, come find me. I'm not going any place. I have an apartment next to the clinic." And then he walked off. Left Roger fuming and staring at what he undoubtedly thought was a cover-up. Dan had to smile. Roger was flunking search and seizure. Couldn't happen to a nicer guy.

Dan walked through the barn to check on Shortcake Dream. The stall was empty. He questioned one of the workers, who pointed to an adjoining outside corral. Dan could see the subdued-looking heifer in the far corner. Scared, but safe. Billy Roland would be relieved.

And, then it dawned on him. He hadn't seen the man, not since the encounter on the front steps. It was unlike Billy Roland not to be involved. He should have been out here. Migraine or no, he'd be checking on Shortcake Dream at the very least.

Dan turned back toward the house, and was just crossing the drive leading to the screened-in porch when he heard it. As quickly as his brain registered what the sound was, he refused to believe it, but started to run, tearing at the back screen door when he reached the porch—the shotgun blast echoing in his ears.

Chapter Nine

The door to the study was closed. Dan hesitated; a moment of trepidation slowed him from throwing it open. He swallowed, took a deep breath and willed himself to reach out and turn the knob. Locked. He twisted it again. Then raced for the front door. He hadn't locked the window to the study last night, just shut it. Hopefully, it was still open. But he knew all the hurrying, all the panic, would not change what he would find.

He pulled the window up, threw a leg over the casement and eased himself into the room. It took a moment for his eyes to adjust to the cool darkness. And then he saw what he had expected to see but the shock of it wasn't any the less powerful. Expectation didn't negate horror. He leaned against the back of a chair, took a few deep breaths before slowly walking to the front of the desk. Even the top of the chair had been blown away by the blast. He could hear someone pounding on the door. The noise seemed far away.

He just stood there, thoughts jumbled, trying to think clearly. Trying to form thoughts of "No, not now. It's not what you think...." Billy Roland's words running through his mind: "You promised...said you wouldn't use it...just our little secret." Dan closed his eyes and turned away.

The one typed sheet was on a chair. Dan hadn't noticed it at first. He walked over and picked it up.

"I can't stay in a world where my friends, even my loved ones, betray me, suspect me of wrongdoing, ruin my reputation...I want my Premier Exhibitor's banner draped over my coffin...."

Dan couldn't read any more as tears welled up. The pounding at the door was now accompanied by shouting. He walked over and unlocked it. Roger burst into the room followed by Tom and two other agents.

"Oh, Jesus. Oh, God. Who let this happen? Tom, why weren't you with him?" Roger was truly beside himself. Because an old man committed suicide? Or because it would put a serious crimp in his investigation, and someone might insinuate that he'd blown it. Dan guessed the latter.

"I don't have to tell you how this looks. Just as good as a signed confession. I knew it. Could smell it. The old codger had guilty written all over him." Roger was gingerly picking over papers on the desk, sliding a couple out from under the body with the eraser end of a pencil.

"Looking for this?" Dan offered the note he'd found on the chair.

"Damn it. You know better than to touch anything at the scene. I've had it with you, Mahoney."

Roger had slipped on a pair of rubber gloves. Must be standard issue for field work, Dan thought sarcastically.

"Tom, I want a team on that clinic soon as it's cool enough to get in there. Sift everything. Go over every inch and have a couple of the guys question that vet."

Roger was in his element. Giving orders, gleefully surveying what he termed a cop-out. Dan overheard him describe Billy Roland as someone who just "couldn't face the music." Then Dan left, had to leave, get away to think, mourn in his own way; he walked out to the porch swing. He'd asked Tom about Eric and found out he was in Milford. Even locked up he could wreak devastation. If it hadn't been for Eric, that old man would have lived out his days enjoying the Double Horseshoe, Shortcake Dream, and the Cisco Kid....

"You know where the wife is?" Tom stuck his head out the study window.

"Gone."

"I know that. When's she coming back?" Roger had pushed Tom aside and leaned out, hands on the sill. His need for control was unbelievable, Dan thought.

"She isn't."

"You want to explain that?"

No, Dan thought; but I'm probably going to have to. He sighed. "Iris Stuckey-Eklund was asked to leave by her husband after it was discovered she may have attempted wrong-doing in order to collect on an insurance claim for several hundred thousand dollars." That sounded vague enough but business-like, and it was the truth.

"I'll be dipped. He ran off the little woman. I'll need your statement. In the meantime, you know where we can find her?"

"No."

"Am I supposed to believe that?"

"Believe what you want."

"You know, before you get too carried away being unco-operative, I should tell you Eric Linden will testify that you failed to report a cache of contraband drugs, left it to him to turn over the evidence, and then you told us you found it in a truck."

Dan didn't say anything.

"That sound about right? How it happened?"

Dan shrugged; he could barely contain his irritation at this man, at the situation, the lies and deceit.

"You know of any other places we'll need to look? Besides the hangar? To find any little surprises that you might know about. Like another glove compartment in a truck."

"There should be a small container of crystals of unknown origin in the wall safe in the study." Dan imagined there was a look of surprise on Roger's face, but he didn't turn around to see.

"Should I know how they got there?"

Dan ignored the sarcasm. "I believe they were planted by Eric Linden to do exactly what he's done—get you guys involved."

"Or expose a drug operation that's been in existence for a number of years."

"As I said before, believe what you want."

"I don't think I need to tell you not to disappear." Roger went back into the house.

The rest of the afternoon was bedlam. He couldn't leave but called Elaine from Hank's phone. She wanted to drive out. He didn't want her to be interrogated, but thought everything would be settled down by late evening. He needed to see her, be with someone who knew he hadn't caused this, hadn't gone back on his word to Billy Roland. She said she would be there by nine.

"Want a beer?" Hank stood in the middle of his pullman kitchen with two cans of Coors.

"Sure."

The two of them walked back into the ten by twelve living room that barely held a couch, TV, and coffee table and smelled of smoke.

"Any idea what will happen to all this? The land and stock." Dan was curious. He believed Billy Roland when he said that Miss Iris wouldn't get anything—but nothing had been said about after Billy Roland's death.

"If he hasn't changed his will in the last year, the Double Horseshoe will become an Ag station."

"Ag station?"

"Yeah. Agriculture test area. Run by an extension of New Mexico State."

"That's great. Neat idea."

"Take a look."

Hank walked back to the kitchen, pulled a legal-looking document out of a drawer, and handed it to Dan.

"I'm executor."

And the director of a multi-million dollar project for as long as you want, Dan thought to himself as he scanned the first page of the will. But it was fitting. Hank was the right choice.

"This is perfect for the ranch. I'm glad to see it go this way."

"Miss Iris gets the Wings of the Dove, but only if she stays clean. Has to be tested every six months, three consecutive times a week apart, different labs."

"He thought of everything."

"Left the Lear to that Linden guy. Guess that will go to his wife now."

"How much is it worth?"

"The Lear? A few hundred thousand without much fixing."

Why did Dan feel a rush of elation? It wasn't two million but maybe enough for Eric to start over....

Elaine pulled into the drive a little before nine. There were still agents standing guard, but the body had been removed and some of the household help were cleaning up the study. Word had gotten out when the body reached the funeral home in Roswell, and the first flowers arrived around six-thirty. Judge Cyrus had called and offered his assistance. Dan had thought to call Carolyn and Phillip. They were shocked. But then, everyone was shocked. Billy Roland had seemed exempt, somehow beyond something as mundane as dying. He should have lived forever.

The safe had been opened and the vial of crystals removed. Dan gave a deposition detailing how he'd found them. He didn't need to hide Eric's part in their discovery. He reiterated that he suspected they had been planted, and by whom. He told what he knew about Miss Iris. How the finding of Shortcake Dream figured into the United Life and Casualty claim. By the time he was finished, he was exhausted. The stress of the day caught up with him.

Elaine had fixed a plate of cold cuts and cheese. He'd grabbed a couple of beers and followed her out to the porch. Hank joined them. Supper was quiet, not uncomfortable, but each lost in his own thoughts, Dan decided. Hank ate quickly and went back to the barns.

"There's one more thing I have to do." Dan stood and took her hand. "Come with me."

He led her back into the house but stopped by a phone in the hall.

"If you disagree with anything I say, interrupt." He dialed the number and waited.

The front office at Milford Correctional put him through to Eric without any questions.

"If you haven't heard what happened to Billy Roland by now, you need to know that he committed suicide about four this afternoon."

Briefly, he recounted what had happened. Apparently Eric hadn't known. His shock seemed real. Real because he saw what he thought was his chance at two million go down the drain once and for all, Dan thought.

"A couple other things. I'm going to find out who was behind the two million—not for you, but to clear Billy Roland's name if he's innocent." Then he told him about the Lear.

Elaine gestured that she wanted the phone.

"Eric, I'll have the divorce papers at the front desk by noon tomorrow. I have them with me now." She paused, then continued, "I don't mind the drive over to get this taken care of…I don't want to see you…Eric, I think you *will* sign. My lawyer has suggested that I charge you with having detained me against my will for the last few weeks. They know you had a gun. It would add a few more years…Good, I thought you might see it that way." She handed the phone back to Dan and walked back out to the porch.

Billy Roland had requested that he be buried beside his first wife in a family plot on the Double Horseshoe. The small cemetery in the strand of poplar not far from the house also held the remains of Billy Roland's mother and father, a couple of ranch hands and their families who had died from cholera in the early 1900s. In the corner a small marker rested on the grave of a young woman who had met her death in the woods, on an altar as a sacrifice many years ago.

Judge Cyrus filled Dan in on local lore as they walked between the well-kept mounds. The plots marked with white-washed crosses paled next to the elaborate marble and bronze statuary that adorned the pink quartz mausoleum behind a picket fence and flagstone walk.

"Ol' Billy Roland used to come out here a lot. Fresh flowers every other day, that sort of thing. Never quite forgave himself for weaknesses of the flesh. Thought his first wife would never understand about Miss Iris." Judge Cyrus stood with hat in hand. "Well, they're together now. I hope they make their peace."

The service was held at the mausoleum, Judge Cyrus presiding. More than two hundred people lined the drive, trampled the grass on the knoll and ate from the picnic tables set up around the pool.

Iris arrived with the resident preacher from The Wings of the Dove. Hadn't taken her long to figure out what was hers. Dan wondered if she'd known the terms of the will all along, only now the price was worth it. All eyes were on her as she placed a single white rose at the base of the urn holding Billy Roland's ashes. She stepped back, and bowed her head before Hank placed the urn on a marble shelf above the tomb of Billy Roland's first wife. The fact that Iris was dressed in white added to the drama: white veil to white shoes peeking out from the gossamer skirt.

"The angels are with me now," Iris informed Dan later over a heaping plate of the ever-present potato salad.

"Come again?"

"I'm being guided. I believe my mission is to save poor souls trapped by their carnal desires and earthly ambitions."

She dropped her voice to a whisper. "There are those among us who serve a false God."

He couldn't think of anything to say. He wished her well, but didn't miss the look she gave the young minister who brought her. Adoration and lust. Working on carnal desires didn't seem to start at home, Dan thought.

Carolyn and Phillip paid their respects, appropriate tears, lots of hand shaking. It was difficult to look at Phillip and not see the posturing of a gubernatorial hopeful. The bodyguard was still in evidence and ate his weight in fried chicken. He seemed to have a lot in common with good old Sheriff Ray. It might not be anything more than a love of fried chicken, Dan thought, as he watched the two reload their plates. But chummy didn't quite capture it. These guys were inseparable.

Carolyn didn't miss the fact that Elaine was with him, that he had his arm around her shoulders. She gave them a once-over glance when she didn't think he was looking; lingering, it seemed, overly long. Dan hoped his mother would be pleased since she would undoubtedly have the news by morning.

Someone had dug up Billy Roland's Premier Exhibitor banner and several other rosettes and ribbons. The mausoleum was plastered with them but the display seemed fitting, and impressive. Dan was surprised when a number of dignitaries from the cattle judging circuit made it all the way out to the Double Horseshoe for the service. Billy Roland was respected. And it was this respect that Dan wanted to make certain wasn't tarnished. At whatever cost, he would get to the bottom of the promised two million, prove that Billy Roland Eklund didn't set up Eric Linden or anyone else for that matter.

When he had time to reflect on the day, he decided that Billy Roland would have enjoyed himself, and, then again, maybe he did. He wasn't sure that he didn't believe the dead hung around for a while before taking off to wherever.

When Elaine told him that she would be leaving Monday for a month's tour of Ireland, he understood. Understood and envied her and wanted to stop her, keep her with him. But it was all too soon. There was still a lot of work to do. And Dan would be here when she got back. He'd pick up Simon in the morning.

He walked her to the car and held her, kissed her. She whispered, "I can't say the things to you that I want to say. Not now, not yet."

"I know."

"It's like too much has happened. Eric, Billy Roland...."

"It'll take time."

She nodded. "You understand my wanting to get away?"

"Yes."

"I can't forgive Eric. I'm working on it, but I'm still angry about so much. I don't want that anger to get in the way of our...future."

He had thought she was going to say something else. But it was too soon to add the "love" word. They both knew that.

"Time. Just give it time," he said instead.

"He caused Billy Roland's death."

"In the name of survival. Eric's own. We probably can't say what we'd do in the same position."

She smiled. "I like your sense of fairness."

"Anything else on that list?" He was teasing, wanted to keep her smiling. And then he kissed her, opened the car door, and stood back. Before temptation made him do anything else.

"I think this is the time I ask you to drop me a postcard now and then."

"I've heard phone calls get through."

He watched until the Benz turned onto the county road and was out of sight, and fought the tremendous sense of loss that washed over him, threatened to engulf him. For Elaine? No. He believed that they would have a chance to put something together someday. But for Billy Roland, there were no chances left to exonerate—no chances left to prove that Dan hadn't sold him out.

Monday morning came too soon. Elaine was already on her way to Albuquerque to catch the flight to New York. He had picked up Simon from Elaine's back yard and taken him to Carolyn's. Good old Sis offered to puppy-sit. It would cost him. But he didn't know in what way yet. He was still more or less headquartered at the Double Horseshoe. He'd work out there during the day, but couldn't bring himself to spend the night. Too many memories, too fresh. He needed to finish up and turn over copies of the paperwork, the inventory with a history of losses to the University, and make sure there wouldn't be any pending claims for United L & C. Hank was helping; it would go quickly.

Roger and crew barely waited for the funeral to end before combing the ranch. And that meant every foot of it. He was even sending out riders to check stock tanks. It would be useless. Dan could tell him that, and had, but it fell on deaf ears. Finding a trace of crack in the clinic after the fire made him crazed.

Yet, in front of Dan on the desk in his office at Roswell's branch of United Life and Casualty was proof. Big-time proof that Eric Linden hadn't fabricated his story about meeting with a lawyer seven years ago. A lawyer who supposedly promised him a new life. Someone signing his name Jonathan James Reynolds but whose signature matched, even to Dan's untrained eye, the squiggles and backward slant of one Juan Jose Rodriguez.

He had made copies of all three samples, then cut out the signatures so that he could align them, paste them on a three by five card and study them: the fax from Chicago containing J.J.'s signature on the deposition; the traced copy from the contract offered to Eric; and last the signature of the lawyer in Dallas. The one that didn't match. The true signature of Jonathan James Reynolds.

Now what? For starters he needed to get an expert to agree with his suspicions, testify, if need be in court, that the two top signatures were done by the same individual. He called Eastern New Mexico University and found out they offered an Associate of Arts in Criminal Law. Yes, the professor in charge of the department also did work for a crime lab out of Albuquerque and one of his specialties was signature verification. Dan made an appointment to see him at two.

Dan thought that all small college towns had a charm that emanated from old cut stone facades on buildings with fake turrets. But that's where it stopped. The turn of the century architecture also seemed like "much ado about nothing," a strange posturing that made ponderous buildings sit in the center of vacant fields until decades later civilization reached that edge of town. By then, ugly flat-roofed, fifties-style, cement block barracks cluttered the once austere grounds that properly showed off the original three- or four-story edifices. A good example was Beeman Hall.

Dan parked as close as he could to the back of the building in a space marked visitor, locked the car, walked down a ramp to the basement, pushed open a windowless steel door, and promptly sneezed about a half dozen times. Musty. Unopened windows, and a below ground dampness that added up to mold—about a century of it, Dan thought. He hoped he wouldn't be there too long.

Professor Lang was in the first office on the right, next to the elevators. A small man, wisps of graying hair combed over a very bald crown, sat on a stool in front of a drafting table.

"Come in. Let me finish up here, only take a minute."

Dan found a chair that wasn't covered with papers and sat. The office was tiny but efficient. Outside light was blocked by blackened windows but various lamps were clamped to the edges of the desk and drafting table. A workroom, not just an office, Dan decided. Professor Lang was busy with a magnifying glass that hung from a cord around his neck. He leaned close to a document tacked to the board. As Dan watched, he pulled a larger magnifying glass with self-contained light swinging across the table from where it was fastened to the opposite corner.

"Yes. Much more like it." Seeming satisfied, he switched off the lamp and turned to Dan. "Dan Mahoney, I presume. A signature verification, isn't it?"

Dan handed him the three by five card, and Professor Lang held it out at arm's length, studied it, then tacked it to the drafting table. He turned on a bank of overhead lights by pressing a button on a side panel of assorted knobs and switches anchored to the table and hunched forward using the glass around his neck to inspect each letter of each signature. Sometimes he stopped to make a note of something on a yellow tablet to his right.

"Uh huh. Interesting."

"Problem?" Dan wasn't certain he was supposed to comment but thought he'd try it.

"Open Os."

"Is that bad?"

"Your guy here isn't very self-confident. Probably wasn't breast fed." Professor Lang paused to enjoy his own humor. "And here? See this?" He motioned Dan to bend over the table. "These little loops, here and here, definite indications of insecurity."

Dan wasn't necessarily interested in a personality profile. But he supposed graphoanalysis was a natural offshoot of working with handwriting. And, it wasn't like he didn't believe in it. Next the professor measured the letters, then width and height of the entire signature.

"Don't like to say this but your guy here isn't too nice."

"What do you mean?"

"Probably wouldn't bat an eye at a little blackmail."

"That sounds about right."

"Unlike the real Mr. Reynolds. Bottom signature is from an entirely different type of person. Boy next door, upstanding citizen."

"So you're saying that the same man signed the top two?" Dan wanted to keep him on track. This was the only thing Dan had come to find out.

"Absolutely."

"Certain enough to say so in court?"

"No problem. Must have thought he'd never get caught, had some assurance of it, because this is sloppy work."

On the way back to Roswell, Dan contemplated his next move. A couple things came to mind. Talk to Judge Cyrus and Phillip to get a little background on J.J., maybe even fill them in on what he'd found out so far, what he suspected happened. The drawback would be spilling the beans about Eric. And he wasn't quite ready to do that. Not just yet.

That left one thing—probably what appealed to him most in the first place—he knew before the outskirts of town that he would confront J.J. himself. Screw tipping his hand to others. He wanted to see the reaction on J.J.'s face. Wanted to be there when a ghost from the past came back to haunt.

J.J.'s office was at one end of a strip shopping center on the west side of Roswell. A Furr's Super Market, Sherwin-Williams paint store, Goodwill center, the Praying Hands Bookstore, Walgreen's drug store, and Juan Jose Rodriguez, Attorney at Law, in that order, lined up to face the parking lot. Which in this case was more than two acres of asphalt.

Dan pulled in beside a red Ferrari. Somehow he knew he wouldn't have to ask who it belonged to. Was this a big horse-powered clue right under his nose? Took some bucks to own one.

The receptionist took his name and buzzed an office in the back, presumably J.J.'s. She had indicated that he was in.

"May I tell him what this is concerning?"

"Estate of Billy Roland Eklund."

That wasn't exactly a lie, Dan told himself, but it would have been more honest to say the reputation of Billy Roland Eklund.

"He'll be with you in a minute. You know, it's so much easier for all of us, and you can save yourself some time by calling ahead. Counselor Rodriguez works mainly from appointments."

Just a teeny bit of a snotty overtone, Dan thought as he watched the young Hispanic woman turn back to her keyboard. An attitude probably works with the locals. A buzzer sounded from an adjoining room and the young woman rose, pulled down her mini skirt, and teetered on four-inch spikes toward a hallway.

The rear view wasn't bad. The woman had a fantastic body once you got your attention away from the hair falling almost to her waist, permed into long ringlets and ink black, bangs another six inches above her forehead. Dan chose a chair by the window and picked up a magazine.

The office was tastefully done. A couple original bronzes accented by pedestals obviously built for them. Oils, three end-of-the-trail roundup-type scenes. Dan wasn't familiar with the artist. But they were good, collector quality originals. The furniture was wood and leather, ivory leather with matching ottomans, the coffee table a tree trunk holding a kidney shaped piece of beveled glass. Not cheap. Not one thing. Not even the receptionist, probably.

"Counselor Rodriguez will see you now."

"Mr. Mahoney, isn't it?" J.J. stood in the hall doorway.

Dan wondered why the formalities. J.J. knew perfectly well who he was. The snottiness of the receptionist seemed mirrored in the boss. "Is this something we can handle here? I'm very busy right at the moment."

"Probably not. I think you'll want a little privacy for our discussion." That caught his interest.

"Very well. Hold my calls." J.J. turned on his heel and headed down the hall.

A conference room and small library on the west faced two offices across the hall; J.J.'s office was at the back, expansive, containing more pricey oils and sculpture and leather sofas.

J.J. waved at a chair across from his desk and Dan sat down. He thought J.J. looked thin and drawn.

"May I offer my condolences. I believe you had a close working relationship with Mr. Eklund?" Dan began.

"It's been a terrible shock. But he was infirm. The headaches.... Is there something I can help you with?" There was an edge to J.J.'s voice.

"You can explain this. An expert will testify that the top two were done by the same man." Dan placed the three by five card carefully in front of J.J., and standing over him saw clearly what happened next. Before he could check the gesture, Juan Jose Rodriguez had started to cross himself.

"I don't understand."

"I think you do. But let me refresh your memory. About seven years ago, a lawyer matching your description met with Eric Linden in a jail in El Paso. The promise of two million dollars for taking a fall was guaranteed by the document that this signature was lifted from."

J.J. didn't say anything, just absently ran his finger over the copies of the signatures. But sweat, just a fine misting of perspiration formed on his forehead at the hairline.

"You think this is my signature?" He pointed to the top Jonathan James Reynolds.

"I know you posed as this Mr. Reynolds."

J.J. was now chewing on his bottom lip, trying to think fast, come up with some plan, Dan thought.

"How do you know this?"

"Eyewitness."

More chewing on the lip. "So, why would I do it? Pretend to be someone else? Another lawyer, didn't you say?"

He's checking on what I know, Dan decided. "Because it was safer. You probably knew then that Mr. Linden would never confront you, would somehow be 'taken care of' when he got out. So, the monthly calls, verifications as to how the two million was doing, would never be questioned." Dan leaned both hands on the desk. "Eric Linden was never going to know that the two million wasn't there—hadn't ever been there in Midland Savings and Loan, because he was going to have a little accident before he got to town. Luckily for you guys, a flash flood took care of things."

This last was said just inches from J.J.'s face and the lawyer nervously looked up, briefly made eye contact, then pushed back from the desk and stood.

"Get out."

"Why? I don't think we're finished here, do you?" Dan sat back down. This seemed to make J.J. more nervous, one to threaten but not follow through, Dan hoped as he saw him open a desk drawer, then close it. Had Dan thought he might have a gun?

Probably, or he wouldn't have his tucked in his belt, hidden by his jacket.

"Firearms aren't the answer." Dan pulled out his revolver and placed it on the desk in front of him. He saw J.J.'s eyes dart from the gun to the drawer that he'd just closed.

"I wouldn't even think it, if I were you."

Suddenly, as if all the starch had been removed from his body, J.J. slumped back down in his desk chair, his head in his hands. His breathing seemed labored but Dan let him take his time, collect himself. He wasn't in a hurry.

"I was working for Mr. Eklund. I had no idea that the money wouldn't be waiting." He said it so low that Dan asked him to repeat himself.

"I don't believe that. Can you prove it?"

"If you give me some time."

"What was in it for Billy Roland?"

"The money. He hired the pilot. The pilot was well aware of what was going on. It wasn't his first such trip."

"You're saying the pilot, Eric Linden, knew about the smuggling?"

"That's what I said."

Dan was trying to size up J.J. Did he believe him? If Eric had been so involved, he would have had the evidence, would have fingered Billy Roland up front, when he first survived the flood, instead of hanging around planting a hundred and fifty dollars' worth of crack in an airplane to keep some feds interested until he could get something conclusive. No, Eric Linden didn't have enough to put the squeeze on anyone.

"You're admitting to impersonating another lawyer and promising Eric Linden two million, do I understand you correctly?" Better slow down and get some things straight. Dan waited for J.J. to nod. Affirmative. So far, so good, but the benefactor's name was wrong. Dan was certain of that.

"I'm not sure I believe you when it comes to the mastermind behind the plan. Let's try this scenario. Billy Roland wasn't behind the bust. He didn't know anything about the drugs, the promised two million, until the wire-transfer came in from the Caymans and the bank book was found."

Was it his imagination, or had J.J. paled considerably? Dan continued, "Someone had something to gain by putting Eric Linden away. Someone who hired you to dupe him, keep him quiet, keep him believing that two million was gathering interest in his name. Who were you working for, J.J.?"

"Billy Roland Eklund."

"No. You've got to do better than that. You aren't pinning this on a dead man and walking away."

"Why don't you ask the wife? Eric Linden's wife."

Dan's breath escaped in a rush; he was stopped. J.J. was staring at him. And somewhere behind those dark eyes was the start of a smile. Just a little game of gotcha and J.J. had won this round. Caught him off guard by saying the one thing that he dreaded to hear. The thing he hadn't allowed himself to think. Did Elaine have a reason for having Eric put away? For having him killed?

"You worked for the wife?"

"I didn't say that. Just said the wife has the answers."

But maybe doesn't know she has them? Yes. That could be it. Please, dear God, don't let Elaine be implicated.

"I'll need a statement."

"Not so fast. This is between the two of us." J.J. paused, then, "Why is someone from an insurance company so interested anyway?"

"I'm also doing a little field work for the feds." That wasn't a lie; he was still on their payroll.

"Or trying to clear the girlfriend." Now, the smile was broad, ear to ear, turning into a smirk as J.J. leaned back in his chair. No wonder this man was a lawyer, recognize the Achilles heel and go for it.

The intercom buzzer interrupted. J.J. told the receptionist to ask his next appointment to wait.

"I don't think it will be necessary to clear Elaine's name." And Dan didn't, but he hated the nagging doubts, little effacing worries that tore at their relationship.

J.J. just shrugged, a cheshire-cat smile hovering around his mouth. "Give it some thought. Dead men tell no tales. Might be to your advantage to accept Billy Roland as the instigator and let things drop."

There was truth to that. But Dan knew he couldn't let it alone. He'd be back to see J.J. He'd gotten what he wanted, an admission of involvement. But lies about who was behind it. He had to believe that. Was he backing off now because he didn't want to hear more about Elaine? Afraid to hear how she might be implicated?

"Maybe, I'll take your advice." Dan stood and tucked the revolver in his belt. J.J. made no effort to show him out.

Sometimes, like today, when Dan was sitting at a desk trying to put together the pieces of some puzzle, solve a mystery of who-done-it and who would benefit, a flicker of light would start in the recesses of his mind and then become brighter until a blinding revelation flooded over him. But usually one that made him feel stupid for not having thought of it before. Like now.

Berating himself with thoughts of early senility, he focused on something he'd ignored. But in fairness to himself, it probably hadn't been important at the time. Until now. And that was the tire. The tire that *could* have a bullet hole through it. Put there by the person chasing Eric Linden the night of the flood. Sheriff Ray? Dan had seen him chasing the Caddy. Couldn't the sheriff have returned in the early hours before dawn and removed the tire and rim so as not to arouse suspicion? Dan could be way off base, but when he had inspected the Caddy, it looked like someone had done just that. And, if Dan hadn't missed his guess, probably tossed it onto the pile of tires behind Sheriff Ray's station on Main Street in Tatum. There would have been no reason to destroy it. And if such evidence did exist, ballistics might put Ray at the scene in addition to Dan's eyewitness account. It was worth looking into.

And it gave him another suspect to question. Dan would have the advantage, the leverage, *if* he found a tire with a bullet hole in it, to force the man's hand. He doubted Sheriff Ray would try to kill someone on his own. No, Ray was the type to take orders. And maybe, this time, Dan would get the name of who was giving them.

He arrived at Ray's station right at noon to find it locked and a "gone to lunch" sign hanging in the door. He decided to wait, spend a little time looking things over. He could always say he was going to get a soft drink on his way to the Double Horseshoe. He needed to do a little scouting first but didn't need to arouse suspicion. He'd parked in front of the double glass and metal doors to the service bay and followed a cement walk around to the back of the building.

He almost whistled. He wasn't disappointed; he had remembered tires stacked behind the station. But there weren't just a few. Stack upon stack of tires, some treadless with stitching popping out, some from tractors in a pile by themselves, others showing the cleats of all-weather wear. There had to be hundreds. The search was fast becoming a needle in the haystack attempt to find something he only *thought* might exist.

What was more discouraging was the seven or eight hundred square foot compound itself. Surrounded by ten feet of chain-link fence, the top laced with razor wire, it looked impregnable from the outside. And, there was no gate. Anything stored back there had to first be brought in through the service bay. There were even a couple old junkers up on blocks to the left of the stacks of tires. One man's treasure was another man's eyesore. How would he ever find what he was looking for? If he was in luck, no one would have taken the tire off the rim and a pink rim would stand out in that mess. The Caddy had been a powder pink, he was sure of that. But how would he get in? The honking of a horn startled him.

"You coming out to the ranch this afternoon?" Hank had pulled up in the drive.

"Yeah. Thought I would but I wanted Ray to check the alignment on the Cherokee first." A lie, but necessary, Dan thought.

"Why don't you leave it? I'll give you a ride out and one of the boys can bring you back in town before Ray closes."

"Good idea. I'll write a note."

Dan walked around to the right front tire shielded from Hank's view and let out about ten pounds of air, then tucked a note under the wipers that read, "Having problems with alignment and keeping air in right front tire. Take a look if you have time. I'll pick up later. If I'm not back by six, leave it in the drive."

He wasn't sure how this would work out, but it gave him an excuse to be at the station. The ever-nosey townfolks would see Ray working on the car; they'd expect Dan to be back for it. In the meantime, he'd put in a couple hours on the books at the Double Horseshoe.

One of the ranch hands knocked on the office door at five. Dan turned off the computer, and then the overhead lights. They would get to Tatum a little before six. Dan still wasn't sure how he'd get into the back; he'd just look for an opportunity and hope there would be one.

Two blocks from the station, the driver offered to buy him a beer. Dan encouraged the man to pull into Jack's; but after they were parked pretended to change his mind, and said he probably should pick up his car and go on back to Roswell. The man wanted to drive him over to Ray's but Dan wouldn't hear of it, just a couple blocks. He didn't mind the walk.

Plus, it allowed him to approach the station unannounced. He wasn't sure that would be helpful, but you never knew what might come in handy. It was five to six when he reached the back corner of the lot. Ray was working on a half-ton pickup on the rack in the service bay with music blaring from a radio somewhere inside. Dan's Jeep Cherokee was parked out front.

The lights above the drive that illuminated the gas pumps were off, Dan noticed. Must be getting ready to leave pretty soon. Dan walked along the edge of the station and decided what he would do. If he could get by Ray without him turning around, he'd go to the restroom. The one inside. Employees only. And if he was discovered, he could always say he thought the ones outside were locked and plead a little constipation.

He opened the door to the station and glanced at Ray's back as he slipped by the counter and down a short hallway to the inside john. So far, so good. Dan wasn't sure constipation would cover sitting on the lid in the dark with your clothes on, but he had to hope Sheriff Ray wouldn't check the restroom before he left. Or, worse yet, have to go himself.

The phone hanging on a wall shared by the office and the restroom rang shrilly. Dan could hear Sheriff Ray walking toward it and then in snatches, a conversation that seemed to be the report of a tractor-trailer turned over on Highway Eighteen outside Milnesand that required his being there with a tow truck. From the way Sheriff Ray hung up the phone, he wasn't thrilled to be called out two minutes before he had planned to close up.

Dan waited until the radio was silenced and the sliding doors on the service bay had slammed shut before looking out. He heard Ray start up the tow truck parked along the south side of the station, and watched as he backed in front of the service islands and headed up the street, red and blue lights twirling on a bar above the cab. Would he come back to finish the pickup on the rack? Dan wasn't certain how long Ray would be gone, but he knew he needed to work fast.

The glass-paned door to the yard was unlocked. Always? Or, because of Ray's haste tonight? Dan was beginning to feel he owed a lot to that tractor-trailer. He shut the door behind him and stood a minute in the light of dusk that showed plainly the literal mountains of possibilities that had to be considered. What if the tire had been removed from the rim? He didn't even want to think of that. But a cursory glance around him in the waning light didn't show any rims, with or without tires. He'd have to individually check those in the stacks.

He started with a tower toward the back. Plain tires, some still showing good tread, leaned against the fence. He crawled the eight feet to the top inspecting each one and those in the stack next to it, running his hands along the outside hoping to feel the splintered hole caused by a bullet. Nothing. These tires had been rendered useless by miles, not someone's aim.

He tried another stack, and another with the same result. He had maybe ten more minutes before he'd run out of light altogether. This time he'd look behind the stacks first. Where would you put something out here if you didn't want it noticed?

He leaned against one of the cars on blocks, this one under a canvas tarp. He pulled a corner back. A DeSoto, early fifties. Why was that not surprising? Collector's were hot for them, but with Ray it could just be a touch of nostalgia. That would have been his era.

Dan lifted the tarp over the trunk, only the lid was gone. Original color was salmon pink and white judging from the rim on the spare tire. Pukey color, if Dan remembered correctly. He uncovered a fender; he'd been right about the color, over the years it had faded to a pale peach.

He let the tarp fall and started back toward a stack of tires next to the station. Then he stopped. In this light, pink was pink, salmon or powder. What if Ray put the rim and tire in the trunk of the DeSoto? It'd look like it belonged, natural camouflage.

Dan tore at the tarp, uncovered the tire and rim and ran his hand along the outside of the tread. Yes. The hole was toward the inside edge. It went through the rubber on a diagonal, a clean hole roughly the size of a .38 slug, but in this case Dan was fairly certain that it had been a .357 with the velocity to pierce the tire and keep on going.

But he'd have plenty of time to go over it. Now, he had to get the whole thing to the Cherokee. He lifted the evidence, being careful to replace the tarp, and carried the tire instead of rolling it back through the door. He'd leave by the front.

The bay doors opened from the inside and Dan pulled one door up, hating the noise that seemed to grate, then shriek into the gathering darkness as it followed the dual tracks and disappeared back into the garage roof to rest overhead. He didn't wait but walked quickly to the Cherokee and threw the tire and rim into the back, thanking someone, anyone, that Ray didn't have an alarm system or a guard dog. He took the time to wipe his hands on a towel he kept behind the front seat then went back to pull the door down.

No one seemed to have noticed. Two carloads of teens had gone by but no one had even glanced his way. What is it that all the books say? If you look like you're doing something you should be doing, then others will think the same thing? He hoped he looked for all the world like someone picking up a tire repair from Ray's station.

Chapter Ten

Dan's Roswell apartment was feeling more like home. Not a place he'd like to spend too much time in, but another month and he'd be wrapping things up. Elaine would be back. He felt a twinge of anticipation. He missed her already, and she'd only been gone two days.

The next month was going to be important. A lot would be behind them in a month. Was he being overly optimistic that he'd have answers by then? Maybe not. Between J.J. and Sheriff Ray, he had uncovered two important pieces to the puzzle. Pieces that would interest Roger and Tom.

He switched on the coffee maker and opened the front door to pick up the morning paper, one of the apartment's amenities, the paper delivered to the door. He slipped off the rubber band, unfolded the paper and read the headlines. The familiar face jumped out at him. "Juan Jose Rodriguez Killed in Accident on Highway 380." Dan quickly scanned the article and skipped references to his law practice while looking for details of what had happened.

Apparently, J.J. had left the road after failing to negotiate a turn somewhere among the hilly twists in the highway outside San Patricio. The Ferrari rolled down an incline and burst into flame. It was hinted that a high rate of speed and alcohol were both involved.

Dan put down the paper. It smelled. Maybe stank was a better word. How convenient for J.J. to die. Had J.J. contacted anyone about their little chat? Probably. And action was taken. No, a life was taken. Could Dan prove it? Did gut feelings count? He needed to call Roger and Tom.

He'd reached some conclusions, the obvious being J.J.'s death wasn't caused by Eric, Sheriff Ray, Elaine, or Billy Roland, and the less obvious, someone probably ran J.J. off the road. Someone wanted him silenced. The same someone behind the drug bust seven years ago. Someone who was dangerous, ruthless, and knew that Dan suspected. The phone rang.

"Yes?"

"Did you see the fucking papers?" Eric didn't wait for him to respond. "Prize suspect topples down incline. With a little god-damned help, right? I'm assuming you trotted over there and put the fear of God in him, set him up for someone to take out."

Dan winced at that. It was probably true. But being instrumental in two deaths in one week wasn't something he wanted to dwell on.

"Mahoney, you there?"

"Yeah. And you're probably right. We talked. He was there when you were arrested. Admitted to being the lawyer who met with you, made the promises, then kept up the charade for seven years. But he tried to pin the whole thing on Billy Roland at first."

"And you didn't believe him?"

"No. He as much as finally admitted that it was someone else pulling the strings."

"Like who?"

"Unfortunately, we didn't get that far. He suggested that I drop it. Just accept the Billy Roland theory."

"But you won't, right?"

"Not now."

"Sounds like you got some idea of who hired him. Did he give you a hint?"

"Yeah. Your former wife."

"What?"

"He said Elaine has the answers. Exact quote. Any idea what he meant?"

Dan felt the silence that followed was ominous. And Eric's obvious reluctance to say anything was making him crazy. If they weren't on the phone, he'd have his hands around Eric's throat screaming at him to tell the god-damned truth.

Dan broke the silence. "Talk to me. Is that possible? Could Elaine have some part in all this?"

"Maybe. I don't know. I never thought...."

"What do you mean, maybe? Answer me, Eric. I want a fucking explanation. What happened seven years ago?"

The phone went dead. Eric had hung up.

A second cup of coffee didn't make him feel any better. It was the fourth or fifth time he had walked past the window before he realized he was pacing, hamster-wheel exercise, getting him nowhere. Should he take a day and drive to Milford? Somehow get Eric to talk about how his former wife might have been involved? Or was Eric just pulling his string?

At least, Elaine was in Ireland. She couldn't have had anything to do with J.J.'s death. There was no way J.J. could have reached her after they talked, no way she could have masterminded running J.J. off the road.

When things calmed down, he'd drive over and chat with Eric, when he trusted himself not to kill him. But meanwhile, he had other things to do. He called Roger. Said it was important, told him to be at the Ramada Inn, ten sharp. Then he got in the shower, first ten minutes scalding hot, second ten minutes, ice cold. But it didn't make any difference in how he felt.

◇◇◇

Roger was waiting for him, sitting across from Tom in a red naugahyde booth in the corner, a bronze plastic pot of coffee between them.

"So, what's the good news?" Roger, the ever-eager one, went first, barely gave him time to slide in beside Tom.

"J.J. Rodriguez would be alive today if I hadn't confronted him with his involvement with Eric Linden." Dan showed the two of them the signatures. Said he had an expert's word that the top two were by the same person. Told them how Eric had recognized J.J. at the party and from the newspaper picture.

Then summarized his interview with J.J. He left out the part about Elaine's knowing anything but said that J.J. suggested Dan believe that Billy Roland did it, insinuated that that would be the easiest thing to do for all concerned.

"But implied that Billy Roland *didn't* have anything to do with the two million?" Roger asked.

Dan nodded and reached for the coffee pot. Probably not good for him, but better than a cigarette.

"You've been busy. Got anything else?" This from Tom, whose uncanny sixth sense was about to pay off, Dan thought.

"Remember the flash flood? The one that supposedly killed Eric?" Dan related his earlier suspicions about how the tire and wheel had been removed from the Caddy and how he had just happened to find the evidence in back of Sheriff Ray's station.

"I'd like a lab to go over the tire."

"Goes without saying. You got it with you?" Roger asked.

"Still in the back of the Cherokee." Dan doubted that Sheriff Ray even knew it was gone. Probably, just thought he'd forgotten to lock the bay on his way out the other night. Nothing was disturbed. There wouldn't have been a reason to suspect anything might be missing.

"We also need to set up a little visit with the local sheriff. Probably should wait for the lab results. Nail down the loose ends, make certain the bullet hole wasn't caused by target practice last week."

Roger was right. Cautious, but thorough and less convinced than Dan that Billy Roland was in the clear.

"So, if J.J.'s death wasn't accidental," Roger mused, "who's left to suspect? We know where Eric was and Sheriff Ray according to Dan, and we buried Billy Roland...."

"Elaine's in Ireland." He hadn't meant to say it. Just thinking out loud, but both agents turned to look at him.

"The wife? She's in town."

"Left for Ireland on Monday morning," Dan corrected.

"Short trip. She was back in town that afternoon. We recorded a call to your sister about six twenty. Sis said a bunch of them were going out to dinner—at the Tinnin restaurant on Three Eighty. Some campaign deal. Invited her to go along."

Elaine in town when J.J. was killed? Could J.J. have been at the restaurant, too? Both of them at the same place, leaving at the same time? Dan felt sick, and it wasn't because of the sixth cup of coffee that morning.

"Should we add her name to the list?"

"Not yet. But you guys will be the first to know," Dan lied.

After the transfer of the tire from his car to Roger's, Dan slumped behind the steering wheel of the Cherokee. What did it mean that Elaine had returned to Roswell? And not contacted him. Had the trip been some sort of ruse all along? Play-pretend to get away. But why? He started the car before he could formulate an answer.

But he knew where he was going. Eleven-thirty in the morning and he was going to go by Elaine's. A part of him didn't believe that she could be back. So, what better way to prove ol' Rog wrong than to just stop by her house and see for himself?

The house looked dark as he drove up. He parked in the street; the Jeep was concealed by the five-foot adobe wall that ringed the property. The Benz wasn't in the driveway. He walked toward the garage, a one-car building with flat roof about twenty-five feet from the house and let himself in through a side door.

And there was the Benz. She was back. He walked to the front of the car and felt the hood. Warm. Must have just gotten home from somewhere.

"Stop where you are, turn around."

Dan did as he was told. Elaine. Even in the dim light of the garage, he knew the semi-automatic in her hand wasn't a toy.

"Dan. Oh, my God."

Elaine expertly ejected the clip and popped the round out of the chamber before placing the gun on top of the car.

"You seem fairly comfortable with that." He gestured toward the gun.

"Took lessons after I decided I could shoot my husband if he threatened me again. It was one of the best things I could have done."

Then she fell silent. Dan felt the awkwardness. Not an "oh, my God, I'm caught" feeling, just a reservation at having to explain why she was there.

"I couldn't leave."

"I've gathered that."

"Did Carolyn tell you I was back?"

He nodded. Better to let her think that than discuss the phone tap. In the meantime he was taking in the tight jeans, beaded vest, dark hair swirling around her face which in subdued light made her look twenty, large luminous eyes searching his face. Seeking his reaction? Trying to read whether he was happy to see her, Dan thought.

"Am I being stupid to think that I'm in love with you? That I should be here with you until all this is over?" The husky voice almost whispered the words. She took a step forward but he was beside her.

"No, you're not stupid." He said into her hair before tilting her head back to reach her mouth.

"My flight was delayed and the longer I sat there, the more I knew I wanted to be here with you. That this is where I have to be. Leprechauns can wait." She twisted away, walked to the front of the car, turned back, thumbs in belt loops, a teasing look, shoulders back showing cleavage, a rounded top of one breast where the blouse fell away from being unbuttoned one button too far.

"Fuck Leprechauns," he said as he walked to join her and continued to unbutton the white linen blouse. This wasn't what he had planned. But he didn't care, either. He made eye contact and searched her expression for guilt. But there wasn't any. He'd have to believe that she was a cold-blooded murderer to think she ran J.J. off the road last night. But he knew this woman. She wasn't someone to set up something like that. She couldn't do it. Maybe she got a gun to protect herself from her husband, but that was different—it wasn't premeditation.

She giggled. Then began in earnest to unbuckle his belt, unbutton his jeans, pull down the zipper…after a move to shrug her arms out of vest and shirt, she helped him pull his sweatshirt over his head.

"Oops. This has got to go." She deftly twisted the pop-out Benz hood ornament and tossed it in the corner. "Don't want to get impaled."

"Oh, no?" Crude bedroom humor but she didn't seem to mind. He let her turn him and gently push him back onto the hood before she stooped to give his own ornament a long sucking kiss as she unsnapped her bra and let her jeans fall to the cement floor.

Had she done this before? Fucked on the hood of a car? Did he care? Short of murder, and maybe even that, he could forgive this woman anything. He didn't care where she was last night. Didn't care that she hadn't called him. He moaned, grabbed her arms to help her move to mount him, then watched as she lowered her body using one hand to guide him inside her.

Her movements were slow and rhythmic. She watched him watching her until finally he closed his eyes when the first burst of feeling skyrocketed through his body. Somewhere in the tangle of arms and legs and moans, she had fallen forward to rest on his chest, and he felt her tongue and mouth and the warm kisses as she worked her way up to his neck.

"I love you." He heard himself saying the words. And he meant them. He knew that now. He wouldn't go back on his word. If she was in trouble, he'd be there. Nothing mattered but keeping this woman with him.

"Are you sure? No matter what?"

He felt a twinge. A lot like "until death do us part," but, yes....

"No matter what," he echoed.

"Good. You can get up now." She laughed, slipped backward until her feet hit the floor and held out her hands to help him up.

"You know, this is Dr. Ruth sex."

"How's that?" He pulled her to him.

"I saw her show once where she suggested that a couple try out every piece of furniture in the house."

"I'd be happy to just make it to the furniture." He feigned a pain in the back; they both laughed. He didn't care where they did it. He watched as she snapped the hood ornament back in place and reloaded the gun before she put on any clothes. He thought he was glad her priorities were in that order and that she was comfortable being naked around him—but maybe he shouldn't be.

Back in the kitchen, she put water in the tea kettle and got down a basket of herbal teas. He didn't even care when she asked him if she could smoke. Her first in four days, and he believed her. He knew he would have to get around to asking her questions. Hurtful questions. But not now. Not yet.

He sat at the table and wanted to spend the rest of his life just being with her. But he was being unrealistic. He knew that, too. Sooner or later, his job would have to get in the way.

"Move in with me. Get Simon and break your lease, it'll be up in three or four weeks anyway. I really want you here...with me."

He said, "Yes." What was he thinking of? Then he said, "I love you." Again. Out loud. To get used to it? Elaine walked to him, straddled his lap, and playfully kissed him.

"I know." She nuzzled his neck.

Then she was gone, back to the counter to fix the tea. The ringing of the phone startled both of them.

"Just a minute, I'll let you ask him. He's here now." She mouthed "Carolyn" and handed him the phone.

"A memorial service for J.J.? I guess so." He looked up; Elaine was nodding. Dan listened to directions and made a note of the time before hanging up.

The service was short, held at a local funeral home. A grouping of pictures among candles and flowers made up a kind of altar in the front of the chapel. The pictures were of J.J., some as a child, alone and with family, others from graduations, high school, then college. Diplomas and law degree were displayed in gilt frames—this, instead of a body. This because there wasn't a body. How convenient for someone, a charred car and no body. A feeling of almost unbearable sadness hung in the room.

Mass was scheduled for the following morning. Dan was relieved to see crosses and other religious paraphernalia of Christians very much in evidence. Signs of witchcraft were simply not present. He wondered, though, if there might not be some special rite, something deep in the woods, planned for later on.

A woman, who was probably J.J.'s mother, was supported by a man Dan didn't know on her left, but on her right was Jorge. The tall good-looking foreman didn't look up as Dan walked down front to place flowers near a podium. Dona

Mari stood next to them wrapped in a black shawl. J.J. was her sister's boy. The old woman seemed shaken, almost befuddled fumbling with a rosary; perhaps the shock had been too much. Or maybe, she, too, suspected he had been killed. But Dan wasn't going to think about that, not tonight.

Carolyn and Phillip invited them to their house after the service, insisted on it, said it had been too long between visits. Carolyn seemed thrilled to see Dan and Elaine together. Took credit for it, Dan decided. But, at least, his mother would sleep better. And so would Simon, who threw himself at Dan, then chased around in excited circles.

The early October night was too cool to sit outside. The four of them moved to the living room, Elaine and Carolyn trading "son at college" stories. It was comfortable. More comfortable than it had been with the two bimbos, as his sister had called his first wives. He had missed this feeling of family closeness. Maybe his mother and Carolyn had been right to be concerned. He settled back into the sofa cushions. Funny, how he seemed to be seeing things in a different light all of a sudden.

Carolyn rose to get ice and a bottle of white wine from the fridge; Elaine went with her. There were no servants tonight. Even the ever-present bodyguard had disappeared and they had left Dona Mari at the service with her family.

Dan asked Phillip about campaign contributions. Not that he was interested, but he was making a concerted effort to be brotherly. Maybe in the past, Dan hadn't tried hard enough. Wasn't that what dear old Mom had always said? Been too wrapped up in his own life? Time to change that. He was thinking about time, how much they had lost; time that they could have spent getting to know one another; time being a family when they heard the sound of breaking glass. He made it to the kitchen just ahead of Phillip.

"Clumsy of me." Carolyn was dabbing at a trickle of blood that escaped down her ankle from where a sliver of glass had grazed her leg. "The bottle just slipped." She was leaning against a hand-carved oak table.

Elaine was picking up the pieces of tinted glass that seemed to have gone everywhere. Dan got a whisk broom and dust pan out of the pantry and was squatting down to help Elaine when Carolyn said, "Tell Phillip what you just told me." The way she said it; the urgency in her voice made Dan look up.

And he knew Elaine had confided that Eric was alive, sitting back in prison, in Milford. He had a sinking feeling in the pit of his stomach, but didn't know why. Elaine was saying that it was a long story but because he was still alive, she was finally divorced, had served Eric with papers last week and because of the circumstances, the waiting period was waived. And then she happily shared that Dan was moving in with her, tentatively, looking at him first, but he smiled reassuringly.

Carolyn bounced up to kiss Elaine on the cheek but the enthusiasm was fake. Dan knew his sister well enough to know that. She suddenly didn't care about his love life. All her attention seemed to be on "poor Eric." Phillip had reacted more strangely still. After listening to Elaine, he excused himself to go get his drink. Or compose himself, Dan wondered which. He appeared shaken. But wasn't Eric his best friend?

They finally ended up back in the living room. Curiosity seemed to have restored Carolyn, who was now peppering Elaine with a question a second about Eric.

"I can't believe you didn't tell us. I just thought Dan was being his usual nerdy self about women."

Thanks a lot, Dan thought.

"When all this time you were being held against your will—no, you forget I know you." Carolyn had seen Elaine shake her head. "You were being held, all right. And to think how brave you had to be."

"I don't know whether I really thought he was dangerous. I suppose I did." Elaine seemed uneasy with painting Eric the villain.

"Of course you did. I can't even imagine how you lived with him. Not after everything…." Carolyn bent to dab at her calf.

"What was your part in all this?" Phillip had turned to Dan. "I'm sure you know about the two million that Midland Savings and Loan was supposed to have waiting for him."

"What two million?" This from Carolyn, who now was completely revived, the cut on her calf forgotten. Elaine filled her in on the details.

"And you knew about this as a bank trustee, and didn't tell me?" Carolyn seemed genuinely irked at Phillip.

"Thought the fewer people who knew, the better. Sorry to say, but it did cast suspicion on Billy Roland."

"Sounds like he did it, if you ask me. A cover-up. Wouldn't be the first time someone wondered where he got all his money." Carolyn added, "Haven't we all seen the wife? He'd need a second income just to keep her in collagen implants." Carolyn hammed an exaggerated pout.

"For God's sake, Carolyn, drop it. We're maligning the dead," Phillip barked, then recovered and sheepishly reached over to tousle his wife's hair. "How many times in the last twenty years have I had to remind you that this isn't Chicago? Small towns, Carolyn, have—"

"Big ears." She was smiling, none the worse for her husband's shortness, Dan thought. "And a governor-to-be's wife shouldn't have opinions—controversial ones, that is." She smiled up adoringly at Phillip. Dan wondered vaguely if she practiced that in front of a mirror. Was it real? It reminded him a little of Pat Nixon.

"Eric asked me to help him out—" Dan realized he hadn't answered Phillip earlier—"find the proof that Billy Roland was behind it all."

"And?" Carolyn leaned forward.

"Didn't find anything that pointed a finger at the old man. No wrongdoing of any kind."

"Are you saying the investigation for United Life and Casualty cleared Billy Roland of anything shady with those dead cows?" Phillip asked.

Dan briefly told them about Miss Iris.

"And no comments, Carolyn. I don't want to hear 'I told you so,'" Phillip said.

"So you're finished out here?" Carolyn asked.

"Almost."

"Then what? Will you stay on for a while?"

Did Carolyn know what she was asking? Was she trying to figure out how serious he was about Elaine? It was something he hadn't discussed with Elaine, but would have to face; that is, if the love of his life didn't turn out to be a killer. He thought of Billy Roland and J.J. and fought back a wave of despair.

"We haven't gotten that far," Elaine said. She was watching him closely; could she suspect what he was thinking?

"Where do you think all this will lead?" This from Phillip, and Dan knew he wasn't talking about his affair with Elaine, probably hadn't noticed his lovely wife trying to pry into her brother's love life.

"Not sure." Dan paused. "J.J. might have had some answers."

Carolyn and Phillip listened to his account of J.J.'s part in the promise of the two million.

"His death was just an unbelievable coincidence or…?" Carolyn shuddered.

"I can't think of all this happening in Roswell. I grew up here. Seems hard to imagine someone wanting to harm someone else." Phillip got up to put another splash of both scotch and water in his glass. "Do you have any other promising leads?"

"One," but it's not for discussion, Dan thought.

"Can you talk about it?" Carolyn must have read his mind.

"Not yet."

"You know, I hate to think of Eric sitting in Milford. This has got to be hard on him. Psychologically, I mean. Can you imagine serving seven years—and let's say he *was* set up, only to be freed and caught in a flash flood, and then have things happen around him that are out of his control." Phillip paused. "What if Billy Roland masterminded the whole thing, where does that leave Eric now?"

"Up the proverbial creek, when it comes to the money or even knowing, for sure, who was behind it." Dan was feeling uneasy. Elaine had said very little, just watched the rest of them pick over her husband's misfortune. Misfortune? Was he going soft on Eric, too? Was he feeling magnanimous because he was sleeping with the wife, former wife? He had to keep reminding himself about the former part.

"I don't see why Eric should be in prison now."

"Phillip, he threatened Elaine," Carolyn said.

"Maybe if I visited him, talked some sense into him."

"That might be helpful, Phillip. I think Eric would appreciate your interest." Elaine added to Dan, "Shouldn't we be rounding up Simon and leaving soon?"

Dan agreed.

They were on the way home, Simon's head between them from his perch on the back seat, when Elaine put into words what was bothering him.

"What if Phillip gets Eric out? Would it be safe for him?"

Dan felt a twinge of something. Of course, she cared about Eric. He was Matthew's father. But still.... And would he be safe? A lot depended on what the feds found out about the tire. But didn't Elaine say she got a pistol after she realized she would have the nerve to shoot Eric? How had she meant that question?

Dan was beginning to think he could be easily sidetracked. The days after J.J.'s funeral were filled with a little work at United L & C and a lot of play—long walks with Elaine and Simon, candlelight dinners even if it was only good wine and a frozen pizza, a trip to the Double Horseshoe to put flowers on Billy Roland's grave. And sex. Lots and lots of good banging. And, if he was being honest, he had never been as happy.

Then the call came from Roger. A disgruntled Roger, who had found him at the office, a little pissed that Dan had moved out of his apartment and in with Elaine and had removed the tap. Tough. Dan wouldn't expect agents to be too open to change. But Roger seemed to get over it when Dan asked him about the tire. Exactly why he was calling; he wanted to meet in half an hour. He'd come to Dan's office.

Roger was without Tom this time. A virus was keeping Tom out of action for a few days.

"Here's the report. Gotta hand it to you. You were right on."

Dan scanned the page, bullet hole not the result of a recent shooting, difficult to pinpoint date but educated guess put the puncture at two to four months old; tire contained traces of deposits consistent with river water; rim was likely from a sixty-nine Cadillac. Too bad for Sheriff Ray that he didn't realize how helpful he was being keeping the tire under a tarp. He handed the page back.

"Looks good. Will you question Sheriff Ray?"

"That may be hard to do."

"Why?" Dan fought the mounting fear. Something was wrong.

"He's disappeared. Thought you might know something you aren't telling."

"Me? Like what?"

"Thought you might have taken things into your own hands and had a little talk with him."

"No."

"You didn't do us any favors with that J.J. guy. He's sort of worthless to us all now, isn't he?"

"I didn't say anything."

"Well, who knows, Judge Cyrus seems to think Sheriff Ray has gone back to Massachusetts to visit family. Says he took his wife, closed up the station for a while. Thought he'd had this vacation planned for some time. We can't find anything to the contrary."

"Get someone on it." Dan was surprised to hear the urgency in his voice.

"One ahead of you. Got an all points out from here to Mass. So far, nothing. Could be they just took a detour, Texas maybe, wanted to see Six Flags, the Alamo, that kind of thing. Judge thought he had a sister in San Antonio."

"He's the one honest-to-God link that we have. Not to mention, you could get him on a little attempted murder with my testimony."

"Hey, calm down. We're doing everything we can."

Dan sat at his desk a long time after Roger left. He didn't like it. The disappearance of Sheriff Ray bothered him. Not for one minute did he believe the vacation story. Ray was on the run, pure and simple. And, now it was going to be interesting to see who found him first—the good guys or the bad guys.

Abruptly, Dan stood, grabbed his jacket from the back of the door, then returned to the desk to dial Elaine's number. He let it ring; she had said she was going shopping, no problem, he preferred to leave a message anyway, he heard the familiar click and a recorded voice telling him what number he'd reached. The message was simple—he'd be home late. No need to upset her by telling her he was on his way to Milford Correctional.

Dan drove northeast out of Roswell toward Clovis, New Mexico, then across the state line at Texico and continued through wide spots in the road called Falwell, Muleshoe and Olton. He didn't need a billboard welcome sign to know he was in Texas. Oil wells, ranches, cattle, everyone wearing Stetsons and driving big sedans. He passed a Lincoln with three-foot-wide horns for a hood ornament. The product of some Longhorn steer. He shrugged, only in Texas....

Scrub oak and other deciduous trees were yellowing, some had dropped almost all their foliage; but for the most part, summer was lingering, warm days, comfortably cool nights. There hadn't been a hard frost. What was really needed was moisture. The flooding of mid-summer was only a memory.

The Jeep had a thick coating of dust by the time Dan pulled into the long road that ended at a guard station with sprawling cement block buildings spreading behind it. Minimum security didn't mean without electrified fencing and lookout towers; the soccer field could be misleading. It was still a prison.

He hadn't called ahead, wanted as much of an element of surprise as he could get even if it would take an extra thirty minutes getting processed. He was asked to sit outside one of the administrative offices while someone checked his credentials. The chairs were spartan, wooden jobs without cushions, the backs hitting you at the lower edge of the scapulae. No luxury here.

Finally a young woman asked him to follow her and led him back through two more secured gates. By now he was without driver's license, keys and gold Cross pen, leaving such items in gray metal trays to be kept in thick reinforced glass booths. Finally, they reached a small conference room. They had asked if he preferred an office setting. It didn't really make any difference. They all had surveillance cameras. He just wanted a halfway comfortable place to talk.

He thanked the girl and had another ten minutes to wait before Eric appeared. He was already back in prison denim.

"What are you doing here?"

Eric wasn't exactly being friendly, but what did he expect? He probably still blamed Dan for J.J.'s death.

"We need to talk."

"We may have said just about all we need to say."

"I don't think so."

Dan moved a chair closer to the table and sat down waiting for Eric to do the same. Eric made a ritual out of lighting a cigarette and bringing an ashtray to the table, but he finally sat down.

"I found a tire from the Caddy you were in when it got washed off the bridge." He paused to watch Eric's reaction. There was a flicker of interest. "There was a bullet hole in the left rear. Lab puts the time and place about three and a half months ago and near river water."

"Didn't you believe me? Seems like I remember telling you I was shot at."

"Just thought you'd like to know the evidence is there." But Eric didn't seem to care. Didn't seem to want to find out about his potential killer.

"Why are you really here?"

"To find out why J.J. implicated Elaine, said that she knew why you were set up."

"You don't want to know."

"Try me." Dan wondered at Eric's reluctance. Something was going on and he was beginning to fight an urge to slam Eric against the wall, cameras or no cameras.

"I've given it a lot of thought. You started me thinking when you asked if there was someone I'd pissed off, someone who would like to see me put away." Eric methodically rolled the ashes from the tip of his cigarette, before looking up. "Well, there might have been back then. But that was eight years ago. And it was over before the bust. I can't think it could have anything to do with what happened. I know the people involved too well."

"I'm listening."

"Just remember, you're the one who wanted to know." Eric put the cigarette out, rubbed the butt around in the ashes. Then abruptly said, "I was having an affair with your sister." He kept his head lowered.

"Jesus. Carolyn?"

"How many sisters do you have?"

Sarcasm, Dan let it pass. "I wish I wasn't hearing this." He suddenly felt sick. Baby sister dropping her drawers for this scum? He wasn't a prude, but he was shocked. Hadn't they all been friends, Elaine, Carolyn, Phillip? Did friends do that to each other?

"You asked. You wanted to know."

"Go on."

"We'd known each other for years. I don't know why it happened. It just did. It was pretty hot for awhile. Meet in motel rooms away from Roswell, sneak around in town. It was over in three months."

"Did Elaine know?"

"I didn't think so at the time. But she found some stuff Carolyn had written to me. She's the one who told Phillip."

"What did he do?"

"Acted like nothing had happened. Never confronted me, if that's what you mean. I never knew that Elaine had given him the letters until she told me last month."

"And Carolyn?"

"Went on with life. We decided that the relationship could be harmful. You know, the kids and all. Roswell is a small town. I was never fooled into thinking she was really interested in anything more than sex with a different partner. She's always known how her bread is buttered."

Dan knew it was true. Carolyn would find excitement, play at something dangerous until it looked like it might hurt her "position." It wouldn't dawn on her until later that her impulsiveness might hurt someone. Or more than one.

"And Elaine?"

Eric pulled another cigarette from the pack, lit it and leaned back in his chair.

"The beginning of the end."

"How so?"

"Never forgave me. A few months later the plane was brought down. There was lots of news coverage. Then the trial. Within a year, I was here."

The silence seemed oppressive. Eric didn't offer any more. Hadn't he said he thought he might know who was behind the two million? Who did Eric suspect? He'd just mentioned three people who would all have a motive. Dan couldn't put it off any longer. "Could Elaine have set you up?"

"Not her style."

Eric had answered quickly and conclusively. Was that good enough for him? Dan couldn't argue with someone who knew her well. Not when it was also something he wanted to believe. But his sister and brother-in-law? What would he do if faced with pointing a finger at his own family?

"What about Phillip or Carolyn?"

"Let me ask you the same thing. What do you think?"

Dan was quiet, he tilted his chair against the wall. The stakes were right. It would be a problem to become governor if the little woman had a past. Worse yet, erred with the same man again. Or maybe Phillip had been angry. That blinding anger of one cuckolded. But could anyone be angry enough to set the playboy up? Get him out of the way for a while. Have a laugh as Eric fell for the bait, ruined his own life, and lived on false hope for seven years. The ultimate joke, a ploy to get even. But that part was almost harmless compared with trying to kill him when he got out. Or kill J.J. and Sheriff Ray? Could his sister or her husband do that? Could Elaine?

"You know I leave this dump tomorrow."

Dan jerked his chair upright. Had he heard correctly?

"Out? How?"

"Thought you'd like to know."

"How'd you manage that?"

"Phillip pulled some strings. I'll be in his custody, so to speak. The two of us are going to take a run at getting the Lear ready to fly. At least, figure out what needs to be done." Eric paused. "Phillip's buying it. Campaign write-off. So, maybe, I should just let bygones be bygones, know what I mean? Bury the bitterness, dance at your wedding...." The old smirk was back. Eric seemed relaxed.

Dan couldn't help feeling a little unsettled at the wedding part. Strange to be getting encouragement from the ex. But why was Phillip doing this? Was it a conscience move? Paying a few hundred thousand to sleep better at night? And help Eric out in the meantime? Go back to being buddies, help his pal put it all behind him. If Eric refused to testify or Sheriff Ray didn't turn up...was there a case?

Suddenly, Dan was weary of it all. Tired of the duplicity. Too tired to second-guess Carolyn or Phillip, or Elaine. But there was one other thing, something he'd been curious about.

"Do you have a transcript of the trial? Or even notes, some play by play of highlights?"

"Yeah. I'd kept it in storage until a couple weeks ago. It's in Elaine's garage."

That explains the keys in the safe deposit box, Dan thought.

"What if I wanted to take a look?"

Eric shrugged. "Okay by me. Do you know what you expect to find?"

Dan had to smile, "Not even the foggiest. But there might be something. It's worth a look. If I need to get a hold of you, where will you be?"

"At the Double Horseshoe, Phillip arranged it. Don't worry, I realize it would be a little crowded at Elaine's." The smirk again but not unfriendly.

All the way back, Dan tried to put into words what he was feeling. Dread? A foreboding? If he could turn the decision around, he'd keep Eric in Milford, keep him there until he had some answers. Dan didn't believe that he would be safe on the outside. Possibly all the wrong people knew he was alive. But it wasn't just that, a fear for his life, there was something else.

Eric's attitude. It came to him in a rush. Yes, the anger was gone. But why? Was he reconciled to Billy Roland's death and the way things had unfolded—the fact that the two million was lost forever? Or was he making people believe he didn't care anymore. That was what was difficult to buy, that Eric Linden would give up on what he thought was owed to him, that he'd spent seven years looking forward to, and docilely accept his fate.

Dan remembered the Cisco Kid. That was revenge, and that was the way Eric thought, the way he approached a problem. Had anything changed? He didn't think so. Did that put Elaine in danger? Or Carolyn and Phillip? They would all have to be careful. What was Phillip thinking of? It just might prove to be one of the dumbest things he'd ever done.

Dan had gotten back to Roswell late. If Elaine thought it was odd that he'd gone to Milford, she didn't say. He told her he had talked to Eric but didn't go into detail. She offered that she thought Eric's getting out of Milford at this time might be a problem. He agreed. She seemed to sense he wasn't telling her everything, but she didn't push. He appreciated that. But he hated having secrets. If they were going to make it as a couple, there couldn't be anything between them.

Elaine went to bed at ten. Dan sat in the dark of the study and thought, sifted through the possible combinations—who had the most to gain, the most to lose? He tried to decide what Billy Roland would want him to do next. If he were Eric, what would he do? He was just about ready to give it up for the evening when he saw Elaine in the doorway.

"Would you like to talk?" The white oversized t-shirt hit her at the knees; she looked waif-like leaning against the doorjamb illuminated only by a street light, but Dan knew she wasn't wearing anything underneath. He also knew she wasn't trying to be seductive.

"I'd like to." And it was the truth. It would make a difference hearing her side of the story. He had been putting it off. Afraid, maybe, of what she might say.

She went to the kitchen and brought back two tumblers of scotch, handed him one then curled up at the end of the couch.

"I'm not sure there's an easy way to begin."

"Try me. I'm fairly resilient."

"When I talked with J.J. the day before he died, he said that you knew who was behind sending Eric to prison." Dan watched her closely.

"That *I* did?" She frowned, then shook her head. "I don't think I know what he meant."

"Think back to what was happening at that time. Was there anyone who might have wanted Eric put away? Was angry enough, felt cheated, whatever, to set him up? And could pull strings to get it done?"

He saw the flicker of realization and waited while she formulated an answer. Would she tell him the truth if she was behind it?

"This is hard to believe, but…."

"I know about Carolyn."

A look of surprise, then, "Did Eric tell you that I'm the one who told Phillip?"

"Yes."

"Do you think Phillip could have done such a thing? Ruin Eric's life?"—Elaine paused—"Ruin mine, too. Or maybe that I…." She said the last softly and Dan watched as the magnitude of what she was saying started to sink in.

"You never thought that I was behind it, did you?" There was a mixture of hurt and surprise in her eyes as she searched his face but didn't find what she'd hoped for. He couldn't lie to her.

"I didn't know what to think."

"And now?"

"If you say you weren't involved, I believe you."

"I wasn't. Maybe, I thought I hated Eric, but I wouldn't have ruined us as a family. It was never as important to me to have a husband as it was that Matthew have a father. Can you understand that?" Tears welled, caught by the rims of her eyes, then singly rolled down her cheeks.

Dan nodded. He hated to see the hurt, but there was nothing he could do.

"Did those FBI men think I was involved in drugs?"

"They check out every lead, everyone involved."

"And Eric? Does he think I could have set him up?"

"I don't think so."

"So, that leaves us with Carolyn or Phillip."

"Tell me what happened when you told Phillip about Eric and Carolyn."

She was silent, no tears now, just quiet, pensive. Then, "It was awful; it may have been the only truly spiteful thing I've ever done." Dan waited while she padded on bare feet to the bathroom and returned with a wad of Kleenex, then blew her nose.

"I realized later that Phillip was shocked, rocked to the core. He really had no idea that Carolyn would do such a thing. And, I think the bedroom was, maybe, sacred—I'm not saying this very well." She settled herself on the couch. "Phillip is the type to take vows seriously. I've never heard a rumor about any womanizing. Frankly, he wants one thing in this life and that's to have political power, be governor, for starters. He's ruthless when it comes to that."

"And couldn't this be an example of his ruthlessness?"

She thought a moment. "I suppose. It could have ruined everything, his chances to get what he's always wanted. Small towns aren't very forgiving."

"What did he say when you told him?"

"That he'd take care of it. Guess that takes on new meaning now, huh?" She blew her nose again before going on. "He took the letters, read two or three while I was there. He asked me who else knew about the affair, and did Eric know that I was coming to see him. I told him I didn't think anyone else knew and, no, Eric didn't know I was there. I didn't know for sure, but Eric always assumed I was in the dark."

"Did Phillip say anything about Carolyn?"

"Only that he found it hard to believe, thought that she wanted the same things he wanted. Couldn't believe she would throw it all away."

"Did he give you any idea how he would take care of things?"

Elaine was silent.

"He told me that if I had been a better wife, it wouldn't have happened."

"Nice guy with just a little free advice. That sounds like Phillip, holier than thou."

"He was hurt. I was the messenger. I couldn't blame him for lashing out."

"What happened next?"

"Nothing really. Eric was suddenly attentive, back home playing baseball with Matthew, helping with homework. Honest." She made a feeble attempt at a scout's honor. "Absolutely nothing was ever said."

"And Eric was the model husband after that?"

"I didn't say that." The smile was rueful when she turned to look at him. "Sex was...maybe, still is...an addiction for Eric. Somewhere along the line, I realized that I was the wife, probably the only wife there'd ever be, but never the only woman. I suppose we should have sought help. Realized that he needed help. There are clinics that treat those kinds of problems. But I'm not sure he would have gone."

"So, you looked the other way." It was a statement. She just nodded and worked at the rug with a bare toe.

"My shrink would like me to explore fear of abandonment some more. Eric and I both had pretty awful childhoods.... I think I tried to be understanding...there was a sensitive little boy under all that impulsive behavior."

Dan didn't want this to be a third degree on spousal indiscretions, but he had to ask, "Are you saying there was someone after Carolyn?"

"Yep. Sandwiched in between baseball and homework. But not someone who really counted according to Eric, really was threatening. Just one of his usuals."

"Which was?"

"This time a domestic at Judge Cyrus's. I found a scarf in his truck. He had smuggled her into the States on one of his trips down South. When I asked him about her, he said he was teaching her the alphabet, teaching her English, and sex was the only way she knew how to pay him. You have to admit that's novel."

"What happened to her?"

"She disappeared, I guess, probably went to Albuquerque or over to Dallas. It's easier for illegals to find work in big cities. Then, the drug bust. You know the rest."

"Did you ever think that Phillip might have had something to do with the bust?"

"No. It looked like Billy Roland was the one to suspect. But, I thought Eric saw a way to get money, made a deal with a drug lord, acted on his own. Things were too easy flying in and out of South America. He would have made contacts, that sort of thing."

"The transcripts of the trial are in the garage?"

Elaine nodded. "Do you think they might be helpful?"

"I don't know. I thought I might look through them."

"Tonight?"

"Why not?"

"Want me to help?"

They dragged the first of seven heavy cardboard filing boxes in from the garage. They were dated and a brief description of what each contained was outlined on their lids. Elaine took the one marked "Testimony on seizure; detailed account of drug findings." Dan picked "Character references: Phillip Ainsworth, Judge Franklin Cyrus, Mr. Billy Roland Eklund, and the names of several people not familiar."

"Sure you're up to this?" Dan asked.

Elaine was sitting cross-legged on the floor, a pile of folders in her lap. "Couldn't make me go away if you wanted to." She smiled and opened a folder with a transparent blue tab.

"Listen to this." Dan had been leafing through the testimony of Judge Cyrus. "Eric Linden was 'detained' for possession of marijuana at age sixteen, not arrested; caught with a gang of kids in a stolen car at seventeen, again not arrested but the use of drugs was suspected...then, later represented the coalition to legalize the use of marijuana for the terminally ill...."

"Believe me, it didn't help his case. At the time I felt it was wrong to dredge up all that old stuff but that always seems to be a part of it, our legal system, I mean."

"And here, Billy Roland had fired him?"

"Eric worked summers at the Double Horseshoe and 'borrowed' a plane without permission. Eric was only twenty-three at the time, last year of law school, had his pilot's license. He took a crop duster on a joy ride that ended with a crash landing. His aunt bailed him out, and then, of course, by that time I was around. No one wanted to give the bride away to someone in prison. How's that for irony?"

"Did you feel that the judge, Aspen, wasn't it, was too strict? Eric didn't have a record. A lot of near misses, but not a record exactly."

Elaine pushed the folders aside and leaned against the couch. "I always thought so. Yes, all the youthful pranks came out, but a man almost thirty-four was on trial, not a kid. It seemed like a lot of things were brought out that were purposefully hurtful to his case."

"Who was the prosecuting attorney?"

"Albert Reyes. Still practices in Albuquerque. You saw him at J.J.'s funeral. He was standing beside Dona Mari."

Dan shut the folder and excitedly leaned forward. A link. It might mean something.

"Were they related?"

"J.J. and Albert Reyes?" Dan nodded. "Cousins, I think. The sons of Dona Mari's sisters."

"But J.J. wasn't on the scene yet?"

"Still in law school, I think. I don't remember meeting J.J. until after Eric was in prison. He took over the job that Eric had had with Phillip's company."

"It might prove interesting to pay Mr. Reyes a visit."

Chapter Eleven

Dan got up at six, left Elaine asleep, and grabbed a cup of Circle-K coffee on his way downtown. The minute he got to the office, he was glad he'd come in early. Five phone messages from Roger. At six-thirty, Dan rang Roger's motel.

"Too early? You've got to be kidding. I do five miles at least three times a week. Only good thing about pulling duty in the sticks, I stay in shape out of absolute, total boredom."

Dan couldn't think of anything more boring *than* running and fought back a vision of a taut-stomached Roger racing along the back-streets of Roswell in flashy trunks, and said, "You've been trying to reach me?"

"Yeah. Finally caught up with the sheriff. He was in San Antonio visiting the sister."

"Did you pick him up?"

"Well, there really isn't a reason to."

"Now, wait, I saw the man chasing a car that got washed away. He must have been doing eighty. He was *shooting* at the Cadillac. You have the fucking proof, and you didn't bring him in?" Dan hadn't meant to raise his voice, but he heard himself almost yelling into the receiver.

"He doesn't deny it."

"What? What doesn't he deny?"

"That he was shooting at the car."

"And that isn't reason to bring him in?"

"Calm down and listen for a minute. He says he was shooting at the car to stop it."

"Stop it?"

"He had been contacted about the flood waters. Dam burst above Caprock. Says he knew the bridge was in bad shape, that it could go any minute and was patrolling County Five to warn people. Makes sense to me. Says there's always someone parked out there smooching it up, someone who wouldn't be paying attention to the weather. Our friend Eric fits the description of someone out to have a little fun with jail-bait."

"She was twenty-three."

"That's young when you're forty."

Obviously, Roger's morals were coming into play. He better get him back on track.

"Did he say anything else?"

"Only that that's what he thought when he saw the Lott girl's car. He'd seen her with Eric Linden at the Double Diamond dancing. When he was leaving to begin his patrol, he saw them turn onto County Road Five, figured they'd be going that way to spend a little time in the back seat."

"So, why was this great savior shooting at them? What's wrong with a little horn honking? Blinking of headlights? I bet old Ray has a portable siren and light on the Dakota."

"I guess he tried to catch up with them. Says they acted like he was chasing them. Acted scared. He hadn't meant to turn it into a race, but he was concerned as hell they'd get into trouble because of the water."

"So he shot at them?"

"Said there wasn't anything left to do. Admits up front that he took the tire out, but they were too close to the bridge, didn't do any good."

"All done in the name of a warning."

"Come on, Dan. It makes sense to me. How else you going to save someone's life going eighty in a car headed for disaster?"

"Makes a good story."

"Dan, the man was all choked up. Took the death of that girl real hard. Blames himself. Says if he was only there sooner."

"And you're convinced?"

"And you're not?"

"I was there, God damnit. I was there heading in the direction of the washed-out bridge and nobody warned me. You understand? Mister do-good Sheriff didn't stop, didn't honk, blink his lights, nothing."

"Maybe he didn't see you."

Dan thought of that rainy evening and could recall the sheriff passing him. He had almost run Dan off the road. Was he absolutely positive that it was Sheriff Ray? Yes. The fact that he hid the tire and rim at the station made him look guilty. But it wasn't going to make a difference to Roger. So, he just said, "Could be" and hung up.

Then picked the phone back up and called Elaine. It rang four times before the answering machine kicked in. She was probably still in bed; they had read transcripts until almost three.

"I'm going to run up to Albuquerque to talk with Albert Reyes. I'll be late again." And then he added something he'd been thinking about. "Get the locks changed on the front and back doors. On the garage, too. Humor me, I'll feel better about leaving your sexy body in bed alone. See you tonight." It was just a precaution. Maybe nothing more than something to make him feel better. But he'd learned a long time ago to trust his sixth sense. And since he'd talked to Eric, he hadn't felt very secure.

The trip to Albuquerque took a little under three hours.

He'd gone up to Vaughn and took the interstate from Clines Corners on into the city. Only about sixty miles of the drive was interesting. Roswell to Vaughn was nothingness, cactus, sandy soil, stubby vegetation; but he had made good time. It wasn't heavily patrolled. The last leg was through the mountains on a good four-lane highway. But he could have been driving the Alps and wouldn't have known the difference.

He had no idea what Albert Reyes could tell him and felt he was chasing leads that kept evaporating. Was it still so important to prove that Billy Roland wasn't involved? Moot question. He was doing it for lots of other reasons, too; not the least of which was to satisfy his own investigative curiosity. He was taking a chance that Mr. Reyes would be in, but again, a call ahead would be a warning. And he couldn't risk it. He couldn't help thinking this was probably going to be the best thing he'd done so far—or a bust—no in between.

He filled up with gas on the outskirts of Albuquerque and called the offices of Reyes and McCandless. For some reason, the second name rang a bell, but he couldn't place it. Mr. Reyes would be out of the office until eleven, would he like an appointment then? Dan said yes, and ducked having to say what the visit was concerning when the receptionist had to answer another call.

The offices were modest, efficient more than a statement of self-worth. Reyes and McCandless shared a receptionist who was seated behind a circular desk with a bank of lighted buttons. The first floor foyer was the only trendy spot in the somewhat austere highrise. But possibly offices on the ground level had a little added prestige.

Dan wasn't kept waiting. Albert Reyes appeared at exactly eleven to personally usher him back to a conference room that opened onto a small enclosed patio containing a tree, sculpted bench, and tiered planting area. Brown and lifeless this time of year, it was probably a delightful spot spring and summer. This was obviously the plus for rooming on the ground floor.

"I don't believe we've met?" Albert Reyes held out his hand. He was tall and handsome, reminiscent of Jorge rather than J.J., dark hair parted on the side. He wore the navy business suit with ease.

"I was at your cousin's funeral."

A small flicker of recognition, then, "May I ask how you knew J.J.?"

"I'm Carolyn Ainsworth's brother, but met J.J. while doing some work for Billy Roland Eklund." Dan was brief but gave Albert Reyes a little background. "I'm here today because I think your cousin might have been murdered."

Albert Reyes didn't flinch but also didn't say anything, just returned Dan's gaze. And in that instant before he said, "Why do you think that?"—Dan knew that the possibility of it not being an accident had crossed his mind, too.

Dan filled him in on his conversation with J.J. the day before he died. How he had not denied being involved with the promise of the two million, meeting with Eric Linden, pretending to be someone else, using a false name on a document.

When he was finished, Albert Reyes shook his head. "I don't know what to say." He paused. "I guess I'd like to be able to say it doesn't sound like J.J., but I'd be lying. Our practices were very different. He got involved...represented some people with questionable backgrounds here and there. I honestly thought he'd stay out of trouble working for Billy Roland and Phillip Ainsworth. It doesn't look like he did. But I don't see how I can be of help?"

"You were the prosecuting attorney at Eric's trial. Someone, I'm guessing J.J., provided you with damaging information about Eric, played law clerk, helped you build a case, encouraged you to make him out to be a menace to society."

"That really wasn't necessary. Eric dug his own grave trying to represent himself."

"But why the stiff sentence?"

"Keep a misfit out of the community. Those were close to Judge Aspen's exact words."

"Misfit doesn't equate to dangerous. Someone wanted him put away, put away and set up to keep him quiet. What do you know about that part of it?"

Albert didn't answer right away. Dan waited; he wasn't in a hurry.

"I believe Judge Aspen was encouraged by friends."

"Who?"

"The circuit court judge down your way, Franklin Cyrus."

Judge Cyrus. This was getting interesting.

"What makes you say that?"

"I overheard a conversation. Judge Cyrus can be pretty convincing, convinced Aspen, anyway, that Eric shouldn't get a light sentence."

"But why? First time offender. You know the user charges were teenage offenses that he wasn't cited for."

"It was morals, if I remember correctly. Judge Cyrus said Mr. Linden suffered from a sexual addiction, probably needed clinical treatment for chronic promiscuity. I remember the judge saying that such problems are usually caused by abuse or neglect as children. Eric had just cited his dysfunctional childhood in testimony that morning. He didn't know it, but it worked against him. I remember Judge Cyrus saying it was only a matter of time before the charge would be rape."

"Strange that Judge Cyrus would use something like that. What was that to him? Promiscuity didn't have anything to do with the trial."

Albert shrugged. "There was something about him having a mistress, no, 'coercing' was the term used, someone underage. Judge Cyrus made it sound like it was a child, or at least a teenager. If you knew Judge Aspen, it wouldn't take much to put an errant lawyer away, especially one suspected of drug smuggling *and* sexual misconduct. He really had a thing for cleaning up the profession. A fellow Yale alumnus seemed to be a double black eye."

"Do you remember if any more was said about this child?"

"No. I wasn't supposed to overhear as much as I did. I just happened to be in the lunch room outside Judge Aspen's chambers."

"So, J.J. didn't need to help you with the case?"

"I didn't say that. He provided some…insights into the defendant's character like what you mentioned earlier. All on the up and up, all on the books. He was apprenticed to

Judge Cyrus at the time. Did some clerking for him before he took the bar."

"Why Judge Cyrus? I wouldn't think a young man would find Tatum very interesting."

"Judge Cyrus has always been a supporter of the family. My family and my wife's. The judge has been generous by making school possible for us. My wife even clerked for him."

McCandless. The farm couple who took in the refugees from Haiti—the Voodoo priest. It was becoming a small world.

"Was there anything else unusual about the trial?"

"Other than all of Roswell was in shock. Eric was a hometown product. Local boy makes good, goes back East to school. Everyone knew his great aunt, the one who raised him; she was a pillar of the community...the wife was well liked. Believe me, it was the talk of Roswell for months."

"Do you know of a reason that anyone might have had to kill J.J.?" It was time to ask again. Bring the focus back where it needed to be.

"I'll admit I've thought about it. It was ruled an accident. Of course, there wasn't much left of the car."

"I don't think you believe it was an accident."

"I guess I believe it might have been intentional. He could have taken his own life."

"Why do you say that?"

"J.J. had been despondent recently. His practice was struggling and he could have just wanted out. Maybe he was in over his head." Albert paused, then shrugged. "I just don't know."

Or maybe he knew I was close to finding out what really happened eight years ago, Dan thought. Knew, and couldn't face the consequences.

Why would Judge Cyrus try to influence the sentencing in Eric's case? Say that he had an addiction, a teenage mistress? According to Elaine, there had been a young girl, one of Eric's stowaways. But she had disappeared. Disappeared. Somehow the word bothered him. She seemed to have vanished about the time Eric was busted. Was that a coincidence or was there a chance that she'd never made it up north to work in Albuquerque? Or any place else, for that matter.

Dan had the three-hour drive back to Roswell to decide on his next move, and that was to stop by the coroner's office at the courthouse. Dan wasn't sure what he'd find, but if his hunch was right, it would suddenly be a whole new ballgame.

The office, tucked away in a back corner on the second floor, proved to be an efficiently run archive of clinical records, masterminded and protected with gusto by the tall, gray-haired woman standing in front of him, arms crossed over a flat chest.

"I usually need a little more identification than this. What you're asking for is highly confidential, highly volatile information." She was peering at the card that said he was a senior investigator with United Life and Casualty but was also an independent contractor. Her lips were tightly pressed together, not a good sign.

"It has some bearing on our investigation of the deaths of several cows owned by Billy Roland Eklund. One, as you might have heard, died by mutilation."

She pursed her lips and frowned, but he'd bet she knew what he was talking about.

"And you think these sacrifices of humans might, in some way, be connected?"

"Mr. Roland shared with me before he died...God rest his soul..." Dan had reverently lowered his eyes when he said this last and through lowered lashes saw that she had done the same. Just a moment of silence but it may have made an ally.

"...that on several occasions the bodies of young women had been found in his woods, on an altar of sorts, suggesting that their deaths had been the result of some kind of cult worship, a ritualistic killing. I understand that their bodies were brought here to Roswell, were autopsied by the coroner? That your office often sent photos and prints to Mexico trying to identify the girls?"

He thought he had won her over. She was just looking thoughtful now, not adversarial.

"There have been five that I know about, and I've worked here for nineteen years. A couple date way back before my time. The last was two months ago, the one you mentioned. But before that, it must have been seven or eight years since we'd had an incident."

Dan caught his breath. Seven or eight years. He felt the excitement rising. "Would you be able to look up the dates for me?" Go easy, don't get too eager; it might be nothing, just coincidence, Dan warned himself.

"I suppose it would be all right. It's the kind of thing people around here don't like to admit to. Makes outsiders shy away from investing in the community, makes us seem unsafe, if you know what I mean." She looked at him, then added, "I was against the UFO museum at first, thought visitors would think all of Roswell ran around looking up at the sky to point at shiny whirling things." She laughed, then added, "I'd hate for there to be any adverse publicity because of this...information."

Dan smiled. "I understand, but this information might just mean the end to these senseless killings." That had gotten her attention. She pushed a clipboard toward him.

"Sign here. Give your address and phone in Roswell. We keep a record of all inquiries."

Dan signed and watched her go through an archway to filing cabinets that lined the walls of a back room. It seemed like she was gone overly long or was it just his excitement?

"Here it is," she called out after he had heard several drawers being opened and slammed shut. "Thought for a moment that I'd misplaced the file."

She walked back into the room carrying several green pendaflex folders. "There's a new procedure in place after this last killing. In the cases of unexplained or violent deaths, bodies must be sent to the Office of Medical Investigation in Albuquerque. In the old days, everything was handled here, locally. The body was examined, kept at the morgue a decent length of time, and if no next-of-kin presented themselves, someone would provide a burial plot."

"Do you remember the names of people who might have done that?"

"Oh yes, people with private cemeteries. Billy Roland offered a resting place for one young girl many years ago. Seems like I remember Judge Cyrus has, too."

"Does he have a family cemetery?"

"Not really. He set up a memorial garden. Pretty spot right next to the bank. The citizens of Tatum weren't too pleased. But it's nice to have someone concerned about the dead, the discarded ones who will never rest with their families."

Dan agreed and hoped she couldn't see his hands shake as he pulled a folder out of the file marked with a date a few days before Eric Linden was framed. First time he had used the word, framed; but suddenly he was sure that that's what had happened.

The file was complete. A description and several photos attested to the young girl's beauty, even in death. She was probably sixteen. It was easy to imagine Eric accepting a little thanks for teaching her the alphabet, and he would bet anything that this was the stowaway, the one he brought to this country to start a new life. The one he accepted a few favors from, and the one Judge Cyrus used to sway his sentencing. He asked for a copy of the autopsy and turned to the other files.

The first death had occurred thirty-two years ago. That placed it a few years after the Voodoo priest moved to the community. The others were spaced at five to ten year intervals.

Nothing unusual. All were attributed to rituals practiced by those who strayed north of the Mexican border. In each instance there was an investigation. A handful of men tried to track down wrongdoers. There were never any suspects found.

"I'd like to borrow a photo of this victim." Dan pointed to the girl that he hoped Eric would be able to identify.

"That's not our usual procedure." The woman turned back to the copier.

"I'll be able to have the photo back in two days." Unless it becomes evidence, he thought.

"I suppose it would be all right. We have four others here." She was thumbing through the stack of papers on the machine in front of her, then removed an eight by ten glossy and put it in an envelope along with the copies of the investigation and autopsy.

"Here you go. I hope this will be helpful."

Not as much as I do, Dan wanted to add as he walked out the door. He tossed the envelope onto the front seat of the Cherokee and backed out into traffic. He knew where he was going; he had one last thing to check before he went out to the Double Horseshoe to confront Eric.

The offices of the *Roswell Sentinel*, the city's one newspaper, were downtown in a beige brick building probably built in the fifties. He had about an hour before they closed to the public, but what he wanted to see wouldn't take long.

The receptionist directed him to the library, a room off of a long hallway that held a microfiche reader, long heavy oak tables and several uncomfortable chairs. The cabinets of film were protected by a counter that stretched across the width of the room. Someone had to be called from the back to help him, but soon he was seated in front of the screen moving through a month's worth of *Sentinels*—all seven and a half years old.

The first headline about finding the girl was two inches high: "Satan Lives Among Us." A local group of ministers had banded together to protest the killing and vowed to get some answers. There were public outcries against satanism and ungodly ritual, lots of quotes from upstanding townspeople. Sheriff Ray supposedly took an active part in tracking down the killers, was quoted as saying he had several "hot" leads.

The second day headlines were even larger. "Community Vows Revenge," a quote from the Tatum mayor. By then, the horror of the death had attracted state-wide attention. Sheriff Ray now had the help or hindrance of a local vigilante group. One more day and that was the end of headline news for the apparent sacrificial death. A total of three days. The next edition of the *Sentinel* had the news of the killing on the back page of the front section. This time the two-inch headline read: "Roswell Attorney Accused in Drug Smuggling."

Dan scrolled through another week's worth of headlines. Eric Linden had indeed been big news. It seems like all of Roswell was captivated by the story. Even editorials chose themes of temptation and greed. The ritualistic death of a young girl from somewhere south of the border was no longer of interest. But a lawyer, well known in the community, suddenly was.

Dan was beginning to see the sense of it all. If someone had wanted, *needed*, to divert attention from a heinous crime; say, one where authorities were getting too close—what better way to do it? The newspapers were proof that it had worked. One day, the community was up in arms about the killing; the next it was in shock about one of its own gone wrong.

"We're closing in ten minutes. Is there something else I can help you with?"

"No. I have everything I need." Dan hadn't seen the young man come in the room. "On second thought, how long would it take to make copies of these three editions, front pages only?"

"Could you pick them up tomorrow?"

"Sure." Dan left his name and paid for the copies, but he was already thinking of talking with Eric. He could just be the last piece in the puzzle. What did Eric know about the young woman's death? He was out of the country when she was killed. And someone made certain that his attention was diverted when he returned. If the killer thought he could identify him...wouldn't that have been worth the promise of two million to keep him quiet?

When Dan pulled into the long curving front drive of the Double Horseshoe, the house was dark. And, for the first time, looked empty, lifeless and forsaken, in the subdued light of dusk. No one had removed the hanging terra cotta pots of petunias, summer leftovers, that now shed dried leaves onto the porch. The cornshuck wreath on the door had been shredded by the wind. This wasn't the same house he had pulled up in front of just four months ago on a sultry summer's day. He drove around to the back fighting the sadness that seemed to settle around him.

He was surprised to see two cars parked next to a couple of ranch pickups: Elaine's Benz and Phillip's white Buick. He pulled in and headed back to the house. They must have brought Eric out. This was turning into a reunion of sorts.

The back screen door was unlatched, and Dan walked through to the kitchen. There was a faint odor of stale food, garbage not removed. There were even dirty dishes in the sink. Whoever lived in the house now wasn't too tidy. The door to the study was closed. Dan knocked, then opened it. A floor lamp was on and had been moved to the middle of the floor. White sheeting covered the furniture. Someone was in the process of packing Billy Roland's library; books were stacked everywhere.

The bar had been dismantled. A large slab of gray-green marble rested against one wall. All the bottles of liquor had been removed. Not the sort of thing a state school would want to inherit, Dan guessed. He wondered who had helped themselves. Billy Roland's walnut desk was gone, leaving a lighter patch of carpet underneath. The drapes were down and the windows seemed naked with only tightly closed venetian blinds. It was a room with all the life sucked out of it.

He stepped into the hall and called out for Elaine before switching on a light. He stood and listened; but it was evident that the house was empty. There was dust everywhere. He was leaving tracks on the fine oak parquet flooring. The chandelier was dimmed by a dusty powdering. He turned and walked back through the kitchen turning out lights as he went.

The barns were a different story. He walked into the first one and saw that the horses had been recently fed. Baby Belle nickered in greeting, and he stopped to rub her nose. It seemed like there were fewer horses. He couldn't be sure. He hadn't paid that much attention before.

The first of the cow-barns was brightly lighted and bustling with activity. Charolais, some getting bathed, others exercised, were everywhere. And the men working with them were young, not quite acne-free Future Farmers of America members who had gone on to an agricultural college. There were even two young girls working together sudsing up a half-grown bull. College kids wearing cowboy hats and Levis. The crew who usually worked in the barns was absent.

"Things have changed." Hank had walked up to stand beside him.

"It's a shock. What's going to happen to the house?"

"Somebody turned up some distant relative of the first wife and we're just waiting for her to come out and go through the household things before we turn it into offices. The Tatum library will get his books. Out here we've already transitioned to university ownership. The kids are doing a pretty good job, don't you think?"

Amid squeals of delight, the two girls washing the young bull turned the hose on each other.

"Different atmosphere," Dan admitted.

"We've even converted one of the bunk houses into a dormitory. Come with me." Hank paused to unlock a door to the back of a second barn. "I want to show you something."

Dan followed Hank back toward the clinic, which was framed in already with rough white drywall panels hanging from sturdy two by fours.

"Difficult to imagine there was a fire."

"Yeah. We were able to shake some money loose from the trust and go ahead with the repairs."

Hank was leading him toward the show ring, a regulation-size arena of sawdust over sand flanked by bleachers.

"Sit here, I'll be back."

Dan hadn't meant to be sidetracked by Hank, but he guessed that Eric would be down at the hangar and would probably still be there when he got through. Hank could barely contain his excitement when he returned to sit beside Dan.

"You've got to see this." Hank pointed toward the double gate at the back of the arena.

As both men watched, the gates opened and two young college students entered leading a magnificent Charolais that glistened silver in the overhead spotlights.

"Shortcake Dream?" Dan couldn't believe it; he sat forward. This heifer was sparkling white with only the characteristic dark shadings on knees and hocks.

"How'd you get rid of the dye?"

"She's been bodyclipped. But look how she's filled out." Hank leaned back. "That's the best example of what this ranch is all about. I know he always said it, but I agree—she's the best Billy Roland ever produced." This last was said reverently. "What more could a man want than a living memorial to his work?"

Dan knew he didn't have to say anything. Hank's way to deal with the grief of Billy Roland's death was to devote his life to maintaining, maybe improving, what his benefactor had started. Actually, the more he thought about it, it wasn't a bad goal.

"What's next for Shortcake Dream?"

"A few shows in the spring. Motherhood can wait until next year. Until she's really ready."

Hank was staring at the heifer with something akin to adoration. It was like Shortcake Dream was family. Dan hated to break the spell but he needed to find Eric.

"Did you happen to see Elaine Linden, or Eric, this afternoon?"

"Elaine was up at the house working on the study. But I think she's out somewhere looking for that dog, now. I told her I thought he followed some folks over to the hangar a while back."

"Guess I'll head out that way." Dan had the envelope of copies from the coroner's office under his arm.

"Want to take Baby Belle? She'd like the attention."

"Not a bad idea."

The barns' peripheral lights were on, some thirty spots strategically placed to illuminate work areas not under cover.

Dan was glad because the night was moonless, one of those velvety dark, "thick" nights with heavy clouds pushing in on the horizon.

Dan thought there was supposed to be a full moon hiding under all that fluff somewhere, but there was no hint of it now. It was only a little past eight; it could clear later.

Belle seemed spooked by everything, snapping twigs, crunch of the gravel in the drive, flapping of the flag against the pole in front of the house. He was just about to decide to take her back when she appeared to settle and trust his judgment. Probably just hadn't been ridden in awhile.

He kept Belle to a slow trot, which wasn't her most comfortable gait as his tailbone would tell him in the morning, but he had better control that way. As they crested the last in a grouping of small hills to the south of the house, Dan looked down on the runway and hangar still three-quarters of a mile away. It was ablaze with light.

Lights twinkled along the strip of asphalt as it stretched to the west. Could the Lear be ready to fly? He somehow didn't think so. The hangar glowed a soft yellow through the small-paned windows along its side. The sight was eerie against the darkness of the night. Belle was snorting and side-stepping now, and it took all his determination to guide her down the incline.

"Must be some party," he muttered to himself as he got nearer. And then he noticed what was odd, what must have been bothering Baby Belle. The lights in the hangar were flickering, winking, and wavering, causing shadows to drift across the windows.

"What the hell?" Dan now had to urge Belle forward, all the while talking encouragingly. He walked her around to the back and tied her to a utility meter next to one of the two ranch pickups parked beside the door. He started to slip the envelope out of his saddlebags, then decided to leave it; instead, he checked his revolver and felt better.

But not for long. Dan stepped into the domed metal building and, squatting to look under the carriage of the cargo plane, saw the candles. Some in tall glass holders with religious pictures on their sides, others in shallow dishes; they were placed to form the outline of a cross on the cement floor to the right of the front entrance.

Sitting in the center of the cross on a wooden straight-backed chair was Phillip Ainsworth, barefoot, hands resting on his knees, palms up, eyes unseeing, staring out of some hypnotic trance, a white handkerchief draped over his head. And around him in rhythmic motion moved a figure in flowing white robes who, as Dan watched, made the sign of the cross first at Phillip's forehead, then his temples, elbows, palms, and feet.

Dan crept forward and crouched beneath the cargo plane and watched as the dancing figure turned his way. Dona Mari. But not the woman he was used to seeing; this one wore a crown of sparkling beads and tall plumy ostrich feathers over her braided silver hair, each cornrow caught at the end with a brightly colored, shiny bow. And more beads, strings of them hung from her neck and wound around her wrists and ankles. A surplice threaded with gold had been placed around her shoulders, its belled sleeves softening the jangle of her bracelets.

In the reduced light, filtered through the smoking candles, she looked beautiful, young, even. A high priestess from another land, another time. And she danced lightly, the springy steps of youth. He watched her turn, eyes closed, holding a brass plate full of fruit to the sky, an offering probably, before placing it at Phillip's feet. Dan imagined how she must have looked standing beside her Voodoo priest-husband years ago. Was she carrying on his traditions? Or, like he suspected, had brought in help to carry them on?

He hadn't seen the figure also in white sitting cross-legged in the shadows about twenty feet in front of him until the drumming began. A slow mesmerizing beat just a fraction of a second slower than a normal heart. The sound seemed to reverberate in the steel building, and he thought he felt his own heart slow to match the echo. It would be easy to fall into a trance; he took a deep breath and continued to stare at the back of the drummer's head. The hair was just a shade or two lighter, now a white-blond, but the gold cord that nipped the white satin robe at the waist belied the dynamite body of Iris Stuckey-Eklund.

The Wings of the Dove must have taken on a new dimension. Was he surprised? Maybe not. Religious extremes in the name of whatever deity seemed to meld, to attract the same sort of converts, offer the same rewards. He was probably watching some guarantee that Phillip Ainsworth would be elected governor. He just wished he had a camera. He wondered how much a picture of all this would be worth to the candidate?

The tug on the sleeve of his jacket all but made him lose control of his bladder. He was reaching for his gun when the figure behind him hissed, "Dan, it's me. Carolyn." With a finger to her lips, she motioned for him to follow her outside.

The cool clear air felt like a slap after the murkiness of the hangar. The full moon had poked through the clouds to hang low in the night sky. He leaned against the steel building and took several deep breaths. Carolyn didn't say anything, just watched him.

"What the fuck is going on in there?"

"There's no need to curse—"

"It's bad enough I find out you dropped your drawers for Eric Linden eight years ago. Now, I find out you're into some kind of hocus-pocus."

He heard her sharp intake of air. The Eric Linden thing. Good. Didn't he owe dear old Sis a few? A payback for insinuating that he was a regular at the Ranch. That he had to pay for sex.

"It's a cleansing."

Was she going to ignore his reference to Eric?

"What does that mean?" He motioned to the hangar behind him.

"It's an act to purify—"

"I know what the *word* means, Carolyn. I want to know what's going on." He didn't even try to keep the anger and impatience out of his voice. He kept thinking this kind of thing goes on all the time in California, but this is New Mexico. But hadn't people told him that healings were common out here? That Santa Fe was a second L.A.?

"I've been a believer, follower, of certain aspects of the Santera. Their herbal treatments are better than any homeopathic care I've ever had. Over the years I've persuaded Phillip to try some of the…cures. I believe it has strengthened our marriage."

"So in the name of homeopathy you drug your husband and let women in white robes dance around him and beat on a drum?"

"Hypnotized. He isn't drugged." Then she added, "You weren't supposed to see this."

"What kind of an answer is that? Does 'not seeing' make whatever is going on in there right?"

"Why does everything have to come down to right or wrong? Can't people think differently than you do and still be okay in your assessment? You're too judgmental, rigid, if you want to know what I think."

He ignored the "judgmental" and decided he'd give some thought to the "rigid" part later.

"Where's Elaine and Eric?" For the moment, it was easier to change the subject.

"Elaine may have started home by now. She was out chasing down Simon about a half hour ago over by the woods. And Eric could still be with Judge Cyrus."

"What's the judge doing here?" He asked the question and tried to stop the tiny finger of fear from skipping up his spine. "He's overseeing the transfer of the estate to the university. The trust is at Midland Savings and Loan. He's been spending a lot of time out here. We're all pitching in. I'm bringing Dona Mari out twice a week to clean and help pack."

"I'll check the house again."

"Dan...don't mention any of this to Phillip later." She gestured toward the hangar. "He won't remember anything when he comes out of the trance, and I'm afraid your descriptions might upset him." Her voice had that whiny, wheedling tone he hated, but she didn't wait for his answer, just hopped down from the fender of the pickup and walked back through the door.

Dan watched her go then untied Baby Belle. He was glad he had an excuse to leave. He had a problem with candles and feathers and women in white robes. And he guessed if that made him rigid, so be it. For not the first time in his life, he wondered how in the hell Carolyn had ever gotten to be his sister.

The moon had slipped behind the bank of clouds again, but the runway flanked by a hundred lights kept the night from closing in on him with its blackness. He was just trying to decide whether to go back up to the house to look for Eric and Elaine when he saw a flicker of lights at the edge of the trees and felt Belle stiffen.

Fifty feet from where they were standing, the dense stand of cottonwood and elm marked the beginning of the woods. The infamous woods that held the secrets of things done on altars.... He didn't let himself finish the thought but swung into the saddle and kneed Belle into a canter. It might be nothing; then again, it might be best to check it out.

He guided Belle behind the hangar and into the dark to approach the woods from the south, through the waist-high brush that formed a marsh of sorts during wet springs. Horse and rider would be concealed, not totally but enough as to not attract attention. But he had a feeling that the owners of the flashlights were long gone, now deep in the trees and concentrating on other things. But where was Elaine? Could she be over there somewhere chasing down Simon?

He slowed Belle to a walk at the edge of the woods, then slipped to the ground and tied her to a clump of scrub oak. He'd have to find his way on foot; the horse would make too much noise. He wasn't sure he knew where he was going. He remembered the first time he was here, the group had followed the stream, so he worked his way to the right until he found the narrow ribbon of water, still barely a trickle, and, sticking to the shadows of the bank, hurried south.

Chapter Twelve

"The god-damned runway wouldn't be lit up like Christmas if somebody didn't expect something big." Roger flicked on the flashlight to read his watch.

"I hope you're right. Seems like we've been sitting out here forever." Tom shifted his weight and continued to clean his binoculars.

"Only an hour. It's a quarter to nine."

"You got to be kidding. Didn't think I could get this stiff and cold in an hour."

"We'll sit out here as long as it takes." Roger's voice had an edge to it, but he didn't care. They had been all set to get out of New Mexico, next assignment was hinted to be Seattle, when a street drop totaling about ten million turned up in Houston. And it was suggested that they give the ol' airstrip the benefit of another week's close surveillance.

"Want some trail mix?" Tom was picking through the bag to find all the almonds.

Roger waved him away. The black theatrical makeup itched after it dried and on top of a close shave drove him almost nuts by stinging.

"Think you can do without me for a few minutes? Nature calls." Tom stood and shook a half dozen errant raisins from the creases in his camouflage jacket before grabbing a flashlight and heading toward the streambed.

"Keep that light aimed at the ground." Roger heard himself sounding peevish. Well, damn it, he was. All the accolades had slipped away. Eric Linden had turned out to be a bomb. Didn't have any more information than the next guy on drugs being smuggled into this country by way of the Double Horseshoe. Every lead had turned to shit, that sheriff, the wife. Roger no longer thought that sitting out here in the cold and damp would make a difference.

Then, tonight, the runway lights had been on, and Roger allowed himself a glimmer of hope, a second thought about promotion. He picked up the discarded trail mix and ate a date.

He heard something thrashing around in the brush toward the stream. They had surprised a wild pig earlier. Maybe Tom had peed on something that didn't appreciate it. Roger chuckled.

Suddenly, Tom came stumbling through the thicket, his fly still open.

"Rog...Come quick. I need some help."

"What...?" Roger was instantly on his feet and followed Tom, who was moving quickly back the way he had come.

"I had to hit someone. He scared the piss out of me."

"Who?"

"That insurance guy, Dan, what's his name, Mahoney. But that's not all, there's some god-damned huge dog that won't let me near him."

By now the two of them had reached the slumped body of Dan Mahoney lying under the watchful eye and bared fangs of an enormous Rottweiler.

"What'd you hit him with? He's out cold."

"Just these." The field binoculars sported a bent rim on one lens.

"Get some water. Help me bring him around." Just maybe if Dan Mahoney was sneaking around these woods, they were onto something big. How many times had Roger been in the right place, right time? Could this be his lucky night?

"Come on, boy. I'm your friend. Just let me help your master." A snarl indicated that the dog didn't believe him.

"What are we going to do?" Tom had returned with a dripping handkerchief.

"You got anything beside the trail mix?"

"Hey, maybe I do." Tom was rummaging in the pockets of his field jacket. "Beef jerky."

"Let me have some." Roger pulled a six-inch piece of dried meat from the packet. The dog was definitely interested. He licked his chops once, then drooled, mouth slightly open; but his expression had changed. The eyes that followed Roger's every move were softer, the eyes of a hungry puppy.

"Here you go, pal." Roger held out an inch of the treat in the palm of his hand and the dog looked uncomfortable, shuffled back and forth, half-standing, whined, then lay down.

"Why don't you try to go closer? Go to him so's he won't have to leave Mahoney." This from Tom, who was standing in back of him. Roger thought of letting Tom try since he was so know-it-all brave, but he didn't, he crept closer himself, still keeping the jerky outstretched in front of him. And it worked. As long as he was being fed, they could get close to Dan.

"Hope the jerky lasts until we can get him to come around."

Tom pulled Dan to a sitting position and applied the handkerchief that he'd dipped in the stream to the back of Dan's head. The dog glanced at him but apparently decided that he wasn't hurting Dan and turned back for another treat.

"How's he doing?" Roger had exactly two strips of jerky left.

"Back among the living."

Dan opened his eyes, shut them, then kept them open and looked from Tom to Roger to the dog.

"Simon, where'd you find Al Jolson…two of them?"

When Carolyn had called that morning to ask for her help, Elaine jumped at a chance to take Simon to the ranch. Someone was needed to go through Billy Roland's personal items, including books, and take an inventory of what was there, especially in the study, and then box up books that would be appropriate for the Tatum library. A few family friends were being asked to help over the next couple weeks. Dan had gone to Albuquerque and would be late. Why not help out if she could?

It was a perfect day, warm and clear; she arrived at the Double Horseshoe just after lunch. She left Simon at the barns. Hank said he thought he'd be fine, and he'd keep an eye on him. She unloaded her car, book boxes, labels, pens, tape, everything she'd needed when she had moved her office last year. She stuck a six-pack of Diet Coke in the fridge and after surveying the kitchen was glad she'd thought to bring something to drink.

The library was dusty. First, she opened the blinds and a couple windows, and felt immensely better. The room smelled fresher. The whole house was beginning to suffer from being shut up. She spent an hour running the vacuum she'd found in the hall closet, then aligned the empty boxes against the walls and began to pull down a row of books.

Sometimes, she'd give in to temptation and sit and read from some author that caught her eye. Billy Roland had a little of everything, best-selling paperbacks, a turn-of-the-century leather bound set of Goethe, two complete sets of Shakespeare, the Comedies and Tragedies; one wall held nothing but law, economics and farm management books, she'd leave that till last. It was at least a week's work; she'd volunteer to come back.

She took a break around two when Carolyn and Phillip arrived with Dona Mari, who was to begin cleaning the upstairs bedrooms. They also had Eric in tow. He was moving out to the hangar, and he and Phillip would begin to assess the plane's needs that afternoon. Apparently, Phillip was sincere about wanting to buy it.

She and Carolyn took cans of Diet Coke out to the porch and sat in the swing. They shared memories of the Double Horseshoe from finer days.

"Doesn't look like there's much work going on around here."

The booming voice made her jump, but it was Carolyn who invited Judge Cyrus to join them. He must have been down at the barns.

"Can't, but I thank you ladies. Got to go meet with that vet and see how much money he needs. He's down there now working on the figures. Managing this trust is becoming a full-time job." But Elaine could tell that he didn't mind. He had been close to Billy Roland. The judge touched his hat and gave a slight nod, then paused like he'd had second thoughts about joining them and walked back up the porch steps.

"Did I see Eric Linden with Phillip just now?"

"They're taking a look at the Lear," Carolyn volunteered.

"I remember when Billy Roland bought that thing over by Dallas. We all thought it was just one more white elephant. The boys got plans for it?" Judge Cyrus said.

"If they can get it together, Phillip's going to use it during the campaign."

"You don't say." The judge leaned against the porch railing. "Either of you lovely ladies know Eric's intentions after the plane gets fixed?"

"Why do you ask?" Elaine leaned forward.

"Oh, no reason, really...might have a job for him if he's interested." He looked at Elaine. "I can't believe he survived that flash flood. You'd have to have more than nine lives to do that, wouldn't you think?"

Elaine shrugged.

"Did he ever figure out who promised him that two million that he thought was waiting for him in Midland Savings and Loan?"

"He has some ideas," Elaine said and then wondered immediately why she said it. Judge Cyrus had never been a favorite, and he was beginning to irritate. If she'd just kept quiet, he'd probably have gone back to the barns.

"And what would those be, if I can be snoopy here?" He was watching her with shrewd, narrowed eyes, and Elaine felt just a little discomfort.

"Dan has uncovered a new angle. Something to do with J.J. Rodriguez. He's in Albuquerque now talking with Albert Reyes."

It wasn't her imagination—the judge's pudgy fingers tightened around the porch railing.

"You don't say. Thought that Mahoney character was a smart one...smart enough to catch the eye of the prettiest almost-widow in the county." He was the only one laughing as he reached over to poke Elaine's knee.

Elaine got up abruptly. "I better get back to work."

"Me, too. Didn't mean to break up the sewing bee." More laughter, as the judge hopped down the steps.

Carolyn and Elaine watched him walk back toward the barns in that peculiar swinging gait of persons with abnormally short legs.

"I've never liked him," Elaine volunteered. "Aside from the sexist stuff, he just gives me the creeps."

"I know what you mean." Carolyn yawned and stretched and said she was going down to the hangar if she could find the keys to a pickup. Elaine went back to the study and heard a truck drive by the window about fifteen minutes later and guessed the keys had been found.

She didn't mind working alone; in fact, she rather enjoyed it. Sometimes the packing went quickly. Sets of anything, she listed in their entirety and barely opened each book, just checked its binding and overall wear and tear. Some of the older collector's items needed gluing along their spines.

She wasn't keeping track of time and was faintly surprised to realize it had gotten dark. She closed the windows and the blinds and moved the floor lamp more to the center of the floor, where she was just beginning to catalogue a rather involved set of personal papers in leather binders, a collection of essays on grazing and grazing rights by Billy Roland's father.

She listened but couldn't hear Dona Mari upstairs. Perhaps she had finished; it was almost seven. It might be a good idea for her to do the same. She walked down the hall to the kitchen. There was a basket of fresh fruit on a sideboard. A leftover from the funeral, probably, because there was little else to eat. She finally found some crackers in the pantry and a half-eaten round of New York cheddar in the back of the fridge. It crossed her mind to make a picnic and go down to the hangar and see how the work was progressing. Then she smiled. There was no reason to feed Eric. He needed to learn to take care of himself. There were just some habits that died hard. She sat at the kitchen table, peeled an apple and ate a hunk of cheese.

She walked out the back door a little after seven and continued down to the barns. She'd round up Simon and head back to Roswell. Dan would probably be getting back in the next hour or so.

"You're going to kill me. I got busy. Last time I saw him he was heading after a pickup going out to the hangar."

She felt like strangling Hank but all she said was, "Thanks. I'll check out that way," and got a set of keys to a pickup, there was no taking the Benz across the fields. She knew that Simon wouldn't get lost. At least, she hoped he wouldn't. He wasn't used to wide open spaces, but more than likely he was at the hangar.

But he wasn't. Phillip and Carolyn had seen him chasing along the edge of the woods sometime earlier, maybe an hour earlier.

"Where's Eric?"

"Went off someplace with the judge," Phillip said.

Elaine felt a twinge of uneasiness, but couldn't figure out why; the judge was probably offering him work. "I'm heading back to town after I find Simon. I'll be here tomorrow."

She sat in the pickup trying to decide what to do. It was a safe bet that Simon was somewhere in the woods. She was kicking herself for not watching him more closely; the woods stretched for five miles along the creek. Maybe if she drove along the edge and got out and called him every once in a while...she was anxious to get back to Roswell and Dan; and she still had a two-hour drive ahead of her. Kids and pets could both be a pain in the ass, sometimes.

His head didn't just hurt; it throbbed in between sharp daggers of pain that seemed to have dimmed the sight in his left eye. Dan held the cold cloth against the fast-rising knot at the crown and filled in Roger and Tom with his suspicions.

"So you think the judge might have had a reason to keep Eric undercover for awhile? Might have had something to do with the ritualistic killing?" Tom was talking and eating trail mix at the same time.

"As good a guess as I can come up with. I can place the death of the girl four days before the bust. She worked for Judge Cyrus. Eric will be able to tell us if she's the one he knew."

"And you think this altar place out here is worth checking tonight?"

"Couldn't hurt." Dan was beginning to feel some urgency to find Eric, headache or no. And, since Simon was with him, where was Elaine?

"How much farther is it?" Roger held the flashlight in his face.

"A mile, maybe more." Dan reached up and Roger helped him stand.

"You going to be okay?"

"Yeah. Let's get going." Dan wasn't too thrilled that Simon was coming along; might ruin any surprise element, but it was too late now, or was it? "Either of you have some rope or something I can use to tie Simon? Might be better to leave him behind and come back for him later."

Tom produced a twenty-foot piece of nylon rope and Dan secured Simon to the trunk of a young cottonwood. Dan used the commands they had learned in school and hoped Simon would obey; then the three of them angled back toward the stream to begin following it south. If Dan wanted to be really truthful, he wasn't sorry he had company. Maybe it was the memory of what he had seen in the woods recently, or what he knew about human offerings in the past, but whatever it was, he felt uneasy.

The first mile was uneventful. Fallen leaves muffled their steps and the overgrown brush hid their movements, but the going was slow. Branches tore at their clothing and caught in their hair. Dan felt the sleeve on his windbreaker get snagged on a branch that he'd tried to duck.

"Just a minute. I'm caught here. It's torn through to the lining."

Roger and Tom helped him get untangled.

"What was that?" Roger switched off his flashlight.

"Sounded like drums."

The three of them stood silently straining to hear.

"There it was again. Did you hear it?" Tom whispered.

"It's coming from over this way." Roger had already turned and began to thread his way through the brush away from the stream.

"Must be one doozy of a drum. Big mother," Roger said.

"Brass gong."

"What?" Roger turned to Dan.

"That last ringing sound must be a gong of some sort. The sound carries like a tuning fork." Instinctively, Dan dropped to the ground. "If we're going to get any closer and not attract attention, we better do it this way."

Crouched low Dan ran forward, then suddenly motioned for Tom and Roger to hit the ground beside him.

"Holy shit." Tom let his breath out in a low whistle.

"What's going on?"

"Service of some sort." Dan wasn't comfortable talking, but they were a safe seventy-five feet from the altar and had a panoramic view of what was happening.

Five drummers, naked except for loin cloths and body paint, knelt beside three-foot-high hollowed logs with taut animal skin coverings, striking their instruments at rhythmic intervals. He had been right, a five-foot brass plate hung between two sapling cottonwoods and every three minutes was struck by someone dressed in a flowing white robe.

Most of the congregation, if that's what they could be called, wore headdresses imbedded with slivers of glass that caught the light of the hundreds of candles that marked the boundaries of the pit-like sanctuary. Excluding the drummers, there had to be thirty people, men and women, dressed in white, wearing masks, body paint, or both, kneeling on mats in a semicircle facing a dais.

The altar in the center was covered with flowers and ribbons that trailed along the ground. The strange, bitter yet fragrant odor of incense hung in the air and wafted to where Dan was crouched. It was intense and penetrating, roses, gardenias, sandalwood, cloves and probably half a dozen other ingredients; he only hoped he didn't start sneezing.

Suddenly four people with tambourines stepped from the woods to stand behind the drummers and began to hit their instruments with the heels of their hands. Their robes were hooded and fell forward, hiding their faces. Dan couldn't help but feel he might recognize some of the people without their finery.

Dan felt the reverberations before he realized that the drummers had increased the tempo. Now, the sound enveloped them, filled the sanctuary, escaping up through the trees to drift out over the night. Dan huddled with Roger and Tom and watched as the congregation began to sway and wave their arms, increasing in speed until two women carrying enormous wicker baskets walked toward the crowd from behind the dais and sprinkled something in sweeping motions over their heads. Rose petals, Dan guessed, as the scent of the flowers reached him. This offering seemed to appease the crowd, which fell silent, but not for long.

Dan's ears were ringing even before a young man stepped up beside the gong and struck it, not once but three times. Again, silence, only the humming until the sound gradually wore itself out. But this time Dan could almost feel the anticipatory excitement as the crowd murmured and shifted position to lie flat in a supplicant's pose, all thirty people face down, arms extended, palms up.

In a burst of fragmented light that danced in the air and sizzled and popped from the tips of the sparklers embedded in the edge of the dais, six warrior-men stepped forward, each supporting his side of a portable throne, an enormous stool with curved arms and no back on a miniature platform secured to three four by fours that extended beyond the base to become carrying poles.

Dan couldn't take his eyes off the figure in the middle in a violet cassock of satin trimmed with gold scrolling and what looked like thousands of beads or buttons sewn along the hem, his long legs encased in white satin breeches and knee-high black riding boots. But on his head was a three-foot-tall headdress of deep purple that flowed train-like behind him, forming a tent around his shoulders and spilling over the edge of the airborne platform. A mask of white feathers covered every inch of his face and he sat sphinx-like, long arms folded in his lap, hands encased in white gloves, only moving his head to nod here and there blessing his followers.

Slowly moving with the beat of the drums, the warriors carried their impressive leader through the crowd. Acrobatic dancers, their green and purple costumes covered with tiny bells, waved additional sparklers and frolicked around the throne turning somersaults over worshipers. The result was a cacophony of sound. But it wasn't just sound. Dan marveled at how all his senses were assaulted, pushed to their limits, making his head ache with overload.

The chants reached a crescendo as the sparklers sputtered to darkness and were replaced by tall white candles in front of the throne. The warriors returned to the dais, but it soon became evident that they would continue to hold the man on the throne aloft and not place him on the ground. It probably wasn't such a bad idea, Dan thought; it certainly added to the majesty of it all.

Next, six women, naked to the waist in diaphanous skirts, nipples erect in the chilly night air, and garlands of flowers encircling their heads, danced around the throne, finally coming to rest at the feet of a warrior. After each pushed a jester away and feigned reclaiming her rightful spot, she offered flowers and a lighted candle to the man seated above her, who accepted her offering with a nod of his head. Yet, Dan had a feeling that it was all just a prelude for something else—a warm-up act, and he didn't have long to wait.

Bursting through a thicket of trees behind the drummers, a bronzed man, his body painted in chevron stripes of yellow and red, swung a machete-long knife above his head, circling and dipping to the low beat of the drums as he made his way to the altar and kicked up flower petals with each step.

Then as someone struck the gong, four more warriors carried a stretcher containing what looked like a body in a white satin robe to the base of the stone mass, where it took all four of them to heave the body upright and place it on its back over the altar.

"Give me the binoculars," Dan hissed. He was suddenly frantic. It didn't take a rocket scientist to figure out that there was going to be a sacrifice. A human one, if the shape of the bundle didn't lie. He focused on the altar and watched as the topless dancers moved forward to caress the body while they anointed it with some kind of oil.

Then they covered the body with theirs, pretending to what? Keep it safe? Shield it from harm? They moved in a mesmerizing circle, arms waving, scattering more flower petals before stopping on cue and stepping back. It took Dan a moment to realize that there was suddenly no sound. The worshippers were still prone and absolutely motionless. The man on the throne was staring in front of him. A light wind moved through the branches overhead, ruffling the feathers of the costumes and picking up tiny swirls of flower petals; in the distance a coyote called to a mate.

Then trance-like a dancer stepped to the altar and working slowly pulled apart the white satin robe, exposing the neck and finally the head of the body that had been tossed across the pile of stones. Eric Linden. In a rush of sound the drummers rolled to a crescendo as the warrior with the machete swung the heavy knife over his head and approached the altar.

Dan was on his feet, running, crashing through the brush, yelling for the craziness to stop. But that was when he saw Elaine, gun cradled in her outstretched hands, drop to one knee and take aim at the high priest. The rest was bedlam. The dancers scattered, stumbling over worshippers. The knife-wielding warrior dashed into the woods. And before Elaine could shoot, the warriors facing her saw the gun and dropped their poles to follow the others.

The throne tilted violently to the right, but as Dan watched, only the head of the priest slipped from view. His body remained stationary—massive squared shoulders, folded arms, gloved hands, legs in high leather boots—nothing moved. It was a shell. A hollowed-out facade that allowed the diminutive body of a dwarf, in this case Judge Franklin Cyrus, to stand upright behind it, looking for all the world like a six-foot-six ruler of the underworld.

It was late before Eric, Elaine and Dan returned to the house. Roger and Tom had taken a few key players and the judge into custody. Most of the audience in the woods had turned out to be former workers from the Double Horseshoe. Disgruntled at their termination and eager to celebrate the demise of the man they, no doubt, were told had caused it. But that part really couldn't be proved, so those who hadn't escaped into the woods at the start were detained as illegal aliens and faced deportation.

The Roswell sheriff's department sent help, manpower and transportation. Roger and Tom were in their element, giving orders and accepting the kudos. No doubt sensing their imminent fame.

Phillip and Carolyn watched all the excitement but begged off coming back to the house. They were taking Dona Mari home, probably secretly relieved that she was with them and not caught in the woods.

Dan was the last to reach the house after going back for Simon and Baby Belle. By the time he got there, Elaine had produced a bottle of Glenlivet that she'd found hidden in the bookcase, and brought ice and glasses in from the kitchen. Dan helped her uncover the furniture. It seemed like the right place to be, in Billy Roland's study, now that they had all the answers.

He silently toasted his friend with two fingers of good scotch, and fervently wished Billy Roland could be there to enjoy it with him. Dan wondered how much his old friend had known about the judge, the strange rituals in his woods. Had he suspected? Let them turn the runway lights on in the past as a signal to gather? Billy Roland had lived out here a little too long not to know the peccadilloes of his friends.

Dan passed the picture of the girl to Eric and instantly saw that he recognized her.

"You know, she was Enrico Garcia's granddaughter. She ran away to the States. I felt responsible; I had known her for some time."

Dan vaguely wondered if that was in the Biblical sense but guessed that it was.

"Before that last trip she begged me to take her back home...she hated it at the judge's. But I never really knew why or didn't pay attention. I could have saved her life."

Dan thought he heard real remorse in Eric's voice.

"Grandpa wouldn't have been too pleased, might have caused some problems. Do you think he ever found out?" Elaine asked.

"Probably not. It was hushed up pretty fast. In fact, that's what gave it away," Dan said. "Three days of coverage and then Eric. It dawned on me that it would take something big to cover something big—especially if the authorities were getting a little too close to the truth."

"So what happens now?" Elaine turned to Eric.

"I'll be reinstated, Eric Linden, attorney at law...probably have a little chat with Judge Aspen...of course, I'll sue the estate of Judge Cyrus."

"I don't suppose a round figure like two million has crossed your mind?" Dan asked.

"I think seven years of my life is worth more than that, now."

Dan knew he wasn't kidding and would probably get it.

"But how do you think he did it? Got the drugs on board without you knowing it?" Elaine asked.

"It could have been done after they brought me down. A few connections with border patrol, someone borrows from the cache from other busts, stuff that's supposed to be locked up. It's difficult to keep an accurate inventory. It would have been easy to repackage, plant it, and get it back without much notice. I have a feeling that J.J. Rodriguez could have shed some light on that."

"Guess we'll never know if Sheriff Ray was warning you or trying to take you out," Dan mused.

"Let's give him the benefit of the doubt," Eric grinned.

There didn't seem to be a lot more to say. They finished their drinks in silence, and Dan stood to go. "You going to be all right out here? We can give you a ride back to Roswell." He looked down at Eric, still pale and obviously shaken by his brush with death, but oddly complacent.

"You two go on. I'll stay up here at the house for tonight. I'll be all right…haven't made a dent in the bottle, yet." Elaine walked toward the door, looked back as if to say something, then didn't. Dan caught her eye and she smiled. In relief? There was a glint of something….

"Leave the Benz and ride back with me." Dan had his arm around her as they walked out the front door, and he realized that nothing had felt quite that good in a long time. "I need your advice about something."

He handed her the packet of airline tickets that he'd picked up in Albuquerque and watched as she hurriedly scanned them under the Jeep's interior light.

"Ireland?"

"For two." And he turned her toward him and realized that they wouldn't make it much farther than a motel room in Tatum that night.

To receive a free catalog of other Poisoned Pen Press titles, please contact us in one of the following ways:

Phone: 1-800-421-3976
Facsimile: 1-480-949-1707
Email: info@poisonedpenpress.com
Website: www.poisonedpenpress.com

Poisoned Pen Press
6962 E. First Ave. Ste 103
Scottsdale, AZ 85251